Starstruck

in

Willow Falls

PAT NICHOLS

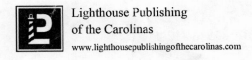

Lighthouse Publishing
of the Carolinas
www.lighthousepublishingofthecarolinas.com

STARSTUCK IN WILLOW FALLS BY PAT NICHOLS
Published by LPC Books/A division of Iron Stream Media
100 Missionary Ridge, Birmingham, AL 35242
ShopLPC.com

Cover design by Elaina Lee

Iron Stream Media serves its authors as they express their views, which may not express the views of the publisher.

This is a work of fiction. Names, characters, and incidents are all products of the author's imagination or are used for fictional purposes. Any mentioned brand names, places, and trademarks remain the property of their respective owners, bear no association with the author or the publisher, and are used for fictional purposes only.

Library of Congress Cataloging-in-Publication Data
Library of Congress Control Number: 2020950644
Nichols, Pat
Star Struck in Willow Falls / Pat Nichols 1st ed.

ISBN-13: 978-1-64526-311-1
eBook ISBN: 978-1-64526-312-8

Praise for *STARSTRUCK IN WILLOW FALLS*

Pat Nichols weaves a refreshing story in Willow Falls with intriguing characters that stick to you. It seems there are no new stories, but when you find one that has a unique twist, you don't want to put it down. Well-written, interesting, and engaging.

~ Cindy K. Sproles, best-selling author of
What Momma Left Behind

Whether you're a new reader or one returning to Willow Falls, the sweet essence of small-town Georgia will embrace you like an old sweater in Pat Nichols' heart-tugging series newest edition. Emily juggles new motherhood, her job as newspaper editor, and a book release that's almost swept away when a major motion picture comes to shoot in town. Meanwhile, her twin sister stage actress, Rachel, snags a secondary role in the film that just might jeopardize her engagement. Serving as hometown movie liaisons, both sisters attempt to navigate family relationships and a delightful if demanding assortment of locals. Willow Falls is just the sort of cozy escape we're all looking for these days!

~ Denise Weimer, Managing Editor, LPC historical
imprints and multi-published author

Starstruck in Willow Falls is the third book of the *Willow Falls* series by Pat Nichols. Willow Falls, Georgia, already held me captive with its mix of winsome personalities. Throw a few quirky ones into the bunch, like local mail carrier, Mirabelle Paine, aptly named. Add a cast of characters straight from the silver screens of Hollywood, and you have the perfect combination for dramatic antics, some on-screen and some off. The plot twists are so skillfully woven, you'll be begging for more when you reach *The End*. Another winner.

~ Debra DuPree Williams, Author, *Grave Consequences,*
A Charlotte Graves Mystery

Starstruck in Willow Falls by Pat Nichols has everything I love in a novel—family drama and a small town filled with quirky characters, with one egocentric woman I'd like to throttle. Yep, it's got it all, along with some humor.

~ Ane Mulligan, Author of *In High Cotton*

Readers who fell in love with the folks of Willow Falls in Pat Nichol's first two books of the series are in for a treat! *Starstruck in Willow Falls* continues the story of twins Emily and Rachel as they seek to live out the fulfillment of their dreams. As I read, I often found myself wishing I could step into the town of Willow Falls and spend time with its inhabitants face to face. They seemed so real, warm, and inviting, making it easy for me to empathize with their struggles and joys. I look forward to another book from Pat Nichols, as she writes with sensitivity and with wonderful insight into the desires of the human heart.

~ Ann Tatlock, novelist, editor, and children's book author

Dedication

To my loving parents, Bette and Jim Hamilton,
whose unconditional love, inspiration, and faith taught me
what is important. I miss them both and will be with them again when I,
too, pass on to eternity.

Acknowledgements

Six years ago, when I abandoned retirement and launched career number two as a writer, little did I realize the impact the journey into this wonderful world would have on my life. I have met and connected with so many friends and mentors. Readers whose comments make my heart sing. Members of American Christian Fiction Writers of North Georgia, whose friendship and wisdom enrich my writing experience. Word Weavers International, Greater Atlanta Chapter members whose critiques strengthen my skills.

I am grateful to my managing editor, Ramona Pope Richards, for believing in me. To my editor, Andrea Merrell, thank you for your amazing insight and attention to details. My faithful Beta Readers, Pat Davis, Bev Feldkamp, Kitty Metzger, and Kathy Warner, you are an integral part of my writing experience, and I will forever be grateful.

To Iron Stream Media, it is an honor to be part of your family. Thank you for all the support and encouragement. To all the book clubs and organizations that invited me to speak, thank you for the opportunity to share my story.

A special thanks to my amazing family. To Tim, my husband and best friend, who has been the wind beneath my wings since the day we met all those years ago. To our son Greg, daughter Shelley, and son-in-law Ed, whose love of family and faith in God inspire me every single day.

Above all, I thank God for His grace and the gift of eternal life.

Chapter 1

Tomorrow's edition of the *Willow Post* loomed large in Emily Hayes' mind as she drove past Willow Falls' picturesque, century-old storefronts. No one—other than the mayor, the town council, and the paper's reporter—had a clue about the chaos scheduled to descend on this quaint little town. As editor of the weekly newspaper, she knew all too well that more than a handful of residents would blame her for keeping the news under wraps.

Emily circled the block a second time and pulled into an empty parking space in front of Pepper's Café. She grabbed her purse and picnic basket and stepped beside the rear bumper. A horn blast and screeching brakes made her flinch. Exhaust fumes from a rattle-trap pickup forced her to cover her nose and mouth.

Crazy drivers. And it's only going to get worse. Emily spotted an opening in the traffic and dashed across Main Street. She breathed deeply and moved on to Hayes General Store. The bell jangling over the door mingled with the antique player piano's rousing rendition of "Chattanooga Choo Choo." Emily set her basket on the soda fountain bar stretched along the sidewall between the front window and the check-out counter and climbed onto a stool.

Gertie—one of the town's favorite senior citizens, dressed in a nineteenth-century dress with a high collar—greeted a family and promised to deliver the best milkshakes in Georgia.

Emily's husband, Scott, settled beside her. He brushed a strawberry-blonde curl away from her cheek. "Still concerned about Rachel?"

One more worry souring Emily's mood. "I wish she'd talk to me."

"Maybe you're overreacting."

Emily shook her head. "My twin has lived with us for the past year. Believe me, I recognize her moods."

"Amazing." Scott propped his elbow on the bar and rested his chin on his fist. "For thirty years you and Rachel had no idea the other existed. Now, even though she was raised in the city and you're a country girl, you two are so much alike folks who don't know would swear you grew up in the same family. Two peas in a pod."

"The miracle of matching DNA." Emily forced a smile, skimming her fingertips over her husband's dimple. "Looks like another busy day."

"Best month yet. Thanks in part to Gertie and her famous chocolate sodas." He pointed to the picnic basket. "Did you bring cookies?"

"Fresh-baked."

He opened the lid, releasing brown-sugar and vanilla scents. "Yumm. Oatmeal raisin, your mom's recipe." Scott stood and reached for the basket. "We have time for a quiet lunch in my office before your shipment arrives."

The ancient wood floor creaked and moaned as they passed barrels, antique cabinets, and wooden shelves displaying old-fashion tools, housewares, and country-style accessories. Emily breathed in the lavender scent of old-fashioned soap bars.

They made their way through the back room to Scott's office. He plunked the basket on a worktable and removed his black frock coat, one of three he wore to signify the store's history. "Are you ready for your big book signing?"

"You know when our paper hits the street tomorrow morning, my event will turn into instant old news." Emily removed two chicken salad sandwiches from the basket and handed one to Scott. "I'm not convinced the town council made the right decision to meet in private and keep everything a secret."

"Remember how residents reacted when they learned the Atlanta TV station wanted to shoot a segment about our town?"

Emily groaned. "Yeah. They nearly drove us crazy with questions we couldn't answer."

"Which is exactly why we didn't hold a public meeting and start a dispute that would stretch way past the decision deadline." He unwrapped his sandwich. "If we had turned the offer down, we'd get our butts kicked all the way to South Carolina."

Emily fiddled with the wrapping on her sandwich. "At least half the population would give you the boot. The other half is still complaining about crowds and traffic."

Scott took a bite, then reached for his drink. "Everyone will come around when they discover the benefits."

Willow Falls' number one mail carrier and purveyor of gossip swooped in carrying a stack of mail. "What benefits?"

Emily flinched and turned at Mirabelle Paine's voice. "Do you have my shipment?"

"Two big boxes. I need Scott's help to bring them in."

"Yes, ma'am," he said to Mirabelle, then winked at his wife. "I'll be right back with the goods."

Emily released a long breath, relieved Mirabelle didn't press for an explanation. She wiped her damp palms on her jeans as the year-long journey from rejection to published author played in her head. Unlike Rachel's dream, hers had taken a giant leap forward.

Scott returned and deposited a box on the table. "Personal delivery for Georgia's soon-to-be-famous author."

Emily's heart pounded.

Mirabelle plopped down the second box and propped her hands on her ample hips. "Well, what are you waiting for? I don't have all day."

"To do what?"

Mirabelle gestured toward one of the boxes. "Buy a book."

"You know you have to wait 'til Saturday." Emily placed a protective hand on one of the boxes.

Mirabelle looked from Scott to Emily and frowned. "Why can't I buy one right now?"

"And have you upstage my book-signing event? Not a chance."

"My wife is one smart lady." Scott whipped out his pocketknife and sliced through the tape. "At least you'll see it up close before all your neighbors."

Emily lifted the flaps and reached for a book. Her heart soared as she traced the artist's rendition of a horse-drawn carriage in front of the family store. She touched the title. *Percy's Legacy.* She could hardly believe it was finally here.

Scott removed his phone from his belt clip. "Hold it up, honey, so you can share this occasion on social media."

"Wait a minute." Emily pulled lipstick from her purse and reapplied color. She held up the book and smiled at her husband. "Okay, I'm ready."

"You look gorgeous." He snapped a series of photos.

Mirabelle reached over and removed a book from the box. "Great cover, and your name is big."

"My name on a book." Emily pressed the novel to her chest. "It's surreal."

"I still want to buy one today."

"Like I said, you have to wait." She snatched the book from Mirabelle's hand.

"What's with the attitude?"

Emily softened her tone. "Sorry, I don't mean to seem ungrateful."

Mirabelle huffed. "I can't imagine why you won't give one of the town's *star* performers first dibs."

Scott closed the box. "Try to understand what a big deal this is for Emily. As a compromise, I bet she's willing to reserve the first spot in line for you."

"That's a great idea, Scott." Emily touched Mirabelle's arm. "I promise to sell you the first signed copy."

"Okay. That's better than nothing." She sniffed and ambled to the door. With her hand on the knob, she glanced over her shoulder. "Sadie told me the Mirabelle suite is booked all the way through the end of the year. That means lots of Willow Inn visitors will read my story and know I'm a Willow Falls VIP. See you guys Saturday."

Emily waited to hear the click of the door closing. "At least she didn't press us for the latest scoop."

"Give her time. The day's not over yet." Scott reopened the box, lifted a book, and touched the photo gracing the back cover. "You look like a successful author."

"A published book doesn't automatically lead to a profitable writing career. I need to rack up sales. Starting with all these copies."

Scott grinned at her. "And I thought managing this store was a tough business."

Emily placed the book in the box and imagined standing at a crossroad. "I've made a decision about my next project."

"Should I alert the media?" Scott slammed his palm against his forehead. "Oh, wait. As the *Willow Post* editor, you *are* the town's media."

"Very funny." She studied the book cover. "Instead of writing a sequel to *Percy's Legacy*, I plan to write a contemporary novel about Willow Falls' transformation, with a different name for the town and fictional characters of course. A multi-book series, filled with fun and drama."

"Uh-huh, and what happens when the book is published, and half the people in town swear the story is about them?"

"I haven't figured that part out yet." She pinched her chin. "If I start writing next week, I can finish a first draft by January and pitch it to my publisher by the end of March."

"You're forgetting one big issue. After your sister marries Charlie and moves out of our house, she won't be around to help you take care of our twins."

"Hmmm. Good point." Emily sat at Scott's desk and removed paper and pen from the drawer.

"Are you planning to write chapter one now?"

She shook her head. "I'm making a list of everything I need to accomplish before the wedding."

Scott moved closer and placed his hands on Emily's shoulders. "I don't want you take on too much. *Again.*"

"Don't worry. I won't commit to anything I can't handle."

"I'll believe that when I see it."

Chapter 2

Rachel Streetman strolled to the gazebo railing and admired the year-old grapevines stretching across acres of rolling hills. She closed her eyes and let her imagination soar. Rows of fans cheered as she appeared on a Broadway stage—the lead in an award-winning play. She pressed her palms together and held her fingertips to her lips, delighting in the thunderous applause, living the dream she'd first envisioned as a preschooler, twenty-eight years earlier.

Her imagination continued to soar until a fluttering sensation akin to a butterfly invasion assailed her chest and plunged her back to reality. Her acting career consisted of a once-a-week performance in a small-town playhouse. Suspended in anonymity. Going nowhere.

In six weeks, she would marry the man she adored, the manager and vintner of his father's retirement project. Charlie was content to live in this small town two hours north of Atlanta. While she'd grown to care about Willow Falls and the people who lived here, she feared her dream would drift into oblivion and leave behind bitter regret.

Tires crunching the gravel driveway winding from County Road to the winery's paved parking lot drew Rachel's attention. Time to put on a happy face. She moved her cooler from the steps and spread a blanket on the gazebo floor, then waved to her identical twin and Mama Sadie—the name they'd given to their birth mother to distinguish her from each of their adoptive mothers.

Emily scurried up the steps and handed Rachel a book. "What do you think?"

"The cover makes me want to dive right in and start reading, and I already know the story." Rachel embraced her sister. "You're an honest-to-goodness author. I'm so proud of you."

Sadie Liles reached up and brushed away a tear. "The day you two were born, I signed papers to give you up for adoption and returned to prison believing I'd never see you again. Then thirty years later, miracle of miracles, we were reunited." Mama Sadie's chest puffed out. "Now I know our little family is not only meant to be but loaded with talent. How many mamas can claim two famous daughters?"

"At this point, our fame is limited to Willow Falls," Emily said.

"You have to start somewhere." Mama Sadie swept her arm toward the vineyard. "Yesterday, I saw a picture of a Napa Valley vineyard in a travel magazine. I declare it wasn't as pretty as this view."

Rachel took in the view, then turned to her new family. "Our wedding will take place right here in the gazebo overlooking the vines."

Emily settled on the blanket. "I don't think so."

Rachel sat beside her. "And why not?"

Emily swept her arm around the gazebo much the same way her mother did toward the vineyard. "I'm guessing you couldn't squeeze more than a hundred chairs in here."

"I only ordered seventy invitations. You know not everyone who's invited will show up."

Emily wagged a finger in her sister's direction. "Have you forgotten that you and Charlie are two of the town's four celebrity darlings?"

"And your point is?"

"If you don't invite everyone, you'll break a lot of hearts."

Rachel's eyes narrowed to a slit. "What do you mean by *everyone*?"

"The whole town," Emily said as if that settled the matter.

"You're joking, right?"

Mama Sadie sat cross-legged between her daughters and brushed a lock of hair—tinted to its original auburn color—away from her cheek. "Emily's right."

"Yeah, well, maybe Charlie and I should ditch the whole wedding idea." Rachel removed a pitcher of lemonade and three glasses from the cooler.

Emily thumped her sister's arm. "Are you experiencing a case of bridal jitters?"

"I wasn't ten minutes ago." Rachel filled the glasses. "I decided to hold on to my townhouse. The next time I land a role in an Atlanta play, I'll need a place to stay. Besides, there are days when I miss big-city anonymity."

"Heavens to Betsy, honey," her mother said. "When you move into that gorgeous house up on the hill, you'll have all the privacy you need."

Rachel looked into her mother's eyes, blue-green like the eye on a peacock feather. "Except for all the tourists flocking to the winery and wandering all over the property."

Emily chuckled. "You might have to enforce a big-city habit and keep your doors locked."

"Like half the Willow Falls natives are doing now that strangers are roaming the streets," Rachel said.

"Enough talk about locks." Emily set her glass down. "Other than a snafu on invitation count, how are the rest of your wedding plans coming along?"

"Not so swift, now that you're telling me I have to invite everyone within a five-mile radius. What am I going to do when half the town shows up expecting to eat? And how big a cake can Patsy bake?"

"You mean *cakes*, and I imagine as big as you want." Emily grinned.

"What about all the other food." Rachel glared at her sister. "You know Charlie and I are paying for everything, and there's no way we can afford hundreds of catered dinners."

"Not a problem," Mama Sadie said. "We'll invite everyone to bring a covered dish."

"Oh, great." Rachel rolled her eyes. "A southern-fried wedding."

"Hey, don't knock it." Emily thumped her arm again. "You'll make a lot of people happy and save a ton of money."

Her mother pointed to the parking lot. "We can put a big white tent over there and rent all the chairs we need."

"Better yet, I'll return the white gown I paid a fortune for and opt for pigtails, a gingham dress, and a dandelion bouquet. With a country-western band to boot."

Emily giggled. "My sister, the hilarious city slicker."

Mama Sadie patted Rachel's hand. "You don't need to worry, honey. I'll form a committee to help with the details."

Rachel groaned. Were these two serious? "You do know the wedding is six weeks away."

"Piece of cake." Mama Sadie chuckled and reached for her lemonade. "No pun intended."

Rachel shook her head. "I won't agree to anything until I talk it over with Charlie."

"Don't wait too long." Emily set her glass down and refilled it. "Everything's about to go bonkers around here."

"Maybe with the new spectacle in town, no one will give a hoot about our wedding."

"Not a chance." Emily tilted her head toward the winery. "Don't look now, but your handsome fiancé is headed our way."

Rachel turned and eyed Charlie walking from the two-story winery, its old-world look created by the building's stone façade and high-pitched, red-tiled roof. Her gaze shifted to the structure sitting on a hill overlooking the Willow Oak property, the house she would soon call home.

Charlie climbed onto the gazebo, followed by his vineyard protectors—Buster, a yellow lab, and Merlot, a border collie. "The three prettiest ladies in Georgia. How lucky can a guy get?" He dropped to one knee beside Rachel.

Those hazel eyes and earthy scent sent a tingle through Rachel's limbs. "Do you want to join us?"

"And interrupt girl talk? No way. Besides, with the winery's grand opening a few weeks away, I'm up to my eyeballs in work." Charlie handed her a shoebox-sized container, then brushed strong fingers through his thick brown hair. "The tile samples for our master bathroom. Stop by my office before you head back to town and let me know which one you want."

She jiggled the box. "Do you have a favorite?"

"Whatever you pick." He stood and responded to Buster's nudge and tail wag with a head scratch. "It's good you two mutts do most of your work at night."

Rachel's heart warmed at the sight of Charlie scratching the dog's muzzle. Along with Brownie, her golden retriever, she could now lay claim to three lovable dogs. A far cry from the pet goldfish her father had allowed.

"I'll let you gals return to whatever earth-shaking discussion I interrupted." He blew a kiss at Rachel, then left the gazebo and headed back to the winery.

"Your young man is a real charmer," Mama Sadie said.

"Family trait." Rachel playfully nudged her mother. "You know we're all waiting for Charlie's dad to propose to you."

A flush crept across her mother's cheeks. "What makes you think Brick's planning to make such a move?"

"Are you serious? The whole town knows he's crazy about you." Rachel looked to her sister for affirmation.

"I've a mind to tell everyone to tend to their own business." Mama Sadie sighed and plucked a piece of lint from the blanket. "You know his wife broke his heart when she divorced him and ran off with another man."

"Charlie's first fiancée dumped him." Rachel fingered her engagement ring. "It took him a while, but he recovered."

"A fiancée is a far cry from a wife. Anyway, dads and sons don't always act the same."

"Speaking of dads." Emily eyed her sister. "Is your father coming up for the weekend?"

"He didn't commit. Something about a big contract he's finalizing. Although you'd think he'd want to check on his latest Willow Falls investment." Rachel swiped her hand across the condensation on her glass and pressed her palm to the back of her neck. "It seems Streetman Enterprise still holds him captive."

Mama Sadie stretched her legs out on the blanket. "Give him more time, honey."

"The way he pushes himself to achieve ... well, enough talk about men." Rachel eyed Emily. "Did you make a decision about your second novel?"

She nodded. "I'm going the contemporary route."

"At least the next eight weeks will give you a boatload of material."

Chapter 3

The next morning, Emily dropped the cordless phone on her desk. "That's the ninth call to the office phone in fifteen minutes, plus six to my cell." She closed her eyes and pressed her fingers to her temples. "At this rate, the whole town will drive us bonkers before lunch."

Mary Dixon, the newspaper's only reporter, ran a finger along the edge of her stylish haircut. "I couldn't answer a single question. Don't they know we included all the information we have in the article?"

"That won't keep everyone from bugging us. Uh oh." Emily pointed to the mail truck pulling into a parking space in front of the *Willow Post* headquarters. "The temperature in here is about to heat up ten degrees."

Mary huffed. "Try twenty."

Mirabelle clutched a newspaper in her right hand, her lips pinched. She stormed into the office. "How long have you known about this?" She slammed the paper on the table in front of Emily and drummed her finger on the headline. "*Director Selects Willow Falls to Film Feature-Length Movie.* Did you keep it a secret to give your sister an advantage?"

"What are you talking about?"

"The article says the director plans to audition locals for minor roles. Did Rachel finagle a copy of the script so she could beat everyone out?"

Emily glared at the woman. "Your outlandish reaction is exactly why the town council kept the news under wraps."

"You didn't answer my question."

"No, she doesn't have the script." Emily crossed her arms across her chest and continued to glare at the irate woman.

Mirabelle's eyes narrowed. "What's the movie about?"

"Obviously, a small town. Beyond that, no one knows."

"Is it true auditions begin early next week?" Would the woman ever run out of questions?

Emily silenced her phone and pushed it to the edge of her desk. "Unless the director changes his mind, yes." She grabbed her half-empty cup and headed toward the coffeemaker.

Mirabelle yanked her cell from her pants pocket. "It says here that Robert Nordstrom has three Oscar nominations and one win."

Mary—who had remained silent during the entire exchange—placed a blueberry muffin on a paper plate and handed it to Mirabelle. "He's a world-renown director with lots of successful films under his belt."

"Why does he want to shoot a film in a town that doesn't even have a movie theater?" Mirabelle looked at the muffin, then stuffed half of it in her mouth.

"Why don't you ask him when he arrives." Emily refilled her cup and returned to the desk. "He plans to show up this weekend to gain a sense about the town's vibe."

Mirabelle stared at Emily's vibrating phone. "Aren't you going to answer?"

"They'll leave a message."

The front door swung open, emitting a blast of warm air and drawing Mirabelle's attention. "Are you here as the pastor to pray or as our mayor to beg forgiveness?"

Nathan laughed. "I take it you've read this morning's paper."

"You should've clued me and other *important* citizens in."

Nathan planted a quick kiss on Mary's cheek, then turned back to Mirabelle. "The next time a movie crew wants to swoop into our little town, I'll give you a heads up."

"Hmph." Mirabelle turned on her heel and moved toward the door. With her hand on the knob, she stopped and turned toward Emily. "The director and the man Sadie shot have the same first name. Strange." She pulled the door open and trounced to the sidewalk.

Nathan shook his head. "Don't let her under your skin, Emily."

Mary patted her husband's cheek. "Did you come to rescue us from our town's most *important* citizen, my dear?"

"Since when did you gals need rescuing? Actually, I need to talk to Emily." He sat across from her and stared at her vibrating phone.

Emily held up both hands. "I've answered enough phone calls. What's on your mind?"

"Nordstrom called me an hour ago."

"Let me guess. He heard about the town's uproar and cancelled."

"Hardly. He wants to hire a local to function as his community liaison. Someone with acting experience. Your sister meets half the requirements. She ..."

"What aren't you telling me?"

"She agreed to take the position, but I need someone who knows this town to partner with her." He propped his arms on the table and leaned forward. "As the newspaper editor, along with all the research you've done for your novel, you're the most qualified person. Rachel agrees."

Emily stared at Nathan as she mentally ticked off her to-do list. She couldn't possibly squeeze one more responsibility into her overloaded schedule. "I appreciate your confidence. It's just, my plate is full. *Really* full."

"I wouldn't ask if I didn't need your help keeping Willow Falls grounded." Nathan eyed the muffins, then his wife.

Emily's phone vibrated again. Nathan's request played in her mind as Mary handed her husband a muffin. "I ... I don't know."

"Will you at least think about it?"

She breathed deeply and released a stream of air. "All right. But don't give me a hard time if I turn you down."

"I promise." He stood, wrapping his muffin in a napkin. "I have to head over and open my store. So far, this is a banner year. Thanks to tourists' fascination with antiques." Nathan waved to his wife and headed out the door.

Emily watched him pass the front window. The idea of postponing her writing career to play nursemaid to a bunch of adults gripped her chest like a giant vice. "There's no reason to keep hanging out here." She popped up and motioned toward Mary. "We need to close up shop and come back next week."

"Hopefully, folks will calm down over the weekend." Mary walked over and turned off the coffeemaker.

"Or end up more riled." With Mary's promise to lock up, Emily tossed her phone in her purse, shouldered the bag, and left the building. A break in traffic gave her a few seconds to dash across the street. She turned toward Hayes General Store, passed Florentine's—the town's first Italian restaurant—and stopped beside Willow Falls Tourist Headquarters.

JT Brown waved her inside. The popular tour guide's navy shorts exposed his famous artificial leg. His white teeth stood in stark contrast to his coffee-colored skin. "The news is plunking crazy." His newest adverb kept him from spouting profanity his friend Jack Parker would smack him for uttering. "Guess I'd better bone up on the movie industry."

"And figure out how to keep tourists focused on local attractions."

He removed a publicity brochure from a display. "Beginning today, we need to pitch our town as the capital of Georgia's movie industry."

Emily held back a laugh. "That's a stretch."

JT nodded toward four strangers passing the front window and approaching the door. "Looks like the next tour group is right on time." He leaned close to Emily. "What do you want to bet their first question is about the big announcement."

A twenty-something young woman hustled in. "Do either of you know what movie stars are gonna show up next week?"

"Told you," he whispered.

"We don't have a clue," Emily said. "One thing I do know, you're in for a real treat. JT is the best tour guide this side of the Mississippi."

The young woman pointed to his artificial limb. "How does that work."

"I'll show you."

Emily's heart warmed at the sight of JT captivating his audience with a demonstration. They'd never believe a year earlier he lived in an Atlanta homeless shelter. She slipped away and returned to the sidewalk. At the corner she paused and glanced at planter boxes filled with flowers, freshly painted facades, and colorful awnings adorning Main Street. The perfect setting for a movie.

Her chest tightened at the thought of struggling to smooth residents' ruffled feathers. Why did Rachel agree to take on that role? She moved on to Scott's store.

Inside, Gertie chatted with tourists while adding scoops of ice cream to tall glasses half-filled with seltzer and chocolate syrup. She pushed the sodas across the counter. "Did you folks read this morning's newspaper?

Robert Nordstrom is coming to town. He's Hollywood's most successful director."

Scott emerged from the second story and met Emily beside a cabinet displaying an array of mason-jar candles. "Too bad we can't harness the force today's news unleashed and create an alternative energy source."

Emily gripped his arm. "We need to talk."

"Uh oh. I can't tell from your expression if you're confused or annoyed."

"Try both." She led the way to his office, then relayed Nathan's request. "I told him I'd think it over."

Scott hiked his hip on the corner of his desk and crossed his arms. "I don't know how you can possibly take on more responsibility, and I'm not wild about you spending more time away from Clare and Jane."

"That makes two of us." She plucked a photo off his desk and traced her finger over her toddlers' faces. "I have to tell Nathan no."

"What about your sister?"

She set the photo down. "She'll understand."

"Don't count on it."

Emily shrugged. "You're right. Guess I need to show up with a peace offering."

"What do you have in mind?"

"Something sweet." Emily kissed Scott's cheek, then walked out the back door and headed up the alley. As she rushed across Main Street to Patsy's Pastries and Pretties and Old-Fashioned Christmas Shoppe, she caught snippets of conversation focused on the morning's news. Once inside, she tuned in to two locals hunched over one of the three ice-cream-parlor tables in front of the glass case filled with pastries and desserts. "What if the director makes R-rated movies with bad language?"

"Or nude scenes with lots of sex?"

Emily paused at their table. "You ladies can relax. Robert Nordstrom is known for PG13 films, a lot of them comedies."

"I hope you know what you're talking about," the older woman said. "Otherwise, Willow Falls will be right up there with Sodom and Gomorrah."

Emily stifled a chuckle as she moved to the counter.

Patsy Peacock adjusted her red hat sporting two peacock feathers and smiled at Emily. "Everyone has an opinion about the coming celebrity invasion. If you ask me, it's another big plus for our little town."

"You are one of our more enlightened citizens."

"Darlin', I haven't kept my store open all these years,"—she nodded toward the entrance to her new Christmas Shoppe—"or expanded it without a good head on my shoulders. What can I bring you?"

Emily pointed to a displayed cake.

"A slice?"

"The whole thing."

Patsy removed it from the case and placed it in a white box. "Special occasion?"

"More like a consolation."

Chapter 4

Rachel sat on the couch in Emily's den between her twenty-three-month-old, identical-twin nieces and read the last page in their favorite book. "The end."

Clair tugged on her sleeve. "Again, Auntie Rach."

Rachel hugged her tight. "One more time, sweet girl."

"I have a better idea." Emily walked in, smiling.

"Mommy's home." Jane climbed down and toddled over.

Emily scooped her off the floor. "I brought a yummy treat for my favorite girls."

Rachel gathered Clair in her arms and followed her sister to the kitchen. She pointed to the cake on the counter. "Is that lemon—"

"With buttercream frosting." Emily set Jane in her booster seat.

"Our all-time favorite dessert. Either your mommy needs a sugar rush or she's celebrating good news." Rachel placed Clair beside her sister.

Emily removed plates from the cabinet, then cut and served four pieces.

Rachel sat at the kitchen table across from her sister and savored the sweet taste of the melt-in-your-mouth dessert. "Delicious as ever. So, which is it? A sugar rush or celebration?"

Emily dipped her fork into the cake. "I talked to Nathan—"

"About Nordstrom's offer?"

Emily nodded.

"Can you believe he'll pay us to collaborate on a project and hobnob with celebrities? Only this time we won't have to ..." Rachel's fork stopped halfway to her mouth as she noticed her sister staring at her plate, her brows scrunched. "The light just came on. The cake is meant to soften the blow. You turned him down, didn't you?"

"You have to understand." Emily eye's pleaded. "I didn't have a choice."

Rachel dropped her fork. "Do you have any idea what working with an influential director would mean to my career?"

"You're a stage actress."

"Doesn't matter." Rachel pushed away from the table and moved to the sliding glass doors leading to the back yard. She eyed Brownie and her cousin Cody, Emily's golden retriever, stretched out on the patio. At least they remained loyal to each other.

Emily stepped beside her. "You know better than anyone how busy I am."

"How can you do this to me?" Rachel's voice quivered. "After everything I gave up last year when you needed me, begged me to help you finish writing the town's play."

"Because you were the only qualified person I knew."

"And now you're the only person I'm comfortable teaming up with." Rachel turned to Emily. "Don't you see? We understand and trust each other. I know we sometimes bicker and disagree, but we always have each other's back. No matter what."

Emily blinked, her lower lip clamped between her teeth.

"It's only eight weeks—"

"Away from my babies."

"Part-time. And when you need a sitter, I'll pay." Rachel grasped Emily's hands. "How about Missy Gibson? Other than her lead in the play, she's not working more than a few hours a week. Plus, she adores Jane and Clair."

"What about your wedding preparations and you helping Charlie at the winery. You don't have a ton of spare time either."

Rachel shrugged. "That's all manageable, especially with Mama Sadie's help."

"I assume Charlie agreed to the wedding changes we talked about."

Rachel released her sister's hands. "I haven't told him."

Emily's eyes widened. "Why not?"

"With the grand opening hanging over his head, I didn't want to stress him out."

"Are you kidding? Easy-going Charlie?" Emily sighed. "Unless he hears it through the grapevine before you tell him. That would give him a giant case of heartburn."

"Good point. Guess I'll bring it up over dinner. Back to Nordstrom's offer." Rachel fingered the emerald and diamond tennis bracelet she and her father gave her mother on her last birthday before cancer stole her from their lives. "If you can't accept it, I'll find another way to boost my career."

"I didn't realize how much the assignment meant to you." Emily wiped a smudge off the glass. "If you hadn't helped me take care of my babies all those months I would never have finished writing my book. I guess tonight, we both need to break the news to our guys."

"Thank you." Rachel pulled Emily into a hug. "How will Scott react?"

"He'll complain about me taking on more than I can handle. But he won't stand in my way." Emily returned to the table.

Rachel followed her. "Maybe you'd better whip up a batch of oatmeal-raisin cookies."

"No need." Emily winked. "The cake and some extra sugar from me will do the trick."

***

Rachel sat across from Charlie at a candle-lit table in Florentine's. "A year ago, did ordering a pizza in Willow Falls ever cross your mind?"

"Nope. Especially in an Italian restaurant owned by a chef named Billy Bob." He removed another slice from the pan.

"According to my sister, he was one of Scott's high-school buddies who moved away, then came back after the town began to thrive."

Charlie swallowed a bite. "Who knew a southern guy could make a pizza this good. Maybe we should ask him to cater our wedding."

Now's the time. Just do it. "We ... uh ... need to talk ... about the wedding."

"Uh oh. Don't tell me my fiancée has cold feet."

"Heavens no. Don't be silly. The thing is, Emily and Mama Sadie sort of brought up a new plan." Rachel relayed their idea. "What do you think?"

His jaw dropped. "Invite the whole town?"

She nodded.

"Sounds more like a county fair than a wedding. Maybe we should include an auction and a pie-eating contest. Maybe even cattle roping."

"We could always fly to Vegas and tie the knot in one of those cute little wedding chapels."

"That makes sense." Charlie reached for his wine glass. "Except for one thing. You've been in Willow Falls long enough to know what happens when residents get riled up."

"Yeah." Rachel cut a piece of pizza. "Nathan calls a town hall meeting, and the natives go at each other like a giant dysfunctional family."

"At least they always kiss and make up. Anyway, the winery opens in a few weeks, and we can't afford to tick off a town full of supporters."

Rachel's muscles tensed. "Are you saying it's okay to turn our wedding into a spectacle because it's good for business?"

"Dad has a lot of money, and I have a year of my life invested in the vineyard and winery." Charlie reached across the table and took her hand. "This is our town, and these are our people."

"I suppose it would be worse if no one wanted to come."

"A whole lot worse."

Rachel sighed as she reached for her wineglass. "Then I guess we're going forward with a southern-fried version of a royal wedding."

He clinked his glass to hers. "With the world's most beautiful bride walking down the aisle to a country version of the wedding march."

"Sorry, Charlie, that's where I draw the line."

Chapter 5

*E*mily checked her image in a full-length mirror—the white skirt and teal blouse she wore for the photo on her novel's back cover. "Too casual? Should I wear a jacket?"

Scott leaned on the doorframe. "It's not too late to back out of the Nordstrom deal."

"Last night you supported my decision." She turned and peered over her shoulder at the mirror. "Did you change your mind?"

"We don't know anything about the guy. After your sister's disastrous experience with the Atlanta director last year, call me more than a little skeptical."

"That was different. He was a scumbag."

Scott moved toward her. "I don't want you involved in something you'll regret."

"Stop worrying." Emily laced her fingers behind his neck. "I'm more concerned about the movie crew upstaging my first book-signing."

"Are you kidding? You're the town's newest celebrity." Scott kissed the tip of her nose. "Everyone will love you."

"We'll see how long that lasts." She unlaced her fingers. "Will you load my books in your truck?"

"I'm on it."

"Thanks, sweetie." She checked her image one more time before moving to the kitchen, where she found Rachel scooping scrambled eggs onto two plates. "I appreciate you helping out with my babies this morning."

"Glad to." Rachel set the plates on the table in front of the twins. "Dad texted me a few minutes ago. He's on his way up. He grabbed a last-minute cancellation at Willow Inn."

"Is he staying through Labor Day

"He didn't say." Rachel reached for a cloth and wiped a spill off the table.

Scott stepped in from the garage. "Books are loaded."

"Your big day." Rachel embraced her sister. "Break a leg, Sis."

Emily stepped back and frowned at her twin. "How does that phrase apply to writers?"

"Today, you start *acting* like a world-class author."

"Who's nervous as a puppy cornered by a twenty-pound alley cat." Emily kissed Clair's cheek, then Jane's. "Aunt Rachel will take good care of you while mommy signs some books." She waved goodbye to her girls and followed Scott to his truck. Once settled in the passenger seat, she grabbed her husband's arm. "What if no one shows up. If they do, I might forget names or make a mistake and misspell a word. My pen doesn't spell-check."

"Relax." He loosened her grip on his arm. "Everything will work out fine. It always does."

"Easy for you to say. You don't have two boxes of books to sell."

"No." Scott chuckled. "Just a store full of merchandise."

Emily clasped her hands and tried to focus on the passing scenery. Other than Mirabelle, would anyone in town even care about her book, especially after blaming her for keeping the movie news under wraps. It was almost time to find out.

When Scott pulled to the curb beside the hotel, she released a heavy sigh. "Now or never," she said to her husband with more courage than she felt. Emily stepped out and headed up the front walk. Light shining through the double doors' beveled glass created a warm glow and eased the tension in her shoulders. Inside, she walked past the high-back circular seat set under the massive chandelier highlighting the gold veins in the marble floor and headed toward the back.

Kat Williams was busy attaching black skirting to a pair of tables set three feet from the floor-to-ceiling windows spanning the back of the lobby. "Is this spot okay?"

"Perfect. Our town and this hotel conquered a heap of problems to arrive at this time and place."

"We should nickname Willow Falls the second-chance city." Kat set the last clip in place, then scratched her dark brown cheek. "Especially for folks like me and Missy."

"Mama Sadie knew what she was doing when she suggested I hire you straight out of prison."

Kat's smile lit up her face. "Your mother is an amazing woman with a huge heart."

Emily smiled back. "Yes, she is."

"Morning, Kat." Scott set two boxes on a table. "You picked a good spot."

"Best in the lobby." Kat opened one of the boxes. "Are you sticking around to watch your wife in action?"

"Can't. Got a store to run. I appreciate you helping her."

"For a few hours of fun, an up-and-coming author is giving me a free book," Kat said as she removed a stack of books from the box.

Scott caressed Emily's cheek. "You're gonna wow them, sweetheart."

"Thanks for being my number one fan."

"Always. I'll leave you ladies to finish unpacking the goods."

Emily opened the other box and pulled a book out. She stared at the cover as a twinge of anxiety pricked her conscience. What if people don't like the story? Or show more interest in the movie than her.

Kat set a stack of books on the table. "I imagine you're excited about today."

"I will be if anyone shows up." In between glancing at her watch and rearranging the display a half dozen times, Emily looked out at the rear veranda and beyond the lawn and lake. During the past three years her life had changed more than she could ever have imagined, and now she stood only moments away from her first live experience as a published author.

"Your fans are arriving early," Kat said. "We could start before ten."

"Not before Mirabelle shows up. I promised her the first book." Emily's palms moistened as she tuned in to conversations and discovered her book played a distant second to the pending celebrity invasion. With seconds to spare before the official start time, Mirabelle stormed in and moved to the front, triggering shouts and grumbles.

Emily held her hand up. "It's okay, folks. I promised to give her the first signed copy." She opened a book and picked up a pen.

Mirabelle pointed to the title page. "Write, to the star of *Percy's Legacy*."

Emily added the words *one of* to the request, then handed the book over. "Thank you for your support, Mirabelle. I hope you enjoy my novel."

The next person stepped forward. "I hear some famous people are planning to stay at the hotel. Do you know if a movie star reserved the room my husband and I decorated?"

Kat accepted the woman's check. "We have a block of reservations, but no names."

Emily opened another book to the title page. "How do you want me to sign?"

"To my good friend, Bertha. I read the director likes to discover new talent. Is your sister planning to audition for a part?"

"I don't know." Emily smiled and handed her the book. "You'll have to ask her."

The next woman in line pushed forward. "Enough, all ready. It's my turn. We hear you and Rachel are working for the director. Sign the book, to my friend Alice. What do you know about the movie's theme?"

So much for my celebrity status. "Not a single thing."

"How's that possible? You're our our paper's editor."

"Unfortunately, that doesn't qualify me for privileged information." Why don't these people understand that? "Thank you for buying my novel. I hope you enjoy it."

As each resident stepped up to the table, one undeniable truth became clear. A local girl who wrote a book couldn't compete with famous Hollywood luminaries. At least a few out-of-town guests made a fuss over her book.

A woman's shriek made Emily jump, wreaking havoc to her signature. "What the heck?"

"That's him!" shouted the woman. "Robert Nordstrom."

Half the people standing in line rushed toward the director.

Kat closed the cash box and handed it to Emily. "Sorry, my friend. I have to rescue our guest from this mob of crazies."

The next woman in line, Emily's neighbor, shook her head. "Our town's population is on the verge of becoming one giant, irritating band of groupies." She leaned close to Emily. "In my opinion, you're the real celebrity in the room. Would you like me to help you sell the rest of these books?"

"Bless you, Bonnie." She signed *to my hero*, then whispered, "This copy is on the house."

Chapter 6

The moment the doorbell echoed through the house, Rachel shooed Cody and Brownie to the back yard, then rushed to Emily's foyer. When she opened the front door, her breath caught. Greer Streetman's neatly trimmed white beard and mustache did little to conceal his pallid complexion. His crow's feet and forehead creases were more pronounced than ever, making him look older than his years. Though he still stood ramrod straight, he appeared thinner.

"Hello, Strawberry Girl."

She looked up into his brown eyes and smiled at the pet name he'd called her for as long as she could remember. "Hi, Dad. It's good to see you."

He leaned down and kissed her cheek. "Been a while."

"Too long." She stepped aside and motioned him in. "Would you like a cup of coffee or a glass of tea? How about a sandwich?"

"No thanks. I need to head downtown before the afternoon heat sets in. Want to join me?"

"I'd like that."

Clair toddled into the foyer, clutching a miniature replica of Buster—the newest item in the winery gift shop. Jane followed close behind, carrying a sippy cup.

"As you can see, I'm niece sitting, so we'll have company. If that's okay with you."

He shrugged. "Why not?"

"Come on in the kitchen and keep the girls occupied while I get ready."

After packing toddler gear into a pink bag, Rachel and her father carried the twins to Emily's car and secured them in their toddler seats. While backing from the garage, Rachel caught another glimpse of her father's sallow skin. "Are you okay?"

His brows furrowed. "Why are you asking?"

Uh oh. I touched a nerve. "No reason. Have you heard the latest? A crew is planning to roll into Willow Falls and film a full-length movie."

"The entertainment industry is good for Georgia and aspiring performers."

"I've accepted an interesting position." She relayed her liaison role. "The value of contacts and relationships are two of the many lessons I learned working for you."

"At least those seven years weren't a complete waste of your time."

His harsh tone triggered a twinge of remorse. After all, he had spent years grooming her to follow in his footsteps ... and forcing her to ignore her dreams. She gripped the steering wheel, determined not to blame him or give him one inch of control. "Is Streetman Enterprise the country's top real estate development firm yet?"

"Getting close."

Would that satisfy his ambition? Or would he aim for number one in the world? Relieved to arrive in town, Rachel searched for an available parking spot. "Typical Saturday. The tourists are taking over."

"You think it's bad now." He fingered his Rolex. "Wait until the film crew shows up."

After circling the block again, Rachel turned onto the street behind the church. She drove past the rear entrances to the two-story row of stores facing Main Street and parked behind Hayes General Store.

Her dad removed the stroller from the trunk. He helped transfer the twins to their ride and pushed it up the alley to the sidewalk.

"Our wounded veteran found his niche as the town's tour guide," Rachel said as she pointed to JT entertaining a group of tourists.

"A man with an artificial limb is bound to draw attention." Greer loosened his shirt collar. "Downtown looks prosperous. No more vacant stores."

"A big change from a year ago. We now have a coffee shop and an Italian restaurant. Pepper's Café and the hotel dining room couldn't handle the growing crowds."

"Tourism done right is a cash cow and a boon for real estate." Rachel's dad pushed the stroller across the street and parked it beside the vintage cast-iron mailbox. Father and daughter carried the twins to the carved mahogany door situated between the bank and adjacent store. Inside the vestibule, they passed a staircase and rode the newly installed elevator to the second floor. Miniature chandeliers illuminated the carpeted hall.

Rachel shifted Clair to her hip. "Definitely upscale. How many condos have you created?"

"Two across the street." He nodded to the right. "Two on this side. Patsy Peacock wouldn't sell her apartment above her store."

"She never will. Too many memories."

"Her loss. After these units sell, I'll make an offer on the space beyond her apartment." They moved down the hall on the left.

Baby Jane giggled. "Lanta Grampa make offer." She palmed his beard.

His eyes widened. "Did she call me Grandpa?"

"Uh-huh. Emily showed them your picture and told them Atlanta Grandpa was coming to visit."

His eyes shone with a tenderness Rachel had seen during his surprise visit to last year's surprise family Christmas party.

"Emily and Scott welcome you in their daughters' lives. And if Charlie and I have children, we want you in theirs as well."

He broke eye contact. "I need to check out my investment."

And the moment ends.

Inside the first of three units, he set Jane on the floor and embarked on a detailed inspection of the luxurious condo.

Rachel placed Clair beside her sister. She moved to the window and peered at the row of storefronts across the street. "I can barely hear the traffic noise."

"Thanks to top-notch materials and triple-pane windows." He squatted and examined the five-inch baseboard molding. "I'm expecting a hefty profit."

Rachel turned to check on the girls. "I assume these units are on the market."

"I'm meeting with the local real estate agent late this afternoon." He moved to the kitchen island and ran his fingers along the granite countertop. "Have you sold your townhouse?"

A sore subject with Charlie, and not one she wanted to discuss with her father. "I decided to hang on to it."

"Good idea. You'll need a place to stay when your career takes off. Why don't you let me pay off the mortgage?"

Rachel's jaw tightened. "Like I told you last year, I either have to make it on my own or abandon acting altogether."

"Suit yourself. How's the winery coming along?"

She tempered her tone. "Close to finished and looking incredible. The grand opening is approaching fast."

"And your wedding plans?" He opened a drawer and tested the self-closing mechanism.

"That's another story." She relayed the latest developments.

Her father's eyes zeroed in on hers. "You're opting for a carnival side-show instead of a ceremony?"

"Emily prefers to call it country sophistication. At least I'm still counting on you walking me down the aisle." Rachel pulled her pinging phone from her purse. "Uh oh. Seems my new role just kicked in. I need your help, Atlanta Grandpa. Will you take the twins back to Emily's?"

He hesitated.

Is he refusing? "If you'd rather not—"

"I've got you covered." He lifted the twins into his arms.

"Thanks, Dad." She tossed him the car keys and scurried from the condo, hoping spending alone time with Emily's toddlers would soften her father's heart.

Chapter 7

*E*mily dropped her pen at the sight of residents and tourists scrambling across the lobby to the hotel's front door. "Are Martians running rampant in our streets or did a neighboring town declare war on Willow Falls?"

Kat rushed over. "I called Rachel. She's on the way. I'll take the remaining books and money to my office."

"So much for selling my entire stock." Emily shook her head as she dashed toward the front door. Outside, the hiss of air brakes preceded three eighteen-wheelers and two smaller trucks braking in the middle of Main Street. The driver in the second rig climbed down and meandered to the front of his cab. He lit a cigarette and hiked his foot on the bumper.

Emily caught sight of Rachel rushing toward her. "Where are my babies?"

"With Dad. He'll take good care of them."

The sheriff's patrol car screeched to a halt beside the hotel, the blue and red strobe lights flashing. Mitch climbed out and slammed the door. Robert Nordstrom—sporting a stubble beard and salt-and-pepper hair curling over his shirt collar—approached him. Mayor Nathan dashed between the first and second truck and turned the duo into a trio.

Emily switched to reporter mode and shot a series of photos. "This week's headlines: *Giant Motorized Monsters Invade Willow Falls*."

"You can take pictures later." Rachel grabbed her arm. "Right now, we have to start earning our pay."

"It's already clear we need to demand a big fat raise." Emily's pulse pounded in her ears as she followed her twin and pushed through the horde gathering on the sidewalk.

Six-foot-four Sheriff Mitch glared down at the director. "We were expecting one decent-size truck, not five. Where in the devil do you think we're going to park these behemoths?"

"Someplace downtown."

The veins in Mitch's neck stood out. "Are you out of your mind?"

Robert glanced at Nathan, then Mitch. "Look, I apologize if my staff failed to give you an accurate picture of our needs. But we expect the mountain of cash we're pumping into this town to compensate for a little inconvenience."

"Inconvenience?" Mitch removed his cap and swept his hand through his hair. "You mean insane disruption."

Nathan nodded toward the nearest truck. "What's in those big rigs anyway?"

"Equipment."

Rachel stepped forward. "A few years back I watched a crew film a segment in downtown Atlanta. It took half a day to set up an hour-long shoot. These guys are shooting an entire movie."

"Which requires a ton of gear." Robert removed his sunglasses and set them atop his ball cap. "You're not suggesting we can't count on the town's full cooperation, are you, Sheriff?"

"No one's reneging on the deal. At the same time, we can't shut down the entire town for two months."

"Understood." Robert pointed toward the park. "I remember seeing a decent size parking lot around the corner, beside a church."

Nathan massaged his chin. "I suppose you could fit two rigs in that space."

Mitch eyed Nathan. "I understand you're speaking as the town's mayor, but that's asking a lot."

"My parishioners can put up with a little inconvenience for a few Sundays. The third truck can park on the next street over, across from my store."

"I suppose we can make that work." Mitch set his cap back on his head. "We'll locate the two small trucks on Falls Street."

Dressed in a black leather skirt, silver tank top, and a cropped jean jacket, Pearl—owner of the town's one beauty salon—pushed past Emily and stared up at Mitch. "Just a cotton-picking minute, Sheriff. You're talking about taking up customer parking spaces for every business on that street. Including mine."

"I know it's not ideal, Pearl. The problem is our limited options." Mitch pointed to the street. "This entire section of Main is only two lanes wide. Any vehicles parked here will create a traffic nightmare for both tourists and residents."

"I see your point." Pearl waggled a manicured finger at the director. "Mr. Nordstrom, is there a hair salon in your movie, like the one in *Steel Magnolias*?"

"No, ma'am."

"Well then, I suggest you write one in and pay me to film the scenes in my place."

Robert grinned. "I appreciate your suggestion, ma'am, but it's too late to go changing the script."

"Pity." Pearl clutched her jacket lapels. "Because everyone knows the local beauty shop is a vital hub in a small town."

"I'll keep that in mind for my next movie. Tell you what, if you agree to let us park on your street, I'll guarantee you a spot in the movie."

Pearl's eyebrows shot up. "A speaking role?"

Robert shook his head. "I can't make that promise."

"Will my name be in the credits?"

He nodded. "That I can promise."

"Okay then, we have ourselves a deal."

Rachel leaned close to Emily and whispered, "And there's the first morsel for your new novel about life in Willow Falls."

From the corner of her eye, Emily spotted an elderly curmudgeon trudging to his car. He opened the door and laid on the horn, sending a not-so-subtle message to the invading vehicular horde. "Uh oh, looks like trouble." She kept her eyes glued on the offender. "Mr. Nordstrom, your truck is blocking our grumpiest, least flexible citizen. I suggest you ask the driver to move it before the old guy drives up on the sidewalk and knocks down a light pole."

"Got it covered." Robert and Nathan hustled to the scene.

Mitch pulled Emily and Rachel aside. "You two come with me. We have to find the owners for all those cars parked on Falls Street."

"It's not too late to back out on this deal," Emily said as they hustled to keep up with Mitch's long strides.

Rachel snorted. "And miss all the fun?"

"We definitely should've negotiated for more pay."

Following a half-hour of ruffling and smoothing feathers, the sheriff and the director's liaisons had the section of Falls Street cleared and the two smaller trucks parked.

Mitch removed his cap and swiped his hand across his forehead. "Glad that's done."

"For the moment," Rachel said. "You know you'll have to do this again in a couple of days."

He glared at her. "What do you mean *again*?"

"Didn't someone warn you about the number of vehicles needed to support a movie shoot?"

"Yeah, the director's assistant said a few. And a few have arrived."

"Are you sure he didn't say fleet?" Rachel asked. "Because that's what you're going to end up with."

Mitch's eyes narrowed. "How are you defining *fleet*?"

"Enough vehicles to fill this entire section of Falls Street, and then some."

He popped his cap back on. "What in blazes have we gotten the town into?"

Emily released a long sigh. "One thing's for sure. The next eight weeks will put residents' patience and hospitality to the ultimate test."

Chapter 8

Sunday morning, Rachel awakened, stretched her arms over her head, and scolded Brownie for sneaking in beside her in the middle of the night. "You know you have to stay in your doggie bed." Her pup barked once and wagged her tail. "You'd best adjust to the idea before we move in with Charlie, or you might find yourself banned from our bedroom."

Brownie's head cocked.

"Don't pretend you didn't hear me." Rachel slipped into her robe, moseyed to the kitchen, and opened the sliding glass doors to let her naughty pet in the back yard with Cody.

"Hey, sleepyhead." Emily removed a tray of cinnamon rolls from the oven, releasing mouth-watering aromas. "Is your father coming to church with us?"

"When I invited him, he said it's not Easter, so what's the point?"

"I take it church isn't his thing."

"Never was." Rachel poured a cup of coffee and stirred in honey and vanilla creamer, a habit she had adopted from her twin. "Charlie's meeting us at the winery this afternoon to give Dad a tour."

Emily spread icing on the morning treat. "I imagine he'll be impressed."

"Especially since Streetman Enterprise had a hand in finding the property for Charlie's dad."

When the buns cooled, Emily gave one to each twin and carried the rest to the table.

Rachel reached for one herself. "The Hayes' decadent Sunday ritual." She closed her eyes and savored the sweet cinnamon and vanilla flavors. "I might have to keep this routine going for the Bricker family."

"They're not as good as Patsy's coffee cake, but they're easy. Pop the carton, lay the buns on a cookie sheet, and let the oven do the rest."

"That's my kind of cooking. Fast and easy." Rachel took another bite.

Emily sat across from her sister. "I hope your dad survived a couple of hours alone with my rambunctious toddlers."

"Even if he won't admit it, I think he enjoyed playing grandpa."

"Maybe it will entice him to spend more time away from work."

"Don't hold your breath." Rachel wiped her mouth with a napkin. "Thanks for the morning sugar rush. I need to change out of my jammies. I'm picking Dad up at ten."

"Why don't you invite him to join us for dinner Monday night."

"I will ... if I can convince him to stay in town one more day."

***

Rachel parked in front of Willow Inn, across from the grand home transformed into the town's hospital. She climbed the stairs to the inn's front porch, its roof supported by white columns. The neighbor's black cat stretched out on the railing, licking a white paw.

Her father sat in a rocking chair, holding a coffee mug in both hands. "Did Sadie adopt a feline?"

"More like Mittens adopted her. This is the kitty's favorite daytime hang out." Rachel stroked the cat's back, eliciting a purr. "It seems she's taken on the role as the inn's official greeter."

Her father laid his cup on a table dedicated to the parents who raised Emily and moved to Rachel's side. "Or guard cat to keep rodents away."

"There's that too. Are you ready to go?"

"I am." He escorted Rachel to her car and opened the driver's door.

After he rounded the front of the vehicle and eased onto the passenger seat, she drove between five of the seven grand houses lining both sides of Main. "JT says visitors claim the history and beauty of this street rival any they've seen in Georgia." She slowed and pointed to the home owned by a famous southern artist. "Since you own a Naomi Jasper original painting, you should visit her museum. It covers the entire first floor. Her studio is out back, along with a garage turned gift shop."

"Maybe next trip. Is the house next to Naomi's the one Charlie's old man bought?"

"It is." *And if Brick ever decides to propose, it'll be Mama Sadie's too.* Rachel turned onto County Road and passed a dozen small homes on clearings carved from heavily wooded lots. Two miles from town, the vineyard came into view. "Did you notice the sign when you drove in yesterday?"

"*Willow Oak Vineyard and Winery.* Couldn't miss it."

She drove down the winding driveway to the lower parking area. "Charlie's waiting for us downstairs."

They moved past the planters filled with colorful perennials set in the middle of a wide walkway to a row of tall, arched wooden doorways on the lower level of the winery. Rachel opened the first and led her father into a windowless room with stone walls matching the building's façade. Pendant lights suspended from the dark, beam-supported ceiling shone on the red-tile floor.

Rachel laid her purse on the three-sided, granite-top bar. "The tasting area turned out great, don't you think?" She pointed to a mural adorning the wall behind the bar—a replica of the gazebo and vineyard. "A Naomi Jasper original."

He moved closer. "That's worth a fortune."

"Her gift for bringing JT, Dennis Locke, and Jack Parker to this town. It's heartwarming how those three homeless guys have become the sons she never had."

"Naomi is an interesting woman."

"And a Willow Falls native."

Charlie entered from an arched doorway and held his hand out to his future father-in-law. "Glad you could make it, sir. You're our first official guest."

The man accepted, then released Charlie's hand and aimed his thumb at three open cabinets holding wine bottles with the Willow Oak label. "Your grapes?"

"Purchased. We'll begin harvesting in a few weeks. Next year's production will come from our vineyard, thanks to the fortune Dad invested in soil prep."

A nod showed approval. "It appears my old client didn't spare any expense on the building either."

"It cost a pretty penny, all right. Come on. I'll show you around." Charlie led the way through the extraction area to the fermentation room.

Grateful her fiancé and father had begun to forge a friendship, Rachel tuned out Charlie's monologue about wine production and ran her hand along a stainless-steel tank's cool, smooth surface. She found the entire winemaking process fascinating.

After Charlie described filtration, he led the way to a long, dark room. Rachel breathed in the rich scent of aged oak from rows of small and large barrels waiting for fermented juice. Ten minutes passed before they moved to the bottling apparatus. More explanations, until Charlie opened a door to a private staircase and led the way to an office. He placed his hand on his future father-in-law's shoulder. "What do you think of our winery?"

"First-class all the way. Is this your office or Brick's?"

"Mine. Dad's is across the hall."

Jack Parker stuck his head in the door. "The restaurant furniture is scheduled to arrive Tuesday."

"Thanks, man," Charlie said. "You remember Rachel's dad?"

"I do." Jack stepped inside and shook the man's hand. War-souvenir burn scars rendered his smile lopsided. "Welcome back to town."

"I take it you're on the Willow Oak team."

"Yes, sir. Charlie hired me six months ago."

"Jack's one of the smartest, hardest-working guys I've ever met," Charlie said. "He already knows as much about winemaking as I do."

"Except for darn near spraying the rose bushes to kill the bees."

Charlie chuckled. "I caught him in the nick of time. The bees help control the destructive bugs."

Jack laid a folder on Charlie's desk. "Have you guys toured the restaurant?"

"We're heading there next."

Rachel followed Charlie as he escorted her father to an area with a coffered ceiling and partially plastered walls revealing random sections of stone. She moved to the row of tall windows affording a panoramic view of the vineyard. "In my opinion, this is the most stunning sight in Willow Falls."

"Those stairs lead down to the tasting room," Charlie said. "Our gift shop is between the restaurant and the upper parking lot."

Rachel turned her back to the windows.

Her father leaned against a dark-wood, floor-to-ceiling cabinet, with doors on the bottom half and open shelves on top. "Brick's outdone himself, and you, young man, have a big job ahead of you. I imagine running a successful winery requires a lot of hard work."

"Not all that difficult when you love what you do. I've definitely found what I want to do for the rest of my life."

"Like Rachel and her acting career." Those intense eyes locked on hers. "You need to audition for Nordstrom. A movie role would boost your career."

Charlie crossed his arms, his jaw set. "You know she's a superstar right here in Willow Falls."

Rachel's skin prickled at his harsh tone. The comment he made the night he proposed exploded in her mind. *Whether you choose to pursue your dreams here in Willow Falls, in Atlanta, or on Broadway, I want to be with you.* Was he withdrawing his promise? "I haven't decided what I want to do."

"Whatever your decision," Charlie's tone softened, "I'll support you."

Rachel turned back toward the windows. Did he mean it? Or was he trying to save face in front of his future father-in-law? She vowed to find out before making a commitment she might live to regret.

Chapter 9

$\mathscr{E}$mily stopped on the sidewalk fronting the hotel, folded her umbrella, and pointed to the rainbow gracing the sky above Hayes General Store. "Brick would call that a good-luck omen." She hoped so. They could certainly use one.

"Today, my soon-to-be father-in-law's superstition might actually have merit." Rachel shook water from her umbrella.

"How so?"

"This is the quietest Labor Day I've ever witnessed. Not a single business, other than the hotel and inn, is open."

"Don't you remember? Up here, Labor Day actually means no labor."

"What a concept." Rachel lowered her sunglasses from the top of her head. "Hopefully, the town's day of rest also means our first official duty as Nordstrom's go-betweens won't be challenged by over-eager residents."

Emily guffawed. "Don't count on it. There's always the Mirabelle factor." The woman was bound to show up sooner than later.

"How does that woman manage to dig up scoops on nearly everything that goes on around here?"

Emily flicked a water droplet from her cheek. "She has eyes and ears in every nook and cranny."

"If she does manage to disrupt us, she'll give you plenty more material for novel number two."

"If I ever have the chance to start writing it."

Dressed in jeans and a light green golf shirt, Robert Nordstrom stepped outside and strolled to their side. "Kat told me today would be quiet."

"For the moment." Emily pulled her ball cap closer to her eyes. "Are you ready for a tour?"

He donned his wire-frame Ray-Ban sunglasses and black ball cap. "Lead the way, ladies."

Before they made it to the end of the hotel, a half dozen women appeared from around the corner, with Mirabelle leading the way.

"That didn't take long," Rachel muttered.

Robert halted, sandwiched between his protectors, as the town's self-appointed newscaster and her cohorts gathered around him.

A woman with short, dark-brown hair moved close. "Mr. Nordstrom, my daughter has a lead role in the high school's fall play. She's the prettiest girl in town and loaded with talent. I'm telling you she'd be perfect for your movie."

An older woman thumped the mother's arm. "There are lots of pretty girls in Willow Falls, Lizzy." She eyed Robert. "My granddaughter—who's a natural beauty—was on last year's homecoming court. She acts *and* sings."

Lizzy's eyes narrowed. "My daughter has way more experience than your skinny little granddaughter."

The grandmother crossed her arms. "That's a matter of opinion, and yours is seriously misguided."

"Oh, yeah—"

"Give the poor guy a break." Gertie, Scott's soda-fountain specialist, stepped between the two women. "We don't want a famous director thinking we're a bunch of country bumpkins."

"Don't get all high and mighty, Gertie." Lizzy huffed. "He's a director who needs to know who's who around here."

"Like he needs you to tell him what to do." Gertie looked up at Robert. "I suggest you use Hayes General Store in your movie, sir. It has a fascinating history, and if you're looking for a place that's country perfect, it fits the bill."

"Thanks for the tip, ma'am. Fact is, I'll make film location decisions during the next few days." He eyed the two women acting as talent agents. "Regarding the daughter and granddaughter you mentioned, they're welcome to show up for auditions."

Rachel tucked her umbrella under her arm. "We appreciate your enthusiasm, ladies, but Emily and I are functioning as Mr. Nordstrom's intermediaries. If you have any more suggestions or requests, you can run them by one of us. In the meantime, you need to let him carry on with his mission."

"My daughter's name is Jenny," Lizzy said. "If you don't pick her, you'll be missing out." She squared her shoulders and sashayed toward the park.

Mirabelle stood her ground as the others moved out of earshot. "You'll have to excuse my friends. They're way too pushy. I don't know if anyone told you, but I'm one of the stars in our town's play." She glanced at Rachel. "Ask her. She knows I can act."

The director chuckled. "Like I told the others, you're welcome to audition."

"I'll do that." She started to step away, then hesitated. "By the way, my name is Mirabelle Paine."

Emily stifled a laugh as Mirabelle walked away. "Sorry for the disruption." Actually, this one was pretty mild. But she knew the woman would not give up so easily.

"It comes with the territory, which is why I hired you two."

"Good thing you understand." Rachel pointed toward the street. "Because another ambush is headed our way."

A gaggle of teenagers rounded the corner and scampered in their direction. A girl, her blonde ponytail swaying, stopped two feet from the director. "We've all been trying to guess which big stars are in your movie. We hope they're famous. Please tell us who's coming to town, Mr. Nordstrom. We *have* to know."

Frenzied pleas from the youngsters erupted.

Robert raised his hands in a defensive mode. "Hold onto your saddle, kiddos." He waited for them to fall silent. "I assume you're familiar with Justin Brooks."

The blonde shrieked. "He's the sexiest guy alive. Am I right, ladies?"

Connor, the town's seventeen-year-old-wannabe FBI agent, shoved his hands in his jeans pockets. "He's not so great."

"You're just jealous," said the blonde.

"Oh, yeah?" The young man's eyes shifted to the director. "Is there a sexy lady in your movie?"

"Is that how you'd describe Carrie Fleming?"

"Now you're talking." Connor yanked his phone from his pocket and tapped the keypad. "Take a look at this." He held a photo inches from the blonde's face. "That's what I call sexy."

A pretty brunette shook her finger in Connor's face. "Like Carrie Fleming would have anything to do with you."

"And you think Justin Brooks will give any of you chicks a second look? Not one chance in a gazillion."

Emily stepped forward. "Okay, kids, settle down and give our guest some space."

"Come on, guys." Connor held his phone up. "We'll find lots of hot Carrie photos."

The teenage pack dispersed, the guys heading in one direction, the girls in another.

"Just what we need, boys with raging hormones surfing the web," Emily said. "It seems in one day my hometown has become starstruck."

Robert adjusted his Ray-Bans. "Maggie will have a ball with these folks."

Emily's brows raised. "Maggie?" *Surely he's not talking about …*

"Warren."

"Oh my gosh." Rachel pressed her palms together. "She's been one of my favorite actresses as far back as I can remember."

"She's a gem all right." Robert sadly shook his head. "But this will likely be her last performance."

Rachel's eyes widened. "Why, is she ill?"

"Nope. Ready to retire and lead a normal life for a change."

Emily noted Rachel's faraway stare and suspected the director's *normal* comment gave her sister pause.

The trio resumed their stroll and settled into a routine as residents continued to emerge to sweet-talk the director and offer not-so-subtle bribes. Robert's reaction didn't vary—smile, respond to questions, and promote the audition.

By late-afternoon, Emily teetered on the brink of exhaustion as the threesome sat on the lake's retaining wall. "I know this is all normal for you, but I still want to apologize for our residents' aggressive behavior."

"No need." He removed his Ray-Bans and wiped the lenses with his shirttail. "Believe me, enthusiasm beats the heck out of resistance or apathy."

Rachel plucked a pebble off the wall. "One thing I've learned about Willow Falls, residents don't suffer from a lack of passion."

"That's one reason I like to film in small towns."

Emily crossed her leg over her knee and massaged her calf. "We'll do our best to keep folks from becoming too disruptive. Rachel and I are hosting a casual family dinner at my house Monday night. We'd be honored if you'd join us, and I promise we won't bombard you with a single proposition or request."

"You're on." Robert slipped his sunglasses back on. "Thanks again, ladies, for showing me around town. In a couple of days, I'll need your help selecting two houses to use in the film."

"That's when I'll be tempted to toss my cell phone in the lake." Emily sighed, knowing the task would end up making two families happy and half the town madder than a cage full of hungry squirrels.

Chapter 10

Following dinner and lively conversation with Robert, Rachel invited her father to Emily and Scott's backyard. She settled on a patio chair. He sat beside her.

Brownie yawned and plopped her head in Rachel's lap. She stroked her dog's muzzle. "One thing's certain. Today's been interesting."

"That's an understatement." Greer set his wine glass on the table. "A year from now, Willow Falls residents will look back and recognize this weekend as a major turning point in their future."

Rachel brushed a stray curl away from her cheek. "Is that good or bad?"

"Depends on one's perspective."

"Are you suggesting a few weeks of rubbing shoulders with Hollywood types will take this little town in a whole new direction?"

"Not suggesting, predicting."

"I don't know." Rachel watched a cloud drift past the half-moon and tried to imagine the changes her father was suggesting. "Folks around here are set in their ways. The influx of tourists hasn't changed them all that much. Although it has amped up complaints about traffic and busy downtown sidewalks."

"Trust me." Greer planted his right ankle on his knee and fingered his Brunello Cucinelli loafers. "Fame and newfound fortune are intoxicating motivators."

The story of Willow Falls' unique beginning and the subject of Emily's book floated through Rachel's mind. One young man's nineteenth-century plan to snub the rich and famous and create a refuge for the woman he loved. She hoped the town wasn't teetering on the brink of transforming into something its founder worked hard to escape. "I'm guessing you had a good time playing grandpa to Clair and Jane Saturday afternoon."

"I managed to keep up with them."

Rachel smiled as she pictured the threesome. "They're a bundle of energy all right." She glanced at her father's profile, the glow of moonlight accentuating his pale complexion. Did the twins wear him out? Did he have a physical problem? Impossible. As far back as she could remember, she had never seen him sick with anything other than one bout with the flu. "I've been thinking. Perhaps you could slow down and spend more time with our family."

"You should know by now that slowing down isn't in my DNA." He picked up his glass.

Rachel fingered her tennis bracelet. "Still, it'd be good if you could enjoy the fruits of your labor. Goodness knows, you have more money than you'll ever be able to spend."

"It's not about the money." He paused for a long moment. "Streetman Enterprise is on the verge of becoming the largest real estate development firm in the country. Number one. Do you have any idea what that means?"

More power and status. Was it worth sacrificing his personal life? She didn't answer.

"I'm flying to the west coast in a couple of days to close a deal on a small company. The acquisition will open doors in a dozen states."

"Some people think less is more."

He planted both feet on the ground and slid to the edge of his chair. "That's a copout for anyone who can't make the grade."

Her father's monologue espousing explosive growth generated a sinking sensation in Rachel's stomach and forced her to question her own ambitions. For years she had found comfort in believing she possessed her mother's characteristics—until she discovered the truth about her birth. Now she understood that her life had been influenced far more by environment than genetics.

"No matter what you think, you're a chip off the old block."

Rachel's mouth went dry. Had he read her mind? Impossible. "What are you saying?"

"You don't need my blood circulating through your veins to possess my penchant to reach extraordinary heights. I just didn't expect you to target your ambition to the entertainment world."

She cringed at his condescending tone. "I thought you had come around to supporting my career choice."

He leaned forward and rested his elbows on his knees. "Seems I overestimated my influence on you."

"Don't feel bad. You taught me the value of hard work and laser focus."

"Both critical skills." He remained silent for a long moment. "Did you and your sister inherit your creativity from Sadie?"

"She does have a keen eye for decorating."

His brows shot up. "The Willow Inn?"

Rachel nodded. "She and Emily collaborated."

"It's first-class all the way."

The sliding glass door opened behind them. "Hey, you two." Emily stepped outside. "Is this a private conversation or can anyone jump in?"

"We're talking about Willow Inn's amazing décor," Rachel said.

"Thanks to Mama Sadie's keen eye and decorating skills."

"She is a fascinating woman." Rachel's father stood. "Time for me to go."

"Please don't let me scare you off," Emily said.

"You're not. I'm leaving town before the crack of dawn and want a good six hours of sleep. Thanks for inviting me to spend the evening with your family and the town's newest celebrity. Nordstrom is an interesting character, despite his status as a Hollywood mogul."

Rachel flinched at his second unmasked reproach and sprang to her feet. "You're coming back to walk me down the aisle, right?"

He tapped the tip of her nose like he did when she was a little girl. "Why wouldn't I, Strawberry Girl?" He turned toward Emily. "You take care of those little girls for their Atlanta grandpa."

"I promise, and thank you for babysitting this afternoon."

"You're welcome."

As Rachel watched him leave, a notion took hold and sent an ice-cold sensation surging through her limbs.

Emily frowned. "You look like you spied a coiled snake rattling its tail."

"Sometimes I wonder if I'm more like my father than I realize."

"That's nuts. I can't believe you let him upset you."

Rachel gripped the back of her chair. "He spent twenty-nine years molding me in his image—"

"And last year you found the courage to follow your own path."

"Thanks to you and Charlie."

Emily reached for her sister's hand. "What do you say we go back inside and enjoy another glass of wine with our two favorite guys?"

"Now you're talking."

Chapter 11

Rachel's jaw dropped at the sight of residents and tourists filling every seat in the Redding Arms ballroom and lining up along the walls. "Looks more like a convention than an audition."

"Seems half the town showed up." Emily slipped her purse off her shoulder. "How will Robert decide who to cast?"

"Beats the heck out of me." Rachel lowered her voice. "One thing's for sure. If everyone in here expects to land a part, a lot of these folks are in for one gigantic disappointment."

"Maybe their small-town sensitivity will keep them grounded."

"Like my father said, don't underestimate the lure of fame, no matter how miniscule."

Emily pointed to a pair of empty seats in the back row. "That's the best we can do."

"Lead the way, Sis."

After scooting to the center, Emily dropped onto a seat and set her purse on the floor. "Help me understand what to expect."

"This is a whole different ballgame than auditioning for a play, so I don't know any more than everyone else in here." A tap on her shoulder made Rachel jump. She turned and faced the mother who had accosted Robert the day before.

"Which twin are you?"

"Rachel."

Lizzy glanced from one to the other. "How do people tell you two apart?"

"Freckle count," Emily and Rachel responded in unison.

The woman shifted her attention to Emily. "You told us to bring requests to you, and you'd handle them."

"That's not exactly what we said, but we're listening. What's on your mind?"

"My daughter is prettier than Carrie Fleming, and she's a better actress than anyone in this town. You have to make sure the director picks her for a speaking role—"

"Stop right there, Lizzy. Rachel and I don't have any say in casting decisions."

"Rumor is you two are earning big bucks to influence the director."

Emily stared at the woman. "You ought to know by now that rumors aren't worth their weight in cotton."

Lizzy huffed. "Are you going to promote my daughter or not?"

"Casting isn't our responsibility," Rachel said. "Besides, no one has a clue which roles Mr. Nordstrom needs to fill. The script might not call for a pretty teenager."

"By the way"—Emily eyeballed the room—"where is your daughter?"

"In the front row with her friends."

"Does she know you're talking to us?"

Lizzy's face flushed. "I'm doing this for her own good."

"I'm sure you are." Emily snickered. "In which case, you need to relax and let this whole thing play out."

"I still believe you two have way more pull with the director than you're letting on." Lizzy sniffed, then backed away.

Rachel leaned close to Emily. "If Nordstrom doesn't cast her daughter, that woman will hound the dickens out of us for the next two months."

"Just what we need. Hey, looks like this event is ready to kick off."

Robert stepped onto the riser, tapped the microphone, and waited for the audience to fall silent. "From the look of this crowd, it's obvious Willow Falls is populated with movie fans."

"Why'd you pick our town?" shouted a woman sitting in the third row.

"It has everything we need. A picturesque downtown with a nice park. A row of magnificent homes, and as a bonus, some experienced actors. Couple of months ago I drove up and watched a performance of *Percy's Legacy*. The professionalism impressed me."

Emily leaned close to Rachel. "I wonder why he didn't mention that yesterday or last night?"

"Most likely because he was too busy fielding questions from the natives. And during dinner we promised not to talk shop."

"Good point."

Connor, the teenage sleuth, popped out of his seat. "Everyone wants to know what your movie is about."

Robert lifted the mic and moved to the edge of the riser. "A romantic-triangle comedy involving a restaurant owner accused of killing her missing fiancé—a hot-shot attorney—and his sophisticated girlfriend. Toward the end of a chaotic trial, everyone learns the fiancé fled town to escape his wealthy, overbearing mother. Carrie Fleming plays the suspect. Justin Brooks is cast as the defense attorney, and Maggie Warren as the mother."

Cheers erupted.

Connor remained standing. "A trial has to have a prosecutor. Who'd you pick to play that role?"

"Max Grover, an up-and-coming young actor. Ben Foster, the well-known character actor, plays the crusty old judge."

"That's a great cast," whispered Rachel. "Did you notice he didn't mention the attorney's girlfriend?"

"Maybe after watching you perform as Lilian, he has you pegged for that role."

Rachel gawked at her sister. "Where'd that come from?"

"An educated guess. A significant part in a Nordstrom movie would send your career soaring in a whole new direction."

Goose bumps popped up on Rachel's skin as Emily's comment resonated and sent images of stardom dancing in her head.

"You're thinking the same thing, aren't you?"

"No. Maybe." Rachel refocused on the director.

"Auditions for speaking roles are limited to those who have actual acting experience," Robert said. "Professional or amateur."

Grumbles and protests resounded.

He held his hand up. "Hold on, everyone. The painful truth is budgets don't allow us time to teach people how to act. However, you can rest assured that I'll need a good number of extras, some with a decent amount of camera time."

The grumblers quieted.

"Good, you folks understand." He moved back to the mic stand. "If you have acting experience and want to audition, join me in the meeting room across the hall. If you want consideration as an extra, please remain in here. My staff will begin the selection process."

"Mr. Nordstrom," yelled Lizzy. "Will you pay everyone who makes the cut?"

"Yes, ma'am. We'll erect a notice board in front of the hotel. In two days at noon, we'll post our decisions. Those selected will need to meet our attorney back here to sign contracts." He scanned the room. "Any more questions?"

Silence.

"No? Okay, let's get the ball rolling." He placed the microphone in its stand and stepped off the riser.

"Time for you to go showcase your talent, Sis," Emily said.

Rachel watched Robert maneuver through the crowd. "What about you? Are you vying for a cameo appearance?"

"Heck no. I'm too busy taking notes for my book." Emily watched Lizzy rushing toward Robert. "Besides, if you land a speaking role, I'll have to cover for both of us."

Rachel blew a puff of air. "That doesn't seem fair. Maybe I should forget auditioning."

"That's crazy talk. What did you say last year when I questioned if I should continue writing?"

"Enlighten me."

"You told me to quit being such a namby-pamby and get on with it." Emily stood and locked eyes with Rachel. "So, get up off your fanny and go knock the director's socks off."

Rachel grinned at her sister. "You sure are bossy."

"Someone has to light a fire under you, which you also told me. Besides, it'd be awesome to have a movie star in the family."

"One little speaking role won't make that big a difference." The moment the words tumbled out, Rachel knew they weren't accurate. Most successful film actresses began their careers acting in bit parts.

Emily nudged her sister's foot with her toe. "Is the fire burning enough to make you walk across the hall?"

"If I don't, you'll bug the daylights out of me." Rachel slipped from the back row and walked out of the ballroom. Two feet from the door she stopped and watched residents entering the meeting room. As far as she knew, none of them had any experience. Which gave her an advantage. Maybe her acting career was destined to veer in a different direction. She squared her shoulders and walked into the room.

The butterfly invasion returned the second she caught Robert's eye. His face lit with a smile. "I'm glad you showed up."

Heat rose to her cheeks. "I don't have any film experience."

"You can act. That's all that counts." He handed her a script. "Page fifteen. You're up in ten minutes."

She opened it. Her palms moistened. Her throat went dry. A famous director wanted *her* to audition for a key role. She breathed deep to slow her pounding pulse.

"Yes, sir. I'll be ready."

Chapter 12

*E*mily pressed the speaker icon and laid her phone on the kitchen table. She braced herself for what was to come. "Slow down, Gertie. My sister and I are both listening."

"The whole town's going bananas."

Rachel leaned over Emily's shoulder. "Over what?"

"All the changes the film crew's making. You two better come down here and calm the natives before they sure enough start a riot."

"Thanks for giving us a heads up." Emily rolled her eyes as she pocketed her phone. "At this rate, every nickel this gig pays will go for childcare."

"I got you into this, so I'll split the cost with you. Call it compensation for a year's worth of room and board."

"Deal." Emily speed-dialed her babysitter. "I hope you're available, like right now."

"I'm on my way."

Ten minutes later, the sisters parked behind Hayes General Store and rushed up the alley to Main Street. Emily halted and gaped at huddles of citizens shouting at men charged with completing tasks.

"Oh my gosh," Rachel said in a panicked whisper. "Where do we begin?"

Emily glanced left then right. "We could go in different directions."

"No way I'm facing any of those crazies on my own."

Her sister was right. "I suppose strength in numbers is best. Come on." Emily led the way across the street.

A man balancing on a ladder leaning against a light pole glared down at Mirabelle. "What's your problem, lady?"

"Why are you taking all our town's flags down?" she shouted.

"We're replacing them with Floral Springs banners. That's the name of this here burg in the movie."

Mirabelle planted her fists on her hips. "How will people know it's Willow Falls?"

He ignored her and continued installing the new flag.

Emily stood by as Rachel caught Mirabelle's attention. "Audiences will know from the credits."

"What are you talking about."

"You know. At the end of the film."

"Don't you know nobody reads those long lists?" Mirabelle tilted her head toward Pepper's Café. "Look what's happening over there. They're painting a new sign on the window. What kind of name is Joanie's Joint anyway?"

Emily turned toward the crowd gathered in front of the café. They were giving owner Pepper Cushman an earful. "There's no need to go ballistic, Mirabelle. I'm sure she's given the film crew permission."

A salesclerk from the clothing store gripped Pepper's arm. "They're changing a whole bunch of signs. Are they gonna put everything back after the filming's done?"

"Yes." Pepper's head shake accentuated her answer.

"Are you positive?" someone from the crowd asked.

"A hundred percent." Pepper held up a sheet of paper. "Every business that's undergoing even a miniscule change has a signed contract."

Mirabelle's brows shot up as she approached Pepper. "Are they filming inside your café?"

"Lots of scenes."

Emily tapped the mail carrier's arm. "Don't you remember the director explaining that the lead character is a restaurant owner?"

"Of course, I do. Is the director also gonna change the name of your husband's store?"

Emily spotted Robert crossing Falls Street with Patsy Peacock. "I'll ask him. He's heading over now." She stepped away from Mirabelle and leaned close to Rachel. "This should be interesting."

"Should we intervene?"

"More like watch the show. Patsy's small in stature, but mighty in persuasion. You're in for a real treat and not just the tasty kind."

The sisters moved to the front of Patsy's store.

Robert tipped his cap. "Good morning, Emily, Rachel. I trust you have everything under control."

Emily shaded her eyes with her hand. "We're working on it. Do you mind if we join you two?"

"Not at all." Patsy unlocked the door and held it open. "Have a seat while I fix you a delicious treat." She locked the door behind her—leaving the *closed* sign visible—then slipped behind the glass display case.

Robert pulled two chairs out from an ice-cream-parlor table and motioned Emily and Rachel to take a seat. He pulled up a third chair and laid his ballcap on his lap.

"I'm curious." Rachel glanced toward Patsy. "How did she manage to lure you here?"

"She cornered me in the lobby and insisted I visit her shop. One thing I do know, it's not wise to upset sweet, elderly ladies." Robert placed his arms on the table. "What's with her peacock feathered hat?"

"You mean hats," Emily said.

His eyes widened. "How many does she have?"

"Dozens. She wears them in honor of her husband, Tommy."

"Where is the guy? I'd like to meet him."

Emily looked up at the ceiling. "He's been with the angels for decades. Patsy claims he was her true soul mate, and she never remarried."

"A real-life love story." Robert glanced around the space. "This is an interesting business—sweets, gifts, and a Christmas store all rolled into one." He turned back toward Emily. "I couldn't resist Miss Peacock's invitation. Call it professional curiosity."

The rich scent of chocolate sweetened the air as Patsy returned with plates and a tray of brownies. "Fresh from the oven." She served three slices while Robert moved a fourth chair to the table.

Emily dug her fork into the fudge-like decadence. "Patsy is the best dessert chef in all of Georgia."

Robert tasted the dessert, then nodded. "I'd say the whole country."

"Why, thank you, sir." Patsy sat with her ankles crossed and her hands folded in her lap. A demur smile warmed her face and crinkled the lines around her eyes. "You're quite a gentleman, as well as a gifted director.

Our little town is blessed beyond belief to have such a talented young fellow pick us for his next successful film."

Emily stifled a grin as she recognized Patsy's ploy to reel Robert in. Big time.

"I'm not so young, ma'am."

"Honey, compared to me, you're a spring chicken. Or should I say a young buck." Patsy chuckled. "What do you think of my humble little establishment?"

"Charming. Lots of peacocks."

The owner looked pleased. "They're magnificent creatures, so statuesque and colorful."

He grinned. "Indeed, they are."

"I hear you're renaming the café next door to Joanie's Joint. The name is unique and definitely memorable." Patsy unfolded her hands. "Kind of like Patsy's Pastries and Pretties. It flows off the tongue like beautiful poetry, don't you think?"

Emily swallowed to keep from choking with laughter, wondering if Robert had a clue he'd been hooked.

"Yes, ma'am." His brows lifted as if the light suddenly came on. "Are you suggesting I leave your store's name alone?"

"I knew we'd see eye to eye. No wonder you're the smartest director in Hollywood." She patted his hand. "You stay right here, honey, while I fix you a delicious cup of hot chocolate." She popped up and disappeared behind the counter.

Robert leaned forward. "Did I just get snookered by one crafty little senior citizen?"

"I'd say you did." Emily looked at Rachel, and they shared a laugh.

"Let me guess. Everyone in town adores her."

Emily nodded. "She's like a folk hero. Her shop is one of the few that survived a long, painful, dry spell. Folks bought her pastries and gifts when they could ill afford to do so, just to keep her from going under."

"Which means if I go changing the name for the movie, I'll be considered the biggest fool this side of the Mississippi."

Patsy returned before Robert's question was addressed and set a mug topped with whipped cream on the table. "There is one more downtown location with a name your movie fans will love. And it's the subject of our signature play and Emily's novel."

"Let me guess." He grinned. "Hayes General Store?"

"Precisely. It sounds so humble, yet important."

"Miss Patsy Peacock, I've decided to keep both names and film a segment right here in your store." Robert pointed his fork toward his plate. "With you serving a slice of this delicious brownie to my lead characters."

"Why, I'm deeply touched."

Robert burst out laughing. "You are the shrewdest, most charming little lady I've ever had the privilege of meeting. If there are many more like you around here, this will be one delightful experience." He laid his fork down, then removed a folded document and a pen from his back pocket. After spreading the stapled papers on the table and making a notation, he handed it to Patsy. "This is what I'm offering for the use of your store."

Patsy adjusted her glasses. "Oh my, that's a lot of money."

"I take it you'll accept the contract."

"Of course." She reached for the pen and signed.

He added his signature. "Oh, one thing that's not in writing. I expect delivery of one decadent dessert to my hotel room every single day."

Patsy held her head high. "Excellent arrangement, young man."

Emily grinned and made a mental note to add the exchange to her growing list of scenes for her new novel.

Chapter 13

Rachel halted in Willow Inn's foyer beside the antique-cherry desk Emily inherited from her grandfather. She glanced at her watch for the umpteenth time, then rolled her shoulders and resumed pacing.

Mama Sadie came in from the dining room and set a cut-glass vase filled with fresh flowers on the desk. "You're fixing to be slap worn out by the time noon rolls around."

"I know." Rachel paused and admired the splinters of light the elaborate crystal chandelier cast on the marble floor. "Landing a speaking role in a Robert Nordstrom film is a big deal." She moved to the curved staircase and plopped on the second step. "Last year, when I turned down that lead in the play at the Alliance Theater, I pretty much slammed the door shut to my acting career."

"Putting your sister and the town's play ahead of your own ambition was a brave and unselfish act."

Maybe so, but ... "I understand I made the right choice. Still ... I've never admitted this to anyone." Rachel's shoulders slumped. "Sometimes, I regret that decision."

Her mother sat beside her. "Regret can eat at your insides. I spent thirty years behind bars because I didn't want anyone to know the truth about my crime. When I look back ... what I'm trying to say is Robert casting you would be a blessing that could open a lot of doors."

Rachel straightened her back. "Even if I'm selected for the part, there's no guarantee it will lead to anything or if I'll even like acting in a movie."

"I don't know squat about the entertainment business. What I do know is you need to find the best way to let your light shine through your gift."

Rachel gave her mother a playful nudge. "Are you practicing for Nathan's preaching job?"

"Hardly. I'm just saying, you shouldn't ignore opportunity."

"You're a wise woman." Rachel slid her arm around her mother's shoulders. "I'm curious. Does it bother you that the director and your deceased stepfather have the same first name?"

"You mean the man I shot? Don't you know that character, not a name, defines a person?"

"Is that a no?"

"A big, fat no."

"Good." Rachel stood, pressed her thumbs to her lower back, and stretched. "Time to go discover my fate. Do you want to come with me?"

"Thanks, but I have to prepare the inn for Carrie Fleming and Maggie Warren."

"Wow. When did you find out they're staying here?"

"Ten minutes ago." Mama Sadie pushed up from the step. "Carrie's assistant sent me an email with a long list of instructions. I'm putting her downstairs in the Carlie suite. It's the biggest."

"And Maggie?"

"In Emily's other mother's room. It's the prettiest." Mama Sadie clucked her tongue. "Mirabelle's gonna throw a hissy fit when she finds out I didn't put a movie star in her namesake."

"Unless Robert casts her in a role. Sometimes she's more irritating than fingernails clawing a chalkboard, but at least she learned how to act. I'll text you the results."

"I'm still amazed at how much the world changed while I was locked up." Mama Sadie stared at her cell phone. "Who'd have believed a little thing the size of a Hershey's candy bar could deliver messages in a nanosecond. It sure beats the heck out of Western Union."

"You're a treasure, Mama Sadie. I love you so much."

"That goes both ways, sweet girl." She gave Rachel a quick hug. "Now scoot. Go find out what Robert Nordstrom has in store for you."

"I'm on my way." Rachel left the inn and skipped down the porch steps to the sidewalk. She slowed and gawked at the mob crowded around the message board on the hotel's front lawn. Shrieks of joy and angry shouts of protest rose as movie-star wannabes discovered their fate. Resisting the urge to turn around and climb back onto the porch, she crossed the driveway and eased into the crowd.

Lizzy, her eyes narrowed to a slit, tapped the glass door on the board. "That director isn't worth a plug nickel. My daughter ended up with nothing better than a measly role as an extra."

Mirabelle faced the woman. "At least she's in the cast."

"That's easy for you to say. You're one of the chosen ones."

Rachel squeezed her way to Mirabelle's side. "Are congratulations in order?"

"Big time." A grin lit Mirabelle's face. "The director chose me to play the jury forewoman. That's an important part in a movie about a trial."

"Indeed it is."

Mirabelle's lips drew into a thin line. "While I was growing up, nobody around here believed I'd amount to much on account of my no-good father and alcoholic mother. Now, not only will tourists who buy a ticket to our town's play know about me, people all over the country, maybe the entire world, will see me in a movie and know ... that I'm somebody."

The raw emotion in her voice caught Rachel off guard. She placed her hand on Mirabelle's arm. "You, my friend, will forever be known as a star juror in a major motion picture."

"I like the sound of that. Wait. You don't know, do you?" Mirabelle pointed to the message board. "You're cast as Justin's sophisticated girlfriend."

"Are you serious?" Rachel stared at her name, topping the list. A major speaking role in a Robert Nordstrom movie. She had no idea how Charlie would react or how much the part would interfere with their wedding plans. At least she would discover if marriage and an acting career could coexist. Her eyes moved to the next two names, Naomi Jasper and Missy Gibson—Mama Sadie's other ex-con friends and stars of *Percy's Legacy*. Both chosen for speaking roles.

"Rachel and Emily obviously had a heap more influence than they claimed." Lizzy's tone oozed contempt.

Pearl, cast as one of the jurors, knuckle-thumped the woman's arm. "Emily's name isn't up there, so you know good and well that's not true."

"All I know is my Jenny has acting experience, and the director overlooked her for one of Sadie's jailbird buddies."

"Honey." Pearl waggled her finger at Lizzy. "Missy can act circles around your girl. Besides, she has something else going for her."

"Yeah." Lizzy's eyes narrowed. "She's a good friend of Rachel and Emily."

"Nope. Missy isn't saddled with a whacky mother who'd drive the director bat-crazy. Everyone knows about your little scene on Labor Day. Heck, I'm shocked the director cast Jenny in any kind of role."

Lizzy glared at Pearl. "Are you insinuating I'm a meddlesome parent?"

"If the girdle fits, sweetie pie."

"Hmph." Lizzy spun and stomped away.

"Who knew you had it in you, Pearl?" Rachel's brow scrunched. "I hope you didn't lose a customer,"

"Not a chance. A quarter-inch of gray roots will send Lizzy racing to my salon in a heartbeat."

Rachel chuckled as she pulled her ringing phone from her pocket. "Hey, Sis."

"Congratulations for landing a plum role."

"How'd you hear? Oh yeah, I almost forgot. News around here travels telepathically." She moved away from the lingering natives. "Did you also hear about the dust-up between the town's hairdresser and the stage mother?"

"I think I'm about to."

Rachel relayed the conversation. "That would be a great scene for your book."

"No kidding. If their reaction is any indication, this town is on the verge of movie-madness meltdown."

Chapter 14

*E*mily steered her car around a corner and glanced at Robert Nordstrom sitting in the passenger seat with Rachel behind him. "It would help if we had an idea what you're looking for?"

"A home suitable for a young, small-town restaurant owner," Robert said. "I'll let you know when I see it."

Emily crept through neighborhoods for twenty more minutes without hearing a peep from him. "You need to know I'm running out of options."

"Stop the car." Robert tapped the passenger window. "Who lives there?"

Rachel opened the rear door. "The Petersons. Wayne composed the music for our town's play."

"Interesting." Robert grabbed his leather satchel, stepped from the car, and walked along the picket fence adorned with blooming vines. An array of layered bushes and annuals created a profusion of color in the front yard. "If the inside is half-decent, we've hit the jackpot." He opened the gate and moved down a winding stone walkway lined with pink begonias. A double swing hung on the front porch. The leaves on a potted lemon tree stood in contrast to white wood siding.

Emily scooted around him and rang the bell, hoping this would go well.

Agnes opened the door and pressed her hand to her chest. "Oh, my goodness. What a pleasant surprise."

"Good afternoon, Mrs. Peterson. I'm Robert Nordstrom"

"I know. I saw you when you checked into the hotel." She stepped aside. "Won't you come in?"

He removed his cap and entered. "Your front yard is picture perfect."

Agnes' face beamed. "My pride and joy. You must meet my husband. He's a retired high-school music teacher and a composer." The wide-plank, wood floors creaked as she led her trio of guests to the front room. "Dear, we have company."

Wayne eased off a recliner, hobbled forward, and extended his gnarled, arthritic hand. "I recognize you from your picture in the paper."

Robert accepted his hand. "The music you wrote for *Percy's Legacy* is excellent."

"A work of love. What can we do for you?"

The director laid his satchel on the piano bench and explained his mission. "If your house fits the film's requirements, I'll offer you a contract for its use."

"How marvelous." Agnes clapped her hands together. "My husband built this little house while we were engaged. Can you believe we've lived here since the day we were married?"

Robert smiled warmly at the woman. "Your home is lovely, Mrs. Peterson. Will you show me around?"

"Please call me Agnes." She began the tour with a story detailing the day they moved in, their voices fading as they left the room and moved down the hallway.

Emily settled beside Rachel on a couch upholstered with red and gray velvet damask.

Wayne returned to his recliner. "I'm old and set in my ways. Having a crew of Hollywood types traipsing around for who knows how long doesn't sit well."

Emily scanned the living room, then the dining room across the narrow foyer. The small spaces, packed with furniture and a lifetime of memorabilia, didn't seem like an appropriate setting for a young twenty-first-century woman. "Maybe he'll only want to film scenes outside."

"My wife won't take kindly to folks tramping through her garden."

"She does have the prettiest front yard in Willow Falls." Emily picked up an embroidered throw pillow and fingered the intricate floral design. "This is sweet."

"A gift from Agnes' mother."

"Reminds me of the pillow Mama Sadie's grandmother stitched." She held it to her nose. "Without the floral scent." She handed the pillow to Rachel.

"He says our home is perfect, dear," Agnes said as she returned carrying a plate of cookies.

Robert sat on the piano bench and opened his satchel. He retrieved a document and handed it to Wayne. "This is what I'm prepared to offer for the use of your home."

Wayne pushed his glasses up his nose and flipped through the pages. "This is a lot of legal mumble-jumble. I need to run it by a lawyer."

Agnes propped her hip on the recliner arm. "Don't be such an old fuddy-duddy. Look at how much he's going to pay us. That's a lot of money."

"It's a standard contract," Robert said. "I'd be happy to have my attorney explain it to you."

"Nonsense." Agnes nudged her husband. "Go ahead and sign it, dear."

"Without reading the fine print?"

"Mr. Nordstrom is a nice young man. He wouldn't do us wrong."

Wayne shook his head as he accepted a pen from Robert. "I hope we don't live to regret this."

Agnes pressed her palms together. "Just think, we'll invite all our friends over for a party in a house that's starring in a movie."

"We'll take good care of your home, sir." Robert dropped the contract in his satchel and bit into a cookie. "I don't know which of your talents is more magnificent, Mrs. Peterson, gardening or baking."

A pink hue crept up Agnes' cheek. "You're a real charmer."

"Thanks for your hospitality, folks." Robert stood. "My crew will contact you in a few days. Right now, I have one more home to select."

"We're so glad you chose ours." Agnes' face beamed as she escorted her guests to the front gate.

"I'm surprised Robert chose their house," Emily said as she settled in the driver's seat and turned toward Rachel sliding into the back. "I mean, it's so old-fashioned."

"He obviously saw potential."

Robert donned his hat and bid Agnes goodbye, then climbed into the passenger seat. "Next stop, Main Street. I'll direct you to the house that caught my attention the day I arrived in town."

Five minutes later, Emily braked in front of an elegant Victorian-style home painted pale teal with white trim.

Robert opened his door. "Who owns this beauty?"

"Reginald Bricker, my future father-in-law." Rachel stepped out of the car. "He bought it last year. He owns a successful business, so money won't impress him."

The threesome climbed onto the porch.

Brick, his thin, wiry frame clad in shorts and a T-shirt, responded to the doorbell. "Let me guess. You want to use this house in your movie."

Robert laughed. "Either this town has the fastest rumor mill in Georgia, or you have great instinct."

"Let's just say my hand's been itching all morning." He stepped aside and motioned them into the house.

"Ah, yes. One of the more interesting superstitions." Robert stood in the grand foyer and took in the view. "So far, this looks like the perfect setting for Maggie's character. The only other room I need to see is the kitchen, Mr. Bricker."

"Everyone calls me Brick. Right this way."

Emily entered the front parlor decorated more twentieth-century antique than Victorian. She eyed the original Naomi Jasper oil painting displayed above the ornate plaster fireplace. "If the kitchen meets with Robert's approval, we'll finish today's assignment."

Rachel settled on a wingback chair. "Don't count on it."

"Other than two houses, what else do you think he needs us to do?"

"I'm sure something will come up."

The men returned, discussing art and antiques. Robert sat on the sofa, opened his satchel, and removed a contract. He flipped a page, crossed out a section, and made a notation. "This paragraph doesn't apply to you. Your home is perfect the way it is." He handed it over.

Brick fingered his white goatee while reading through the pages. "Looks good."

Robert handed him a pen. "Been a pleasure doing business with you, Brick."

"Likewise. I'm donating the money to Infinite Heroes." Brick signed the last page. "Military veterans deserve all the help we can give them."

Rachel pressed her hand to her chest. "That's a beautiful gesture."

"Driven by respect for JT, Jack, and Dennis. Willow Falls is fortunate those three guys settled here," Brick said as he returned the contract to Robert. "They're among the hardest-working men I've ever met."

Rattling glass and flashing blue lights sent Emily bolting to the front window.

"Sounds like the rest of the crew is ahead of schedule," Robert said.

Rachel stepped beside her sister. "What did I tell you? Our day isn't over by a long shot."

Chapter 15

Emily stood in Brick's front yard beside Rachel, gawking at a convoy of trucks, trailers, and RVs idling behind a deputy's car. Was this really happening? "You weren't kidding when you said a fleet was headed our way. I hope Mitch had plenty of warning."

Robert adjusted his ballcap. "We'll find out soon enough."

Emily and Rachel scurried behind Robert to the intersection of Main and Falls Street and found Sheriff Mitch shouting into his shoulder radio. "We need every parking spot vacated ASAP!" He released the speaker button and glared at Robert. "Who do those RVs belong to? Didn't the cast and crew book rooms at the hotel and inn?"

"Carrie and Justin's mobile dressing rooms."

"They can't dress in their other rooms?" He pointed to the line of vehicles. "What's in those trailers?"

"Production, make-up, wardrobe. One of the trucks hauls equipment from the rigs to film sites. Another is loaded with golf carts, our preferred mode of transportation."

"Your fleet will fill every parking space halfway to the waterfall." Mitch's jaw clenched. "I suggest you open your wallet and compensate the businesses your intrusion is bound to affect. And while you're at it, you might want to give Pearl a couple of lines in your movie."

Robert clutched his satchel to his side. "Do you people expect me to write words for every Tom, Dick, and Harriet who has some sort of beef? My staff already cast Pearl as a jury member, which, by the way, is a prime non-speaking role with plenty of camera time." He thrust a thumb over his shoulder. "Odds are those stores on Falls Street will enjoy a boost in business when people hang around to get up close and personal with a movie star."

Time to earn my pay. Emily's pulse pounded in her ears as she stepped between the two men. She locked eyes with Robert. "You have to understand, a year ago no one knew Willow Falls existed. Although we've become a tourist destination, this kind of chaos is new to us." Her gaze traveled to Mitch. "You know the town, as well as a fair number of residents, are benefiting financially from this deal."

"Look, I understand your concern, Sheriff." Robert nodded toward the left. "I suggest we close off traffic to Falls Street until the crew is forced to shut down Main for filming."

Mitch crossed his arms over his muscular chest. "Then what? We barricade the entire town?"

"We'll do our best to avoid too much disruption. One good thing, the bright young man with the artificial leg, JT, will turn this invasion into a lucrative tourist attraction and promote the town's businesses in the process." Robert clasped Mitch's shoulder. "What do you say we give my idea a shot?"

Mitch hesitated, then lowered his arms. "I'll give it two days." He pressed his shoulder mic. "We need to clear Falls Street and set up barricades."

Emily wiped sweat from her upper lip as the two men headed in opposite directions. "We for sure need to lobby for more pay."

"Or at least better working conditions," Rachel said. "Do you want to hang around and watch what happens?"

"More time away from my babies?" Emily released a long sigh. "Only because I need to gather details for another front-page story." They crossed Main Street and settled on a wrought-iron park bench. Emily picked a dried leaf off the seat. "You haven't said much about landing the girlfriend role."

Rachel blew out a long, slow breath. "I have mixed emotions."

"What does Charlie think?"

"We haven't talked about it." Rachel crossed her leg over her knee. "I don't know how I'll adapt to the new kind of acting. In live theater you start at the beginning of a story and move logically to the end. Movies are shot in short segments. Nothing's in chronological order. None of the Willow Falls cast will know the full story until the film is released, and some of the extras will discover their scene ended up on the cutting-room floor."

Emily crumbled the leaf and let it fall to the ground. "You might enjoy the experience as much as or more than performing on stage."

Rachel flattened her palm against her thigh and fingered her diamond engagement ring. "In a way, that terrifies me. If I'm drawn to the movie business—"

"You make it sound like a fly caught in a spider's lair."

"It could take a toll on my relationship with Charlie. Most celebrity marriages don't last long."

"You're getting a little ahead of yourself, don't you think?" Emily reached for her sister's hand. "Even if this opportunity leads to something bigger, I can't imagine you letting a career, or your ego, destroy your personal life."

"I suppose you're right. Besides, I can't worry about something that will probably never happen."

The sisters fell silent as Emily focused on the scene unfolding along Falls Street. By the time the invading vehicles were parked, dozens of onlookers had gathered on the sidewalks. After Mitch set up barricades, she and Rachel joined residents and tourists meandering in the center of the street, reading names inscribed on doors. Dozens of teenage girls snapped selfies beside Justin Brooks' RV.

Emily aimed her phone and snapped a series of photos. "What do you think all those girls will do when the actor shows up in person?"

"Go ape crazy, I suppose." Rachel nodded toward Carrie Fleming's RV. "Look at those boys trying to act cool and not go all hyper."

"We'll see how long that lasts. Do you want to give me a hand?"

"Doing what?"

Emily handed over her phone. "Snapping photos while I interview folks and capture tidbits for Thursday's paper."

"Does this assignment come with perks?"

"Yeah, a slice of Patsy's lemon cake."

"Now you're talking." Rachel slid her arm around Emily's shoulders and snapped a selfie.

Following an hour of collecting comments from locals and tourists, Emily had formed one undeniable impression. The next eight weeks would do more to reveal Willow Falls' soul and its future than anything in its hundred-plus-year history.

Chapter 16

Rachel leaned close to the lighted mirror in the playhouse dressing room and applied the last touch of stage makeup. Over the past few months her enthusiasm for playing the role of Lillian in *Percy's Legacy* had morphed to a sense of obligation. The casts' dependence on her as their director had taken a toll and become a burden.

As she watched the female lead fashion her blonde hair into a nineteenth-century style, memories came rushing back of the day she first met the pretty, young woman and Kat, the dark-skinned woman who had unofficially adopted her. Missy's role in the play helped her transition from a frightened, timid girl who was an ex-con to a confident woman.

Rachel's mind shifted to Missy's co-star, handsome Dennis Locke—the brown-haired, homeless vet she plucked from an Atlanta homeless shelter. The two young people had become the town's darlings and ongoing fodder for the rumor mill. Everyone wondered when Dennis would emulate Percy, the character he played, and propose to Missy. Until the movie crew rolled into town, that topic frequently topped the list during social gatherings.

In her role as director, Rachel had transformed Missy and Dennis from mediocre performers to players with star quality. As she listened to Missy hum a tune, a deep sense of satisfaction warmed her heart, knowing she had played a role in helping the girl who had spent most of her life being mistreated find her place in the world.

A female crew member opened the door. "Ten minutes till curtains up, ladies."

Missy stood, smoothed her period costume, and left the dressing room.

Rachel checked her image one last time. She meandered backstage to the spot where players and stage crew gathered to hear her pre-show pep talk. Her eyes scanned the faces she had come to adore. "Tonight, we have another full house with guests eager to watch the Willow Falls story unfold. They're expecting a top-notch performance. We need to live up to our reputation and give them a show worthy of a Tony. Forget all the Hollywood hullabaloo going on outside. Go out there and break a leg, kids."

While cast members scrambled to take their places, Charlie approached Rachel. "Your inspirational talk could use a boost in enthusiasm."

"I'll work on it. You don't think they noticed, do you?"

"Hang around for a few minutes after the show." His arm encircled her waist and pulled her close. "We need to talk."

She swallowed. "Why? Is something wrong?"

He shook his head. "Everything's cool." He released her and stepped away.

The theater lights flickered and dimmed, signaling the beginning of the musical overture. The players moved into position on stage. Rachel tamped down her angst and whispered under her breath. "Another night, another performance."

As the curtains parted, her mind drifted back to opening night, when every nerve in her body tingled with excitement and expectation. She longed to experience those sensations again. She shifted her attention to the stage as Missy and Dennis performed their roles as Percy and Peaches to perfection.

Acts one and two ended with audience cheers and applause.

Charlie, costumed and wearing stage makeup, moved to Rachel's side again. "Two acts down, one to go." His tone apathetic.

She crossed her arms. "Now who needs a big shot of enthusiasm?"

"Don't worry. I'll slip into character before I step foot out there."

"Sorry for being snippy. I have a lot on my mind." She unfolded her arms and turned her attention to the crew, busy changing scenery for the final act. With her own zeal meter teetering in the red zone, she had no right to snap at Charlie. Questioning her ability to deliver a noteworthy performance, she considered asking the understudy to take Lillian's role. *Pull yourself together and deliver what you demand from your cast.*

"Two minutes till curtains up," announced her assistant.

Missy and Dennis—wearing wigs and makeup to reflect a twenty-five-year passage of time—moved into position. Charlie, playing their son Everett—Scott Hayes' great grandfather and founder of Hayes General Store—joined them on stage.

The curtains opened. Rachel closed her eyes and mentally pictured the grand mansion standing at the end of Main Street. The actual home Percy built for his beloved Peaches. Willow Falls' colorful history served as far more than the subject of Emily's novel and their play. It provided the impetus behind the town's rising popularity. She questioned if Robert Nordstrom's movie would replace Percy's Legacy as a main attraction. And if it did, would it matter?

Missy and Dennis finished their scene and exited stage right, signaling Rachel's entrance. She filled her lungs and exhaled slowly. *You can do this.*

Professionalism and experience kicked in the moment she slipped into character and skipped onto the stage. Toward the end of the final act, a fly buzzing above Charlie's head caught her attention and sent her mind wandering into the abyss.

Charlie squeezed her shoulder. Startled, she blinked and realized he had covered her missed cue. *Get your mind in gear, Rachel.* She held her chin high and spoke the next line with over-the-top exuberance.

After delivering his line, Charlie held his hand over his lavalier mic and whispered, "Do you need to guzzle some ginger tea?"

She stifled a laugh, realizing her next words were the perfect response to his reference to the pre-performance drink she often sipped to calm her nerves. "Of course, I do, darling." They finished the scene with a passionate kiss and ended the play to rousing applause.

Following the final curtain call, Charlie stretched his arm across Rachel's shoulders. "You were in rare form tonight."

"Tell me about it. Thanks for rescuing me."

"Don't mention it. After all, you covered my butt more than a few times."

Rachel squeezed his hand. "Nine, to be exact."

"Does that mean after you mess up eight more times, we can call it even?"

She patted his cheek. "My one is equal to your nine."

"In that case, are you ready for our autograph-signing session?"

"Lead me to the lobby, Everett." She flipped a stray curl away from her face. "Do you suppose our guests will shower us with compliments or grill us with questions about the movie?"

"I'm guessing fifty, fifty."

Five minutes after mingling with the audience, it was clear Charlie had nailed the estimate. When the last guest left the theater, Rachel dropped onto a padded bench. "Do you want to talk now?"

He propped his foot on the bench and leaned on his knee. "It can wait."

"Good, because my feet are killing me." Rachel unlaced her gold, nineteenth-century boots. "I don't know how women endured these torture chambers."

"Or all these clothes." Missy sat beside Rachel and loosened her collar. "Are you excited about being in a movie?"

"It's growing on me. How about you."

She shrugged. "I only auditioned because Dennis wanted me to."

"Good for him. You're a talented actress. Who knows where it might lead?"

Missy folded her hands in her lap. "Before I came to Willow Falls, no one except Kat and Sadie cared about me. Then you gave me a part in this play, and now lots of people love me." She sniffed. "I don't ever want to leave this town."

"You're an amazing young woman. I admire your sense of priority."

"When you find where you belong, why go looking for something else."

Is that what I'm doing? Looking for something else? She stood and caught Charlie smiling at her. Heat crept up to her cheeks. Had he read her mind? "What?"

He moved to her side, leaned close, and caressed her hair. "Have I told you recently how much I love you?"

Missy's declaration and the sounds and sights around her vanished. His touch, the twinkle in his eyes, and the musky scent of his aftershave awakened every nerve ending in her body. At least for the moment, all seemed right in her world.

Chapter 17

Applewood-smoked bacon and maple syrup aromas launched a stomach grumble as Rachel sauntered into the Willow Inn dining room. An antique brass chandelier with etched glass globes cast a warm glow on an elderly couple, the inn's remaining guests.

Mama Sadie refreshed her visitors' coffee and set the silver carafe on the carved mahogany buffet with lion-claw feet. "Good morning, honey. Are you hungry?"

"I wasn't until I walked in." Rachel embraced her mother. "Breakfast smells too good to pass up."

"I'll fix you a plate."

"Thanks." Rachel sat across the table from the out-of-towners. "I recognize you from Saturday night. You're the couple from New York."

"Upstate." The woman wiped her hands with a napkin. "You're Rachel, the one who played Lillian. I have to admit the play and performance were quite unexpected for a small town. Are you aware Maggie Warren is checking in today? We saw her in a Broadway production last year. Are you related to Sadie?"

"I know about Maggie. And yes, Sadie's my mother."

"She's a delightful innkeeper. So attentive. Don't you just love her accent? She's so southern."

Mama Sadie slipped back into the dining room, set a plate in front of Rachel, then returned to the kitchen.

Rachel savored the pancakes while listening to the woman across from her carry on about all the famous people she had entertained in her home. Her husband passed the time reading the local paper and glancing sideways at his wife, with a cocked brow and subtle head shakes. When

Rachel finished her last bite, he folded the paper and pushed his chair away from the table.

"Come along, dear. We need to give this young woman's ears a break."

"I do tend to carry on when talking about our wonderful friends." The woman stood. "My husband and I will wait for Maggie on the front porch."

When the couple disappeared around the corner, Rachel gathered the dirty dishes and carried them to the kitchen. "Based on your guest's tales, she's the most famous hostess in the northeast. By the time she returns home, odds are she'll claim Maggie Warren as her new best bud."

"That woman should take up acting." Her mother loaded plates in the dishwasher. "Speaking of performing, how did Saturday night's show go?"

"Let's just say it wasn't one of my best performances."

"Whoops, did you forget a line or trip on stage?"

"My mind blanked out. Thank goodness Charlie rescued me." Rachel washed her hands. "He said he wanted to talk to me, then changed his mind."

"Must not have been anything serious."

"Unless ..." Rachel's brows raised as she dried her hands with a paper towel. "Do you suppose he's having second thoughts about our wedding?"

"Charlie? No way."

"I suppose you're right." Rachel eyed the new laptop sitting on the desk. "Are you ready for your celebrity arrivals?"

"I am. That is if Carrie's assistant doesn't send me another email. Can you believe her boss insists on silk sheets, brand-specific towels, and sandalwood-scented candles? Oh, and her suite temperature must be set at exactly seventy-two degrees. Those are just the first four instructions out of twenty-six."

"She sounds like a pampered prima donna."

"Guess it goes with the territory." Mama Sadie removed her apron and tossed it on her desk chair. "Thank goodness Maggie didn't demand special treatment."

"Maybe she's more grounded in reality."

"If not, the next two months will drive me nuttier than a bushel of Georgia pecans."

"And a whole lot saltier." Rachel chuckled as she accompanied her mother to the foyer.

Mama Sadie leaned back against the desk and pointed straight ahead. "I've a mind to start a wall of fame, pictures of famous people who slept here."

"That's a great idea."

"I'll start with Maggie." She withdrew five gold bags from under the desk. "In case you're wondering, I'm giving Carrie the same welcome gift as every other Willow Inn guest."

"I wouldn't expect anything different from the South's most gracious innkeeper."

The front door swung open, emitting a blast of warm air. Mirabelle swept in.

"You're early."

Mirabelle handed over a stack of mail. "Have you seen the crowd hanging out on your front lawn? What people will do to rub shoulders with celebrities."

Rachel snickered. "Too bad you have to finish your route."

Mirabelle eyed Rachel as if she'd taken leave of her senses. "I'm not leaving until Maggie and Carrie are all checked in. Which movie star is staying in my suite?"

Mama Sadie glanced at Rachel then flipped through the mail letters. "The VIP."

"Oh goodie. Carrie?" Cheers sent Mirabelle racing to the door. "They're here."

"Saved by their arrival." The mail was tossed on the desk. "Will you hang around and help me greet my guests?"

Rachel grinned. "I wouldn't miss it."

When they stepped out to the porch, Rachel witnessed a throng rushing toward a black, stretch limo. Mirabelle stood at the top of the steps glaring at the woman from Upstate New York.

Rachel nudged her mother. "It appears your guest and our mail carrier are vying for Mitten's role as Willow Inn's official greeter."

"As long as they don't scratch each other's eyes out."

The crowds parted. Dressed in black slacks and a red, tailored shirt, the tall, silver-haired actress—who had aged gracefully and could still turn heads—climbed the stairs and pushed sunglasses to the top of her stylish cut.

"Welcome to Willow Falls, Ms. Warren. I'm Mirabelle Paine, one of the stars in our town's play."

"How marvelous. I must watch you perform."

The New Yorker stepped forward. "I saw you perform on Broadway, Ms. Warren. I'm a huge fan. We live close to the city." She handed Maggie a business card. "You must come visit us sometime."

"Thank you for the invitation." Maggie smiled and moved to the door. "Which one of you lovely ladies is Ms. Liles?"

"I am." Mama Sadie moved closer and extended her hand. "This is my daughter Rachel. I'm delighted to meet you, Ms. Warren."

"The pleasure's all mine, and please call me Maggie." She stepped into the foyer. "What a magnificent inn."

Mama Sadie moved to the desk. "For the next two months, consider the inn your home away from home."

"You're a sweetheart, Ms. Liles."

"No need for formality. You can call me Sadie."

Maggie locked eyes with her hostess. "I have a feeling we're going to become good friends. I hope you're giving Carrie the grandest suite. She's a bit demanding. The rest of us will be happy anywhere. Do you mind if I look around while you welcome the princess?"

"Go ahead and give Maggie a tour," Rachel offered. "I'll greet the rest of your guests."

"Your daughter is beautiful and thoughtful."

Mama Sadie beamed. "Mr. Nordstrom cast her as the defense attorney's girlfriend."

"Good for Robert. He's an excellent director with a keen eye for new talent."

"My daughter is an amazing actress. Her twin sister's a published author. I'll put a copy of her book in your room," Mama Sadie said as she led her guest into the parlor.

Maggie's comment about the director ignited Rachel's imagination. If she met Robert's expectations, her career could soar. Deep down she knew she'd be crazy not to consider movie acting. And yet ... Missy's comment about finding where you belong still gave her pause.

Applause erupted out front. Rachel returned to the door as the crowd parted again. A stunning blonde—decked out in metallic-leather skin-tight pants, stilettos, and a low-cut blouse—emerged and sashayed to the porch.

The New York maven's elbow jab to her husband's ribcage didn't stop him from gawking at Carrie as she paused on the top step and flashed a smile. "Thank you all for welcoming me to your sweet little town." She glided past her greeters, her blue eyes locking with Rachel's as she held her chin high. "I assume you received my list."

"We did."

Carrie stepped inside, stood under the chandelier, and turned in a slow circle. "This is more sophisticated than I anticipated."

What did she expect, hillbilly heaven "I'm glad you approve."

Her mother returned to the foyer with Maggie. "Welcome, Ms. Fleming. I hope you enjoy your stay."

Carrie flicked a hand toward the limo driver and three women schlepping in with luggage. "My assistant and publicist will take care of any details. Right now, I'd like to freshen up before my lunch date with Robert."

"Of course." Mama Sadie removed a key from a hook and handed it to Rachel. "Will you show our guest to the Carlie suite while I check everyone in?"

"My pleasure." Rachel moved past the desk, unlocked the door, and stepped aside.

Carrie swept past her and sniffed. "Is this the largest suite?"

"It is."

"Then it will have to do. Have my assistant bring my luggage in."

What else does her highness demand? Rachel pressed her lips tight and nodded, then closed the door.

Mirabelle and the New Yorkers hovered in the background while Mama Sadie welcomed the newest arrivals.

A pretty young woman, her dark hair cascading over her shoulders, stepped forward. "I'm Ms. Fleming's publicist." She nodded toward a middle-aged woman. "My friend here is her personal assistant."

Maggie slipped her arm around an attractive, older woman's shoulders. "Meet my administrative genius. These three ladies are the real VIPs."

"We're delighted y'all are staying with us. Let me know how I can make your visit extra special." Mama Sadie distributed gift bags and turned a leather binder toward the newcomers. "Won't you please sign our guest book?"

Rachel marveled at the stark distinction between Maggie's gracious demeanor and Carrie's sense of entitlement. She questioned if it resulted from a difference in their age or something more profound and made it her mission to find out during the weeks ahead.

Chapter 18

Grateful for a respite from the chaos, Emily sat at her desk in the *Willow Post* headquarters and opened her computer. Six months earlier, the influx of tourists provided enough content to expand the bi-monthly newspaper to a weekly edition. Although she had delegated a good bit of reporting responsibility to Mary, the additional twenty-one issues a year added to her workload and tested Scott's patience. While her small salary still came in handy, the prestige rather than the money kept her from calling it quits.

Emily read her latest editorial, a work-in-progress stalled by an attack of writer's block. Nothing clicked. "Maybe I need to change the subject," she mumbled.

A flock of teenagers racing past the front window caught her eye. She grabbed a camera and dashed outside, heading toward the park. Emily pushed through the crowd amassed on the sidewalk. The sheriff escorted a couple off the lawn and headed straight to where she stood.

"What's going on, Mitch?"

"You're not gonna believe this." He relayed the latest celebrity demand.

Emily gasped. "Are you serious? Is there enough room?"

"Barely." Mitch led Emily through the crowd to the sidewalk's edge.

Rachel dashed from behind the hotel. "I assume you're clued in about Justin's arrival."

"I guess a car isn't dramatic enough for a male publicity hound." Emily shot a photo of the crowd. "One good thing, it will make a great front-page story for next week's paper."

Rachel faced the lake and shaded her eyes with her hand. "At least he's not parachuting in. One thing to be thankful for."

"Actually, that might be a lot safer." Emily snapped another picture.

Mitch raised his megaphone and aimed it at the crowd. "Listen up, people. Anyone who steps one foot on the grass before I give the okay will end up with a hefty fine." He pointed to a gaggle of teenagers. "Are you kids paying attention?"

"Yes, sir," Connor shouted. "Me and my buddies have it under control."

"I'm counting on it." Mitch lowered the megaphone. "This better go off without a hitch or heads will roll." He responded to his shoulder mic's squawk and rushed toward his deputy.

Emily kept her eyes glued to the horizon. "How'd everything go at the inn?"

Rachel snickered. "I spent the last hour with an interesting cast of characters. One thing in Carrie and Maggie's favor, they chose a normal arrival."

"Rumor is they showed up in a stretch limo."

"Nearly as long as a bus. I hope one of those trucks has an air-conditioned and heated golf cart to haul Princess Carrie around town."

Emily continued to snap photos. "You're obviously not a fan."

Rachel shielded her eyes with her hand. "Let's just say she takes herself way too seriously. Maggie, on the other hand, is down to earth and delightful."

"Like any other career, success affects people differently."

Gertie sidestepped her way past the teenagers and stood beside Emily. "Things around here get a little crazier every day."

"Movie madness," Emily said with a grin. "Are you a Justin Brooks fan?"

"Honey, I don't have a clue who the young man is. But I figure anyone coming into town with this much fanfare is worth a look."

"Excellent point." Emily squinted and spotted movement in the sky. "Get ready. Here he comes."

A distant rumble intensified as a bright-yellow helicopter swooped down and skimmed over the lake. The rotor wash sent ripples cascading across the grass as it eased over the retaining wall and set down in the park.

Conversations ceased. The crowd stilled. The whirring rotors slowed and halted. Mitch reactivated his megaphone. "All right, everybody, try to keep your composure and behave like this is nothing out of the ordinary."

"Like that's gonna happen," mumbled Emily.

Mitch and his deputy approached the chopper. The door opened. The masses held their collective breath as a tall, muscular young man, dressed in jeans, a tight button-down shirt, and cowboy boots stepped down.

"That's him!" someone shrieked. Squeals accompanied a pack of teenage girls—and some not-so-young women—bolting off the sidewalk.

They surrounded the newest celebrity arrival, cutting off Emily's view. She swept away a strand of hair plastered to her cheek by the helicopter's wash. "What happened to waiting for Mitch's okay?"

"My goodness." Gertie adjusted her glasses. "You'd think Elvis Presley just descended from heaven in a fancy whirlybird."

Rachel laughed. "Good one. Maybe Emily and I should go rescue the town's newest arrival."

"What makes you think he wants rescuing?" Gertie scooted closer to the twins. "Don't you know that a man who pops on the scene like he did craves attention?"

Emily shouldered the camera and gave Gertie a sideways hug. "You are one wise woman."

"I didn't live this long without learning a lesson or two. When things calm down, bring him to the store so I can take a good look at what everyone's going all gaga over?"

"By all means. Right, Rachel?"

"Absolutely. What about Carrie and Maggie?"

"I'll check them out later." Gertie lifted her long skirt off the sidewalk. "Right now, I need to return to work. All this hullabaloo is likely to stir up hankerings for milkshakes and chocolate sodas. Too-da-loo, ladies."

Rachel's eyes gleamed. "Don't you just love her?"

"She's definitely one of a kind." Emily slipped the camera strap off her shoulder and waited for Mitch and Justin to emerge from the parting crowd. The young actor's dark hair, along with his stubble mustache and beard, accentuated his rugged appearance.

"He is handsome. I'll give him that," Rachel said.

Emily snapped a series of photos until fans closed the gap between the sidewalk and the men. "So much for getting up close."

"Do you have a badge identifying yourself as a reporter?"

"In Willow Falls? I never needed one."

"Until now. Come on." Rachel grabbed her arm and led her sister to the crowd's edge. "Excuse us, please. Press coming through."

Emily's cheeks flushed as friends and neighbors stepped aside and stared. She mumbled apologies while Rachel continued to push their way to the center. Her instincts kicked in the moment she looked up and locked eyes with their target. "Welcome to Willow Falls, Mr. Brooks. I'm Emily Hayes, editor of the local newspaper. Why did you choose to arrive by chopper?"

He grinned, revealing perfect teeth. "It's faster than galloping in on a stallion."

"I see. Are horses your preferred mode of transportation?"

"The four-legged kind." He winked and raised his voice as if he wanted to be sure his adoring fans heard him. "And the six-hundred under the hood of a sports car."

He's charming and more than a little full of himself. "From your accent, I'm guessing you're from the southwest."

"Born and bred Texan." Justin's brown eyes drifted to Rachel. "Are you in the news game, like your twin?"

"She's an actress," said a woman standing behind Rachel.

"Huh." His grin widened. "I hope Robert casts you in the movie."

Rachel brushed her hair out of her eyes. "As a matter of fact, I'm playing your girlfriend."

"A fiery redhead. Way to go, Nordstrom. What say I treat you and your sister to lunch so we can all become better acquainted."

"That's a terrific idea," Rachel said. "There's a great little café right across the street."

"Lead the way, ladies."

The crowd murmured their disappointment as the trio walked away.

Emily eyed her sister's smile and wondered how long it would take her to tell her faux boyfriend about her engagement to real-life Charlie.

Chapter 19

Rachel pulled off County Road onto Willow Oak Vineyard and Winery's winding driveway lined with newly planted cherry trees. At the private residence sign, she turned and eased toward the two-story house—the beige and gray brick façade complementing the winery's stone. She parked beside the three-car garage and mentally ticked off the issues she needed to address with Charlie.

"Here goes." She slung her purse over her shoulder and followed the curved stone sidewalk to the front porch.

Charlie, wearing his *Mr. Good Lookin' is Cookin'* apron, met her at the stained glass door. He swept her into his arms and kissed her with abandon. When he released her, his lips bloomed into a smile. "Hey, gorgeous."

"Wow. Is this how you greet all your lady callers?"

"Just those I'm weeks away from marrying."

He pressed his hand to her back and led her from the foyer to the empty living room, pointing to the newly installed crown molding. "What do you think?"

"Looks great."

"Dennis finished the work yesterday."

Rachel smiled as memories bubbled up. "The day I first saw him on the sidewalk in Atlanta, I had no idea he was a talented builder."

"Lucky for Willow Falls you didn't ignore the guy."

"Funny how some things work out." Hopefully, her conversation would work out as well.

"Like you and me. Dad buying all this property is what brought us together." His arm slid around her waist as they walked through the dining space to the back deck that stretched from the corner to the master bedroom's French doors.

Rachel noted a round glass-top table set for two. "How lovely." She breathed in the aroma of smoking cedar drifting from the grill. "Are you planking salmon?"

"Yep." Charlie stooped and lit a fire in the stone fireplace, adding warmth to the season's first cool evening.

Rachel moved to the railing and gazed down at the winery and acres of grapevines beyond.

Charlie brought her a glass of wine.

"I'm imagining what it will be like waking up every morning and sipping a cup of coffee while drinking in this view."

"I plan to move in next week after our new furniture is delivered from Nathan's store."

She swirled the red liquid. "You were sweet to leave your bachelor furniture with your roommates."

"They insisted on paying for it, compensation for letting them live with me for the past year. Plus, they've been paying the rent since May."

"They're all good guys. Obviously, Dennis isn't going anywhere. I hope JT and Jack decide to stay in town."

"I don't know why they wouldn't." Charlie moved to the grill. "Dinner's ready."

"Good. I'm starving." Rachel carried her glass to the table and took a seat.

Charlie lit two candles and set plates with salmon and sweet potatoes beside salads. He removed his apron, tossed it over the back of a chair, and said a short blessing—a habit he had picked up after moving to Willow Falls.

Rachel savored a bite of salmon. "This is delicious. You're definitely upping your game as a grill master."

"I'm thinking of trying bar-b-que ribs next."

"Maybe you should take on the role of winery chef."

"Not a chance." He cut a piece of salmon. "When it comes to cooking, I'll stick with the grill."

During dinner, Charlie shared his ideas for the dining room menu and outlined his grand-opening plans. The gleam in his eyes and his enthusiastic tone confirmed he had found his calling. When they finished eating, they settled on a double chaise lounge facing the fireplace.

As Rachel snuggled close to her fiancé, her list loomed large in her mind. She couldn't wait any longer. "We have a lot to talk about."

"Starting with the conversation I postponed after last week's play." Charlie paused and studied her. "You know weekends are the busiest times for wineries that open to the public. Which means during peak season, I'll be tied up every Saturday and half a day on Sunday. I know it puts you in a tough spot, but you need to replace me as Everett."

"Wow, I didn't see that coming."

"I hope you're not angry?"

Rachel watched a burning log split and tumble into the ash. "Maybe it's time to replace both of us."

"That's a good idea. What I mean is, our understudies are chomping at the bit to perform."

His exuberance triggered a heavy sensation in Rachel's chest. "Are you sure there isn't another reason you want someone else to play Lillian?"

"I'm just saying we both have a lot going on." Charlie stood and moved to the fireplace, adding another log to the fire to rekindle the flame.

Rachel's chest tightened as she listened to logs pop and crackle. "There's one more subject we have to discuss. My role in the movie."

He returned to the chaise and sat silent for a long moment. "When were you going to tell me about your lunch with Justin Brooks?"

Her body tensed. "You mean *his* lunch with Emily and me. How did you hear about it?"

"Have you forgotten that Mirabelle delivers my mail? Did you know the guy's in-between wives and on the hunt?"

Rachel's back stiffened even more. "What's your point?"

"You're playing his girlfriend."

"And?"

"Chances are you'll be doing love scenes with him."

She zeroed in on Charlie's profile. "Are you jealous? Or don't you trust me?"

"I don't want him to get the wrong idea, that's all."

"Not a problem." She held up her left hand and splayed her fingers. "He noticed my ring. In fact, he wants to meet you."

"To check out his competition?" His tone hinted of sarcasm.

"That's absurd."

"Look, I'm not wild about my beautiful fiancée locking lips with a handsome, egotistical superstar. You know he met both his ex-wives on movie sets. One was married."

Rachel's jaw tightened. "Did you research him, or did Mirabelle give you a rundown?"

"I'm just trying to warn you."

An unsettling sensation ripped through Rachel's chest like a swarm of angry bees. "You need to understand ... this role could open new career doors for me." She wished Charlie would look at her.

"How do you know you'll even like movie acting?"

"I don't. But if I do ..." She cringed as the image of invisible shackles inching toward her ankles flashed across her mind. "I spent most of my adult years denying my dreams to live the life my father laid out for me. I don't want to start our marriage fearing I might one day have to do the same for you."

Charlie bolted to his feet and glared down at her. "You should know by now that I'm nothing like Greer Streetman."

"Are you saying you'll support my career decisions?"

His eyes narrowed. "How many times do I have to answer that question?"

"Until I'm convinced you mean it."

He refilled his wine glass and trudged to the railing.

Rachel watched another log implode into a heap of ash. She wouldn't give Charlie a hard time if the roles were reversed and Robert had cast him to play a role involving a passionate love scene with Carrie Fleming. Would she? Goose bumps popped out on her arms. *Does acting mean more to me than the man I love?* She set her glass on the table and moved beside him.

Charlie stared at his wine. "I love you more than life itself, and I'd be a lousy husband if I didn't support whatever path your career takes. The thing is ... the idea of another man pressing his body against you, then looking deep into your eyes and kissing you makes me nuts."

She swallowed the lump forming in her throat. "Do you want me to abandon the role?"

He turned toward her, his eyes wide. "You'd do that?"

"If it threatened our relationship." She locked eyes with him. "In a heartbeat."

"Then the answer's no. I don't want you to quit." He pulled her into his arms and kissed her deeply, sending ripples of desire charging through her.

When their lips parted, he stroked her cheek with his fingertips. "But you'd for sure better be thinking about me when you're swapping spit with that helicopter-flying Texas dude."

She grinned and breathed in his musky scent. "I promise."

"Okay then, how about dessert?"

"What do you have in mind?"

"Something I guarantee you can't resist."

Chapter 20

*E*mily pushed the stroller through Hayes General Store's back room to the fenced play area set up in the corner of the retail space. The twins climbed out and toddled to their favorite toys while she yanked her vibrating phone from her pocket and answered the call. When it ended, she plodded to the counter and scooped a handful of lemon drops from a jar.

"Your candy heist must mean another resident gave you an earful." Scott stooped, picked up a box, and set it down on the counter.

"Sixth call from a disgruntled resident since nine." She popped a drop in her mouth and let the sugary coating dissolve. "The problem is Agnes made a big deal about all the money Robert's paying to use their home. The way some people are acting, you'd think the Petersons stole a ticket and won a multi-million-dollar lottery. Can you believe one of our neighbors accused me and Rachel of steering Nordstrom to their home because Wayne's involved with our play?"

"Even in Willow Falls, envy rears its ugly head." Scott removed a bag of gourmet jellybeans from the box and refilled a candy jar. "None of us who agreed to this craziness considered the negative impact. There's nothing we can do about it now except try to smooth all the ruffled feathers."

Gertie sidled over from the soda fountain. "We haven't had a single customer all morning."

Scott popped the lid back on the candy jar. "Like two years ago when we didn't have enough business to pay the light bill."

"Maybe we should close up and watch the big scene out on Main Street," Gertie said.

"You go on." He stashed the box back under the counter. "I'll keep things buttoned down in here in the event a stray tourist decides to wander in."

"I'll go with her and gather more editorial material." Emily reached across the counter and took Scott's hand. "Is it okay to leave the twins here with you?"

"I don't expect much traffic while the circus is going on out there. I'll call if I need you to come to my rescue."

"Fair enough. As for you and me, Miss Gertie, let's find out what the clowns are up to."

A crowd filled the sidewalk and spilled onto the grass. Some observers stood while others sat in lawn chairs. Barricades blocked traffic from entering the section of Main Street separating stores and the park.

"My goodness." Gertie shaded her eyes with her hand. "It looks like everyone's waiting for a parade."

"Good thing it's a school day or every teenager in town would be hanging out over here."

They found Rachel explaining a tall, motorized boom to a group of residents and tourists. Gertie pointed to a two-man crew laying track in the middle of the street. "Is there a little kid's train in the movie?"

Rachel shook her head. "That's called a dolly track."

"It's used as a platform to shoot movement without bounce," said a portly older man wearing an Atlanta Braves ball cap.

Gertie eyed him. "You're not from around here, are you?"

"No, ma'am, I'm a set designer. Name's Bert. My crew prepares film locations for shoots."

"That's a big, important job." Gertie latched on to his arm. "How about taking a break and coming with me, sugar. I'll show you a location that doesn't need any fixing up. Do you like chocolate sodas?"

"Thanks for the offer, but I don't have time to—"

"Nonsense. Everyone has time for a soda."

Emily eyed the man. "Gertie makes the best in Georgia, and she doesn't take no for an answer."

He patted his protruding belly. "In that case, lead the way, little lady."

Rachel pulled her sister aside. "Are you gonna warn Scott?"

"Heck no, he's used to Gertie. Although I'm surprised she isn't staying to watch the show."

"She won't miss much." Rachel nodded toward the street. "Today, they're shooting background and non-speaking scenes. Like Justin stepping out of his fancy car and other mundane stuff."

"Sounds boring." Emily caught sight of a truck hauling a large, white water tank. "I haven't seen that before."

"It just pulled into town. You know they wet the streets before filming."

"I do now." Emily's phone rang. She checked the screen. "The same angry woman I talked to an hour ago. Do these people actually believe their complaints will lead to results?"

"Call it hopeful thinking." Rachel fingered her engagement ring. "Last night, Charlie and I talked about my role."

"And?"

"He's not crazy about me and Justin acting in a love scene."

Emily shot photos of a film crew setting up cameras. "I assume there is one."

"Yeah."

Emily raised her brows. "In a bedroom?"

"No, of course not. But it is steamy."

"Charlie will get over it." Emily's phone pinged a text. "Our mother is looking for us." She typed a response.

Moments later, Mama Sadie circled around the crowd and headed in their direction. She stepped between her daughters. "Carrie Fleming is driving me batty."

Emily pocketed her phone. "What does she want now, caviar for breakfast?"

"That'd be a whole lot easier than the disgusting energy drink I have to fix for her every morning. She wants a personal tour of the town after today's shoot. JT's booked, and I've already had my fill of her whacky demands." She eyed Rachel. "Will you take her on?"

"I promised Charlie I'd help him with grand-opening plans."

Pleading eyes turned to Emily. "I'll babysit the twins if you agree to play tour guide for the princess."

"I'd rather spend the day cleaning sidewalks with a toothbrush." She slipped her arm around her mother's shoulder. "However, I can't refuse letting Clair and Jane spend the afternoon with their grandma."

"Bless you, honey. You'll keep me from landing back in jail for strangling that woman."

Sheriff Mitch moved a barricade aside to let the water truck pass.

Mama Sadie craned her neck. "Why are they watering the street?"

"Standard practice for outdoor shots," Rachel said. "Wet streets film better than dry."

"This movie-making business is mighty peculiar."

"And disruptive as a swarm of yellow jackets during a fall picnic." Emily plucked her pinging phone from her pocket. "This celebrity invasion is turning too many residents into irrational nutcases. At least it's good press material." She ignored the text and switched her phone to record mode, then transitioned to newspaper editor and moved through the crowd questioning residents, tourists, and members of the film crew.

Chapter 21

*E*mily turned off the sidewalk to Willow Inn's front walk and parked the stroller at the bottom of the stairs. The twins climbed out, grasped their mother's hands, and scrambled up to the porch and into the foyer.

"I'm in here with Maggie," Mama Sadie called out from the parlor. "We're talking about Mama's favorite picture." She scooted to the edge of her wingback chair and held her arms out. Clair and Jane scampered over and climbed onto her lap.

Emily entered the elegantly furnished room.

Maggie set her teacup on the vintage neoclassical coffee table's smoked-glass top. She pointed to the oil painting over the fireplace—depicting a compote filled with pears, apples, and grapes sitting on a marble table with a rose, a white lace napkin, and a fancy paring knife. "Gorgeous piece. I presume it's worth a small fortune."

"You obviously know art." Emily sat in the second wingback chair facing the chocolate-colored settee with gold inlaid wood trim. "Have you seen Naomi Jasper's work?"

"Only the piece in the dining room. Sadie told me all about her."

The twins climbed off their grandma's lap and toddled to the basket of toys stashed in the corner. Mama Sadie watched until they were busy entertaining themselves. "Maggie and I plan to take my grandbabies to visit Naomi while you entertain Carrie."

"You two are obviously hitting it off."

"Your mother is a breath of fresh air in this crazy world I live in." Maggie removed a plate of cookies from the coffee table and held it out to Emily. "She invited me and Ben—"

"Foster?" Emily reached for a cookie.

"Uh-huh. He and Max Grover are coming to town tomorrow. Ben and I are old friends, so Sadie invited us to Sunday dinner at Brick's house."

Sadie nodded. "I figured they'd appreciate a home-cooked meal. I want you and Rachel and your guys to join us."

"I wouldn't miss it."

Carrie—wearing skin-tight white jeans and an off-the-shoulder gold sweater—breezed into the parlor. She laid her phone on a cabinet and pulled her blonde ponytail through the back of a gold, sequined ball cap. "Is my tour guide here?"

Sadie eased off the chair. "My daughter, Emily, is a published author. You're fortunate she's taking time from her busy schedule to show you around town."

The actress cocked her head. "You and your twin are Robert's local lackeys, right?"

No wonder she's driving my mother crazy. "I prefer to think of us as his in-town assistants. Did you know my sister is a gifted actress? She landed a key role in the movie."

"Yes, I know." Carrie nodded toward her publicist as she wandered in carrying a camera. "I hope you don't mind Bev taking pictures of our little jaunt. For publicity."

Like I have a choice. "Not a problem."

"I hear you have a little waterfall close by."

"If you call fifty-feet high little." Emily pointed to Carrie's gold tennis shoes. "Based on your footwear, I suggest you save that trek for another day. We'll begin with a tour of the mansion at the end of the block."

"I assumed our first stop would be more interesting than a tourist attraction." Her tone hinted of arrogance.

Emily bit her tongue to keep from telling Miss Fancy Britches they'd go where and when she decided. "Believe me, it's way more than a sightseeing venue. In fact, it's an important piece of Willow Falls history. The town's founder built it for his wife. If you go see our play, you'll learn all about Percy and Peaches and discover how talented my sister is as an actress and a director."

Carrie fingered a gold hoop earring. "If I manage to carve time out of my busy schedule."

Don't strain yourself. Emily kissed the twins and escorted her assignment to the porch.

"Is that Caddy our ride?" Carrie donned a pair of sunglasses and pointed to the red fifties convertible Cadillac sporting white-wall tires parked at the curb.

"After we visit the mansion and our art museum."

During their stroll to the end of the block, Bev shot dozens of photos while Carrie inundated Emily with descriptions of her Hollywood mansion and her vacation homes in the Bahamas and southern France. "I adore French wine. Have you been to Europe?"

"I've been too busy raising a family and writing a novel."

"What a sweet little life." Again, Carrie's tone hinted of arrogance.

"Believe me, there's plenty of excitement around here. Plus, we have a first-class winery ready to open a short distance from town."

"Georgia wines." Carrie sniffed. "Who'd have guessed?"

"We're full of pleasant surprises out here in the country."

The moment they arrived at Percy's Mansion, Carrie turned on the charm for a group of tourists clamoring for autographs.

Bev snapped a series of photos before the hostess—dressed in a nineteenth-century gown—led the group through the home. At least Carrie acted interested in the town's history. Most likely for show.

When the tour ended, Emily escorted her charge across Main Street and climbed onto Naomi's front porch. "You're about to meet our town's number one celebrity. Not only is she a famous artist, she dabbles in live theater. In fact, she landed a speaking role in your movie."

"Casting locals is Robert's thing. Interesting approach."

Inside the foyer, the museum's guide summoned the owner. Naomi glided in wearing white bell-bottom slacks and a multi-colored, thigh-length shirt. She extended her hand to Carrie. "Welcome to my family's home."

The actress glanced around wide-eyed. "You live here?"

"Upstairs." Naomi swept her arm in an arc, sending her bracelets into a symphony of jangles. "My boys—JT, Jack, and Dennis—transformed this floor into the museum. I'll show you my Christmas room first. All the decorations belonged to my mother."

Naomi escorted Carrie to the dining room and launched into stories about the antique ornaments decorating the Christmas tree, the pink glass collection, and Christmas Around the World china set on an elegant dining room table.

Carrie fingered a fragile angel ornament. "Back in my hometown, some people still drape strings of popcorn on their trees."

"Tinsel covered trees in Mom's day. I'm glad that fad passed." Naomi led the way to the large room across the foyer. "Welcome to my art gallery. Most pieces are available for purchase."

Carrie strolled among the free-standing displays, examining each work of art. She stopped in front of an original watercolor depicting a seaside village. "This is magnificent."

"My newest creation."

"The colors are perfect." Carrie pressed her palms together. "I must have it for my home in the Caribbean."

"Excellent choice," Naomi said. "We'll work out the details later." After viewing Naomi's personal art collection in the den, the trio walked to the backyard to see the miniature two-story, gingerbread-style structure painted pale green with pink and white accents. She opened the door and stepped aside. "Welcome to my studio. My father built it for my sixteenth birthday."

Sun shining through a row of floor-to-ceiling windows along the back wall illuminated the space filled with artist tools, paint, and canvases.

Carrie moved to a canvas resting on an easel in the corner, partially covered with amateur sketches.

"The interactive corner," Naomi said as she stood beside the actress. "Go ahead and draw something."

Carrie picked up a stick of brown chalk off the table beside the canvas and drew a tree trunk and limbs. She added darker accents and topped it with puffs of green leaves.

"Marvelous. If you sign it, I'll keep it as a permanent display."

"Seriously?"

"A Carrie Fleming signature and a drawing will give our tour hostess something new to share with our visitors." Naomi handed Carrie a piece of blue chalk while Bev captured the moment. The actress signed with a flair and posed with Naomi for a publicity photo.

The women ended their tour in the garage-turned-gift shop where the actress added two numbered prints to her purchase. After accepting Carrie's credit card, Naomi smiled at her newest fan. "I've enjoyed doing business with you. Where is Emily taking you next?"

"I think to that gorgeous red Caddy parked across from the inn."

"Ah yes, my daddy's pride and joy."

"Naomi donated it to the town," Emily added.

Carrie locked eyes with the artist. "You should create a painting of that car parked in front of your museum."

"What a marvelous suggestion."

"Thanks for the tour, Naomi. I have a lot more to show our guest." Emily escorted Carrie up the driveway to the sidewalk. "I'm guessing you didn't expect to find a first-class art museum in the north Georgia hills."

"Can't say I did." When they arrived at the Caddie, Carrie sent Bev back to the inn, then climbed into the front seat. She ran her fingers over the soft leather. "I want to keep the top down."

"We're likely to draw a lot of attention."

Carrie stared at Emily as if her IQ had suddenly dropped fifty points. "That's the point."

Excuse me for thinking you possessed a modicum of humility.

Locals and tourists clamoring for the star's attention stalled their ride a dozen times before they finished driving through town. Emily gripped the steering wheel, then turned onto the street leading to the back of Scott's store. She glanced at her passenger. "Do you ever tire of living in the limelight?"

"Why would I?"

"I don't know, maybe so you can relax a little."

Carrie crossed her arms tightly across her chest and stared straight ahead. "I can't afford to relax. Without fans I'm nothing more than another pretty face in a giant sea of actresses."

That explains a lot. "I think I understand."

"How could you?"

Emily bristled at Carrie's condescending tone. "As an author, I compete with thousands of authors and millions of books. Which means I have to work hard to reach readers who don't know I exist."

"It seems we have something in common after all." Carrie unfolded her arms. "What's our next stop?"

"Another historical landmark." Emily parked behind Hayes General Store and led Carrie up the side alley to the front. The actress stopped to eye the display in the window featuring a treadle sewing machine, an ancient typewriter, and an array of eclectic antiques. "Looks like another museum."

"The building hasn't changed much during the past hundred years, so in a way it is." They stepped inside and meandered toward the soda fountain.

"Oh my gosh." A young woman gasped and flew off her stool. "You're my all-time, most favorite actress." She wrapped her arm around Carrie's shoulder and snapped a selfie. "Wait till all my friends see this. They'll die from envy."

Gertie wiped her hands on a towel and stepped from behind the counter, her period dress brushing the floor. "Welcome to the most famous store in Georgia."

"I heard all about it during the tour of the mansion." Carrie removed a bar of scented soap from a wooden barrel and held it to her nose. "Lavender."

"My favorite," Gertie said. "Come on over, and I'll fix you an old-fashioned chocolate soda."

"That's sweet of you, but I stay clear of desserts."

"Goodness gracious, honey child, a soda isn't a dessert. It's food for the soul." She led the actress to the counter. "Don't you know that here in the South, hosts always feed their guests? And proper guests oblige."

Emily captured the moment with her phone. "Gertie won't take no for an answer. You might as well agree."

"All right. But only one teeny sip." Carrie climbed onto a stool next to the selfie fan and answered a flurry of questions.

Emily spotted Scott escorting a woman carrying a handmade quilt down from the second-story consignment shop. A man followed close behind. After the couple paid for their new treasure and left the store, Scott moved to Gertie's side and smiled across the counter at their famous guest. "What's your verdict on the South's best soda, Ms. Fleming?"

"Yummy. Is this your family's store?"

"My great-grandfather built it."

"Charming." Carrie pushed her half-empty glass across the counter and flashed a smile at Scott. "I'll let you show me around and tell me all about the store's fascinating history."

Scott cleared his throat. "I think I'll leave that honor to your guide, who's also my wife."

Carrie slid off the stool and faced Emily. "I didn't know he's your husband."

"And the father of those adorable twins you met in Willow Inn's parlor."

Gertie scooted from behind the counter. "I'll give Carrie the five-dollar tour and tell her everything she needs to know about this historical site." She steered the actress toward the player piano.

Emily hiked onto a stool, rested her chin on her knuckles, and locked eyes with Scott. "I do believe the pretty movie star flirted with you."

"Fat chance." He removed Carrie's soda glass from the counter. "Is she as demanding as Sadie insinuated?"

"Oh, yeah." Emily glanced around, confirming that Carrie had moved out of earshot. "Maybe that's how she copes with insecurity."

"Are you kidding? I doubt that woman has an insecure bone in her body."

"You might be right. On the other hand ..." As Emily watched Carrie pose for pictures with adoring fans, she sensed a deep-seated vulnerability lurking beneath the star's confident pretense.

Chapter 22

Rachel parked behind Willow Inn and climbed the stairs to the two-room garage apartment. She knocked on the door before pushing it open. "I'm here."

"Be ready in a jiffy," Mama Sadie called from the bedroom.

Rachel passed the miniature kitchen anchoring one end of the living room, laid her keys on the coffee table, and settled on the loveseat. She adored the cozy room, artfully decorated with a mixture of furniture from Emily's parents' home and local garage sales. Her eyes focused on the bookcase displaying her sister's novel beside three Francine Rivers books. On the shelf below sat framed photos of Sadie and her mother. The woman died before she and Emily were born, yet they knew their maternal grandmother through Sadie's stories.

Mama Sadie came in, carrying her cell phone. "Ben Foster and Max Grover checked into the hotel a few minutes ago. Kat said Max looks like a young Denzel Washington. Too bad he's not ten years older, or Kat ten years younger."

"Age differences aren't a big deal anymore. For example, you and Brick."

"You're not exactly subtle."

"You two have been dating for the better part of a year. You deserve to have a loving relationship with a man who adores you."

Sadie tossed her phone beside Rachel's keys, then settled on a slipper chair. "Brick and I are what you might call ... close friends. Besides, I'm okay with the way things are, so I'd appreciate it if you and your sister would give me a break and stop barking up that tree."

"Subject closed." Rachel zipped her fingers across her lips. "I'm curious about Princess Carrie. How's she behaving?"

"Like royalty." Mama Sadie tapped her lips with one finger. "But I wonder if under her too-big-for-her-britches attitude lurks a sweet, vulnerable girl. If you have a chance to work with her, you'll find out if I'm on to something or flat-out wrong."

"We'll see." Rachel grabbed her keys and popped up. "Are you ready to watch the princess and helicopter Justin make some movie magic?"

"What is it you actors say?" Mama Sadie plucked her phone off the table. "Let's go watch them break their legs?"

"You're a trip."

They left the apartment and walked to the corner of Main and Falls Streets where a mob of teenage girls congregated behind a row of steel barricades separating onlookers from the celebrities' RVs. The sheriff's deputy stood guard beside Justin's mobile dressing room.

"Am I missing something?" Sadie looked confused. "Isn't it a school day?"

Rachel nodded. "Some high schoolers are cast as extras in today's park scene, so the principal released everyone early."

A golf cart rounded the corner and stopped beside the deputy.

The RV door opened.

The girls stood motionless. Staring.

Seconds passed.

Rachel aimed her phone at the scene. "We're about to find out if those barricades will restrain a horde of teenage groupies."

Justin appeared in the doorway and descended to the bottom step. He paused, then waved and blew kisses.

The girls erupted in a collective scream. One scurried over the barrier and ran toward him. Five more followed.

The actor's assistant climbed out of the golf cart and stood shoulder-to-shoulder with the deputy guarding the RV's door.

"I can see the paper's new front-page headline." Rachel signified quotation marks with her fingers. "Local Law Enforcement Rescues Helicopter Superstar from Starstruck Sweeties."

A second deputy rounded the corner and rushed toward the commotion.

Justin emitted a shrill, two-finger whistle.

The girls froze in their tracks.

"I appreciate your enthusiasm, ladies, but I have to go to work. If you let my assistant drive me to the set, I'll return later and pose for pictures with you."

The girls shrieked, then backed away from the golf cart.

"Well, I declare." Sadie grinned. "That young man knows a thing or two about creating and controlling crowds."

"Superstar survival, I suppose." Rachel checked an incoming text. "Emily needs me to meet her in front of Scott's store. Something about a problem with the extras."

They passed the crowd gathered in front of the park and found Emily in a heated conversation. Rachel's eyes shifted from her sister to Lizzy. "What's going on?"

Lizzy's nostrils flared. "The director doesn't know what he's doing. He has my daughter facing away from the camera. She's the prettiest girl out there. How will anyone recognize her?"

"She's in a crowd scene, not a starring role," Emily said.

"I don't care what you call it. I want the audience to see her face. I'm going to give Robert Nordstrom a piece of my mind."

Emily gripped Lizzy's arm. "That's not a good idea."

"How else will he know he needs to make some changes." She yanked her arm from Emily's grasp and spun around.

Rachel stepped in front of her. "Hold on, Lizzy. Before you go doing something you'll regret, look at the scene again. Tell me what you see."

The woman huffed. "What are you talking about?"

"Your daughter and the other girls, what are they doing?"

Lizzy squinted. "They're standing around."

"Precisely," Rachel said. "Because the crew is still blocking the scene. And that boom camera can shoot from any angle. Which means no one other than the director and the camera crew knows how it will look."

Lizzy's brows shot up. "Are you saying they might end up with a good shot of Jenny?"

Rachel nodded. "That's exactly what I'm saying."

"How will I know?"

"That's a no brainer," Sadie interjected. "Watch the movie when it comes out."

Scott wandered over. "What's all the fuss about?"

Lizzy glared at him. "For one thing, your wife and her sister turned Willow Falls' only theater into a playhouse."

"Why are you grumbling about transforming an old, abandoned movie theater into a successful tourist attraction?"

"Because now everyone will have to traipse out of town to see my Jenny's big movie debut."

"The whole town is going off its rocker." Scott shook his head and returned to his store.

Lizzy huffed and moved closer to her daughter.

"She does have a point," Emily said. "It's a shame we can't hold a big fancy premiere right here in town."

An idea emerged and began to take root. Rachel tucked it away, saving it for a father-daughter discussion after the wedding.

Chapter 23

Alone in the theater dressing room, Rachel finished applying her stage makeup. She turned in a slow circle, viewing the space she had occupied every Saturday night for the past year. Tonight's performance would mark the end of that phase of her career. She moved to the rack of costumes and slipped into the dress for act three's opening scene. As her fingers caressed the smooth fabric, a lump formed in her throat. Maybe she would miss this more than she realized.

Following a knock, the door opened a crack. "It's me. Are you ready to tell the cast the news?"

She took one last look around and pulled the door open to let Charlie in. "Let's go make two people enormously happy."

"Are you talking about our understudies or you and me?"

"Hopefully, all four."

They found the young, married couple Rachel had recruited and trained six months earlier. "Bonnie, Kevin, do you have a minute? Charlie and I need to talk to you."

The pretty young woman glanced at her husband, then back at Rachel. "Is everything okay?"

"Couldn't be better." Rachel led them to a back corner, away from the other performers. She dismissed a stab of doubt and curved her lips into a smile. "You've both done an excellent job learning every key role in our play, and when you filled in for absent cast members, you performed like champs." Rachel paused and gave them time to process her words. "Now it's time for your names to appear as leads on our program."

Bonnie's eyes widened. "Are you saying ... I mean ... who's quitting the play?"

"Charlie and I have a lot going on with the wedding and the winery opening. So, we're stepping down as Everett and Lillian. Beginning with next week's performance, you two will fill those roles. If you're willing."

"Oh my gosh." Bonnie's eyes lit. "We're way more than willing. Right, honey?"

"It seems our director thinks we're ready," Kevin said.

Bonnie's smile evaporated as she locked eyes with Rachel. "Are we? Ready, I mean? We've never filled in for you and Charlie. What if we aren't up to the task?"

"This play is important to this town." Rachel placed her hand on Bonnie's shoulder. "I wouldn't ask if I didn't think you were fully prepared. Besides, I'll schedule some mid-week rehearsals to help you perfect your lines."

Kevin's arm encircled his wife's waist. "That's all we need. Right, sweetheart?"

Bonnie's smile returned. "This is so exciting. Wait 'til I tell our friends."

"Then it's settled. Let's share the news with the rest of the crew." Rachel waited for her newest stars to join their peers before stepping in front of her team. She caught Charlie's eye. His smile conjured memories from a year ago when he agreed to take a role he didn't want, then struggled to learn how to act. All because she needed him. Tears welled in her eyes. How many men would step miles outside their comfort zone and endure humiliation to please the woman they loved?

Now, it's my turn to pour energy into supporting his career.

Rachel scanned the faces staring at her. "During the past year, Charlie and I have loved performing with all of you. I ..." She sniffed and dabbed her eyes. "The fact is every good idea has its season. The time has come to let others experience the joy of performing in lead roles. To that end, I'm pleased to announce a cast change. Beginning next week, Bonnie and Kevin will take over as Lillian and Everett."

Stunned silence.

Rachel held her breath.

Seconds passed.

Mirabelle stood and clapped, leading the team in praise and congratulations for the show's new stars.

Rachel released her breath as tears spilled and pride filled her heart for the cast of amateurs she had molded into professionals.

Charlie pulled her away from the crowd. "Robert Nordstrom has nothing on you, Director Streetman."

"It was more difficult to let go than I'd imagined."

He wiped her tears with his fingertips. "It's not too late to change your mind."

"And rob Bonnie of the opportunity? Not a chance."

"Five minutes to curtains up," announced her assistant.

The cast fell silent. Rachel transitioned into director mode. She took her place, stage left behind the curtain. While watching the first act, she mentally replayed the weeks of rehearsals before opening night. During act two, Charlie held her hand, as if he sensed her melancholy. Moments before the curtain went up for act three, his arm glided around her waist, awakening every nerve ending. His lips touched her ear. "Are you ready to give the audience a performance they'll never forget?"

She drew in a deep breath and released it slowly to ease her pounding heart. "Let's give them all we've got, Everett."

"You're on, Lillian."

When the act ended, she knew they had truly delivered the performance of a lifetime. Following the final curtain call, Rachel pulled Charlie aside. She touched his cheek and gazed deep into his eyes. "Tonight, I fell in love with you all over again."

He pulled her into his arms. "Falling in love with you is the best thing that ever happened to me."

She nuzzled his neck, trusting that whatever challenges their future presented, they would find a way to overcome them together.

Chapter 24

Rachel and Charlie parked in Brick's driveway and climbed the steps to his front porch moments before Maggie and a grandfatherly looking man with white hair, blue eyes, and deep lines in his suntanned face sauntered up the sidewalk.

Dressed in white slacks and a red sweater set, Maggie stepped onto the porch. "I want you to meet Ben Foster, one of my oldest and dearest friends."

Rachel extended her hand. "Welcome to Willow Falls."

"Thank you." He sandwiched her hand between his. "Are you the writer or the actress?"

"The latter." *This man is utterly charming.*

"Welcome to the crazy world of show biz." He released Rachel's hand and clasped Charlie's shoulder. "I take it you're the lucky fiancé."

"And mighty proud of it, sir."

"I hear you and our host own the Willow Oak Winery." Ben removed his hand. "I passed it on the way into town. Great looking vineyard."

"Thanks. My dad's the owner. I manage the property."

"Don't let him kid you," Rachel said. "Charlie's the brains behind the entire operation."

"Smart young man." Ben's smile widened. "I'm a bit of a wine connoisseur myself."

"In that case, you have to let us give you a personal tour."

"I'd like that."

Mama Sadie—looking radiant in a teal dress, high heels, and dangly, gold earrings—opened the front door. "Welcome, everybody."

Rachel made the introductions.

Charlie embraced his soon-to-be mother-in-law. "You look like a million dollars."

"You're a real charmer." Sadie led them from the foyer to the renovated kitchen that opened to the den.

While her mother introduced Ben to Emily's family, Rachel leaned close to Charlie. "Not only is my mother gorgeous, she's right at home as lady of the house. It's hard to believe my mother and your dad aren't more than good friends."

"Guess he never recovered from my mother walking out on him."

"How is that possible?" Rachel's brows furrowed. "That happened a long time ago."

"Contrary to what some might think, when a woman shatter's a man's heart, it's hard to put the pieces back together."

Charlie's tone gave Rachel pause. How much damage did his mother inflict on her two sons when she abandoned the family? She held his hand while they moved to one of three couches forming a U in front of the slate fireplace. She watched Brick uncork two bottles of white wine and fill eight glasses. Was it possible he was incapable of falling in love with someone else?

"I hope y'all are hungry," Mama Sadie said as she carried a plate of appetizers from the kitchen and laid it on the massive coffee table centered on an oriental rug.

For the next half hour, everyone gathered in the den and launched into lively conversation about families, wine, and antique cars. Maggie and Ben acted more like old friends than Hollywood superstars. When everyone gathered in the dining room, Rachel discovered Mama Sadie had learned a thing or two from her mama about entertaining. She had set the table with place cards, napkins folded in triangles, and an elaborate centerpiece of fresh flowers. Glasses filled with water and white wine completed each setting.

"Wow," Emily said. "It looks like we're dining in a royal palace."

Mama Sadie's smile was radiant as she and Brick placed Caprese salads in front of their guests. After taking their seats at each end of the long table, Brick said grace followed by a rousing amen and "dig in, folks."

Rachel breathed in the scent of fresh basil, then savored the taste of balsamic, tomato, and mozzarella.

"If this is any indication of the main course," Maggie said, "we're in for a meal worthy of a gourmet editor's accolades."

"Sadie and I figured you and Ben were used to eating in fancy restaurants." Brick cut a piece of tomato. "So, we asked Pepper Cushman to help us out. She's the hotel's executive chef and owner of Pepper's Café."

"And one of my dearest friends," added Mama Sadie.

"Want to know the real skinny?" Ben speared a piece of cheese. "I'll take a delicious meal in a private home with hometown folks over dinner in a grandiose restaurant with a bunch of celebrities any day of the week. Don't get me wrong. I'm grateful for all the perks the entertainment business has given me, and I have a lot of celebrity friends. Unfortunately, the price of fame is high, and showbiz folks often take themselves way too seriously."

Rachel sipped her wine. *Like Carrie Fleming.*

The conversation shifted to food until the host and hostess removed empty salad plates and delivered individual plates artfully arranged with crab cakes, mashed potatoes, and kiwi slices.

Ben dug his fork into the entrée and took a bite. "Best crab cake I've ever tasted. What's the sauce?"

Mama Sadie grinned. "Pepper's secret recipe."

"I'm beginning to understand why Maggie's considering retiring here in Willow Falls."

Rachel watched as Emily's eyes rounded. "Really?" She stared at Maggie. "Is he kidding?"

"Not at all. I'm seriously thinking about it."

"Easy to understand why folks who live here love Willow Falls." Scott slathered butter onto a roll. "What is it about our little town that appeals to a famous star?"

"I imagine a lot of people think everyone who makes movies likes living in big-city mansions." Maggie smiled. "Fact is I grew up in a sweet little village that was swallowed up when the city crept into the suburbs. Willow Falls reminds me of my hometown. And it's far enough from Atlanta to hold on to its identity and has enough going on to keep life interesting."

"If you ever get a hankering to act," Mama Sadie said, "Rachel can cast you in *Percy's Legacy*."

"At this point, I prefer to remain in the audience and cheer others on."

Rachel glanced sideways at Charlie, remembering how easily he had adapted to small-town life. She had to admit Maggie had a valid point. A year ago, she couldn't imagine living miles away from Atlanta. Now, with a theater, a museum, and two clothing stores, Willow Falls held a certain appeal.

Charlie leaned in close. "What do you think?"

She blinked. "Sorry, I took a mini mental vacation. What's the question?"

"I invited Maggie and Ben to a private tour before the winery's grand opening."

"Oh, good idea."

Brick tipped his glass toward Ben. "Maybe you should settle down around here as well."

"Can't. My grandkids are on the west coast. Besides, I plan to follow in Clint Eastwood's shoes and keep acting 'til I'm too old to walk, talk, or remember my lines."

As Rachel considered Ben and Maggie's perspective about their golden years, she wondered how she would spend her retirement. At this point she couldn't imagine ever slowing down. She tuned back into the conversation and watched her mother and future father-in-law steal glances across the table. After they served dessert in the den, they sat beside each other on a couch.

Emily motioned Rachel to follow her to the kitchen. "Did we misunderstand Mama Sadie's comment about her and Brick being friends? I can't imagine there isn't more going on."

"You mean like friends with benefits?"

"I'm just saying they're perfect together." Emily refilled her wine glass. "If they're just friends, I have a feeling their relationship is on the verge of growing into something far deeper."

"Not according to Charlie." Rachel relayed his comments about Brick's broken heart.

"Maybe Mama Sadie understands Brick's limitations and is willing to accept a platonic relationship."

Chapter 25

A cool breeze nipped Emily's cheeks the moment she opened the patio door to let Cody and Brownie out to the backyard. "There's a bit of fall in the air this morning."

Scott glanced at his phone before stuffing it in his pocket and refilling his coffee cup. "Maybe the weather will cool hot tempers."

"Another disgruntled caller?"

"Third one in half an hour. This one complained about residents killing the tourist business by hogging the few remaining downtown parking spaces. Half the locals are starstruck, and the other half are ticked off." He plopped onto a chair at the kitchen table. "And we're facing six more weeks of this chaos."

"If nothing happens to delay filming."

"The way everything's going, I wouldn't bank on smooth sailing."

Emily settled across from him. "Are you second-guessing the whole project?"

"I still believe we made the right decision. I just ... we underestimated the movie crew's impact on everyday country folks."

"On the plus side, not many communities have the chance to star in a Robert Nordstrom movie."

Scott sipped his coffee. "Which makes the long-term benefit worth the trouble."

"As long as something beyond our control doesn't rear its ugly head." She opened her computer and scrolled through her emails. "Hey, good news about my book."

"An offer to turn it into a movie?"

"In my dreams. A message from a woman over in Clayton. She wants me to call her about talking to her book club."

"Your first out-of-town presentation. Congratulations."

Emily pressed the digits and engaged the phone's speaker.

"Hello, Janice speaking."

"Hi, this is Emily Hayes."

"Oh, my goodness. I appreciate you responding so fast. Everyone in our club ordered your book and would love to hear all about your writing journey."

Scott signaled a thumbs up.

Emily grinned. "I'm honored and delighted."

"Are you available a week from today?"

Emily checked her phone calendar. "I am. Where and what time?"

"Actually ... we'd like to come to Willow Falls. You know, to see what's going on in your town and hear your story."

Why did they really want to come here? "I'm putting you on hold a second." She locked eyes with Scott. "Do you think she wants to hear about *Percy's Legacy* or cozy up to movie stars?"

"It doesn't matter. You have to oblige."

"You're right." She sighed and re-engaged with the caller. "Things are a bit hectic with the movie and all, but I can make it work."

"Excellent. There will be nineteen of us."

"Oh my. How about one o'clock at the Willow Inn. You'll see it on the left as you drive into town."

"Looking forward to meeting you."

Emily ended the call, leaned back, and clasped her hands behind her head. "I wonder if they'd want me to talk if celebrities weren't hanging out in town."

"Whatever the reason, you'll have a captive audience."

"Until Carrie makes an appearance or Maggie wanders by."

Rachel dashed into the kitchen, her cell phone in hand. "We have a problem."

Scott shook his head. "What a shocker." His tone was laced with sarcasm.

Emily shifted her attention from Scott to Rachel. "Another complaint?"

"Big time. Bert's at the Petersons' home—"

"Hold on." Emily held up her hand. "Who's Bert?"

"Robert's set designer. Agnes is refusing to let him make any changes to her house."

"What kind of changes?"

"All I know is, one of us needs to intervene, like now."

Emily closed her computer. "I've known the Petersons all my life. I should go."

"This is getting out of hand," mumbled Scott.

"I won't be gone long. Besides, Rachel can stay with the twins." She eyed her sister. "Right?"

"Of course."

Emily grabbed her purse and headed to the garage. Three minutes later she parked behind a panel truck in front of the Petersons' house. The set designer and two men dressed in paint-stained jeans and T-shirts huddled on the front porch. Emily rushed up the sidewalk. "I hear there's a problem."

Bert thrust his thumb toward the door. "It seems the Petersons didn't read their contract."

"What'd they miss?"

"The paragraph about adapting the house to fit the movie. You need to go in there and explain it to them."

"I'll do my best." She knocked on the front door, then stepped inside. "Agnes, Wayne, it's Emily." She found them in the front room, sitting on the couch. "Hey, what's going on?"

Agnes sniffed. "Robert Nordstrom said our house is perfect. Now, that man out there wants to go making a lot of changes."

Wayne waved the contract he held in his gnarled fingers. "I signed this, giving them permission to do whatever they want. If you hadn't been so all-fired excited, I'd have read it more thoroughly, and we wouldn't be in this pickle."

Emily sat on the piano bench and breathed in the scent of chocolate wafting from a plate of cookies sitting on the coffee table. "What do they want to do?"

Agnes dabbed her eyes with a tissue. "Paint this room a light color, replace the furniture and remove all my ... what Bert called knick-knacks. He said they needed to make the room look like it belongs to a young person. Oh, and they don't like the painting over the couch. Said it's not modern enough. If they go changing everything, it could be anyone's house. How will all our friends recognize it as ours?"

Wayne shook his head. "For goodness sake, Agnes, they'll know because we told them. Besides, they're not changing the kitchen ... much anyway. And the outside not at all."

"Why isn't this room perfect the way it is?" Agnes bit her lower lip, her eyes pleading.

Emily leaned forward. "I know you love your home. All the pretty decorations and the memories. If it were up to me, I'd leave it exactly the way it is. But I suspect the director believes your parlor is too fancy for a young, struggling café owner." She moved off the piano bench and sat beside Agnes. "Your front yard is the most beautiful in Willow Falls, maybe the whole state. Just think, millions of people will discover that Agnes Peterson is a gifted gardener." She reached for a cookie. "And that your kitchen is almost perfect for a character who cooks for a living."

"I'll tear this up if you want me to, dear," Wayne said as he tossed the contract beside the cookies. "But if we back out now, we'll have to give the money back and disappoint all your friends."

Agnes stood and plucked a figurine off the piano. "This belonged to my mother. I don't know if it's worth anything other than the sentimental value." She moved to the front window and pulled the curtain aside. "My garden *is* picture perfect."

"You mean movie perfect." Wayne moved beside his wife and wrapped his arm around her. "What do you say? Can we let the men hanging around outside know everything's okay?"

"If Emily will agree to be here when they start filming."

"I promise." She'd have to find a way to make Scott understand. "Right now, I'll deliver the news to the crew." She walked to the front porch, closing the door behind her.

Bert removed his hands from his pockets. "Any luck?"

"Problem solved." She pulled him aside. "If you want on Agnes' good side, I suggest you compliment the heck out of her decorating expertise and baking skills."

"I've been doing this work for years and know how to deal with disgruntled homeowners."

Then why did I have to drop everything and rush over to intervene? "I'm sure you do." She returned to the living room and stayed to console Agnes until the crew moved everything except the piano from the living room, then spread drop cloths on the floor and rolled the first line of paint.

Wayne stood in the foyer holding Agnes's hand. "At least they're giving us a free paint job."

"I guess the room did need some sprucing up. And it is a pretty color."

Emily smiled. "You see, everything is working out okay after all."

Wayne nodded toward Emily. "Thank you for taking time away from Jane and Clair to babysit a couple of old codgers."

"You mean two of my favorite young-at-heart senior citizens." Emily shouldered her purse and walked out the front door. She stopped on the porch to admire the shrubs and flowers and to pray the footage of Agnes' front yard would make it through the editing process.

Chapter 26

Rachel stood on an eight-foot stepladder arranging pewter platters, antique candle holders, wine bottles, and books on the built-in cabinet in the Willow Oak dining room. "What do you think?"

"It looks great." Charlie held the ladder while she climbed down.

She stepped back and assessed her work. "It does, doesn't it? Seems I inherited some of Mama Sadie's decorating skills."

He moved behind her, wrapped his arms around her waist, and pulled her against his chest. "I'm glad you'll be around weekends to help entertain visitors."

"Don't forget. I'm still directing *Percy's Legacy*."

"Someone else can take over. At least until the business is up and running."

"It's not that easy." She pulled away.

"The cast worked together for a year. How much directing do they need?" He folded the stepladder and leaned it against a wall.

"You don't understand."

"I don't understand what?"

"How much the play means to me." Rachel placed a pyramid-shaped centerpiece crafted from grapevines on a four-top dining table. "It served as a life preserver for my sinking career. Walking away cold turkey without a clear path to the future ..." She moved to the windows overlooking the vineyard.

Charlie followed and stood beside her. "You're right. The cast and crew still need you. At least for a while."

She slipped her hand in his. "You're a good man, Charlie."

"I have my moments."

A car pulling into the lower parking lot drew Rachel's attention. "Is that your dad?"

"I forgot to tell you he planned to come over." Charlie moved away from the window.

Watching Brick stroll past the gazebo brought Charlie's comment about men and broken hearts back to mind. She pivoted at the thump of footsteps on the stairs.

"Where's my almost daughter-in-law?" Brick's voice oozed charm as he reached the top of the stairs and moved to embrace Rachel.

"Did I tell you how much I enjoyed the dinner party you and Mama Sadie hosted?"

"More than once." He released Rachel. "Interesting centerpieces."

"One of our residents copied them from a photo she found on Pinterest."

Brick's frown showed his confusion. "Is that some sort of new-fangled website?"

Charlie chuckled. "Dad's not the most up-to-date guy when it comes to social media."

"I prefer my generation's communication methods—person to person." Brick glanced around the space. "Dining room looks good."

"Thanks to Rachel," Charlie said proudly. "She calls it rustic elegance."

"You have a good eye, like your mother." Brick pulled a chair away from the table. "You two need to take a load off. I have something important to discuss with you."

"You've captured my attention." Charlie held a chair out for Rachel, then sat beside her, across from Brick. "What's on your mind, Dad?"

"Sadie's fiftieth birthday is in three weeks. I want to throw her a surprise party. Not too big, just family and a few close friends."

"What a wonderful idea," Rachel said. "At your house?"

Brick shook his head. "Here, at the winery. I know you and Emily have a lot on your plates, but I'd appreciate it if you'd plan it."

Rachel's shoulders tensed as she mentally ticked off her list of obligations. "Sure. I mean anything for Mama Sadie. Are you thinking a sit-down dinner or appetizers and a big cake?"

"I'll leave the details up to you two." Brick leaned back and ran his hand through his thinning white hair. "I threw a surprise bash for my ex-wife's fortieth birthday. Bought her a three-carat diamond ring." A faraway look clouded his eyes. "I loved Cynthia and believed we'd grow old together. After she ran off with a younger man and abandoned me and our sons, I didn't think I'd ever trust or love another woman."

Brick's pained expression tore at Rachel's heart. Charlie was right.

Moments passed.

"Then I met Sadie. She's as different from Charlie's mother as night and day. That's what first attracted me to her." Brick's eyes met Rachel's. "Your mother is an amazing woman. She has a bigger heart than anyone I've ever known. Which is why you and Emily need to make the night special. I don't want anyone besides you two, plus Emily and Scott, to know the real reason for the party." He reached into his pants pocket and pulled out a signature, turquoise Tiffany box.

Rachel pressed her fingers to her lips.

Brick opened the box, revealing a stunning princess-cut diamond ring. "I'm going to ask Sadie to marry me."

Charlie clasped his dad's shoulder. "Good for you, Dad. Good for you."

"Deep down ..." Rachel swallowed hard. "I hoped you were more than friends."

"My dear, your mother and I have been more than friends for a long time."

Thank goodness Charlie was wrong. Rachel kissed Brick's cheek. "Thank you for loving her. I know she loves you too."

"I hope she loves me enough to say yes."

Of course she will. "It seems you'll become both my stepfather and father-in-law."

"Interesting family tree. To keep rumors from spoiling the surprise, I want you and Emily to make the party your idea and only invite folks who can keep it under wraps."

Rachel chuckled. "You've obviously learned a thing or two about small towns."

"I'm smarter than I look." Brick turned to Charlie. "We need to talk about the grand opening."

"I'll leave you two to discuss business." Rachel grabbed her purse and raced down the stairs to the tasting room. She climbed onto a stool, dug for her phone, and pressed her sister's number.

Emily answered on the second ring. "Hey, how's the decorating going?"

"Are you sitting down?"

Emily groaned. "Please don't tell me there's more bad news?"

"The complete opposite." Rachel shared Brick's revelation.

"Oh my gosh, they *are* romantically involved."

"We have to keep the proposal hush-hush." If that was even possible.

"We'll make sure it's the best kept Willow Falls secret since ... ever."

Chapter 27

Rachel laid her script on her lap at the sound of the glass door sliding open. She smiled at the sight of Clair and Jane scrambling toward their outdoor play set, then turned her attention to her sister. "From your expression, I can't tell if you've been sucking on a pickle or are just plain frustrated."

"More like exhausted." Emily set her computer on the patio table and cranked the umbrella up.

"Too much on your plate?"

"You tell me." She dropped onto a chair across from Rachel. "First, I have to write an editorial and preview articles for Thursday's newspaper. I'm speaking to a book club in a couple of days. There's Mama Sadie's party to plan and your expanded wedding. Tomorrow, the crew is filming at the Petersons' house. I need to squeeze a few minutes to plot my next book, and I'm struggling to set up my author website. All that in addition to taking care of two rambunctious toddlers."

"Are you complaining or blowing off steam?"

Cody deposited a ball at Emily's feet and barked. She tossed it high. "I don't know if I need a two-hour nap or six cups of strong coffee to keep me going."

"Hmm." Rachel tapped her index finger to her chin. "Should my stressed-out sister choose sleep or a caffeine rush?"

"How about both."

Cody returned with the ball, tail wagging. "Sorry fella, no more catch." Emily turned her attention back to her sister. "Enough about me. Are you nervous about today's shoot?"

Rachel stared at her script. "My first scene is with Princess Carrie. So, yeah, I'm way more than a little anxious."

"If you're going to pursue a movie career, you'll have to figure out how to work with inflated egos." Emily opened her laptop.

"After today, I might be forced to retire my short-lived acting career."

"Who's the negative Nellie now?" Clair toddled over and climbed onto Emily's lap.

Rachel closed her script and clutched it to her chest. "What if this new gig isn't a match?"

"You're a talented actress. You'll figure out how to make it work."

"I appreciate your vote of confidence." Rachel glanced at her watch. "Time got away from me. I'm scheduled for makeup and wardrobe in twenty minutes."

"Try not to outshine the princess."

"When did you add comedian to your resume?" Rachel pushed up from her chair. "Tonight, we'll celebrate my success or mourn my failure. Either way, I'll bring home a bottle of wine and some of Patsy's dark-chocolate brownies."

Emily tapped the tip of Clair's nose. "What do you say, baby girl. Do you think we'll celebrate with Aunty Rachel?"

Clair sneezed, then giggled.

"There you have it, Sis. We're gonna celebrate."

***

Rachel parked behind Hayes General Store, then dashed down Main to Falls Street. She slowed her pace as she approached, then stepped inside the thirty-six-foot-long, white makeup truck.

A thin, attractive, middle-aged man wearing a pink silk shirt, smelling of a woody, floral cologne, greeted her. "Good morning. I am Antoine." He pressed his palms together. "Please tell me you are Mademoiselle Rachel." His French accent dripped with attitude.

"In the flesh."

He applauded with his fingertips. "How wonderful. I adore working on beautiful redheads. Please, come to my station."

Rachel sat in the first salon chair in a row of four facing a white cabinet and wall of lighted mirrors and stared at her makeup-free image.

Antoine stood behind Rachel and pulled her hair away from her face. "Such magnificent bone structure and intoxicating green eyes. You are more suited as a seductress than a jealous girlfriend. But I must follow Monsieur Nordstrom's direction." He pulled a rolling cart filled with the tools of his trade from beneath the cabinet, raised her chair, and swiveled it toward him.

Rachel looked up at the man with a sheepish grin. "I've never had my makeup professionally done."

His mouth fell open. "Impossible. Have you not acted before?"

"Only in small regional theaters, where we do our own."

"What a pleasure to be your first professional."

She choked back a laugh as he draped a pink bib around her neck.

An hour later, Antoine fluffed her hair, stood back, and pressed his palms together. "*Magnifique.*" He snapped a photo, then turned her chair toward the mirror. "Are you pleased?"

Her face looked natural yet different. She moved close to the mirror and stared at her smooth skin. "I take it Mr. Nordstrom isn't fond of freckles."

"For a country girl, yes." He removed the bib. "Not for a sophisticated city woman."

"Does that mean the real me is better suited for Willow Falls than Atlanta?"

"My magic hands can make you suitable for another planet if the script so dictates. Now scoot, Mademoiselle Rachel. Wardrobe is waiting for you."

"Thank you, Antoine. I'll see you before my next shoot." Rachel rushed to the wardrobe trailer.

A woman steaming a green, short-sleeve dress, glanced up. "Miss Streetman?"

"Yes."

She turned the steamer off and handed over the dress.

Rachel fingered the label. "Prada. Impressive." She read the woman's name badge. "Thank you, Bernice."

Bernice gave her a shoebox. "These also cost a pretty penny."

"Jimmy Choos. I'll finally find out what the big deal is about outrageously expensive clothing and footwear. What about jewelry?"

"Diamond earrings are on the shelf in the first dressing room. They're fake. About your engagement ring." Bernice pointed to a row of lockers. "I'll keep it safe for you."

A twinge of guilt pricked Rachel's conscience as she slipped the ring off her finger for the first time since Charlie proposed. *It's part of this crazy career you've chosen.* She set the ring on the padded shelf and stepped into the dressing room. After changing, she stared at her image in the full-length mirror. At least she looked the part of a rich girlfriend. She placed her clothes in the locker, thanked Bernice, and stepped outside. A golf cart was parked by the door.

"Hop on, Miss Streetman," said the young driver.

"It's only a block. I can walk."

"Sorry, ma'am. I have orders to drive you."

"If you insist." She sat in the rear-facing seat and watched tourists gawk at her as if catching a glimpse of a world-famous movie star. "Sorry, folks," she mumbled. "I'm just a Georgia girl who landed a part in a Robert Nordstrom movie."

The driver rounded the corner and braked behind a silver Porsche 911. She hopped out and joined the director's assistant on the sidewalk. "I assume the Porsche is my character's ride."

"All day long. We'll film out here first."

Robert arrived in another golf cart. After setting the scene, he directed the first shoot. For what seemed like hours, she endured dozens of shots of her stepping from the car, walking on the sidewalk, approaching Pepper's Café—renamed Joanie's Joint—all action without dialogue.

"Cut!" shouted Robert. "Next shoot in fifteen."

"Follow me, Miss Streetman." The assistant led her inside the café, where locals tagged as extras milled around, chatting, waiting for their moment on camera. Their conversations halted as they turned toward her.

Rachel waved to fellow performers occupying four booths hugging the partially exposed brick wall in the café that not long ago served as the town's only restaurant. "Hey, everyone." Following polite responses, they resumed chatting, clearly not impressed with an almost local. She moved to the back wall and glanced around. Other than new signage, production lights, and sound-recording equipment, the space looked much as it did before the movie crew showed up. A row of Formica-topped tables lined up in the center. Swivel stools anchored to the floor provided seating for the counter on the right.

Antoine dashed in, draped a makeup bib on Rachel, and performed minor touch-ups. "Perfect."

Moments later, the main character breezed in, halting conversation and initiating stares. Dressed in a white, waitress-style dress, blue apron, and tennis shoes—her hair pulled into a ponytail—Carrie had transformed from Hollywood superstar to Joanie, a small-town café owner. She eyed Rachel from head to toe. "Expensive outfit. Nice touch."

"Obviously, my character is a fashion fanatic with a high-paying job or a gigantic trust fund. Before moving to Willow Falls, I held the position of vice president in a wealthy company and still couldn't afford these clothes."

"Stories work best if the *other* woman is the complete opposite of the main character."

The café door swung open. Robert and his production assistant entered. They conferred with the camera operators, then relayed instructions to set the scene for the first shoot—rich, city-slicker girlfriend meets poor, country-girl ingénue. Carrie stepped behind the counter. Two men, dressed in overalls, sat on stools. Another production assistant marked a slate and clicked the clapper. The camera rolled.

Carrie slipped into Joanie's character, reciting rehearsed lines with the overall-clad extras. Her feigned southern drawl came across as natural and authentic. Her actions and facial expressions accurately portrayed the character's small-town persona.

Following a series of takes, the director positioned Rachel for her first speaking role. The queasy sensation she often experienced before stepping on stage attacked with a vengeance. Why hadn't she thought to bring a thermos of ginger tea?

The clapper clicked with a loud snap.

Rachel took a deep breath and began her first scene—walking into the café.

"Cut!" barked Robert before it ended. He approached Rachel. "You can't appear tentative and sweet. You're playing a woman who believes small-town folks are beneath her. Which means you need to walk in with an air of superiority."

"Yes, sir, I understand."

"Good. Take two."

Get a grip Rachel. This isn't your first acting rodeo. She breathed deep to slow her pulse and repeated the action. When she finished, Robert gave her a thumbs up and filmed it again.

During four grueling hours, Rachel understood why fans touted Carrie as an up-and-coming Hollywood superstar. Her acting skills were top-notch, and unlike her entitled princess persona, she responded well to direction.

By the time Robert ended the session, Rachel longed to know more about Carrie, thinking perhaps she possessed some of the characteristics she displayed as Joanie—until the actress converted to movie star, signed autographs for the ogling extras, and dashed from the café as if she'd already spent far too much time with the minions.

Chapter 28

*U*nable to find a vacant downtown parking spot, Rachel pulled into Brick's driveway. She dropped her car keys in her purse, crossed Main Street, and closed the distance to Redding Arms. On the sidewalk leading to the beveled-glass doors, she paused and checked the notice attached to the production crew's message board. Updated every morning, it provided cast-call information for the movie extras. A text message informed those chosen for more important roles—one of the perks for the so-called elite.

She spoke to tourists exiting the hotel as she made her way through the lobby to the back veranda stretching the full length of the building. She looked to the right. A row of white rocking chairs—three set in motion from guests—functioned as a spot to relax and enjoy the scenery or make new friends. Rachel turned left and entered the dining room's outdoor space.

Her mother motioned her to a table covered with a white linen cloth. An etched-glass candle holder on a bed of Magnolia leaves served as a centerpiece.

"Thanks for inviting me to join you." She sat beside her mother and across from Maggie Warren. "This is one of the best views in Willow Falls."

"Among others." The actress closed her menu and smiled at Rachel. "Are your ears burning? We've been talking about you."

"Uh oh, what did I do?"

"Oh, nothing much." Maggie winked. "Except impress the dickens out of our director. He called you a star in the making."

An adrenalin rush soared through Rachel's limbs. "Are you serious?"

"In case you haven't heard, he's well-known for discovering new talent."

"I'm flattered and more than a little surprised."

Mama Sadie caught Rachel's eye. "I don't know why. You've been showered with lots of accolades for your role in *Percy's Legacy.*"

"Praises from theater-goers aren't in the same league as compliments from a world-class professional."

"He's not the only person you impressed." Maggie rested her forearms on the table and leaned forward. "The *princess* is also singing your praises."

Rachel's mouth gaped open. "Carrie?"

"The one and only."

Images of the talented actress dashing from the café popped into Rachel's head. "I'm shocked she even noticed my performance."

"Because she comes across as arrogant and aloof?" Maggie reached for her water glass. "Carrie is far more complicated than most people realize. Like I explained to Sadie, acting like a spoiled prima donna is her defense mechanism."

Their waitress approached carrying three glasses of tea. She announced the lunch special.

Eager to hear more from Maggie, Rachel handed over her menu. "I'll take the special."

"Sounds delish," said Maggie.

Mama Sadie squeezed lemon into her tea. "Make it three."

Rachel finger-tapped the table until the waitress collected the remaining menus and returned to the dining room. She leaned forward and locked eyes with Maggie. "What exactly is Carrie defending?"

"Self-esteem that's fragile as paper-thin glass. Have you ever experienced stage fright?"

Rachel nodded. "Big time."

"Try to imagine living in a constant state of fear."

"Talk about fear." Mama Sadie plucked her napkin off the table. "She should try living in a prison for thirty years."

Rachel's eyes shifted from her mother back to Maggie. "You mean Carrie's afraid of not performing up to snuff?"

"To a small degree. The bigger issue is the agonizing dread of becoming irrelevant—last year's news. When Carrie trekked from the heartland to the west coast, she became one more pretty face in a town overflowing with wannabe actresses."

Rachel sighed heavily as she leaned back in her chair. "Likely with a less-than-impressive resume."

Maggie's head tilted. "Is your comment a lucky guess or based on experience?"

"Both. My career never made it out of the basement in Atlanta. Too much competition, one refusal to compromise my ethics ... and one hasty decision. Those are stories for another day. Tell me more about Carrie."

"When she bucked the odds and moved to Los Angeles, ambition compelled her to buckle down, study the craft, and claw her way to the top. Like too many young starlets, she didn't arrive unscathed."

Memories of her encounter with Director Gordon Wells loomed large in Rachel's mind. "A lesson I learned last year."

"This business is filled with heart-wrenching lessons." Maggie's expression spoke volumes. "As hard as it is to reach the top, it's much more difficult to stay there. Especially for young, beautiful women. There's always someone prettier, with more talent, and willing to cross more lines."

"I'm curious," Mama Sadie interjected. "How have you managed to remain a household name for so long?"

"Believe me, I've survived a lot of difficult years." Maggie ran her thumb over her manicured fingernails. "It boils down to three factors, beginning with finding an outstanding agent who had my best interest at heart. Then there's my willingness to accept difficult, unglamorous roles. Which is why I'm best known as a character actress."

The waitress returned with their salads.

Rachel waited for her to leave before she speared a slice of hard-boiled egg. "What's the third factor?"

Maggie sipped her drink. "I could get used to sweet tea." She picked up her fork. "Lifestyle. Like Carrie, I also migrated to California to begin my career and immersed myself in the Hollywood scene. All my friends were performers competing for roles and attention. Although we fed each other's egos, our interaction often led to petty jealousy."

Rachel laid down her fork and listened intently.

"Then I met and fell in love with the most amazing man." Maggie's eyes gleamed. "He owned a car dealership and didn't give a hoot about fame or famous people. Our relationship kept me grounded. After we married, I kept my career in perspective and treated it like any other successful job. His circle of acquaintances became my new friends."

"Sort of like folks in Willow Falls when I returned from prison," Mama Sadie said.

"Good friends make all the difference." The smile crinkling the corners of Maggie's eyes faded. "My husband and I were married thirty-two years before he suffered a fatal heart attack. We never had children. When he passed, I was devastated. To help ease the pain, I poured every ounce of energy into my career." She paused for a long moment. "I've been blessed with a long, successful run. But now, I'm worn out and ready to live the rest of my life in peaceful obscurity."

"I'm curious." Rachel fiddled with her salad. "Do you ever regret your career choice?"

Maggie shook her head. "Show business was the right career choice. But I'm equally pleased I found a way to have a life away from the spotlight."

Rachel stared at the slice of egg speared on the tip of her fork. "If you had to choose between the two, which would prevail?"

"Hands down, the normal life. Fortunately, I didn't have to make that choice." She reached across the table and touched Rachel's hand in a motherly gesture. "Neither do you."

As conversation shifted to life in Willow Falls, Rachel imagined standing in front of a dressing room door with her name scrawled on a foot-high star, then stepping inside and eyeing an Oscar sitting on a gold mantel beside her Willow Falls Wonder Woman trophy. A giggle escaped, sending heat rising to her cheeks. She blinked, grateful Mama Sadie and Maggie gave her a fleeting glance and continued chatting about Willow Falls' transformation from obscurity to movie location.

Chapter 29

*E*mily breezed into the living room, placed two glasses of lemonade on the coffee table, and dropped onto the couch across from Rachel sitting on one of two plush, overstuffed chairs. "The twins are down for their afternoon nap, which means you and I have at least an hour to work on party plans for our mom."

"Sounds good." Rachel reached for her pinging phone. "A text from Carrie Fleming."

"Let me guess. *Her Highness* wants Mama Sadie to redecorate the Carlie suite to better suit her sensibilities. Or is she ordering breakfast in bed? Maybe caviar for afternoon nosh?"

"Enough with the sarcasm. She's not demanding anything."

"Uh oh, did I touch a nerve?"

Rachel laid her phone on the coffee table. "She invited me to her RV tomorrow morning before her shoot."

Emily snapped her fingers. "Ah-ha, she's going to request something outrageous and plans to hold you for ransom."

"Either you've spiked your lemonade, or your writer's imagination is on overdrive."

"Occupational hazard. Seriously, what do you suppose she wants?"

"I don't have a clue." Rachel read the text again. "Maybe she's lonely and needs a friend."

"That doesn't make sense. Carrie has Maggie and a town full of fans fawning over her and kowtowing to her every need."

"Maggie's more like a mother, and fans aren't friends."

"Good point." Emily sipped her lemonade. "Whatever her motivation, I can't wait to hear about it."

"I'll give you an update the second I escape her private domain."

"I'm counting on it. Now on to important stuff." Emily removed a yellow notepad from the end table and handed it to her sister. "What do you think about this guest list?"

Rachel ran her finger down the page. "Eighteen's a good number." She read the list again. Her brow pinched. "Mirabelle's name is missing. You know if you exclude her, she'll throw an earthquake-triggering hissy fit."

"I considered inviting her. Problem is, I don't know if we can trust her to keep a secret."

Rachel handed the notepad back to Emily. "She will if you let her know how exclusive the list is—"

"And that it only includes people who have the discipline to keep it hush-hush."

Rachel nodded. "You catch on fast."

Emily reached for a pen and added two names to the list. "Mirabelle and her husband bring us to twenty." She flipped to the second page. "Pepper and Patsy agreed to provide appetizers and a cake. Charlie's supplying wine and champagne. You and I are in charge of decorations. Do you suppose Brick will propose on one knee?"

"Your guess is as good as mine." Rachel's brows arched. "Oh my gosh, what if Mama Sadie says no?"

"The same thought crossed my mind." Emily's phone pinged a text. "Mary. Wouldn't you know. When everything's going along without a hitch, a new problem crops up."

"What bombshell dropped this time?"

"Connor posted a risqué photo of Carrie on social media, and he's giving all his friends a hard copy. Parents are hopping mad."

Rachel frowned. "This is not good."

Another ping.

"No wonder they're up in arms." Emily pushed her phone across the table. "Check this out."

Rachel's eyes grew wide. "That's the tiniest bikini I've ever seen. A couple of postage stamps would cover more than those strips of fabric."

"Leave it to our teenage super sleuth to dig up a heap of controversy. This is bound to make Carrie the target of rumors and all kinds of ridicule. Although she might consider it good publicity."

"Not for the role of Joanie." Rachel scooted to the edge of the chair. "We have to quash this before it goes viral."

"Are you kidding? You've lived in Willow Falls long enough to know by now the whole town is tuned in."

"We have to take action." Rachel sprang to her feet, her eyes lightning fierce. "That kid had no right."

Emily crossed her leg over her knee and pumped her foot. "You can't lay all the blame on Connor. Carrie posed for the picture. And what's with your over-the-top reaction? She's a celebrity who—in Maggie's words—clawed her way to fame. Which pretty much guarantees this isn't her first bout with negative publicity."

"Point taken." Rachel dropped back onto the chair. "Maybe I am overreacting."

Emily stared at her sister. "You think?"

"It just doesn't seem right to sit back and do nothing."

Emily's foot stopped pumping. "Do you remember what happened last year when Connor uncovered the truth about Kat and Missy being on parole?"

"Yeah." Rachel emitted a long sigh. "He posted details on social media."

"After that."

"Remind me."

"His parents took away his computer and grounded him for a month."

Rachel's eyes narrowed to a slit. "And your point is?"

"One good thing about small-town rumor mills is kids can't hide their shenanigans. By tomorrow Connor will have repossessed every photo, shut down his social media site, and be facing a heap of trouble."

"Exactly how does his punishment help Carrie?"

Emily's gaze probed, then softened. "Is your concern prompted by her glowing comments about your acting ability?"

"No." Rachel broke eye contact. "Maybe. Okay, partially. The thing is, I'm trying to imagine how I'd feel if some kid dug up a nearly-naked photo of me."

Emily pointed to Rachel's phone. "Are you telling me you have pictures like that floating out there in cyberland?"

"Heavens no. I'm just saying if there were, I wouldn't want anyone to see them."

Carrie's *without fans, I'm a nobody* comment and her pained expression the day she played tour guide, trickled up from Emily's memory. "I suppose I could use the power of the press to counter the negative."

"You mean write a story about her?"

"That's too obvious. I'll ask Mary to interview all five of our guest celebrities and write a glowing editorial about their virtues."

"That might help." Rachel reached for her glass of lemonade and ran her finger around the rim. "All those years I worked at Streetman Enterprise, I longed to make it big in show business."

"You still do. Right?"

"Of course." The mental image of an Oscar in a dressing room designated as Rachel's private space resurfaced. "Although sometimes I wonder if the price of fame is too high."

Emily laid the yellow pad on the coffee table. "It won't be if acting is your true calling. *And* if you keep your priorities straight."

Chapter 30

$\mathcal{F}$ive minutes before her scheduled time to meet with Carrie, Rachel stood on the sidewalk between Pearl's Hair and Nail Salon and the star's RV. According to the morning's grapevine, Connor's photo caper ended with a parental recall, a scrub of his social media post, and a two-week computer confiscation. Comments about his victim ran the gamut from empathy to disgust.

Sweat popped out on Rachel's upper lip as she debated the best way to approach Carrie. She swiped the moisture with her fingertips and settled on *act like nothing happened*. She stepped off the curb, rounded the back of the RV, and knocked on the door.

Seconds passed.

A young couple strolling in the middle of the blocked-off section of Falls Street stopped and stared. She smiled and waved. "Nice day for a walk."

They nodded and inched their way forward.

"Rachel?" Carrie's voice echoed through a speaker.

She turned toward the intercom and pressed the button. "It's me."

"Come on in. The door's unlocked."

Rachel pushed the door open and climbed the steps into the custom vehicle, the living room walls expanded to create additional space.

Carrie—dressed in a pink jogging suit, her hair wet, her face scrubbed clean—stood at the kitchen counter. "I have cappuccino and French vanilla pods or orange juice if you're not a coffee drinker."

"Cappuccino works for me."

"My favorite." Carrie popped a pod in a coffee maker. "Make yourself at home."

Rachel settled on a white, leather couch and admired the white marble floor with tan and gold veins glistening in the glow of lights recessed in the shiny gold ceiling. "This looks more like a luxury home than a mobile dressing room."

"It's my refuge when I need to escape." Carrie handed a mug to Rachel and set a second on the end table. "Like last night." She aimed a remote at the window across from the couch and opened the blinds.

"You slept here?"

"I wasn't in the mood to answer questions about the photo." Carrie settled on an overstuffed chair that matched the couch.

"Can't say I blame you. Although by now, I imagine Connor has taken it out of circulation. At least in Willow Falls."

"A lot of good it will do. The image is burned into who knows how many brains." Carrie pulled her left leg up and tucked her foot under her thigh. "If you're wondering why the shot exists, it happened a long time ago."

"An unscrupulous paparazzi?"

"A fly-by-night agent. He duped me into believing a series of racy photos were necessary to stand out." Carrie guffawed. "It worked all right, for all the wrong reasons, by all the wrong people."

Rachel caught sight of JT standing on the sidewalk talking to a group of tourists. Robert's prediction about the town's favorite tour guide maximizing the sudden influx of movie people had merit. "Have you tried to remove the pictures from the Internet?"

"My current agent and publicist attempted. Obviously, they failed." Carrie reached for her coffee cup and clutched it in both hands as if absorbing its warmth. "What'd you think of the first scene we did together?"

"I enjoyed it. Although, I admit I had no idea what to expect, given all my experience has been in live theater."

Carrie sipped her coffee, then set the mug back on the end table. "Landing your first speaking role in a Robert Nordstrom film will give your agent a huge boost in securing movie contracts."

"If I had an agent, which I don't."

Carrie's pointed glare begged for an explanation.

"When I first pursued my dream to make it as an actress back in Atlanta, I didn't have enough credentials to attract an agent. I don't need one in Willow Falls. The truth is, for the past year I haven't put much effort into my career."

"As far back as I can remember, I wanted to act," Carrie said wistfully. "On my twelfth birthday I announced my dream to run off to Hollywood and become a movie star."

Rachel smiled. "Seems we have something in common. My childhood fantasy was making it big on Broadway."

"My parents were convinced I would come to my senses, marry a local boy, settle down to a mundane, small-town lifestyle, and give them a house full of grandbabies. I was nineteen when I kissed them goodbye and boarded a bus to California, with two hundred dollars and a new credit card in my wallet."

"At least no one could accuse you of buckling under parental pressure." *Unlike me giving in to my father's demands the day I graduated from college.*

"I was plenty defiant all right. Until I spent the first two nights in the bus station eating candy bars from a vending machine and scouring want ads for a job and a cheap place to live."

"An inauspicious beginning." Rachel swallowed a sip of coffee.

"No kidding. Anyway, I ended up in a less-than-desirable, three-bedroom, one-bath apartment with five other girls. It didn't take long to discover Hollywood was overrun with wannabe actresses, including my roommates."

"Did you ever second-guess your decision to leave your hometown?"

"More times than I can count. Pride and a mid-western stubborn streak kept me from turning tail and admitting defeat. So, I took a waitress job, enrolled in an acting class, and set a one-year goal to land my first role."

At least she set a goal. "How did that work out?"

"It didn't. By the time one year approached two, I'd become desperate. That's when I met the sleazy agent. He had a long list of names he claimed were successful clients and a surefire plan to make me famous. My need to believe him outweighed my skepticism and led me to sign a contract." Carrie pinched the bridge of her nose. "A week after the bikini photo session, he called with an offer."

A woman stretching her neck as if trying to catch a glimpse inside the RV drew Rachel's eye. "Your first big break?"

"My first dose of reality. A five-thousand-dollar offer to perform in an underground skin flick. For a split-second I considered taking it. Until I pictured someone in my hometown showing it to my parents."

She does have redeeming qualities. "The sign of a good moral compass."

"Not according to the agent. The kindest thing he called me was a stupid loser. Then he threatened to sue me for breach of contract."

"Did he?"

"Thankfully, no. I'm confident he found a victim more afraid of failure than me. A year later, my acting coach encouraged me to audition for a bit part in a Robert Nordstrom film. I landed the role, found a legitimate agent, and launched my career."

That was encouraging to hear. "Did your parents change their tune about your career choice?"

Carrie shook her head. "They're convinced I've been lured into a life unfitting for an innocent small-town girl. How ironic they haven't returned any of the generous checks I've sent them."

"Maybe they'll come around."

"When pigs fly." Carrie planted both feet on the floor and leaned forward. "In case you're wondering why I'm baring my soul, it's because Robert believes you have the talent to make it big in this business."

"Wow." Rachel fingered her engagement ring. "I'm flattered."

"You need to understand that talent isn't enough. There are plenty of one-movie wonders who didn't have the stamina to claw their way to success or the passion and drive to stay there after they arrived. There's always someone with more talent ready to knock you down a peg or two. And if you let them, completely off the ladder."

Silence enfolded the moment as doubt about her career choice niggled at Rachel's conscience and released a horde of butterflies in her chest.

"The reward for those of us who have what it takes is a magical life." Carrie stood at the sound of a knock.

The door swung open, and a young woman breezed in.

"My personal hairdresser and makeup artist. She's worth her weight in gold." Carrie motioned to Rachel. "Come on. I'll show you the real purpose for this outrageously expensive house on wheels." She slid a door open to reveal a fully equipped salon. Beyond that was a luxurious bedroom anchored by a king-size bed covered with a gold, silk spread and an array of green and gold throw pillows.

"You've come a long way from a crowded Hollywood apartment,"

"And I intend to stay here." Carrie sat in the stylist's chair. "Stick around, and I'll tell you how to impress our director even more than you already have."

Rachel leaned against the wall and listened to the superstar share tidbits she claimed would give her career a giant boost and secure her place among Hollywood's luminaries.

Chapter 31

*E*mily repositioned folding chairs in Willow Inn's parlor, then stepped back. She planted her hands on her hips and shook her head. "The room's still too crowded."

Rachel lifted her hands in exasperation. "Enough already. That's the third time you've moved those chairs. You're going to collapse from exhaustion before you welcome your fans."

Emily filled her lungs and exhaled slowly. "This is my first book-club talk. I don't want to blow it." Every nerve in her body was stretched tight.

"You're not delivering a state-of-the-union address. Relax. All you have to do is tell them about your writing journey and answer questions."

"That's what worries me. My story isn't that interesting."

"Do you know how many people dream about writing and publishing a book?"

Emily shrugged. "I don't have a clue."

"Neither do I, but I imagine it's a lot." Rachel dropped onto the settee. "Don't forget, you're a successful playwright *and* a published novelist."

"You mean a play finisher."

"Doesn't matter. If you hadn't accepted Naomi's offer to finish writing the half-finished play she found in her attic, it wouldn't exist, and I wouldn't have stayed in Willow Falls. Think George Baily in *It's a Wonderful Life.*"

"That's a stretch. But I understand what you're saying."

Rachel propped her feet on the coffee table. "Does that mean you've finished rearranging the furniture?"

"I suppose." Emily landed on the wingback chair. "I'm counting on you to rescue me if I come down with a bad case of the jitters."

"Twins tag teaming? I'm game. We could keep them guessing about who's who."

"Better yet, you can play the role of Emily the writer."

"Now there's an intriguing idea, except ..." Rachel held up two fingers. "I didn't read the script and ... oh yeah, improv isn't my cup of joe. I could ask Mama Sadie to fix you some ginger tea. It works for me when my stomach is tied in knots."

The front door swung open, followed by footsteps and female voices.

"Too late." Emily stood, her pulse pounding. "They're here."

Rachel moved beside her sister and whispered, "You'll wow the socks off 'em, kid."

After greeting the arrivals, Mama Sadie led them to the parlor.

An attractive, brunette woman clutching Emily's book approached. "I'm Janice." She looked from one sister to the other. "Wow. Twins. Which one of you is the author?"

"I am." Emily stepped forward with her hand extended. "Welcome to Willow Falls. I'm delighted to meet you."

"Same here. We're looking forward to hearing all about you and your writing experience."

A woman with short, spiked hair stared at Emily, then Rachel. "I saw one of you perform in *Percy's Legacy* a few months back."

"That was me," Rachel answered. "I remember signing your program."

"You do?" The woman's eyes widened. "You are one talented actress. Is it true you were chosen for a part in the new movie?"

"Yes. A minor role."

A short, plump woman held up her copy of *Percy's Legacy*. "I want you to sign my book along with your sister. When you become a famous movie star, it'll be worth a fortune."

Rachel shook her head. "I didn't write—"

"Both of us signing is a great idea," Emily said. "After all, Rachel and I are a team."

"My sister is generous. But today belongs to her." Rachel squeezed Emily's hand before slipping behind the last row of chairs to stand beside her mother.

"Okay, ladies," Janice said. "Let's find a seat and give the celebrity author our full attention."

Emily moved in front of the fireplace and mentally reviewed her notes while the book-club members followed their leader's direction.

A hush fell over the room.

Nineteen pairs of eyes focused on Emily. The overwhelming grip of stage fright turned her palms clammy and her knees wobbly. She locked eyes with the two most important women in her life and drew strength from her mother's wink and her twin's thumbs-up.

She glanced around the room. *Maybe they really are interested in hearing me after all.* "I imagine something happens in every author's life to awaken the writing spirit. For me, it was love for this little town I call home."

The words poured out with ease as her animated gestures punctuated her two-year journey from blank page to published author. When she finished, her new fans awarded her with applause and gave her another glimpse into her sister's life—the thrill of audience approval.

"Thank you, everyone. Before my sister and I sign your books, I'll gladly answer any questions."

Janice raised her hand. "Is it true your town doesn't have a movie theater?"

"We did. Until the owners shut it down. Last year, Naomi Jasper had the old cinema transformed into a playhouse."

The woman's eyes widened. "That means everyone who lives here will have to go somewhere else to watch the film. We have a theater in Clayton—"

"And a vintage drive-in." Spiked hair jumped up. "We should track the director down and pitch our town as the perfect place for a premiere."

A woman wearing a red jacket leapt off her seat. "I want to find Justin Brooks and get his autograph. For my daughter, of course."

Emily's shoulders slumped as a barrage of questions—not one about her book—erupted.

"Are any of the movie stars staying here?"

"What's it like having famous people wandering your streets."

"Is Carrie as pretty in person as she is on screen?"

Rachel scurried to her sister's side and whispered, "Looks like you need a little twin intervention."

"What do you have in mind?"

"Follow my lead." Rachel faced the audience. "Ladies, how about some movie-star trivia."

The women fell silent.

"What mode of transportation do you think *Texas* Justin used to arrive in our little town?"

"An expensive sports car," said spiked hair. "Maybe a Porsche or Corvette."

Janice waved her hand. "He's a Texan. I'll bet he rode in on a horse."

Rachel shook her head. "Try a giant yellow whirlybird."

Red jacket's brows shot up. "You mean a helicopter?"

"Uh-huh. It landed smack dab in the middle of our park. Nearly blew the grass away."

Murmurs rippled through the parlor.

Emily suppressed a laugh. "Here's an interesting tidbit. The crew dumps water on streets for outdoor shots because wet streets look better on film. What do you think is the cast's favored mode of transportation from makeup and wardrobe to location?"

"Stretch limos?"

"Nope. Air-conditioned golf carts."

"I rode in one of those cute little vehicles," Rachel said, staring at her sister. "It didn't have any doors or windows."

"Which made it air-conditioned." Emily grinned, then nudged Rachel. "Hey, Sis, I hear Carrie Fleming invited you to her private RV."

"She did."

"Are you serious?" Spiked hair moved to the edge of the settee. "What's she like?"

"She's a real sweetheart. Would you believe her favorite coffee flavor is cappuccino Rachel eyed her sister. "I have a great idea. I'll call and ask her to come over and sign autographs for all you ladies."

Red jacket popped off her seat. "You have her phone number?"

"Darn tootin' she does." Mama Sadie hustled to the front and stood between her daughters. "In fact, I'll ask my good buddies Maggie Warren and Ben Foster to join Carrie."

A cacophony of chatter followed.

Emily laughed as her mother emitted a two-finger whistle. "I need you ladies to join me in the dining room where Willow Falls' hometown celebrities will sign your books while you enjoy goodies from the best little pastry and gift shop in Georgia."

On cue, the throng vacated their seats and followed Mama Sadie from the parlor, across the foyer, and into the inn's dining room.

Rachel grasped Emily's hand. "It seems our sister act has transformed into a mother-daughter trio."

"Almost good enough to take on the road."

"Come on, hometown celebrity author. It's time to go wow your adoring fans."

"Yeah." Emily sighed. "Until the real celebs show up."

Chapter 32

Rachel stood beside Scott, peering over the railing in his store's second-story consignment shop. Half the size of the first floor, it offered an unobstructed view of light stands, sound equipment, cords, and a dolly track invading the retail space. "Too bad Robert isn't filming a movie about your store's history. Although, if the right people read Emily's book or see our play, *Percy's Legacy* could end up on theater screens."

"I don't know if this town could survive another movie crew invasion." Scott planted his forearms on the railing. "Transforming Willow Falls into a tourist destination has already stretched our charm and hospitality to the limit."

"A small price to pay for saving your hometown from a slow, painful death."

Scott rolled his eyes. "If we can keep from losing our soul in the process."

Rachel turned her back to the railing and gazed at photographs, paintings, quilts, and an eclectic assortment of local arts and crafts. A drawing of Willow Inn caught her eye. "The key is recognizing when the outcome is worth the risk."

"Which is sometimes impossible to know before you're too deep in the process to back out gracefully."

Carrie's revelations about life as a celebrity loomed large in Rachel's mind. "Unless friends with experience warn you ahead of time."

"Your director just arrived. It looks like our Hollywood mogul might need rescuing."

Rachel spun back around and spotted Gertie directing Robert to a soda-fountain stool. "From your sweet, soda-fountain lady?"

"You have no idea." Scott dashed down the stairs. Rachel followed. They reached Gertie as she launched into a story about the store's history.

Scott interrupted her monologue. "I don't think—"

"Let her finish," Robert said. "I'm intrigued by her infectious enthusiasm."

Scott stepped back and whispered to Rachel. "Watch and learn."

Gertie's face glowed as she entertained her audience of one with the entire spiel while preparing and serving him an old-fashioned chocolate soda. When the story ended, she laced her fingers. "And that's why you're smart to film scenes in this historical landmark."

"Thanks for the vote of confidence." Robert scratched his stubble beard. His eyes crinkled with a smile. "I don't remember you auditioning for a part in the movie, Miss Gertie."

"Goodness gracious, honey child, I'm not an actress. But I can tell you a thing or two about where to take the best shots." She stepped from behind the counter. "For example, you should have two old codgers playing checkers over there by the piano and some ladies and children walking around looking at our unique merchandise." She pointed to candles and linens displayed in an antique cabinet. "That's a real pretty spot for a closeup. The background's not too fussy."

Rachel hesitated, then stepped in. "Those are great suggestions, Miss Gertie. But I imagine Mr. Nordstrom already has everything planned."

"He's a bright young man, so I'm guessing he's open to new ideas."

"She's right." Robert looked around at the places Gertie had mentioned. "In fact, I've decided to add a scene with this enchanting lady serving sodas to Carrie and Justin's characters."

"Oh, my goodness." Gertie's hands flew to her cheeks. "You want me in your movie?"

"Absolutely," the director said. "You're a natural."

"Will I need to change clothes? What about makeup? I'm wearing a little. You know we senior ladies want to look our best. Will I have a talking role?"

Robert chuckled. "We'll write a few easy lines for you. Nothing you'll have to rehearse."

"Just think. Me in a movie with real live movie stars."

"Yes, ma'am. One of my assistants will take care of wardrobe and makeup details." He glanced at his watch. "We'll shoot your scene in two hours." He issued directions to a female assistant who then whisked Gertie from the store.

Scott pulled Rachel aside. "What did I tell you?"

"Are you suggesting Gertie was on a mission to get discovered?"

"Not suggesting, stating a fact."

"Wait a second." Rachel's eyebrows furrowed. "If she wanted a part, why didn't she audition with everyone else?"

"Why compete with a crowd when she could showcase her skills up close and personal. I've learned not to ever underestimate the power sweet, elderly ladies wield."

Rachel chuckled. "Who'd have guessed Robert Nordstrom would be played by a small-town senior. Unless ... he let her."

Rachel and Scott moved back to the consignment shop to catch a bird's-eye view of the film crew shooting footage of two white-haired men dressed in overalls playing checkers.

"I'm curious." Scott leaned on the railing. "Do you think your director followed Gertie's advice or had he already planned this scene?"

Rachel shrugged. "I'd call it a toss-up. Given this is your first experience observing the movie-making process, what's your take?"

"It's like watching water struggling to boil over low heat. A lot of effort for a few bubbles."

"Interesting analogy."

"Plus, I have new respect for the people who edit all the footage." Scott straightened. "They need the patience of Job and the skill of a surgeon."

Rachel frowned. "Who's Job?"

Scott glanced at her. "A guy who lived thousands of years ago."

"Before cameras and editing equipment were even imagined?"

"The comparison still fits."

Rachel peered over the railing and watched Carrie stroll from the front door to the soda fountain. Moments later, Justin showed up. "You're about to watch two professionals create water boiling bubbles."

"Yeah, in slow motion."

An hour later, Gertie arrived wearing an up-to-date dress and a white apron.

"We need a closer view." Rachel moved down the stairs to a spot close to the counter, out of camera shot.

Scott followed.

Robert turned to face his newest recruit. "Welcome back."

Gertie patted her new hairstyle. "Don't you think the new do and makeup make me look ten years younger?"

Robert grinned. "I do indeed. Are you ready?"

"Not exactly." She pulled a sheet of paper from her pocket. "I've been thinking about this line you want me to say. You see, here in the South, we like to address people as honey or sweetie."

Robert scratched his ear. "That's an easy fix."

"Good." Gertie hoisted her body onto a stool. "Something else I've been pondering over." She spent ten minutes describing the best way to shoot the scene.

When she finished, Robert stared at her.

"Uh oh," whispered Scott. "He's going to fire her."

Rachel saw a grin forming on the director's face. "I don't think so."

"Miss Gertie, you're a lot like my grandma, full of sweetness and gumption." Robert laid his script on the counter.

"Does that mean you're taking my advice?"

"We'll shoot from different angles and let the editor work his magic."

"I'm certain he'll see things my way." Gertie slid off the stool and made her way around the end of the counter.

Scott leaned closer. "Mark my words, by tomorrow morning the whole town will hear about our soda-fountain expert starring in and directing the most important scene in the movie."

"One fact is certain." Rachel nudged him. "Living in Willow Falls has proven more interesting than living in Atlanta."

"About time you came to that conclusion."

"It took me a while." She watched Robert order six retakes of a short scene with Carrie and Justin sitting at the counter chatting with Gertie. When he announced a final cut, Gertie moved to his side and presented a litany of suggestions. Rachel marveled at his patience and diplomacy.

Scott nudged her back. "He's good."

Rachel nodded, secretly hoping her future would include more opportunities to work with such a fascinating director.

Chapter 33

*E*mily unlocked the *Willow Post* headquarters' front door—a new routine prompted by the influx of strangers—and stepped inside. She tossed her purse on the desk, turned on the coffeepot, and dropped onto the chair. A mounting headache forced her to close her eyes and run her fingers up the back of her neck to the base of her skull. The sudden increase of traffic noise made it clear the front door had opened. She lifted her eyelids and stopped her tension-easing massage.

Mary breezed in and laid her briefcase beside Emily's purse. "You look exhausted. Did the twins keep you up all night?"

How much should I say? She's not family, although she is the pastor's wife and a good friend. "Scott's patience is running on empty." Emily locked eyes with her reporter. "Between writing deadlines, newspaper responsibilities, the director-liaison job, the wedding, Mama Sadie's surprise party ... I barely have time to breathe."

"At least three of those tasks will end soon."

"That's what I tried to tell Scott." The scent of hazelnut and coffee beans drifted from the fresh brew, temporarily diverting Emily's attention.

"Nathan has also been bent out of shape the last few days." Mary poured two cups, added creamer and honey to one, and carried both to the desk. "He's having second thoughts about agreeing to this movie deal."

Emily took a sip. "In the end, I hope everyone will consider it a plus for the town."

"If we survive the process." Mary sat in a chair facing the desk.

"That's one big *if.*" Emily's attention shifted to the mail truck pulling into the church parking lot. Its driver climbed out and dashed across the street, carrying a handful of mail. "I'm guessing we're about to get an earful."

Mary glanced out the window. "One thing about Mirabelle, she has spunk."

Mirabelle pushed the door open. She tossed the mail on the worktable, then trounced to the desk. "Lots of people are upset about Max Grover inviting JT, Jack, and Dennis to lunch. Why did he buddy up with those newcomers instead of longtime residents?"

"His choice makes perfect sense," Mary said. "Max's father and older brother are both West Point graduates. Those three *newcomers*, as you called them, are veterans."

"Yeah, well, he's not the only celebrity whipping up a fuss. Justin's flirting with all the pretty girls and ignoring the rest. And then there's Sadie and Maggie paling around together." Mirabelle glared at Emily. "Is it true Sadie and Brick invited her and Ben to dinner?"

"They figured a homecooked meal—"

"And another thing." Mirabelle scowled. "How did your sister finagle an invitation to Carrie's private dressing room?"

"You know they're doing scenes together." Emily drummed her fingers on the desk. "Doesn't it make sense they'd want some private time to rehearse?"

"I'm telling you folks around here won't buy that story."

Give it a break already. Only one thing will calm her down. Maybe. Emily hesitated before reaching into her purse and removing an envelope. "I have something for you." She held the envelope a foot from Mirabelle. "You are one of the select few receiving this, so you have to promise not to tell another living soul."

"What is it?" Her eyes widened as she reached for it.

Emily snatched it out of reach. "Not until you promise."

"Okay."

"Okay what?" Emily waved the enticement.

"Geeze, you're paranoid." Mirabelle held up her right hand. "I promise not to breathe a word to anyone about whatever's in that gold envelope."

Emily's eyes narrowed.

"So help me God."

"Well now. It seems Robert Nordstrom made a wise decision casting you as the jury forewoman." Emily handed the envelope over.

Mirabelle tore it open. "A surprise fiftieth birthday party for Sadie. Who else is invited?"

"Like I said, a select few we can count on to keep it top secret. You'll find out who the other privileged guests are at the party. And remember, you promised to keep your lips *zipped*."

"Hmph."

Emily caught sight of Lizzy heading to the door. "We have company, and she's not on the list. What are you going to do?"

Mirabelle zipped her fingers across her lips. She stashed the invitation in her pants pocket only seconds before the door swung open. She nodded at the stage mother as she made a beeline to the door.

Lizzy stomped to the desk. "I'm here to lodge a complaint."

Emily rubbed her neck again. "This is a newspaper office, not the town's grievance department."

"I invited Robert Nordstrom and Carrie Fleming to dinner so they could find out more about my Jenny." Lizzy crossed her arms and glared at Emily. "Their assistants turned me down. Said their bosses were too busy. You and your sister need to convince them to reconsider."

Mary smiled at the woman. "Can I pour you a cup of coffee? Our special brew."

"With two sugars."

"Here's the thing, my friend." Mary scooted to the coffeepot. "We know you have your daughter's best interest at heart. But if Emily and Rachel attempt to overrule our guests' personal assistants, Jenny's scenes would likely end up on the cutting room floor."

"If you ask me, that's a convenient excuse to brush me off." Lizzy accepted the cup, then sniffed the brew. "Which means I have to take matters into my own hands. First, I need to find out what time the director goes to lunch. If I arrange to sit at a table near him ... make it look coincidental. Hmm." She set her cup on the desk. "Thanks for the coffee. I have plans to make."

Emily shook her head as Lizzy scooted to the door and dashed toward the park. "Like Robert needs one more irritating resident messing in his business."

"I presume a Hollywood director is accustomed to disruptions." Mary opened her briefcase and extracted a document. "I finished the article about our stars' good works. Did you know Carrie sponsors five Compassion International children, and Maggie's been on seven mission trips to third-world countries? The guys also have their favorite charities."

"You learned a lot in a couple of days." Emily scanned the article. "Good work."

"I hope this defuses the Carrie photo caper and motivates residents to quit squabbling about who's doing what with whom."

"You understand enough about human nature to know it will take more than a well-written article to pull off that feat."

"Like an incident that forces the troops to rally?"

"Yep." Emily pushed the article across the desk. "Which, if Willow Falls' history is any indication, is bound to happen."

Chapter 34

Rachel pocketed her phone and tucked the royal-blue golf shirt sporting a Willow Oak Vineyard logo into white slacks. She hiked down the steps leading from the house to the upper parking lot and entered the winery's gift shop.

The woman standing behind the checkout counter, cleaning a smudge off the glass top, looked up. "Can you believe it? The grand opening's official start is forty-five minutes away, and the lower parking lot is already half full?"

Rachel fingered stuffed replicas of Merlot and Buster displayed in a half wine barrel. "Two years ago, this piece of property was nothing more than a forest and one man's vision."

"A lot has changed in our town since then." The woman stashed her cleaning cloth in the cabinet behind her. "Most of it good, some of it not so much."

Rachel's phone signaled a text, quelling the question she wanted to ask about the not so much. "Charlie's looking for me." She rushed through the dining room, passed staff members scrambling to set up an appetizer buffet, and headed downstairs to the tasting room. JT, Dennis, and a pretty young woman stood behind the three-sided bar serving wine flights to guests while explaining the nuances of each pour.

Charlie snaked his way through the crowd and grasped Rachel's elbow. "Where have you been? Dad, Jack, and I are ready to start our tours. I need you to here to answer questions."

Her eyes remained on his as she placed her hands on her hips. "And greetings to you too, Mr. Bricker."

"Sorry. We didn't expect such big a crowd this early."

"I haven't seen you this uptight since our play's opening night." She touched the logo on his chest. "By the way, the shirts look great. I love the color."

A smile replaced his scowl as his eyes moved south from her face. "You definitely fill yours out nicely."

"And there you have it, folks." Rachel grinned at her fiancé. "Easy-going, flirtatious Charlie Bricker returning from the edge of panic."

"All it took to save me was a gorgeous, green-eyed redhead. Let me restate my request. Is the future Mrs. Bricker willing to charm our guests, answer their questions, and promote our winery for one grateful guy?"

Rachel eased into her Scarlet O'Hara impersonation. "Since you phrased it so sweetly, dahling Rhett, I'd be dahlighted to mingle with all these lovely suitors and entertain them with irresistible tales about this fine southern establishment."

"What was I thinking, proposing to an actress? I'll never know from day to day which character will show up."

"Why, sugar, my talent will provide you with an amazing harem, minus all the drama created by a real entourage of wives."

"Lucky me," Charlie said with a wave of his hand. "I have to go to work and leave you to the adoring fans."

Rachel's heart fluttered as her eyes followed him to the fermentation room entrance. *I really do love that man.*

A young couple emerged from the crowd. "You're Rachel Streetman, right? We were in town last month and attended *Percy's Legacy.*"

The woman looked familiar. "I remember signing your program. Welcome back to Willow Falls."

"Thanks. Is this your place?"

"My fiancé manages the vineyard and property. His father is the owner." She plucked a tri-fold flyer from the shelf behind her. "Their photos are on the second page."

The man glanced at the flyer over the woman's shoulder. "Nice artwork. We've visited nearly every Georgia winery open to guests. So far, we can tell this one's a gem."

"We're delighted you're joining us today." Rachel shifted to hostess mode and sang Willow Oak's praises until a spot opened at the tasting bar.

For the remainder of the afternoon, she schmoozed with locals and out-of-towners until her jaw ached and her feet begged for a break. When the last guest drove out of the parking lot, she joined the staff in the dining room for a victory party.

As she watched her future father-in-law uncork two Champagne bottles and lavish praise on the staff, memories surfaced of her father's event three years earlier when he celebrated her promotion to vice president of Streetman Enterprise. She marveled at the difference between Brick's show of appreciation and her father's formal presentation.

Charlie wandered over and brushed a curl away from her cheek. "I hear you made quite an impression on our guests."

"I charmed so many people you might have to create a new blend and name it after me."

"A blush called Rachel." He winked. "That'd be worth an atta boy from my favorite gal."

"At least one." She touched his shirt logo again. "So, Mr. Accomplished Vintner, are you pleased with today's turnout?"

"The crowd definitely exceeded our expectations. Ten more guests and we'd have run out of food."

"A good sign your dad's retirement dream is a huge hit."

"If we're lucky, we'll turn a profit before I qualify for social security. Thanks for being here for me."

"I loved every minute." Rachel leaned close. "Our next big event is Mama Sadie's surprise birthday party."

"When she becomes my stepmother and future mother-in-law, that will make for an interesting Mother's Day. Do you suppose Hallmark makes a card that covers all the bases?"

"Maybe they should create a spin-the-wheel feature or include stick-on titles."

"Better yet, we'll overwhelm her with a dozen different cards."

"You're promising to turn into one terrific son-in-law." Rachel kissed his cheek.

"And an even better husband."

Brick wandered over and clasped his son's arm. "You did a mighty fine job setting up this event."

"Thanks to Rachel and Jack's help."

Brick's focus shifted to Rachel. "Who knew way back when I convinced you to prepare a publicity package for the *Willow Post* that your old man and I would one day become family."

"Believe me, no one was more surprised than Dad."

"When is my old pal planning to slow down and take time to enjoy life."

Rachel shrugged. "He claims slowing down isn't in his DNA."

"If he's smart, he'll figure out what's important before he works himself to death."

Brick's comment conjured an image of her father's pale complexion and sent a shiver up Rachel's spine. Could tough-as-nails Greer Streetman be plummeting toward a physical breakdown? She dismissed the idea as absurd and shifted her focus to the winery staff celebrating their victory.

Chapter 35

Rachel stood behind the hotel at the lake's edge and eyed dark clouds billowing overhead, bringing early dusk to downtown Willow Falls. The pre-storm wind sent waves and miniature whitecaps cascading across the water and goose bumps popping up on the back of her neck. She turned up her jacket collar and crossed her arms to ward off the chill until raindrops sent her scrambling to Redding Arms' veranda. She glanced at her watch—five minutes before her dinner date with Charlie.

Inside the lobby, soft background music and a warm glow cast by the elaborate chandelier created a welcome shelter from the approaching storm. Rachel meandered to the dining room entrance where the young hostess welcomed her with a smile. "Good evening, Miss Streetman." She stepped from behind her stand and led Rachel to a corner table beside the window. "I hear you and Mr. Bricker are celebrating a successful grand opening. It's amazing how our little town is all grown up and has its very own winery."

"What a unique way to describe it."

"A year ago, I considered moving away. But now, with all that's going on, I think I'll stick around for a while."

"That's good news."

"About tonight's menu, Mr. Bricker and Chef Pepper have a special meal planned for you. It's so dreamy." The hostess pressed her fingers to her lips. "My goodness, I'd better scoot before I spoil the surprise."

Rachel warmed at the notion that Willow Falls was still small enough to make keeping a secret virtually impossible. A lightning flash, followed in seconds by a window-rattling thunderbolt, commanded her attention.

As she slipped out of her jacket, the clouds released a deluge of rain. From the corner of her eye, she spotted Charlie heading in her direction.

"Hey, gorgeous." He stooped to kiss her cheek.

"Looks like you made it in before the downpour."

"With a minute to spare." He sat close, facing the dining-room entrance. "Hope you haven't been waiting long."

"Couple of minutes." She breathed in his musky aftershave. "I hear you and Pepper cooked up something special for dinner."

He reached for her hand and kissed her fingers. "To celebrate our journey thus far."

His touch sent a tingling sensation rippling through her limbs. "Oh my. The romantic sentimental Charlie showed up tonight."

"In the flesh."

Their waiter approached, carrying two stemmed glasses filled with golden wine. "Good evening, Miss Streetman, Mr. Bricker. Are you ready for your first course?"

Charlie's face inched close to Rachel's. "Are we, Miss Streetman?" His voice was barely above a whisper.

"Why, I believe we are, Mr. Bricker."

"Excellent. I'll return momentarily," the waiter said as he backed away.

Rachel's pulse quickened as Charlie's warm breath caressed her cheek. "You've managed to touch my heart and arouse my curiosity."

"I hope that's not all I've aroused."

Warmth rose from her neck to her cheeks. "I ... uh ..."

His eyes danced. "You're blushing."

"Call it a momentary heatwave."

"I'll try to keep it going."

Their waiter returned and set two bowls on the table. The rich scent of lobster and cream wafted from the bisque as the waiter drizzled sherry into each bowl.

Charlie reached for his wine, keeping his eyes focused on Rachel's face.

Rachel swallowed the lump in her throat. "Pepper served this at her café the first time we came to Willow Falls. The night Emily and I discovered each other."

"You remembered." He raised his glass. "To the woman I adore more than life itself."

She closed her eyes and savored the first mouthful. "Do you remember what you said when we first laid eyes on this old hotel?"

"I called it a mess. You said it was charming, with all the ivy climbing up the walls. Turns out we were both right."

"A lot has happened since that day."

They continued to reminisce about their first trip together until the waiter approached and removed their empty bowls. He returned with a bottle of Cabernet Sauvignon and two more wine glasses. "Chef Pepper said this will compliment your entrée." He removed the cork and poured a splash.

Charlie swirled the red liquid, breathed in the scent, and tasted. "Perfect."

"Excellent." The waiter finished pouring.

"Now you've really aroused my curiosity." Rachel swirled her glass and stared at the ruby-red liquid. "What goes with red wine? Spaghetti, lasagna, meatloaf?"

"None of the above," Pepper said as she approached and placed two silver-domed covered plates on the table. "A special presentation for one of my favorite couples. Bon appetite." She lifted the lids, then slipped away from the table.

Rachel bit her lower lip. Her eyes moistened. "Oh, Charlie, our first date ... you remembered."

"How could I forget." He touched her hand. "We both ordered rack of lamb."

"One of my all-time favorites." She cut a piece, then relished the taste. "Melt-in-your-mouth delicious. The best ever ... and it's here in Willow Falls."

Charlie grinned. "Better not let Pepper hear you talking like a city girl with low expectations of us country folks."

She swallowed and playfully pointed her fork at him. "You know ... you're as much a city slicker as I am."

"You mean *was*. Now I'm a certified, yee-hawing, knee-slapping country boy who's head over heels in love with a ..." He dropped his fork. His face turned ashen.

Rachel's heart jumped to her throat. "Charlie, what's wrong?"

"It isn't ..." He blinked. "Possible."

She grabbed his hand as her eyes followed his gaze to a smartly dressed woman engaged in a heated discussion with the dining room hostess.

The newcomer dashed past the young woman and glanced around the dining room as if searching for a companion. She seemed to spot them, then moved in their direction. When she reached their table, she set her gold clutch purse on the table. Her lips curled into a smile. She shifted her focus away from Rachel. "Hello, Charlie."

He stood. His Adam's apple bobbed. "Mom?"

Chapter 36

Rachel gasped. A bone-jarring chill sent a shudder ripping through her body. She glared at the woman who settled nonchalantly beside her as if she had simply arrived late.

The intruder stared intently at Charlie. "You're as handsome as ever, Son." She turned her attention to Rachel. "And who's this pretty young lady?"

Charlie gawked, seemingly unable to find his voice.

The woman extended her hand. "I'm Cynthia Welch. Charlie's mother. Pleasure to meet you, whoever you are."

Rachel stared at the manicured nails and extravagant cocktail ring.

Charlie blinked. "This is Rachel, Rachel Streetman. She's my fiancée. What are you doing here? And where's your husband?"

"You mean my ex-husband. It seems he still prefers younger women. Ironic, isn't it?"

Rachel's eyes probed the woman's pretty face, surprised she appeared closer to Charlie's age than Brick's. *Good genes or expensive surgery?*

"How is your father?" Cynthia's voice broke through the fog in Rachel's head. "He's not married, is he?"

Charlie shook his head. "No, but—"

"Good. I hear you two have ventured into the wine business."

Rachel glared at Charlie, mentally urging him to tell his mother about Mama Sadie.

"I'm curious. Are his decisions still guided by crazy superstitions?"

"Not so much." Charlie's eyes narrowed. "Why did you come here?"

She fingered the diamond ring on her left hand. "Do you recognize this? My fortieth birthday gift from Brick. One thing about him, he was always generous. You know we were madly in love—"

"Until you ran out on him and broke his heart."

"That happened a long time ago." Cynthia signaled to the waiter.

"Good evening, ma'am." The waiter nodded as he approached.

"Will you bring a glass and pour me some wine, young man?"

"Certainly."

Cynthia glanced from Rachel to her son. "Please, don't let me interrupt your dinner."

Charlie pushed his plate away. "Too late. I've lost my appetite."

The waiter returned and poured a round. Cynthia lifted her glass and took a sip. "Good choice."

"Enough with the small talk." Charlie's voice was laced with anger. "You didn't just happen to drop by."

"Of course not." She ran her finger around the wine glass rim. "Under the right circumstances, old flames can be rekindled."

Charlie's nostrils flared. "What are you suggesting?"

"Our family should become whole again."

Rachel laced her fingers and squeezed until the knuckles turned white. "Look, I know we've just met, and you're Charlie's mother. But you need to know that Brick has a new life, with new friends—"

"She's right," Charlie blurted. "Dad's not the same man he was when you left."

Rachel fought the urge to scream. *Why doesn't he tell her about Brick's pending proposal?* Maybe she should spill the beans. She opened her mouth, then pressed her lips tight. If Brick and Cynthia did renew their relationship ... it would destroy her mother if she found out how close he had come to marrying her.

"I want you to take me to see him tomorrow morning, Charlie." Cynthia stood and retrieved her purse, then reached for her wine glass. "Tonight, I need my beauty sleep. I'll meet you in the lobby at nine."

Before he could respond, Cynthia spun around and left the dining room.

Rachel gripped Charlie's wrist. "Please tell me you're not going to show up tomorrow."

He jerked his hand away. "I have to. She's my mother."

"And *my* mother is your almost mother-in-law."

Charlie's eyes grew lightning fierce. "Don't you think I know that?"

"You have no right to raise your voice to me. Your mother is the one creating the turmoil."

He grabbed his wine glass and emptied it in one long swallow, then swiped his palm across his lips. "Even if I don't show up, she'll find him on her own."

"By tomorrow afternoon the whole town will know about the latest invasion—ex-wife shows up to reclaim jilted husband. We have to warn Mama Sadie."

Pepper approached and squatted between them. "Is everything okay? I hear you were accosted by a stranger." She looked from Charlie to Rachel.

"You can't breathe a word to anyone until we talk to Mama Sadie," whispered Rachel.

"The unexpected visitor was my mother." Charlie's jaw tensed. "It seems after dumping my dad more than twenty years ago, she's had a change of heart."

Pepper's eyes widened. "You can't be serious. Everyone knows Brick is sweet on Sadie. Pardon me for saying so, Charlie, but you have to keep your mother's paws off your dad."

"What do you expect me to do? Drag her out of town tied behind the back of Naomi's caddy? Or get Mitch to arrest her for alienation of affection?"

His bitter tone startled Rachel. "Pepper's just saying we care about what's best for Mama Sadie."

"What about my old man? Shouldn't he have a say in his future?"

Rachel's brows shot up. "I can't believe you're taking your mother's side."

"I'm not taking sides." Charlie shot out of his chair. "I'll be in the lobby at nine, Rachel. Be there if you want to go with me. Right now, I have to figure out if I should warn Dad tonight or shock him tomorrow." He stormed from the dining room, drawing stares from other diners.

Rachel propped her elbows on the table and buried her face in her hands. "I can't believe he's running out on me."

Pepper sat in Charlie's vacated chair. "He's in shock and needs time to sort things out. I'll leave the kitchen in the hands of my staff and go with you to break the news to Sadie. Call Emily and find out if she can join us."

Rachel glanced around the dining room. "Everyone's staring at me. They must think Charlie and I had a huge fight."

"They're all out-of-towners, so it doesn't matter. I'll meet you on the veranda in fifteen minutes." Pepper peeked out the window. "It looks like the storm has passed."

"Not the one that threatens to shatter Mama Sadie's world and tear her heart into a thousand pieces."

Chapter 37

A litany of possibilities collided in Emily's mind as she dashed through the hotel lobby to the veranda. "I can't believe Charlie's mother showed up out of nowhere. What is she thinking?"

Rachel's nostrils flared. "That Brick will forget the past and fall in love with her all over again."

Emily stared at the dark clouds drifting away from town. "We can't let that happen."

"According to Charlie, the ball's in Brick's court, not ours."

"Until word leaks out." Emily pulled her sweater tighter across her chest. "You know the wrath of Willow Falls will fall squarely on Cynthia's shoulders."

"That could backfire and send both her and Brick running for the hills."

"Maybe, but we can't let *our* mother go down without a fight."

Pepper approached, carrying a bottle of wine and a corkscrew. "Reinforcements."

Rachel flicked a wet leaf off the railing. "I'm not sure one bottle will do the trick."

"Come on, ladies." Pepper clutched the bottle to her side. "It's time to launch this mission of mercy with as little pain as possible."

Pepper led the twins through the hotel's backyard to the garage apartment. She stopped at the foot of the stairs. "Rachel, you're the one who talked to Cynthia, so you should take the lead. *After* I pour the wine."

"I'm thinking we should wait until we drain the bottle."

Pepper shook her head. "Sadie's too smart. She'll know something's up the moment she lets us in."

They climbed the steps.

Emily knocked.

Mama Sadie, dressed in lounging pajamas, opened the door. She eyed her visitors. "What's wrong? Are my grandbabies okay? Is the inn on fire?"

"No burning buildings or accidents," Pepper said.

"I'm guessing this isn't a social visit."

Emily stepped in and suppressed the urge to gather her mother in her arms.

Rachel followed.

Pepper headed to the kitchenette and opened a cabinet.

Mama Sadie's eyes narrowed. "Somebody had better tell me what's going on before I throw a heart-pounding hissy fit."

Pepper carried four glasses to the coffee table and uncorked the wine. After pouring each glass full, she sat on one of the slipper chairs.

Rachel settled on the other.

Mama Sadie sat on the edge of the love seat beside Emily. She looked from one to the other. "Well?"

Rachel spoke first. "You know Charlie and I had dinner at the hotel tonight."

"Oh my gosh." Mama Sadie clutched her chest. "Did you two break up? Is the wedding off?"

"Nothing like that." Rachel fidgeted with her bracelet. "The thing is ... we had an unexpected visitor."

"What's with all the mystery? Did Elvis come back from the dead?"

Rachel hesitated. "Charlie's mother checked into the hotel."

"Cynthia?" Mama Sadie's shoulders slumped. Her eyelids lowered. "She wants him back, doesn't she?"

Pepper slapped her hand on her knee. "She's crazy to think she can waltz back into Brick's life like she owns him."

Mama Sadie reached for a glass of wine and stared into the bowl. "Brick showed me her picture a while back. She's a pretty lady."

"If you ask me, she's had way too much Botox and one too many skin-stretching facelifts." Rachel's tone oozed with contempt.

"Don't be catty, Rachel," her mother warned. "The woman left Brick for a younger man, so she had to look the part." Her eyes widened. "Wait a minute. Is she still married?"

Rachel shook her head. "Get this. The man she ran off with dumped her for a younger woman."

"I reckon that's justice."

"Darn right it is." Emily's hands fisted. "When word spreads, she'll be run out of town."

Pepper leaned forward, her eyes locked on her friend's. "You are one of Willow Falls' most loved and respected citizens, and your relationship with Brick has captured the town's imagination. So, you know everyone will support you."

"And treat Cynthia like some low-life floozy? Is that what you think I want?" Mama Sadie slammed her glass down, splashing her drink on the table. "Brick and I are good friends." She held up her left hand. "Do you see a ring on my finger? No, because there's no commitment between us."

"What are you trying to tell us?" A nervous laugh bubbled up from Emily's chest. "That you're giving up without a fight?"

"Even if I wanted to, what chance would I have. I'm an ex-con with a high-school diploma and a couple of on-line hotel management courses under my belt. Cynthia is a sophisticated, educated lady. She was Reginald Bricker's first love. If she can make him happy, then good for her."

"What happened to your fighting spirit?" Emily stared at her mother. "Do you remember what you told me three years ago when I accused you of buckling under to Mirabelle's accusations about you stealing her credit card?"

"Something about hanging in there?"

"Bingo. You said I'd make one tough inmate except I spooked too easily. And if I had a shot at getting my way, I'd have to hang in there and not back down."

"This is different."

"It's about what's right." Emily softened her tone. "Everything depends on one simple truth. Do you love Brick?"

Her mother leaned back and pursed her lips. "When I was a little girl, all my friends had two parents. One time I asked Mama why I didn't have a daddy. She told me a handsome prince would find us and make our lives magical. Years later she married Robert Liles. Truth is, I stopped believing in fairytales."

Pepper scooted to the edge of her chair. "Honey, Mitch and I have spent enough time with you and Brick to know he's crazy about—"

"Odd you used the word crazy and not in love with."

"Don't get caught up in semantics." Pepper waved her hand as if brushing away Sadie's words. "It means the same thing."

"No ... it doesn't. Look, I appreciate my daughters and best friend trying to put lipstick on this toad, but what happens isn't up to me. Now, if you'll excuse me, I'm slap worn out and need some sleep." She trudged to her bedroom and closed the door behind her.

Emily leapt to her feet. "We have to bring her back out here and talk some sense into her."

Pepper grabbed her arm. "I know Sadie better than anyone. And right now, she needs time alone to sort through her emotions."

"We can't let her roll over and give in to Brick's ex."

"There is one person who can connect with Sadie on a level we can't." Pepper lifted her wine glass and held it in both hands. "Tomorrow, Kat and I will have a heart-to-heart with your mother."

Emily dropped back onto the loveseat, praying Mama Sadie's two best friends would talk some sense into her.

Chapter 38

A gut-wrenching headache forced Rachel's eyes open before the sun crept over the horizon. She swung her legs over the side of the bed and grimaced. Brownie yawned, stretched, and padded to her. Rachel stood and grabbed the edge of the nightstand until the wave of nausea passed. "I need a jolt of caffeine and a couple of pain pills."

She trudged to the kitchen where she found Emily sitting at the table, her fingers dancing across her computer keyboard. "You're up early."

"Couldn't sleep."

Rachel slid the patio door open to let Brownie out. "Where do you keep your aspirin, or whatever you have for a massive headache?"

"Cabinet beside the microwave." Emily stopped typing. "What did you decide about meeting Charlie this morning?"

"I haven't." Rachel grabbed a bottle of painkiller and poured a glass of orange juice. She downed two pills and dropped onto a chair across from Emily.

"You have to go, as our side's one-woman investigation squad."

Rachel set the glass on the table. "Cynthia isn't a criminal."

"It depends on your interpretation of the word." Emily pushed her computer aside. "In my opinion, she's a domestic wrecking ball. Besides, Charlie needs you."

"The way he stormed out of the dining room last night, I'm not so sure that's accurate."

"How would you expect him to act when the woman who abandoned him and his father charged back into his life without warning?" Emily ambled to the coffeepot and refilled her cup. "One more thing. He'd likely consider you not showing up as rejection."

Rachel sighed. "I suppose you're right."

Emily returned to the table. "While you're supporting your fiancé, you can gather intel to help our mother win this battle."

"If we're going to build a rock-solid case, you need to go with Pepper and Kat when they talk to her."

"I texted Pepper last night. The three of us plan to show up right after breakfast is over at the inn."

Scott walked in dressed for work and headed straight to the coffee. "You're already loaded with more tasks than time." He poured the dark liquid into an insulated cup and eyed Emily. "Why are you adding interventionist to your list?"

"It won't take more than an hour—"

"Until it turns into another project."

"She's my mother."

Scott stirred sugar into his coffee. "You're taking on too much."

"What happens today will have a lifelong impact on our little family."

"And our town," Rachel added.

"Looks like I'm outnumbered. Again." Scott leaned back against the counter.

Emily rose and moved close to her husband. "I promise not to let this get out of hand."

"Jane and Clair need their mother."

"I can cancel the sitter and take them with me. Although they'd distract us from our mission."

"How many missions do you think you can juggle?" Scott gripped his cup and headed to the garage. "I'm going to the store early." The door slammed behind him.

Rachel rolled her shoulders to relieve the tension. "He's in a mood."

"Who can blame him? Most nights I'm too cranky and exhausted to spend quality time with him."

"Tell you what." Rachel stood. "I'll babysit tonight so you two can go out for a romantic dinner at the hotel."

"I have too much to do."

"Wrong answer. I'll make reservations for seven. You text Scott. Right now, I need a hot shower." She escaped before Emily had a chance to protest.

***

Rachel entered the hotel lobby and spotted Charlie sitting on a couch, his forearms planted on his knees, his face aimed at the floor. She sat beside him and laid her hand on his back. "Are you okay?"

"I couldn't spring my mother's return on him without a warning." He plucked a piece of lint off his jeans. "I called Dad last night."

"How did he react?"

Charlie straightened his back. "He didn't."

His clenched jaw and expressionless eyes sent a confusing message. Was he angry or conflicted? Rachel jerked her hand from his back at the sight of Cynthia wearing a red dress better suited for a cocktail party than an early morning outing.

Charlie stood and accepted his mother's embrace.

Rachel struggled to tamp down her anger as she lifted off the couch.

Cynthia leveled a suspicious glance at her, then locked eyes with her son. "I see you brought moral support."

He curled his arm around Rachel's waist. "She's family."

His harsh tone sent a chill skittering up Rachel's spine. She forced a positive note. "I hope your room suits you."

"Interesting, sleeping in a suite decorated for Christmas."

"Every Redding Arms room was adopted and decorated by a resident."
She doesn't give a flip about the hotel, so ditch the small talk.

Cynthia turned her attention to Charlie. "I'm guessing your father lives in one of the lovely old mansions I passed on the way into town."

"Couple of doors away."

"Is he expecting us, or will our visit surprise him?"

"He knows you're here."

Cynthia smoothed her skirt. "Then let's not keep him waiting."

Charlie pulled his arm away from Rachel, squared his shoulders, and led the way out the front door. They crossed Main Street and covered the remaining distance in silence.

When they turned onto the sidewalk leading to Brick's front porch, a knot formed in the pit of Rachel's stomach. The last time she had stepped into the house, he and Mama Sadie were entertaining two famous movie stars. Today, the owner would reconnect with the woman who wanted back in his life after smashing his heart to bits.

They climbed the steps.

Brick opened the front door. "Charlie, Rachel ... Cynthia."

She kissed his cheek. "You're as handsome as ever, in your own unique way."

He stepped aside and motioned them in.

Cynthia twirled in a slow circle. "What a lovely home, so well-appointed. Did you do all this yourself?"

"I had some help."

Rachel tensed. *Yeah, from the woman he's going to marry.*

"I made coffee." He turned and headed toward the kitchen.

His guests followed.

"I hear you retired and left your business in Ronnie's hands." Cynthia tossed her purse on the island and settled on the first stool. "I always thought our firstborn would one day follow in your footsteps."

Rachel stood at the end of the island. Charlie sat on the stool beside her.

"Both our sons went into the business." Brick served the coffee, then stared at his ex. "You're the last person I expected to show up."

"Life is full of surprises." Cynthia lifted a cup to her lips.

Brick continued to stare for a long moment. "Charlie said the man who snatched you from our family found a younger honey. Was she also a married woman?"

"A single, twenty-something gold digger, and not his first affair." She sipped her coffee. "One sugar. You remembered." She set her cup down. "I'm surprised you haven't remarried."

Rachel's eyes narrowed to a slit. *Tell her you're going to propose to my mother.*

He rounded the island and sat beside Cynthia. "Why did you come here?"

Rachel clamped her lips together and summoned every ounce of willpower to keep from blurting the secret plan.

"To make amends." Cynthia studied him. "And renew what we once had."

His silence turned Rachel's skin to goose flesh. She had to break it. "Brick has a lot of close friends here in Willow Falls."

Charlie grabbed her arm.

She glared at him. Why was he defending Brick's silence? Did he want his parents back together?

Cynthia crossed her leg over her knee, sending her dress riding up her thigh. "His infectious charm always did attract people." She kept her eyes glued on Brick, her next words directed to him. "I'm surprised you moved away from the city."

"I needed a change."

"The house on the hill overlooking the winery. I noticed it on the way in. Is it yours?"

"It belongs to me," Charlie said stiffly. "And Rachel. Our wedding's in a few weeks."

"Well then, my timing is perfect. After all, a proper wedding requires the presence of the groom's mother." She slid off the stool and wandered around the kitchen. "Tell me, Brick, have you learned how to cook?"

His eyes followed her. "I'm working on it."

"I understand why the director selected your home to appear in the movie. A chatty room service waiter enlightened me this morning."

Rachel grimaced at the idea of the gossip grapevine snaking its way through town. She glanced at her watch. An hour before Emily, Kat, and Pepper were scheduled to meet with Sadie.

Cynthia opened a cabinet and peered inside. "I see you still have the wine glasses we bought in Napa Valley." She spun around. "I'd like to see the town."

"We have an excellent tour guide," Rachel said. "JT's a wounded vet who knows Willow Falls inside and out."

"That's not what I had in mind." Cynthia returned to her stool. "How about it, Brick? Will you escort me?"

Brick stared at his hands. "That's not a good idea."

"Are you concerned about small-town tongues wagging?"

"By now, half the residents know you're here."

"One big reason I prefer living in the city. We'll give it a few days. In the meantime, you can show me around the winery, unless it's open to the public."

"Only on weekends," Charlie interjected.

Rachel scowled. *What is he doing?*

"I've always found vineyards and wineries to be alluring and romantic." Cynthia reached for her purse. "I'm ready if you are."

Brick shrugged. "Might as well." He grabbed his keys off the counter.

Cynthia snuggled close to Brick as he escorted her out the back door to the free-standing garage.

Flurries of anger built up inside Rachel and exploded. "What is *wrong* with you, Charlie? Why did you send them off to what she called a romantic destination?"

"What would you do if she were your mother? Tell her she's as unwelcome as an ex-con returning to the scene of her crime?"

Rachel felt as if she'd been slapped. "I can't believe you said that."

"I'm sorry. It's just ... Cynthia ... my mother ... isn't how I remember her."

Rachel dropped onto a stool. "You mean a conniving—"

"That's not what I meant."

Rachel's tone softened. "I realize this isn't easy, but I need to know what you want to happen."

Charlie stared straight ahead. "My brother and I were closer to my dad than my mother. He always spent more time with us than she did. I wouldn't call her a bad mom. Just busy with fundraisers, ladies' clubs, social activities, stuff like that." He paused for a long moment. "I want Dad to grow old with a woman he loves as much as I love you."

"Based on everything I've seen so far, Cynthia is the polar opposite of Mama Sadie." Rachel choked back tears. "For all our sakes, I hope the woman he loves is *my* mother, not yours."

Chapter 39

*E*mily parked behind the inn, stepped out, and stared at the back door leading to the kitchen. Her chest tightened at the prospect of blindsiding this woman she loved so much. She feared her mother would view the morning's surprise encounter as an unwanted intrusion on a private matter. Even if she climbed back in her car and drove away, she knew Kat and Pepper wouldn't back out. She dropped her keys in her purse and trudged into the kitchen. "Do I smell your famous cinnamon and apple coffee cake?"

"Today's sweet treat." Mama Sadie closed the dishwasher and pushed the start button. "Is this a social visit?"

"We need to talk."

"I reckon it's not." She pulled a dish towel off her shoulder and hung it on a rack. "I'm listening."

"Not here. In your place."

She eyed her daughter. "Did you eat breakfast?"

"Not exactly."

"Either you did, or you didn't. I'll take this in case you figure it out." Her mother covered the remaining coffee cake with plastic wrap.

They left the inn, walked silently across the rear parking area, and climbed the stairs to Mama Sadie's apartment. Emily followed her inside and eased toward the loveseat, breathing in the rich scent of fresh-brewed coffee.

Mama Sadie halted, her eyes ping-ponging between Pepper standing at the coffeepot and Kat sitting on a slipper chair. "This looks like an ambush."

Kat scooted to the edge of her chair. "I prefer to call it an intervention."

180

"Who says I need one?" The plate went on the counter with a loud thump.

"We're here to fire up your fighting spirit." Pepper filled two more coffee cups.

"Did my ex-con friend turned hotel manager trick you into taking tough-girl lessons?"

"Based on your reaction last night, I'd say *you* need an emergency refresher course." Pepper pointed to the coffee cake. "Maybe a shot of sugar with your caffeine will start your motor running."

"You three are for doggone sure barking up the wrong tree." Mama Sadie meandered across the room and dropped beside Emily. "So, I'll get right to the point and save you a lot of hot air. This thing with Cynthia ... I have to let nature take its course."

Kat waggled her finger at her friend. "That's one big pile of monkey muck."

"That's an apt description." Pepper distributed plates of coffee cake. "To put it another way, Sadie, if you don't go to battle for Brick, he'll think you don't give a flip."

"What do you want me to do, challenge his ex to a duel?"

Kat guffawed. "That's a darn good idea. How good a shot are you?"

Mama Sadie curled her fingers into a pistol shape and tapped her thumb to her index finger. "At close range, deadly."

Emily cringed. "That's not funny."

"No need to get your panties in a wad." Kat dug her fork into the coffee cake. "We need a little prison humor to lighten the mood."

"The point is," Mama Sadie said, "the woman who bore Brick's children wants him back in her life."

"She's also the woman who had the hots for another man and ran out on him." Pepper squared her shoulders and locked eyes with Mama Sadie. "Think about this. If she somehow manages to snare him, chances are she'll find another honey and break his heart all over again."

"People can change. Maybe she's different than she was back then."

"True, some people do." Emily held up an index finger. "However, based on Rachel's description of last night's encounter, I'm guessing Cynthia hasn't changed her stripes one iota. Which means if you care about Brick, you have to keep him from falling into her trap."

Emily's mother stared at her for a long moment, then moved to the dormer window overlooking the inn's rear façade. "Thirty years in prison did a number on my dreams. Including the foolish childhood fantasy about a handsome prince sweeping me off my feet and us living happily ever after in some big fancy castle. I came to accept the fact that romantic love was for other women, not a damaged girl who'd spend half her life behind bars. I was okay with that. Then I met Reginald Bricker, and we became ... close friends." She spun toward her guests. "Until his former soulmate—who, from what I hear looks years younger than me—drops in out of nowhere." She meandered to the loveseat and propped her hip on the arm.

Fearing her mother was seconds away from letting her future slip away, Emily clasped her arm. "You can't give up, not after all you've been through."

"Hold on to your chickens. I'm not finished." She pressed her hand over Emily's. "I'm not worldly or sophisticated, or even all that well-spoken. And I've resigned myself to being life-long buddies with Brick. But one thing's for rock-solid certain. Friends don't let friends down."

"What are you saying?"

"In the end, Cynthia might up and win him back. But she'll have to shoot me down first. Figuratively speaking, of course."

Kat leapt off her chair. "There's the Sadie Liles I know."

Pepper embraced her. "You're a real gem, my friend." She stepped back. "So, what's your first move?"

"Invite Brick to a cozy dinner right here in my apartment and give him a good talking to."

Kat's face beamed. "You go, girl, and save your man from Cynthia's treacherous web."

Emily stared at a photo on the end table—Brick and her mother sitting side by side with Jane and Clair on their laps. She closed her eyes and silently prayed he would choose her mother over Charlie's.

Chapter 40

Seconds after Emily ended a conversation and set the cordless phone on the desk, it rang again. She drummed her fingers on the desk and glared at the offender. "Enough already." The barrage of calls, along with the gloomy gray sky and constant rain patter, sapped her motivation to work faster than a stream of water racing downhill toward a drain. She grabbed her umbrella and keys, stepped outside, locked the door, and turned toward the park.

Grateful for the row of awnings lining Main Street, she paused beside the bank and peered around the corner. An equipment truck and golf cart parked in the middle of the block signaled a late morning shoot at Pepper's Café—or as it had been recast, Joanie's Joint. Her focus wandered past the storefronts to Redding Arms and beyond to Willow Inn. She assumed her mother was in the kitchen cleaning up after serving her guests breakfast. Where was Cynthia? And what was she doing?

A thunderclap disrupted Emily's musing and sent her scrambling across the street. After stopping under the awing hanging over Hayes General Store's front door to shake water from her umbrella, she stepped inside and set it against the wall.

Gertie looked up from a book lying open on the counter.

Emily rambled to a soda fountain stool. "Looks like a slow day."

"More like dead in the water."

"No customers?"

Gertie shook her head. "This is the first time that bell over the door has rung since we opened."

"Too bad the rain hasn't stopped the phone from ringing. What are you reading?"

"Jan Karon's latest Mitford novel. I like reading stories about small towns and lovable characters." Gertie marked the page and closed the book. "I'm thinking about fixing me a root beer float. Want to join me for a sugar rush?"

Emily propped her elbow on the counter and rested her chin on her knuckles. "The perfect cure for my morning malaise."

"Let me guess." Gertie reached for two tall glasses. "Willow Falls' overactive grapevine's been buzzing like a swarm of bees."

"More like angry yellow jackets. Based on dozens of phone calls, the whole town is in an uproar over Brick's ex."

"At least everyone's on Sadie's side." Gertie scooped vanilla ice cream into the glasses. "Right now, folks are thinking up ways to boot that crazy lady clean out of town."

"Ironic, isn't it?"

Gertie added root beer "You mean because a couple of years ago residents wanted to do the same thing to Sadie?"

"Funny how things change."

"Now, your mama and Brick, who brought us that nice winery, are considered locals." Gertie added a tall spoon and straw to a glass and pushed it across the counter.

Emily dipped her spoon into the ice cream. "I remember the day you stood outside our newspaper office protesting a winery in Willow Falls."

"I'm not too old to change. Would you believe I tried a couple of wines during the open house? Can't say I liked them much, except for one that tasted sweet, like dessert." Gertie sipped her float. "I hear Cynthia's one of those fancy city ladies, all decked out in expensive clothes and looking way younger than Brick. Based on Charlie's age, everyone's guessing she's had a few snips and tucks ... if you know what I mean."

"One thing's certain. She's rich fodder for the town's insatiable appetite to gossip."

"Honey, it doesn't matter how many tourists or movie people swoop into Willow Falls. We're still a small town, and we're not about to let outsiders mess with one of our own."

Scott sauntered from the back room and placed a box on the counter. "Root beer floats before noon? Are you two celebrating or commiserating?"

"Gertie's giving me the scoop on the town's latest quest."

"You mean the Cynthia caper?" He removed his pocketknife, cut through the tape, and opened the box. "If this is her first experience with country folks, she's in for a shock."

"The residents' efforts could backfire. I mean, she is Charlie's mother."

"Not to mention the fact that Charlie might not like people giving her a hard time." Scott removed bags of old-fashioned candy from the box.

Emily fingered her straw. "If he gets all bent out of shape and defensive, it could create a huge problem for Rachel ... and their relationship."

"Folks are too riled up to pour spilled milk back in the jug." Gertie swirled her straw in her drink. "Besides, Charlie has lived here long enough to know what to expect."

"Doesn't mean he'll like it." Emily finished her drink while Scott refilled the candy jars lined up on the checkout counter.

The front doorbell jangled, announcing a new arrival.

Mirabelle dashed in. "Have you heard the latest? Brick met Cynthia for breakfast at the hotel." She handed a stack of mail to Scott. "If you ask me, they looked mighty chummy."

Emily drummed her fingers on the counter. "Are you playing super sleuth this morning?"

"Somebody has to keep an eye on things."

"Don't worry, Mama Sadie's—" Emily clamped her mouth shut to stop the rush of words.

Scott shot her a look.

Mirabelle glared at her. "The cat's half out of the bag. You can't shove it back in now. Sadie's what?"

If she blurted that Brick had accepted her mother's invitation to dinner, half the town could take a notion to show up at her apartment. "She's in control of the situation."

Mirabelle's eyes narrowed. "That's not what you were fixing to say."

"Give it a break, Mirabelle," Scott said.

"I don't understand why you two aren't fighting mad. That woman has some nerve coming to our town to steal Brick from Sadie." Mirabelle pointed to a candy jar. "Fix me a bag of those, Scott. Good thing for her, folks aren't satisfied to sit back and let her reel him in."

Emily scowled at Mirabelle. "What kind of crazy scheme are you cooking up?"

"Don't know yet. Maybe some kind of rally."

Scott scooped jellybeans into a small paper sack. "I hope you and your cronies consider the fact that this little town is no longer invisible to the outside world."

"Are you worried about what the tourists might think?" Mirabelle shook her finger at him. "Don't you know protesting is as American as sweet-potato pie?"

"That's a southern dish." Scott pushed the sack across the counter.

"And Willow Falls is a southern town that stands up for what's right and takes care of its own." Mirabelle slapped two dollars on the counter, grabbed the sack, and stomped out the door.

"You sure riled her up." Gertie shook her head. "No telling what she's aiming to do."

Emily groaned. "That's what worries me."

"When I was a young girl, I read every Nancy Drew book I could find." Gertie removed Emily's glass from the counter. "Now it's time to put some of her tactics to good use. So, I'll keep my eyes and ears open. Mirabelle's not the only one aiming to keep Cynthia from messing up our good friend's romance."

Scott shoved the empty box under the counter. "I was smart to hire you, Gertie."

She winked at Emily but directed her words to Scott. "Sweetie, you keep right on thinking it was your idea."

He burst out laughing. "Out maneuvered by a senior citizen, also known as Nancy Drew's apprentice."

Gertie grinned. "Don't forget. I'm also a co-star in a Robert Nordstrom movie. When I hear something important, I'll give you two the scoop." She giggled. "Of chatter, not ice cream."

Emily made a mental note to add a Gertie character to her new novel.

Chapter 41

Rachel curled up on the couch in Emily's living room with an open script on her lap. She squeezed her eyes shut, then blinked, hoping to clear her head enough to learn her lines. After releasing a heavy sigh, she focused on the words. Halfway through the first page, the script was hurled to the floor.

"I'm glad that's not my book." Emily came in and sat beside her.

"My next shoot is tomorrow. I can't concentrate long enough to absorb one line, much less an entire scene. This Cynthia fiasco is messing with my brain, big time."

"I know what you mean. Last night a nightmare about Mama Sadie shooting Cynthia shocked me awake." Emily swept her fingers through her hair. "It took me two hours to go back to sleep. How's Charlie handling this mess?"

"He doesn't want to talk about it." Rachel propped her arm on the back of the couch and rested her cheek on her knuckles. "Any word from Gertie?"

Emily nodded. "The scuttlebutt is Mirabelle organized a cold-shoulder campaign and a letter-writing assault."

"I'm surprised she didn't plan a sign-carrying protest outside the hotel."

"Don't count that out yet."

"I know Mirabelle's a royal pain, but you have to admire her determination," Rachel said. "Did I tell you I'm meeting Carrie for lunch at the hotel?"

Emily nodded. "You and the princess are becoming quite chummy. One good thing about Cynthia's invasion, it slowed complaints about stars cozying up with locals."

"Believe me, I'd rather deal with complaints." Rachel turned her head and peered out the window behind the couch. "The leaves are starting to change color."

"Fall comes early up here."

"I can't stop thinking about Brick's first reaction to Cynthia. He acted like she had never left him." Her eyes met Emily's. "She was manipulative and seductive in front of me and Charlie. Who knows what happened after they headed to the winery?"

"The good news is Mama Sadie is cooking dinner for him tomorrow night."

Rachel sighed. "If he compares her to his ex, our mother might come in second."

"Not if she keeps her fighting spirit alive."

Rachel pulled her arm off the back of the couch. "Mama Sadie deserves to win this battle. The problem is the thirty years she lived behind bars."

Emily frowned. "And your point is?"

"She's ill-equipped to compete with a femme fatale."

The twins toddled in and climbed onto the couch. Emily gathered Jane in her arms.

Rachel pulled Clair onto her lap and breathed in the clean scent of baby shampoo. "Your grandma's surprise birthday party can't come soon enough."

"Gramma's 'prise party?"

"Little ears." Emily smiled at her girls.

"Auntie Rach has big ears."

Rachel nuzzled her niece's neck. "All the more to hear you with sweet girl." Clair's giggle helped ease Rachel's growing anxiety.

***

Following another hour with her sister and nieces, Rachel drove to town and parked behind Hayes General Store. She switched her phone to silent and dropped it in her purse before walking up the alley and crossing the street to the sidewalk fronting the park. An elderly couple holding hands greeted her as they approached. When they passed by, she turned to look at them one last time, fearing Mama Sadie's life-long loving relationship with Brick would end up on the trash heap of lost opportunity.

She bit her lip and quickened her step until she arrived at the hotel and found her lunch date signing autographs for adoring fans.

Carrie motioned her over. "Meet my good friend, Rachel Streetman," she said to the small crowd. "She has an important supporting role in our movie. She'll give you her autograph, so you can tell all your friends you knew her before she became a big star."

The fans shifted their attention to Rachel, clamoring for her signature and nuggets about her future.

"This is my first film. Until now, all my experience has been in live theater. If you folks are in town Saturday, you must buy tickets for *Percy's Legacy*." She touted the play and Emily's novel, prominently displayed in Scott's store and Patsy's Pastries and Pretties.

The tourists promised to buy a copy.

Rachel shook her head as she watched them walk to the exit. "Pitching me as a future star is a stretch."

"Not if you aim high enough." Carrie linked arms with Rachel.

Images of Charlie, the winery, her wedding ... all played in Rachel's mind. "I haven't figured out what I want to do."

"You need to decide before Robert recruits you for another role, and I suggest you find yourself a good agent."

"In this town? That's a laugh."

When they arrived at the dining room entrance, Carrie greeted the hostess by name. The young woman's face beamed as she escorted them to a spot beside the window and presented them with menus.

"A storm raged outside the last time I ate here." Rachel scooted her chair close to the table.

"The night your fiancé's mother showed up?"

Rachel stared at Carrie. "How did you hear?"

"Are you kidding? The entire crew knows. And we're all pulling for Sadie. What's going on around here is a ton more intriguing than the movie we're shooting."

"There's one huge difference." Rachel fingered her engagement ring. "We can't write the ending."

Carrie leaned forward. "Which makes it even more interesting."

"And more than a little scary."

A young woman dashed to their table, gawked at Carrie, and pressed her palm to her chest. "I've seen all your movies. Do you mind if I take a selfie with you?"

"My pleasure." Carrie leaned closer to the woman.

"If you'd like," Rachel held out her hand, "I'll take the picture for you."

"Great idea." The woman handed her phone over.

Rachel snapped three photos before returning the phone. "Are those okay?"

"Perfect. My friends will turn green with envy when they learn I'm friends with a famous movie star." Fingers flew over her phone's keypad as she dashed to the lobby.

Rachel grinned as she watched the woman leave. "What do you think she's telling her friends about her so-called friendship with you?"

"It doesn't matter. She's giving me what I like to call organic publicity." Carrie's eyes widened. "Uh oh. The lead in your town's unfolding story just stepped off the elevator, and she looks hopping mad." She popped off her seat. "We *have* to find out what set her off."

"What about lunch?" Rachel wasn't sure she wanted to get involved.

"What could possibly be more delicious than a first-hand glimpse into a real-life drama?"

Rachel rolled her eyes. "Are we characters in your own private movie or busybodies clamoring for some local gossip?"

"You're so dramatic." Carrie grasped Rachel's hand and led her from the dining room. They approached as Cynthia dumped contents from a plastic bag on the check-in counter.

The clerk eyed the pile of postcards, envelopes, and random pieces of paper. "What is this, ma'am?"

"You tell me. I found them on the floor by my door. What kind of rinky-dink hotel are you people running?"

"I'm sorry, ma'am." The young man was clearly uncomfortable.

"Sorry doesn't come close to making this right. I demand to speak to the manager."

"I'll ask Ms. Williams to come right out."

Cynthia tapped her high heel on the marble floor. "You do that."

Carrie leaned close and whispered to Rachel. "This is a fascinating plot twist."

Rachel tensed. "Easy for you to say. This is real life for me."

Cynthia's head jerked around. Her features grew rigid. She locked eyes on Rachel. "Who's behind this scandal?"

The intensity of the woman's glare raised the hair on the back of Rachel's neck. Her mouth went dry. "I ... I don't have a clue."

The door behind the front desk opened. Kat moved in front of the counter and extended her hand to the disgruntled guest. "Ms. Welch, I'm Ms. Williams."

Cynthia ignored Kat's gesture. "How could you let someone shove all this propaganda under my door?"

Rachel noted a glint in Kat's eyes. "What are these?"

"Notes and letters telling me I'm not welcome in Willow Falls."

Kat picked up one of the notes. "Looks like some sort of juvenile prank—"

"Prank my tushie." Cynthia's eyes narrowed. "This is an organized attempt to force me to leave."

"On behalf of the hotel staff, I apologize," Kat said. "To compensate for this unfortunate event, we'll comp your room for your entire stay."

"Add free room service and meals in your dining room, and maybe I won't file a gigantic lawsuit."

"Yes, ma'am. Whatever you want."

"And another thing." Cynthia pointed to the stack of notes. "Who is this Sadie woman everyone is so all fired up about?" Her tone dripped with disgust.

Rachel's pulse pounded in her ears as she stepped forward. "She's my mother. And believe me, she had *nothing* to do with this."

"Doesn't matter who's at fault." Cynthia's eyes shot daggers. "You tell her I'm not about to cut and run because a bunch of country bumpkins don't think she can stand the heat. For Charlie's sake, I suggest you tell everyone to lay off before I sue the whole wretched town." She lifted her chin, threw her shoulders back, and headed to the exit.

"Wow," Carrie said. "Talk about an award-winning performance."

"I'm caught between supporting Sadie and managing this property." Kat scooped the pile back into the plastic bag, handed it to Rachel, and shot a hesitant look at Carrie.

"Whatever you want to say to Rachel, you can trust me to keep it under wraps." Carrie moved closer. "I come from a small town, so I know what's going on."

"Who'd have guessed you were regular folks?" Kat shifted her focus back to Rachel. "After Sadie rescues her man, she might want to read these."

"If she succeeds." Rachel sighed. "Cynthia is so riled up there's no telling what she'll pull to assure victory."

Chapter 42

Rachel tossed the bag of notes in her trunk, then slid into the driver's seat and turned her phone on. Two missed calls from Emily, five from Charlie. A heavy sensation lodged in the pit of her stomach as she pressed his number.

He answered on the first ring. "I've been trying to reach you for hours." His tone dripped with anger. "Why didn't you answer?"

"I switched my phone to silent before meeting Carrie for lunch." She resisted telling him about the confrontation with Cynthia. "Then we spent a couple of hours in her RV. Rehearsing."

"We need to talk."

This doesn't sound good. "What's going on, Charlie?"

"Not over the phone. Meet me at my house. Now." He ended the call.

The way he spat the word *now* triggered a warning bell in Rachel's brain. She pressed Emily's number. She answered, her tone strained.

"Charlie is in an uproar."

"Did he tell you what set him off?"

"Something about his mother. He didn't make much sense." Rachel filled her lungs, then slowly released the air. "He must know about Cynthia's meltdown."

"What happened?"

"Call Kat. She'll fill you in." Rachel tossed her phone on the passenger seat, backed out of the driveway, and headed out of town. During the drive to the winery, her emotions volleyed between anger and gut-wrenching anxiety. By the time she pulled onto the driveway, her palms were moist and her throat parched. She stepped out of her car and dashed to the front porch.

Charlie yanked the door open before her finger reached the bell. He stepped aside, his hand gripping the curved door handle.

She walked past him, avoiding eye contact.

He slammed the door. "Why did you confront my mother?"

Rachel spun around and glared. "What are you talking about?"

"Don't act like you don't know. You and Carrie ganged up on her."

She aimed her palm at his face. "Stop right there. I don't know what you heard, but—"

"An earful." He trudged to the living room and dropped onto the newly delivered couch, facing the stacked stone fireplace. "She showed up here, hopping mad."

Rachel sat on an overstuffed chair catty-corner to the couch. "What did she tell you?"

"What happened at the hotel. When she left there, she went to Florentines for lunch. She sat there half an hour waiting for someone to acknowledge her. All she got was a cold shoulder and ugly comments. She left and showed up at my door ... in tears."

I doubt the woman's capable of real tears. "Did she happen to tell you she threatened to sue the hotel?"

"Over what?"

"Notes from angry residents. She came close to accusing me of collusion." Rachel crossed her legs and pumped her foot. "Worse, she threatened Mama Sadie."

"She was hurt and upset."

"No, Charlie. Cynthia was irate. And very rude."

"What would you do if you were in her shoes?"

"There's no way I'd ever find myself in her situation because I'd never abandon my family." Rachel uncrossed her legs. "I know this is difficult for you, but you have to understand. Your mother knows how to manipulate emotions."

His stare intensified. "Are you accusing her of using me?"

"I'm saying she has her sights set on snaring your father, and she doesn't care who gets caught in the crosshairs."

The veins in Charlie's neck pulsed.

"You don't believe me, do you?"

He broke eye contact, then moved to the fireplace and ignited a gas-fed flame.

Icy fear built up inside Rachel as she watched him prop his arm on the mantle and tilt his head toward the fire.

"Do you want me to leave?" Rachel worked to keep the pain from her voice.

"I can't reach my dad."

Chills crept up from Rachel's spine. "Did you go by his house?"

"This morning. His car wasn't in the garage. When he's struggling to make decisions, he sometimes takes long drives. Claims it helps him think."

"What are you suggesting?"

Charlie spun around. "You saw my mother. She looks as young as she did when she left him."

"That doesn't erase the rotten way she treated him." Rachel scooted to the edge of the chair. "You have to talk to him, make him understand."

"Understand what?"

"That he's days away from proposing to my mother. The woman who, by the way, won't break his heart into a thousand tiny pieces."

Charlie returned to the couch and slumped against the back. "I can't."

"Why not?"

"It's his life. Not mine. And not yours."

Rachel narrowed her eyes as her muscles tensed. "Then there's nothing more for you and me to discuss."

Silence permeated the room.

She stood. Hesitated. Then hurried out the front door and raced to her car. She headed down the driveway. Seconds after turning onto County Road, she slammed on the brakes and pulled onto the shoulder. Her eyes scanned acres of grapevines spread across the hills. Charlie's passion. His expression before she abandoned him exploded in her head. She gasped for air. "I have to go back."

Rachel pulled a U-turn and sped back to the winery. After racing up the sidewalk, she stopped on the porch to catch her breath before opening the door and stepping into the foyer. She found Charlie on the couch, his elbows on his knees, his face buried in his hands. She knelt in front of him.

He lifted his head. His eyes were red, his cheeks wet.

She had never seen him cry. She reached for his hand.

"I was fifteen when Cynthia abandoned us. The day before she left, I called her selfish and cold." His voice cracked. "I accused her of caring more about her stupid friends than me and my brother. It took me years to stop blaming myself. When she showed up here ... all that guilt gushed back."

Rachel's heart ached. "I'm so sorry."

"You're right about Cynthia. She's calculating and self-centered." He sniffed. "I love her because she's my mother ... but truth is I never liked her."

She stroked Charlie's fingers.

"Tomorrow, I'll talk to Dad and try to find out what's going on in his head."

Relief washed over Rachel as she pushed up and sat beside him. "I have one request." She held his hand and rested her head on his shoulder. "Make it early. Mama Sadie invited him to dinner."

He leaned his head back and closed his eyes.

Rachel watched the flame lick the artificial logs and vowed to stay here with the man she loved for however long he needed her.

Chapter 43

The sun had risen halfway to its peak when Rachel parked in her sister's driveway. She removed the bag of notes from her trunk and hauled it to the kitchen.

Emily looked up from her computer. "I read the text you sent last night. Is Charlie okay?"

"He is now. I invited him to join us for dinner." Rachel opened the bag and dumped the notes on the table. "Willow Falls' silent protest."

"What do you expect me to do with these?"

"You could weave them into your new novel about this town's crazy cast of characters."

Emily unfolded a note. "You have to give residents credit for creativity. This one says, 'Go home, hook a man who isn't already taken, and come back as a tourist to enjoy our town's hospitality.'"

Rachel shook her head. "That's what I call moxie."

"How about this one. 'Ladies who think they can steal a man by dressing fancy and sashaying around town aren't welcome in Willow Falls.'"

"Where do people come up with this stuff?"

Emily reached for another note. "Want to hear more?"

"Can't. I'm due at makeup in half an hour." Rachel opened the refrigerator and removed a bottle of water. "The first courtroom scene and Mirabelle's premiere movie performance is on today's docket."

"Fireworks are likely to explode when Mirabelle tries to run the show."

"She's had enough experience in the *Percy's Legacy* cast to understand the director's role. Maybe she'll respect him and behave herself."

Emily guffawed. "And pink and white striped elephants will parade through town at high noon."

"Do I hear a hint of skepticism?"

"A boatload of reality is more like it."

"If you're right, the movie crew is in for an interesting afternoon." Rachel twisted the cap off the water bottle. "For now, I'm heading to the shower."

"I'll text you with any breaking news about Willow Falls' boot-Cynthia-out-of-town endeavor."

Rachel waved her fingers at her sister. "I'll wait with bated breath."

**

Moments after Rachel's makeup and gabfest with Antoine ended, the town's protest leader pranced into the trailer. "I'm Mirabelle Paine, here for my appointment."

"Ah, yes," Antoine said. "The ex-wife's number one antagonist and chief letter writer."

Rachel's eyes widened. "You heard?"

"Darling, the entire crew knows about the Cynthia caper." He removed her pink bib and tossed it in a hamper. "One of the grips started a pool predicting the number of hours until the woman struts her derriere out of town. I'm guessing forty-three."

"Fifty-six for me," said the makeup artist working the next chair over.

An older, dark-haired woman sniffed. "I hope that ex-wife read *my* note."

The man in the chair next to her chuckled. "I can only imagine what you wrote."

"I told her we don't take kindly to homewreckers messing things up for a fine lady like Sadie."

The man stared at her. "Aren't you one of the protestors who gave our innkeeper a hard time when she showed up in town after her release from prison?"

"That was before we knew the rest of the story. Now, she's one of us."

Antoine pulled a fresh makeup bib from a drawer and nodded toward Mirabelle. "Madame, come to my chair, *s'il vous plaît*."

Mirabelle eyed him from head to toe, then pulled Rachel aside. "Everybody's talking about him being kind of ... you know ... girly."

"What's your point?"

She glanced at Antoine, then faced Rachel. "Should I let him do my makeup?"

"Well now, that depends." Rachel stared at her. "Do you want one of Hollywood's most talented makeup artists preparing you for your big movie debut or one of his underlings?"

Mirabelle only hesitated a moment before moseying to Antoine's station. "You know I play a Newport maven in the town's play where I'm supposed to look ... stern and ordinary."

"In movies, one must look fabulous up close." He draped the bib around her neck. "You shall see what I mean when I work my magic on you."

"He *is* good," Rachel said as she lifted her purse from a hook and stepped outside. She walked the half block to the town's municipal building. Inside the courtroom, she moved into the middle aisle and sat in the last of three rows of oak pews. Shades were lowered on two windows facing Falls Street.

Beth, a member of the *Percy's Legacy* stage crew, slid in beside her. She nodded toward the crew setting up lights. "If it took us this much time to set a scene, our two-hour play would turn into eight."

"No kidding. Are you an observer or a jury member?"

"Observer. Which means I didn't merit a trip to the makeup trailer. It hardly seems fair. I don't understand why the director doesn't want us looking our best."

"Ladies and gentlemen," Robert's voice boomed. "If you're cast as a courtroom observer, please come up to the front."

"I'm going to ask him." Beth joined the extras gathering in front of the judge's bench.

During the half-hour the director spent giving instructions and answering questions, Rachel read and deleted emails, then sent a text to Charlie confirming her dinner invitation.

When Robert dismissed the courtroom extras and sent them to their assigned spots, Beth stepped into the aisle, turned toward the back, and halted. Her eyes bugged. "Wow!"

Mirabelle grinned at Beth as she slid in beside Rachel.

Rachel tried to hide her surprise. "Aren't you glad you let Antoine work his magic. I mean, you look amazing."

Mirabelle folded her hands in her lap. "This is the first time ... I'm not plain."

The female extras rushed toward Mirabelle, gushing over her new look.

"Follow me, ladies," Beth said. "We need to demand time in the trailer or go on strike."

Before Rachel could stop her, Beth dashed toward the front. "Mr. Nordstrom, sir, we want a word with you."

The director's eyes widened as the flock of women accosted him.

"Excuse me, pretty lady," Rachel said. "I need to rescue our director." She slipped past Mirabelle and scurried toward the front.

Robert leaned back on the prosecutor's table and crossed his arms. "What seems to be the problem, ladies?"

Beth stretched her arm toward his jury forewoman. "She is. We want the same treatment she got. Professional makeup."

"That's not necessary—"

"It is to us. This movie is the only time people all over the country, maybe the whole world, will see our faces. We want to look fabulous, like her."

"Yeah," said one of the other women. "My cousin in Birmingham told all her friends about me being in a movie."

A barrage of complaints and pleas followed.

Rachel stepped beside Robert and interrupted the verbal assault. "Ladies, please ..."

Robert touched her arm. "I'll handle this." He stepped out of range and spoke to his assistant.

Beth propped her fists on her hips. "We didn't have a chance to tell him about a strike."

Amateurs. "I suggest you all settle down," Rachel said, "and let him do his job."

"But what if—"

"No what-ifs. You need to exercise diplomacy. Or at least patience."

Beth sighed. "We'll wait to see what happens before we take the next step." The women moved up the aisle and gathered around Mirabelle.

Rachel settled in the front row, ready to intervene if sparks flew. Fighting her body's urge to release beads of sweat, she searched the Internet for tactics to calm disgruntled workers. With each passing minute, the female voices drifting from the back escalated in volume and intensity, making it difficult to focus.

Twenty minutes elapsed without a word from the director.

Rachel stuffed her phone in her purse, stood, and turned toward the female mob. Moments later, Antoine and his three colleagues arrived carrying makeup cases. They scurried to the front.

The women gathered around Mirabelle fell silent as their director faced them. "Ladies, our make-up artists have arrived to make you all look beautiful."

Cheers erupted.

Robert emitted a shrill whistle. "We'll do this in an orderly fashion. My assistant will call you in alphabetical order."

The tension gripping Rachel's muscles eased as she stepped close to Robert. "I'm surprised you gave in to their demands."

"Believe me. It's easier and less time consuming to appease them than select new extras. The makeup crew will show up here every morning an hour ahead of schedule until the courtroom scenes are finished." He glanced at his watch. "The rest of the cast is due in fifteen minutes. If no more off-the-wall demands pop up, we'll knock out setting and mood shots today and kick off dialogue scenes tomorrow."

Rachel pressed her lips together to keep her thoughts from rolling off her tongue. She had lived in Willow Falls long enough to know his gesture would unleash a torrent of requests he would live to regret.

Chapter 44

Exhausted, Rachel dropped on the courtroom's front row the moment Robert shouted, "That's a wrap for today." She rolled her head from side to side as she listened to him tick off a laundry-list of instructions for tomorrow's shoot.

When he finished, Carrie wandered away from the witness stand and sat beside her. She clasped her hands and stretched her arms over her head. "How are you holding up under all the drama going on around here?"

"That depends on which spectacle you're talking about."

Carried lowered her arms. "The Cynthia versus Sadie caper."

"The jury's still out."

"Clever response." Carrie snickered. "You know the entire crew's pulling for your mother."

"Including you?"

She leaned close. "I guessed the ex will bail after sixty-two humiliating hours."

"I'm not convinced Cynthia's capable of humiliation." Rachel sighed. "By now, I'm sure Mama Sadie has gotten an earful."

"She didn't mention it during breakfast. Can you believe this morning is the first time I ever tasted grits? Not as good as my protein shake, but not bad. Anyway, maybe Sadie will mention her rival tonight when she meets me and Maggie for dinner. You're welcome to join us if you're not busy."

"Thanks, but Charlie's joining me for dinner at Emily's."

"This whole mess must be tough on him."

"He's dealing with it." Rachel eased off her seat. "We have another long day tomorrow."

Carrie stood and smoothed her skirt. "For those of us with speaking roles, it will be a lot more fun than today."

The two women walked out of the courtroom and municipal building. Outside, Carrie turned toward her RV, and Rachel headed to the wardrobe trailer. Relieved the lady in charge didn't comment about the ex-wife pool, she changed clothes, then rushed to her car. During the short drive home, a pang of anxiety for Cynthia nudged her soul—until she dismissed the sensation as misguided compassion.

By the time she veered around Charlie's truck parked at the curb and parked in Emily's driveway, resentment toward his mother had reached a new high. She gripped the steering wheel and breathed deeply until her fingers uncurled and her anger diminished.

Rachel found her sister standing at the kitchen counter. Clair and Jane mimicked their mother at a kitchen play set. "Where are the guys?"

"On the patio, nursing beers and likely tossing balls to Cody and Brownie." Emily lifted the crockpot lid, releasing the savory aroma of cilantro and tomato sauce.

"That smells yummy."

"A new chili recipe." Emily stirred the contents, then closed the lid and grabbed two light beers from the fridge. She twisted off the caps and handed one to Rachel. "The perfect accompaniment for tonight's meal."

"Did Charlie mention meeting with Brick?"

"Not a word. In fact, other than *hello,* he didn't say anything before he and Scott headed out back."

"That's not good."

"He has a lot on his mind." Emily added dressing to a bowl of greens. "How'd your day go?"

"Interesting." Rachel shared the Mirabelle makeup drama.

"Robert has no idea what he unleashed. We need to plan how we're gonna deal with all the women in town when they discover the power of a professional makeover."

Rachel agreed. "Maybe they'll flock to Pearl's salon and give her business a big boost."

"When a famous Hollywood makeup artist is within spitting distance? I have a better chance to win the lottery."

"I didn't know you bought lottery tickets."

"I don't. That's the point." Emily cut fruit and a grilled cheese sandwich for the twins, then plated the salad and ladled chili into four bowls. "Let the guys know dinner's on."

Rachel opened the patio door and relayed the message.

Charlie stepped inside and kissed her before he headed to the kitchen table.

Scott grabbed two beers from the fridge, then sat beside his wife and pushed a bottle to Charlie. "Wait till you see what our girls learned this afternoon." He pressed his palms together and nodded to the twins. "Say the blessing Mommy taught you."

Clair and Jane mimicked Scott and recited a six-word prayer, ending with amen and giggles.

Rachel placed her hand on her chest. "These little darlings fill my heart with pride."

"Hopefully, they'll rouse your maternal instincts." Emily pointed her spoon at her sister. "If you and Charlie decide to start a family soon, our babies will grow up together."

"Or we can wait until your girls are old enough to babysit." Eager to change the subject, Rachel turned to Charlie. "How'd the conversation with your dad go?"

"It didn't."

She stared wide-eyed at his profile. "What do you mean?"

"Give it a break, Rachel. I called him after you left this morning. Before I could say two words, he claimed he had another call coming in. He told me he'd call back." Charlie dipped his spoon in the chili.

"And?"

"He didn't. I tried to reach him all afternoon. No response."

"Maybe his phone's dead." Her shoulders tensed. "Or he fell down the stairs—"

"Nothing happened to him, Rachel. I stopped at his house on the way here. He answered the door. Said he had company and promised to call me tomorrow."

"Did he seem angry? Or stressed?"

Charlie shrugged. "I don't know. Maybe distracted."

Emily added a dash of pepper to her salad. "Odds are the company was your mother."

"No doubt," Charlie said.

Images of Brick's ex captivating him with her feminine charm rocked Rachel's brain. "I'm glad he accepted Mama Sadie's invitation to dinner tomorrow night."

"Unless ..." Charlie distractedly stirred his chili.

Rachel zeroed in on his face. "Unless what?"

"Nothing." His eyes met hers for a moment, then cast downward. "Forget it."

Rachel pushed a piece of cucumber around her salad bowl. Did he know something he couldn't or wouldn't reveal? Flurries of icy dread built up inside as potential conclusions to his unfinished comment zipped through her mind.

Chapter 45

*E*mily closed her email and pushed her computer aside. "Less than twenty-four hours and half the town's going bananas."

"What now?" Scott rinsed his mug and set it in the dishwasher.

"Women are fixated on Mirabelle's new look." She meandered to the kitchen counter and refreshed her coffee. "I imagine Rachel's getting an earful."

"I didn't see her this morning."

"She left at dawn. Early morning shoot." Emily's phone pinged an incoming text. "Pearl wants me to meet her at the salon in an hour. Something about cancellations."

"You're not the town's fix-it queen." Scott donned a gray frock coat. "You don't have to show up."

"Yeah, I do."

"As what?" His tone sounded harsh. "Newspaper editor or Nordstrom's go-between?"

"Little of both."

"This town can't return to normal soon enough." He snatched his keys and headed to the garage.

"Whatever *normal* is," mumbled Emily as she pressed the babysitter's phone number.

Forty minutes later, she gave the woman instructions. With her sunglasses in hand, she kissed the twins good-bye and drove into town. Surprised to find empty parking spots and few people on the sidewalks, Emily pulled into a space across from the newspaper office. She crossed the street, walked past Nathan's furniture store, and halted at the corner of Falls Street. Her comment to Rachel about planning ahead exploded in her head as she gawked at the throng of women gathered outside the makeup trailer.

Pearl, dressed in tight black pants, red tank top, and sequined jacket, stood on the sidewalk fronting her salon with her cell phone pressed to her ear. As Emily closed the distance, she heard the stylist's plea to reconsider.

Seconds passed.

Pearl shifted her phone to the other ear. "You don't seriously think ..." Her voice got louder. "Good luck with that." She jerked the phone to her side. "Bunch of ungrateful ..."

"What's going on?"

"That circus." She thrust her thumb toward the trailer. "Can you believe eight customers cancelled their appointments with me?" Her phone pinged. She stared at the screen. "Make that nine. Not a single one of those ladies ever gave a hoot about a makeover until word leaked about Mirabelle. Now they're clamoring for time with that Hollywood guy. Like they have one shot in a million at getting their feet in his door."

"Maybe you should run a two-for-one special."

"Wouldn't help. Everyone wants Antoine to make them look like a hot-to-trot movie star. For what? So they can run off to Atlanta and pay for glamor shots to hang in their living rooms and post on social media?"

Emily's phone vibrated. "I have to take this." She held the phone to her ear. "Hey, Sis."

"Do you have any idea what's going on?"

"You mean the mob on Falls Street?"

"Not just out there." Rachel's voice was laced with tension. "Sheriff Mitch had to evict a crowd of women from the courtroom. I suspect he's standing guard to keep them from storming back in. Robert's none too happy."

Has the entire town gone bananas? "What is he planning to do?"

"Not him. Us. And since I can't leave ... you."

"Why am I not surprised." Emily released a long sigh. "Short of letting them all in the trailer, I don't have a clue how to appease these women. By the way, where are Antoine and his crew of miracle workers?"

"Hiding out in here. Maybe you can convince your friends and neighbors to make appointments with Pearl. After all, she is a professional."

"Won't work." Emily stepped away from the salon owner and lowered her voice. "She's dealing with a heap of cancellations and is hopping mad."

"Who can blame her. Tell you what, we'll have a noon lunch break. I'll meet you at the salon. Maybe we can come up with some kind of plan. In the meantime, will you talk to the ladies and at least try to calm them down?"

"I'll give it my best shot." Emily ended the call and moved beside Pearl. "I've been tasked with crowd control. Want to join me?"

"With all the bailouts, I have nothing better to do."

When they reached the trailer, Emily climbed onto the steps, slid her sunglasses to the top of her head, and faced the crowd. "What's on your minds, ladies?"

Stage-mother Lizzy pushed to the front. "Which twin are you?"

"The author."

"Have you seen the picture Mirabelle texted to all her friends?" She shoved her phone in front of Emily's face.

Emily shaded her eyes with her hand and stared at a photo. "She does look good."

"If Antoine can make her look like that, imagine what he can do for the rest of us." Lizzy lowered her phone.

"I know read exactly what you mean. Lucky for all of you, Pearl's salon is a full-service—"

"Forget it," shouted a woman standing behind Lizzy. "We want a professional."

"In case you're wondering," Pearl said. "I'm not a beauty school dropout."

"We don't mean any disrespect, but you're one of us."

Pearl waggled her finger at the woman. "I happen to have a cosmetology degree, thank you very much."

Lizzy stepped closer. "Then how come you never made Mirabelle look good?"

"Let me think." Pearl snapped her fingers. "Oh yeah, because she never made an appointment for anything other than a haircut. What'd you expect me to do, show up at her house, tie her to a chair, and slap a pound of makeup on her?"

"There's no need to get all huffy."

Pearl glared at Lizzy. "Don't tell me your tail feathers wouldn't ruffle if friends ditched you for an outsider."

A barrage of comments erupted.

Emily held her open palm toward the crowd and shouted. "Ladies!" She waited for them to settle down. "Look, I understand why you're here. The thing is, you have to understand that the people who work in this trailer are hired to prepare cast members for filming, not provide salon services to residents."

"If we'd known about the makeovers, more of us would've auditioned," Lizzy said.

A young woman raised her hand. "We're not trying to act unreasonable. And Ms. Pearl, we're not saying we don't think you're the best. It's just ... well ... this is a once-in-a-lifetime opportunity. Ms. Emily, will you and your sister please try to convince Mr. Nordstrom to let us schedule appointments with Antoine?"

The women's wide-eyed expressions sent a clear message about the crowd's objective. Emily breathed air in through her nose and let air escape through her mouth.

Lizzy glared. "Well, what's your answer?"

"The decision isn't up to us, so I'm not making any promises. However, I'm meeting Rachel for lunch. We'll talk about it—"

"Did you hear that, ladies? Emily and her sister are gonna make it happen."

Cheers erupted as the crowd morphed into a deafening frenzy of excited chatter.

Emily climbed down, skirted the mob, and dashed toward the salon.

Pearl caught up with her. "Now you've gone and done it."

"I can't help it if they drew their own conclusions."

"You're a female. What did you think was gonna happen when you told them you'd talk about it?"

"Scott had it right. I should have ignored your text and stayed home."

"You didn't," Pearl said as she pushed the salon door open. "Which means you're up to your eyeballs in this mess."

"Rachel's meeting us here in an hour. You have a lot at stake. So why don't you stop with the comments and help us come up with a solution?"

"You're on, girlfriend." Pearl flipped the sign on the door from open to closed. "I'll even order us a pizza."

Chapter 46

Playing the role of the defense attorney's girlfriend, Rachel sat in the first row behind Justin Brooks' chair. Other than the disruption from women charging in to demand makeovers, the morning moved at a snail's pace—until Mirabelle raised her hand in the middle of a scene.

"Cut." Robert moved to the jury box and stood at the railing in front of the forewoman. "Is there a problem over here?"

Mirabelle leaned forward. "I have a suggestion."

Maggie slipped in the row beside Rachel. "This should be interesting."

Robert removed his ball cap and scratched his head. "Do you now?"

"Yes, sir. I think the prosecutor should stand closer to the jury when he's asking questions."

"Thank you, Ms. Paine. I'll take your comment under consideration." He popped his cap back on. "Do you mind if we return to filming?"

"Yes, sir. I mean, no, sir."

"Good."

Rachel leaned close to Maggie and whispered, "Unlike Gertie, I doubt Mirabelle reminds our director of his grandmother. I've been around long enough to know he just made a huge mistake."

"How?"

"Wait, you'll see."

Thirty minutes later, Mirabelle interrupted a third time. "Mr. Nordstrom."

He zipped his fingers across his throat, signaling another cut. His eyes narrowed. "What is it this time, Ms. Paine?"

"I have another suggestion."

"Why am I not surprised?"

"Last night I watched an old *Law and Order* episode and ... well ... I think you should film the defense attorney leaning on the jury railing while he's questioning the witness."

"With a shot of you in the background, I presume."

"The jury's reaction is important."

Robert crossed his arms. "Do you mind if *I* make a suggestion?"

"Of course not."

"How generous of you, Ms. Paine. Either we change places, and you direct using the expertise you gleaned from a television show, or ..." He removed a pad of paper and a pen from his briefcase and slapped them on the railing. "You jot your suggestions down, give them to me at the end of the day, and let me continue doing my job."

Mirabelle hesitated as if considering her options.

"Well?" His tone intensified. "What's the verdict?"

"Will you read them?"

He gestured an X across his chest. "Cross my heart."

"Okay, then." She took the pad and pen off the railing.

"I assume we can continue now, *uninterrupted*."

"Yes, sir, Mr. Nordstrom."

Maggie nudged Rachel. "Is it her new look or has she always been this brazen?"

"Yes, to both."

The remainder of the morning ran smoothly, without comments from the self-appointed courtroom expert.

When the director announced a lunch break, Rachel tucked her purse under her arm. She dashed past the ladies hanging out in the hall to avoid an onslaught of questions. Outside, Sheriff Mitch mingled with the crowd gathered at the makeup trailer. Rachel skirted around the RVs and trailers parked on Falls Street and rushed to Pearl's Hair and Nail Salon. She arrived seconds before a waiter from the town's Italian restaurant walked out.

"You're right on time." Pearl carried three bottles of water from the back room and placed them on a card table surrounded by three folding chairs. "My office is barely big enough for one, much less three." She opened a large, thin box, releasing sausage and spicy tomato aromas. "Can you believe Willow Falls now has pizza delivery?"

"One of the good changes." Emily reached for a slice.

Pearl bit a chunk from her piece. "And it's delicious."

Emily swallowed a bite and eyed Rachel. "How'd your morning go after the disruption?"

"Depends on which one you're referring to?" She relayed Mirabelle's meddling.

"Our mail lady graduated from orchestrating a letter-writing crusade to finagling a suggestion-box campaign." Pearl snickered. "Does your director know she'll demand answers?"

"If he doesn't, he'll soon find out." Rachel uncapped her water bottle. "One thing I know for sure, he's dead-set against letting all those women make appointments with his crew."

"That's not good. Especially since your sister promised they'd get their wish."

Rachel glared at Emily. "You did what?"

"Don't give me that look. They twisted my words."

"How convenient." Rachel gulped down mouthfuls of water. "You were right about needing to come up with a plan."

"We could kidnap Antoine and Nordstrom." Pearl nodded toward the back. "And keep them tied up in my office until he agrees to our demands."

"Or you could wear a disguise." Rachel reached for a pizza slice. "Call yourself Fifi, adopt a French accent, and pretend you're a famous Hollywood makeup artist."

"How about we cut the jokes and come up with an idea that won't land us all in jail," Emily said.

"We're trying to lighten the mood, girlfriend."

Emily jabbed her finger toward Pearl. "I left my babies to deal with this catastrophe, not do comedy central."

"She's right," Rachel said around a bite of her pizza. "We have to figure out how to satisfy all those ladies."

The three women brainstormed until they had devoured the pizza, without landing on a single viable solution.

"To use one of Sadie's phrases, maybe we're barking up the wrong tree." Pearl wiped her fingers with a napkin and eyed Rachel. "What's your director's biggest objection to letting Antoine go public?"

"The insane amount of time it would take," Rachel said.

"Uh-huh." Pearl fingered her three-inch hoop earrings. "And what do all those women want?"

"To look as good or better than Mirabelle."

"Exactly. The problem is an Antoine makeover is a one-time thing. It would make a heap more sense if they learned how to look sensational all the time."

Emily's brows furrowed. "What are you suggesting?"

"A giant makeover session in the hotel ballroom with Antoine demonstrating techniques on one person. Everyone else can follow along and apply their own makeup. With me and the other three artists circulating and giving ladies personal attention."

"You watched their reaction when they took my comment wrong." Emily groaned. "I can't imagine your idea will satisfy them."

Pearl eyed Rachel. "Any chance your director will let Antoine take reservations for individual makeovers?"

"Not one in a million."

"Then I suggest you two go along with my idea."

"Seems like a massive undertaking, and Emily and I already have our hands full."

"No need to worry." Pearl grabbed a napkin. "If you convince Nordstrom to approve the plan and kick in some cash, I'll take care of the whole thing."

Rachel closed the empty pizza box. "How much cash?"

"Enough to sponsor the event."

Emily rested her chin on her knuckles and stared at Pearl. "You are one smart businesswoman."

The town's only salon owner hooked her thumbs under her jacket lapels and pointed her index fingers toward her head. "My look fools everyone. Underneath my everchanging hair color is a brain that's hot as a firecracker."

Emily laughed. "Never underestimate a small-town salon owner."

Simultaneous pings on Rachel's and Emily's phones disrupted her compliment.

A text from Mama Sadie. *Urgent.*

Chapter 47

*E*mily exchanged glances with her sister. "We'd better hope your suggestion works, Pearl."

Rachel dropped her phone in her purse. "I'll pitch your idea to Robert this afternoon after we finish filming. Right now, I'm due back in the courtroom." She stood and reached for Emily's hand. "Walk with me."

"Hold on a cotton-picking minute." Pearl bolted off her chair. "If those ladies are still hanging around outside, they'll expect an update."

"I know," Emily said with more courage than she felt. "I'll handle it."

"While you're calming the natives, don't forget to remind them that Pearl's Nail and Hair Salon is still open for business."

The sisters walked out, turned left, and stopped in front of the Willow Falls Theater ticket booth.

Rachel pulled her phone from her purse and stared at the screen. "I can't believe he did this to Mama Sadie."

"Do you think Charlie knows?"

"I haven't talked to him since last night, so I don't have a clue. I'm sorry to dump this in your lap, but you have to talk to her and find out what's going on."

"I will." Emily motioned toward the makeup trailer. "After we update the crowd."

Rachel's eyes narrowed. "What do you mean *we?*"

"You don't expect me to face that mob alone, do you?"

"You know I have to return to the set."

"I'm not letting you off the hook." Emily looped her arm around Rachel's elbow. "Besides, it won't take long."

"This liaison job is taking on a life of its own." Rachel dropped her phone in her purse. "What are we going to tell them?"

"I'm an author and reporter. You're an actress. We'll come up with something."

"You mean we're winging it."

"Do you have a better idea?"

"Yeah," Rachel said. "Consider witness protection and move to North Dakota."

"Not a bad idea." Emily hastened her steps toward the trailer. "At least the crowd has shrunk from a couple of hours ago." Conversations stopped when she climbed onto the steps. "My sister and I had lunch with our salon owner—"

"Only one thing we want to know," shouted Lizzy. "When can we start making appointments with Antoine?"

Rachel stepped up beside Emily. "Here's the thing. Our guest makeup artist's schedule is full."

"Your sister promised—"

"Let me finish," Rachel said. "Pearl suggested an idea we believe will satisfy everyone. Before we share it with you, Mr. Nordstrom has to approve."

"It's obvious you and your sister are trying to blow us off."

"How about ditching the attitude, Lizzy." Emily scanned the faces staring at her. "We know all of you are eager for an answer, but you have to understand it would be foolish for us to reveal anything before we have the details ironed out."

A woman standing toward the back of the crowd held her hand up. "When will you let us know?"

Emily locked eyes with her sister and shrugged.

Rachel hesitated, then faced the crowd. "Maybe the town's talented newspaper editor will share the news in this week's *Willow Post*."

Emily rolled her eyes. "Yeah. Okay, I'll do that."

"Thanks, Sis." Rachel grinned. "Right now, you ladies will have to excuse us."

While rushing toward the sidewalk fronting the courthouse, Emily shot her sister a stern look. "Slick move. Using the newspaper tactic to shirk responsibility."

"Hey, one of us had to come up with a response. Besides, I'm not off the hook. I have to convince Robert and Antoine to go along with Pearl's insane plan."

"As they say in show biz, break a leg, kid. In the meantime, I'm headed to Willow Inn to talk to Mama Sadie."

"Let me know what you find out."

"I'll text you." Emily lowered her sunglasses. After covering the block-long stretch of Falls Street, she crossed Main and turned toward the inn. She found her mother sitting in a rocker on the porch, eyes closed. Mittens, the neighbor's white-pawed black cat lay curled on her lap.

Memories of the weeks following Sadie's parole raced through Emily's mind. How she had navigated through a mountain of obstacles and became a beloved member of the community that once scorned her. She deserved a loving relationship with a man who adored her.

Sadie's eyes fluttered open as a floorboard squeaked under Emily's feet. Mittens stretched, slithered off her lap, and claimed her spot on the railing.

"Sorry I woke you." Emily settled in the white rocking chair beside Sadie.

"I wasn't asleep. Did you read my text?"

"Rachel and I both did. Is there more to the story?"

Sadie set her rocker in motion. "Like what?"

"Did Brick tell you why he canceled dinner with you?"

"His plans changed."

A spider web stretched between two railing posts conjured an image of Cynthia snaring Brick in her manicured claws. "Did he reschedule?"

"I didn't invite him back." Sadie stopped rocking. She stood and moved to the railing where she gently stroked Mitten's back. "A month after Mama married Robert Liles, and we moved here, I had a crush on a cute boy in my biology class. We dated for a while before he flipped over another girl. A majorette. Several years later, they married and moved out of town."

Emily stepped beside her mother. "Why didn't you invite Brick to another dinner?"

"I survived all those years behind bars because I learned not to hold on to impossible hopes and dreams. The promise of freedom was enough for me." A faraway look clouded her eyes. "I'm satisfied with my life the way it is now. I'm reunited with my daughters. I have two beautiful granddaughters. A loving family. Good friends."

A heavy sensation invaded Emily's chest. She wanted to embrace her mother and tell her that Brick loved her, but her arms failed to move. The words refused to form. Maybe because deep down, she feared the ring Brick showed Rachel and Charlie would never find its way to her mother's finger.

Chapter 48

$\mathcal{E}$mily sat on a patio chair in her backyard, watching clouds drift past the moon. She held a glass in one hand and stroked Cody's back with the other. "I don't care if he is your almost father-in-law, he's no longer welcome in my house."

Rachel glared at her sister. "I can't believe you're willing to break up our family because Brick canceled dinner with Sadie."

"He did way more than bail. You didn't see her face. I'm telling you, Brick broke her spirit. She believes he and Cynthia sealed her destiny to remain single for the rest of her life."

"That doesn't make sense." Rachel released a heavy sigh. "No one knows what Brick intends to do."

"Do you honestly think he still plans to propose to Sadie?"

Rachel ran her finger around the rim of her glass. "He didn't answer Charlie's calls again today."

"Two days in a row, Brick ignored his son. What does that tell you?"

"What should we do about her surprise birthday party?"

"Guests have already been invited." Emily refreshed her drink. "We need to continue as planned. Besides, a celebration will remind Sadie that a lot of *other* people around here still love her."

Rachel remained silent for a long moment. "I talked to Robert again ... about Pearl's idea."

"And?"

"He's okay with it as long as Antoine agrees."

"What about him kicking in some cash?"

"He said it was worth the expense to keep the locals from protesting him like they are Cynthia." Rachel sipped her drink. "Antoine's on board. He wants to call it Antoine's Amazing Beauty Bash. He plans to invite Pearl to dinner tomorrow night to flesh out the plans. She'll have her hands full working with him."

"More likely, he'll discover he's met his match."

Brownie sprang to her feet and deposited a Frisbee on Rachel's lap. She sent it soaring across the yard. Brownie chased after the flying disc and plucked it from the air before it hit the ground. Cody bounded to his canine cousin and initiated a tail-wagging tug of war.

"Our dogs will miss each other after you move out," Emily said. "You'll have to bring Brownie back to visit."

"Help me understand. I can bring my dog to your house, but not my father-in-law?"

"Give it a break, Rachel. Brownie didn't crush Mama Sadie's heart. If we're lucky, Brick will move back to Atlanta and only visit a couple of times a year."

"Have you forgotten he owns the winery?"

"Doesn't matter. When folks around here find out what he's done, he'll end up less popular than a room full of cornered skunks."

The patio door slid open, followed by footsteps.

Scott approached and handed Emily her phone. "It's Kat. There's a problem at the hotel."

She pressed the speaker icon. "Please don't tell me there's another fire."

"A break-in."

"In Willow Falls?" Emily stared at the phone. "You've got to be kidding."

"Hold on." Unintelligible mutterings followed. Kat returned. "You need to come now."

"Why?"

"You'll want to cover this for the paper." Kat ended the call.

"Just when I assumed this day would end on a positive note." Emily popped up and moved toward the door.

Scott grasped her arm. "It's after nine."

"News isn't dictated by the clock, honey. Like Kat said, whatever is going on is a newsworthy story."

"Call Mary. She's a good reporter, and she doesn't have two babies who need their mother."

Emily eyed her husband. "She's leading a Bible study tonight. And in case you didn't notice, I put our daughters to bed an hour ago."

"If you insist on going, I'm going with you."

"How's that going to look—frightened newspaper editor needs chaperone."

Scott released her arm. "How many glasses of wine have you had?"

"One. Two."

"Which means you need a designated driver."

"No, I don't."

"Yes. You do."

"Just go, you two." Rachel grabbed the wine bottle and glasses. "And don't worry about the twins. I'm not going anywhere."

***

During the drive to town, Emily stared out the passenger side window, her arms locked tight across her chest.

Scott remained silent until he parked in front of the hotel, behind the sheriff's patrol car. "I know you're hopping mad, but you need to understand. Crime isn't something we're accustomed to around here, and we don't know what's going on inside."

"Did you forget that last year a tourist nearly destroyed the hotel?"

"One big reason why I'm not letting you go in there alone."

Emily's eyes probed his. "I know you want to keep me safe. Just promise me you won't interfere with my job as a reporter."

"You know I won't."

Emily slung her purse over her shoulder. "Time to find out what hard-core criminal is lurking in the hotel's shadows."

They entered the lobby and passed guests huddled in small groups. The desk clerk nodded to the right. "The sheriff took them all to the ballroom."

"Thanks." Emily removed a notepad and pen from her purse. "What do you suppose he means by all?"

"Maybe Mitch broke up a notorious theft ring."

"That would definitely make the front page."

As they neared the open door, a cacophony of high-pitched female voices drifted into the hall, abruptly interrupted by the sheriff's loud voice. "Everyone sit down and be quiet."

Inside, five teenage girls wearing T-shirts sporting Justin Brooks' picture dropped onto chairs set in a row. Kat stood to their right, a deputy at her side. Justin, dressed in jeans and a sweatshirt—his hair wet, feet bare, thumbs hooked in his pockets—stood beside the deputy.

Mitch sat in a chair facing the girls, his right fist on his hip, his left arm planted across his thigh. Five cell phones lay on the floor beside him. He pointed to the girl sitting on the end. "What's your name, young lady?"

"Bonnie. Sir."

"I'm designating you as the spokesperson for this gang of break-in artists. Start from the beginning."

"Like we told you, it's a teacher's workday. So, we drove up from Atlanta."

"You're all in high school, right?"

"Yes, sir."

"And your parents gave you permission to stay overnight?"

Bonnie glanced at her friends, then back at Mitch. "They ... uh ... don't exactly know we're here."

"Exactly where do they think you're hanging out?"

Emily leaned close to Scott. "So much for a gang of thieves."

Bonnie leaned forward and pointed to the girl sitting on the other end of the row. "At her house."

Mitch turned his head toward the girl. "And your parents didn't notice you were all missing?"

She shrugged. "They're sort of ... out of town."

"Which means you're all here without your parents' permission." Mitch shook his head and turned back toward Bonnie. "What did you do when you arrived?"

"My friends hung out by Justin's trailer while I checked into the room next to his. Like, we're all in his fan club."

The girls erupted in a flurry of comments.

Mitch straightened his back and held his hands up. "Silence."

The chatter stopped.

"Can you restrain yourselves for five minutes or do I need to send my deputy for a roll of Duct Tape?"

Scott chuckled.

Emily shot him a stern look.

The girls rolled their eyes and mumbled.

"Starting now," Mitch demanded.

Silence.

"Okay. Let's try this again." Mitch pointed his finger at Bonnie. "After you checked in, what happened?"

She eyed Mitch. "The other girls kind of sneaked into the hotel and up the back stairs. We just wanted to meet Justin and take some pictures."

Emily noted Kat's amused expression and wondered what she was thinking.

Mitch glared at Bonnie. "How did you end up in Mr. Brooks' room?"

"Tiffany watched a YouTube video about how to pick locks." Bonnie fidgeted. "And ... well ... there was this door between our room and his."

"How did you know it was his room?"

"Like, some kid in your town posted it on social media."

"Bet it was Connor," whispered Scott.

Mitch glared at Bonnie. "So, you came here intending to break in?"

"No, sir." Bonnie shrugged. "It just kind of happened. Sir."

"I see. And when you broke into his room and heard the shower, you didn't stop to think it might be smart to get the heck out of there?"

Bonnie lowered her chin. "I guess not."

Mitch pointed to the pile of cell phones. "What were you planning to do with the photos you shot of Justin walking out of the shower?"

The girls glanced at each other, shuffling in their seats.

Mitch pushed up from the chair. "Are you aware that breaking and entering is a felony?"

"We didn't steal anything." Bonnie's voice trembled. "We just wanted to ..."

"What? Invade his privacy?"

"Touch his things ... and ... you know ... take lots of pictures."

Mitch walked from one end of the row to the other, eyeing each girl like a drill sergeant inspecting new recruits.

Two offenders chewed their nails. One picked at a cuticle. A fourth hugged her chest.

Mitch nodded toward Justin. "Mr. Brooks, do you want to press charges against these criminals?"

The actor unhooked his thumbs.

The girls stared at him, wide-eyed.

He shrugged. "They didn't mean any harm."

Mitch stepped toward him. "Is that a yes or a no, young man?"

"A no."

"Okay then. Here's what's going to happen." Mitch faced the girls, his tone stern. "You're each going to call your parents from my office, tell them what you've done, and request they come up and bail you out of jail."

Bonnie wiped tears from her cheeks. "Jail? Are you arresting us?"

"You broke the law, young lady. While you're waiting for your parents to arrive, maybe you'll decide what you did isn't cool or smart." Mitch instructed his deputy to escort the intruders to jail.

Emily snapped photos of the girls shuffling from the ballroom. "So much for taking down a serious crime ring." She caught Mitch's eye. "Are you really arresting them?"

He shook his head. "Just scaring them straight."

Kat approached Justin. "On behalf of our entire staff, I apologize."

"No big deal."

"We don't want it happening again." She gave him a key card. "To the room next to yours. No one will occupy it until you leave."

"Thanks." He pocketed the card and left the room.

"At least they aren't local girls." Emily viewed the photos she had snapped. "The headline 'Five Teens Jailed for Breaking and Entering' is likely to send the town into chaos."

"Run the story on page one." Mitch gathered the cell phones. "Let everyone assume they were arrested. With any luck, the news will keep our kids from crossing the line."

Emily eyed Mitch. "You do know rumors about tonight will run rampant before the *Willow Post* is printed?"

"I'm counting on it."

Chapter 49

*E*mily stood at the *Willow Post* window, pressed her fingers into her lower back, and stretched her shoulder muscles. Three ladies she didn't recognize stopped to stare. She smiled and waved at them. They waved back. "What do you suppose tourists expect to see in a newspaper office?"

"Beats me." Mary scooted her chair away from the table. "Antoine's Amazing Beauty Bash ad is ready for your review."

Emily moseyed to the table and reviewed the announcement. "Good work, Mary."

"About the front-page story. Do you still want to print the shot of Mitch sitting beside a pile of cell phones, pointing his finger?"

"Definitely." Emily sat across from Mary and closed her laptop. "It sends a clear message about the consequences of breaking the law without revealing the girls' identities."

"Makes sense." Mary laced her fingers and stretched her arms out. "This week's release can't come soon enough. The rumors about the break-in are spreading faster than a brush fire in a field of dried hay."

"Some of the stories floating around are so far beyond nuts they defy logic." Emily glanced at her watch. "I'm going to meet Scott for lunch. With the store generating enough business to support two more employees, he broke down and agreed to take a break."

"All the hours he works, he deserves some time off."

"Yes, he does. As an added bonus, Gertie now has someone besides Scott to talk to when there's a lull."

"That will save him a heap of time." Mary placed her hands on her laptop keyboard. "You go enjoy lunch. I'll take care of everything in here."

"You're the best." Emily slipped her phone in her jeans pocket. "I'll see you in a couple of hours." She waved as she made her way to the door. When she stepped onto the sidewalk and turned toward the park, she spotted JT leading his noon tour group across the street to the Willow Falls Historical Museum. One of the ladies raised her hand.

"Yes, ma'am, you have a question?"

"Rumor is those girls that paraded through the hotel lobby last night stole all of Justin Brooks' clothes. Is that true?"

"I heard he invited them to his room for a private party," said a man wearing an Atlanta Braves ball cap. "When he found out they were teenagers, he panicked and called the sheriff."

Another woman shook her head. "These Hollywood types are full of themselves. Why can't they act normal like the rest of us?"

Where do people come up with this stuff?

A flurry of comments erupted.

JT emitted a two-finger whistle. "All I know is the real story will show up in tomorrow's local newspaper. In the meantime, I have a lot of cool stuff to tell you about our town." He caught Emily's eye, winked, then diverted the crowd's attention to the museum window and began his spiel.

Emily moved past the group, relieved no one recognized her. She rounded the corner and spotted Scott scooting between parked cars. He stepped onto the sidewalk in front of the café. She rushed to catch up with him.

"Good timing. Are you hungry?"

"Starving." She slipped her hand in his.

Inside Pepper's Café, they found two empty seats at the counter. Emily sat beside Mirabelle and stared at her new look. "Wow. I almost didn't recognize you."

The woman's face beamed. "My husband says I look like a movie star."

Scott rested his forearm on the counter and peered around Emily. "He's right, you do."

Mirabelle's cheeks pinkened. "No one ever taught me how to put makeup on. I still don't really know."

"In that case," Emily said, "you'll like the announcement in tomorrow's paper."

"About what?"

"You'll see. Rumor is you're taking your role as forewoman seriously."

"I'm more than an actress." Mirabelle's chest puffed. "I'm kind of like the director's advisor."

Emily pressed her lips tight to thwart a laugh.

"So we hear," Scott said. "By the way, we miss your postal delivery expertise. Your replacement seems to scramble the mail a little more every day."

"Everyone thinks delivering mail is easy. It takes a lot of experience to do the job right." Mirabelle glanced around, then leaned close to Emily. "Have you heard the latest?"

There she goes, charging back into her role as the town's gossip queen. "About what? Or should I say whom?"

"Brick's ex."

The hair on the back of Emily's neck bristled. "Can't say that I have."

"Well, it seems one of the crew members couldn't sleep, so he went for a walk. At four. This morning." Mirabelle's voice lowered. "He saw Cynthia." She spat the name. "Leaving Brick's house. Returning to the hotel."

That's not good. "I imagine there's a logical explanation."

Mirabelle's eyes narrowed. "Did you hear what I said? He saw her at four a.m. Why would she be sneaking out of his house before dawn?"

Emily's pulse accelerated as she stared at the menu the waitress laid in front of her. She forced her eyes to scan the list of entrees, hoping to keep her head from exploding with unacceptable possibilities.

Mirabelle squeezed lemon into her iced tea. "My friends and I are making signs and plan to stage a protest outside the hotel first thing tomorrow morning. That'll draw Cynthia's attention and drive her out of town." She glanced at her watch before quickly sliding off her stool. "Time to return to the courthouse for my afternoon shoot."

When Mirabelle was gone, Emily pushed the menu aside. "I've a good mind to make a sign and join the protest."

Scott's shoulders visibly drooped. "So much for a relaxing lunch."

"Sorry, honey." She inched her face close to his. "How's everything going for the world's most handsome, number-one husband?"

"You're over-compensating."

She squeezed his knee. "Are you complaining?"

"Observing."

The waitress arrived and placed two glasses of water on the counter. "Mirabelle looks amazing, don't you think? Rumor is Antoine's going to make all us ladies look good. What can I bring you two?"

Moments after they placed their orders, Sheriff Mitch wandered in. He sat beside Emily and ordered cherry pie with ice cream.

Emily laughed. "I see you still like to start with dessert."

"Start and finish. Don't tell Pepper. She'll make me eat kale for a week."

"For good reason." Emily reached for her glass. "Have all of Justin's groupies returned home?"

"Last girl left an hour ago. Her parents were plenty ticked about cutting their trip to Napa Valley short. They threatened to ground her 'til she's twenty-one." His shoulder mic squawked. "Second fender bender this week. My deputy will handle it."

Memories of another accident skated into Emily's conscience. "At least the town hasn't suffered from a fatal wreck since ... my parents were forced off the road at Devil's Curve."

Scott reached for her hand and kissed her fingers. "I love that you can finally talk about it without falling to pieces."

"Time and faith heal even the most broken hearts." *Maybe the same will happen with Mama Sadie.*

Scott released Emily's hand as the waitress placed a slice of pie in front of Mitch. "That's what I call a proper lunch."

"I do believe Mitch is on to something." Emily picked up the menu again. "In fact, I'm canceling my salad and ordering a piece of lemon meringue pie. With all the drama going on around here, I'm in the mood for a high-calorie, lemony sugar rush."

Chapter 50

Snippets of chatter about the break-in and Antoine's Amazing Beauty Bash accosted Rachel the moment she arrived for the final day of courtroom filming. The rustle of newsprint solidified Emily's declaration about job security. Despite the national decline of physical newspapers, the *Willow Post* remained the town's prime source of accurate information.

Rachel scooted into the last row beside Carrie and set her purse on the floor. She spotted Justin leaning against the witness stand, talking to the director. "What's the male lead's take on last night's hotel caper?"

"His social media post says it all." Carrie handed her phone to Rachel.

She stared at the photo of the bare-chested actor, his muscles flexed. "For my loyal fans who risked arrest to capture a candid shot of their favorite leading man," she read. "Talk about an inflated ego."

"He's a master at self-promotion." Carrie lowered her voice. "Has he hit on you yet?"

Rachel shook her head and returned Carrie's phone. "He knows I'm engaged to Charlie."

"Which makes you that much more enticing. Are you aware both his ex-wives were love interests in the movies they were filming? He lured them during their love scenes."

"What about you?" Rachel glanced at the actress. "Based on what I've read in the script, your romantic scenes with Mr. Big Ego are way more passionate than mine."

"We were an item a while back. In between his wives. Photos of us showed up in gossip magazines and everywhere on social media. Great publicity for both of us." Carrie stashed her phone in her purse and laid

228

it on the floor beside Rachel's. "There's an animal magnetism about him ... consider this fair warning."

"Thanks, but I doubt he'll try anything."

"His first wife was blonde, the second brunette." Carrie pointed to Rachel's hair. "He hasn't snared a redhead ... yet."

"Trust me. He won't snare this one."

"Maybe so, but I'll be shocked if he doesn't try."

As Robert announced the first scene, Rachel found it difficult to shake the image of Justin's bare chest and seductive grin. Their one love scene was scheduled for the following night in the park. She had made it clear her heart belonged to Charlie during lunch following his helicopter arrival. He wouldn't try anything foolish. Would he?

Rachel squeezed her eyes shut until the mental image disappeared and the director called her to move into position behind the defense table.

Carrie settled in the defendant's chair.

Justin stood at the witness stand, ready for the morning's first scene. When he caught Rachel staring at him, he grinned and winked.

Heat rose from her neck to her cheeks. Maybe he forgot about her engagement to Charlie. She had to set him straight. Tomorrow. She blinked and diverted her eyes to a camera operator, vowing to ignore the self-absorbed actor until the script called for their interaction. She leaned back and focused on the cast sitting in the jury box.

During the morning session, Rachel mentally applauded Robert when he cut Mirabelle's one interruption short by motioning her to write her suggestion on a notepad. At four-thirty, he called a wrap and thanked the extras for their participation and patience.

Rachel scooted to the back row, grabbed her purse, and dashed from the courtroom to avoid contact with Justin.

Carrie caught up with her. "What's the rush? Do you have a hot date?"

"No. I mean ... yes. I'm meeting Charlie for dinner at five."

"Lucky you. I'm spending the next couple of hours rehearsing with social media's self-appointed sensation."

"Justin?" Rachel glanced at tourists attempting to peer into Carrie's RV.

"None other. At least we both know there's a better chance Martians will invade the earth than the two of us entering into another romantic relationship."

"Bad breakup?"

"Mutual understanding. Gotta run. Have fun tonight. I'll see you tomorrow." Carrie stepped away and poured on the charm for another group of tourists begging for autographs and selfies.

The price of fame. Rachel made her way to the hotel and entered the lobby. With a few minutes to spare, she settled on the circular seat under the chandelier and dug her phone from her purse. Three texts. One from Emily, another from Kat, a third from Pepper. All with the same message. *Cynthia has checked out.*

Relief surged through her limbs until she looked up and saw Charlie's pinched expression. "You look like you swallowed a stinkbug."

"My mother checked out of the hotel—"

"I know."

"Dad's not answering his phone. We need to find him."

Rachel bolted to her feet. "You don't think he left with her, do you?"

"I don't know what to think." Charlie led her toward the door. At the corner, he waited for the traffic to pass, then held her arm as they crossed Main Street and closed the distance to Brick's front porch.

Charlie rang the bell twice before pounding the antique knocker.

No response.

"We're going in." He fished a key from his pocket and thrust it into the lock.

Rachel stepped into the foyer, quaking at the ominous silence.

Charlie charged upstairs and returned moments later, shaking his head. They searched the rooms on the main level, ending in the kitchen. A coffee cup with a lipstick imprint sat on the counter beside the sink. A lamp on the island spilled light onto the granite countertop. "This isn't good."

Rachel's heart jumped to her throat at the sight of a folded sheet of paper with the name of Brick's housekeeper scrawled across it. She pointed. "Look."

After Charlie read it, he dropped it on the counter and dashed out the back door.

Rachel grabbed the note. Her hands trembled as she read Brick's words. *I need to take care of some business in Atlanta. Not sure when I'll return. No need to change the sheets.*

Charlie bounded back inside. "His car is still in the garage."

"They left together in Cynthia's Beamer."

He dropped onto a barstool and massaged his temples. "Maybe it's for the best."

Rachel glared at him. "How can you say that?"

"If he's determined to run off with my mother, it's better he does it quickly. Like ripping off a bandage."

Rachel's shoulders curled forward. "I'm beginning to think Emily was right. The man who broke Mama Sadie's heart isn't welcome in her home."

Charlie's face reddened. "What about you, Rachel? Are you planning to ban my father from our home too?"

She turned away from him. "I don't know what I'm going to do."

"I suggest you figure it out before we get married." He stormed out of the kitchen.

The front door slamming shut sent icy cold shivers up Rachel's spine. She buried her head in her hands as tears erupted and dripped onto the counter. How could so much go so wrong weeks before her wedding. She pulled her phone from her purse and pressed Emily's number.

Rachel sniffled when Emily answered. "He's gone."

"Who?"

"Brick. He left town with Cynthia."

"How do you know?"

Rachel swiped her fingers under her nose, then read Brick's note. "Cynthia is more manipulative than we imagined. Unless ..." She looked at the lipstick-stained cup. "He never stopped loving her."

Chapter 51

The sun had reached its peak when Emily and Rachel carried the twins up the stairs to Mama Sadie's apartment. Inside, Emily watched Clair and Jane scramble to the basket of toys their grandma kept in the corner. "Spending time with her grandbabies always warms her heart."

"Here's hoping it works again today." Rachel's phone pinged a text.

Emily removed two juice boxes from the fridge. "From Charlie?"

Rachel shook her head. "Carrie."

"How long are you planning to wait for him to make the first move?"

"As long as it takes."

Emily carried the juice boxes to the babies. "I can't believe you're letting Brick's insane disappearance tear you and Charlie apart."

"He stormed out on me, not the other way around." Rachel tossed her phone onto the love seat. "The ball's in his court."

"If you ask me—"

"I didn't."

Pepper swept into the apartment carrying a plate of cookies and a pitcher of lemonade. She eyed Emily, then Rachel. "How do you two expect to cheer Sadie up when you look like you've been sucking lemons and sour pickles?" She removed plastic wrap from the plate and set it on the coffee table.

Emily breathed in the chocolate and brown sugar scents. "From Patsy's?"

Pepper nodded. "Her newest recipe. If grandbabies and sweets don't put Sadie in a good mood, nothing will."

"Except a surprise birthday party." Emily caught sight of her mother climbing the stairs. "She's on her way up."

"Then I suggest you and Rachel put on your happy faces." Pepper carried four glasses from the kitchen and filled each with lemonade.

The door opened. Mama Sadie stepped inside and meandered to the coffee table. Her face wore a scowl and not a stitch of makeup. She glared at the three women. "Is this a pity party or another intervention?"

"More like a southern-style tea party," Pepper said around a mouthful of cookie.

Emily flinched at her mother's appearance. She hadn't seen her without makeup in more than a year. Slumped shoulders and a harsh tone invoked memories of the weeks following her parole—weeks when she didn't trust anyone other than Pepper and Mitch. She snagged two cookies and plopped on the floor beside her granddaughters.

The girls giggled with delight and climbed onto their grandma's lap.

Pepper sat beside her friend.

Intense anger at Brick sent pain shooting up the back of Emily's neck. She dashed to the kitchen counter. Gripping the edge, she stared out the window at the lake, glistening like millions of sparkling diamonds floating on the surface.

Rachel moved beside her carrying a glass and a cookie. "Our mother has aged ten years overnight." Her voice came out barely above a whisper. "It's criminal how much damage Cynthia caused."

"Too bad there isn't a law against what she did."

"We should lobby for one. It would keep men from falling victim to seductive women." Rachel set the glass on the counter. "Or vulnerable women from succumbing to charming, egotistical men."

"You're talking about tonight's love scene with Justin, aren't you?" Emily released her grip and stared at her sister.

"Forget it." Rachel handed over the cookie.

Resisting the urge to probe, Emily glanced at her daughters chattering with their grandma. "If Brick brings Cynthia back to that house down the street ... Charlie has to keep her away from Willow Falls."

"What makes you think he has any say in the matter?"

"He owes it to all of us to at least try." Emily held the cookie inches from her mouth. "Right now, it's up to us to act normal."

Rachel sighed. "I don't know what normal is anymore."

"That makes two of us." Emily crammed half the cookie in her mouth. The chunks of chocolate melting on her tongue failed to ease her angst. She swallowed, then polished off half the lemonade in one long guzzle.

Rachel snickered. "Good thing that's not laced with vodka."

"Too bad it's not." Emily wiped her mouth with the back of her hand.

They moved to the other end of the room. Rachel opted for a spot on the floor beside Pepper. Emily sat eye-level across from her mother.

Clair selected a book from the toy basket and climbed back onto her grandma's lap. Mama Sadie opened to the first page. As she read, the words rang hollow. Her smile didn't reach her eyes.

Pepper's arm slipped around her friend's shoulders as if she sensed the struggle with internal turmoil.

After reading the last page, Mama Sadie laid the book down and locked eyes with her daughter. In that moment, Emily recognized such intense sadness, she feared nothing would mend her mother's shattered heart. Worried her own emotions were seconds from exploding, she pushed off the floor and dashed through the bedroom to the bathroom.

She closed the door, gaped at her image, and imagined staring at her twin. "No matter what it takes, we have to find a way to entice Charlie's dad to come back to our mother."

The image staring back at her refused to answer, solidifying one devastating fact. It was beyond their ability to force Brick to do anything he had no intention of doing.

Chapter 52

Rachel changed into her costume before checking her phone for the fourth time. Still no response from Charlie. *What made me think texting him with a reminder about tonight's shoot was a good idea?* She stashed the phone, engagement ring, and keys in a locker. When she stepped from the wardrobe trailer into the cool night air, a golf cart waited to transport her one block to the film's location. She ignored the driver and forged ahead, counting on a brisk walk to ease her anxiety.

She passed the playhouse and paused in front of Pearl's salon. At least news about Antoine's Amazing Beauty Bash—thanks to Robert Nordstrom's generosity—had been well received by the town's female population. She resumed her pace. At the corner, she crossed the section of cordoned-off Main Street and halted at the park's edge.

Crowds of local and out-of-town observers gathered on the sidewalk, gawking and pointing at the unfolding scene. Tall lights illuminated a section of retaining wall at the water's edge and a blocked-off section of sidewalk fronting Hayes General Store. Sound equipment mounted to booms loomed large. Camera operators, crew members, and the director moved in a flurry of activity.

Reality sent a shiver surging through Rachel's limbs. Robert expected her to deliver a convincing love scene under the scrutiny of a horde of onlookers—with a man known for his romantic prowess. She closed her eyes, filled her lungs, and slowly released air through pursed lips. *You can do this.*

A hand touching her back made her flinch. She opened her eyes and whirled around.

"Perfect night for a hot love scene."

The overpowering scent of Justin's cologne filled her nostrils. She resisted the urge to flee. "You know your character is scripted to act aloof and distracted."

"And yours is desperate to hold on to me."

"Which will take a persuasive acting job."

He grinned. "Because you haven't played a jealous girlfriend, or you've never been one?"

"Yes." *Get a grip Rachel.* "I mean no." Her back stiffened.

"You're way too uptight." His hand moved along her spine to the base of her neck. "A Justin-style massage will relax your tense muscles."

Don't let him get to you. "No thanks. Although I will take a cup of ginger tea. If you have one."

"I'll call my assistant—"

"I'm kidding. And my muscles are fine, thank you." She twisted away from him and headed to the lake.

Justin quickly caught up with her. "I see your point. Physical tension adds dimension to love scenes."

Ignore him. Focus on remembering your lines. She moderated her pace as they closed in on the director.

Robert looked up from his clipboard. "Are you ready, Rachel?"

"Yes, sir."

"Good. We'll start with shots of you entering the park."

She followed Robert to the setting beside Scott's store. For the next hour she poured her energy into action shots and close-ups. When the scenes ended, she mentally patted herself on the back for what she knew had been a good performance. *Okay, Mr. Justin Brooks, I'm ready to take you on.*

A half-hour later, Robert relayed directions about the love scene from a tall director's chair. "Roll cameras. Action."

Justin—his left foot propped on the retaining wall, his forearms resting on his thigh—faced the water.

Rachel slipped into character. She sat on the wall facing away from the water and delivered her first line. Following six more takes, with varying camera angles, they moved to the next scene. Justin lowered his foot to the ground and turned toward her.

This is it. The first move. As directed, she placed her hand on his cheek and looked into his eyes.

A camera moved close.

Three more takes.

I can make it through this.

Robert clarified his expectation for the next shot.

Rachel nodded. She laced her fingers behind Justin's neck and pulled his face toward hers until their lips touched. They repeated the move four times before Robert shouted *cut*.

While the cameras repositioned, Justin leaned close to Rachel's ear. "The next scene won't be easy."

"Why? Is the great Justin Brooks scared of a love scene?"

"That's not the problem." His arm slipped around her waist. He pulled her close. "Coming across as aloof after a passionate kiss with the most beautiful redhead I've ever met will take every ounce of acting skill I have."

Heat crept up Rachel's neck.

Justin tenderly stroked her cheek as his warm breath mingled with hers. "You felt it too. Didn't you?"

"What? No." She pressed her hands to his chest and pushed hard.

Robert slid off his chair and stepped beside them. "Is there a problem over here?"

"Nope." Justin smirked. "Just getting in the mood."

The director focused on Rachel. "Is that what's going on?"

"I ..." She hesitated. "Yes."

Robert frowned at both of them as if not sure what to believe. He returned to his chair.

Rachel crossed her arms and shifted her focus to the crowd on the sidewalk. Her eyes landed on a man sitting on the grass under a streetlight, his arms propped across his knees. *Is that ... Charlie?* She blinked. "I don't believe it," she muttered.

Justin's eyes widened. "My comment or your feelings?"

"Everything's not about you." She glared at Charlie. How dare he ignore her text and show up here unannounced. *If that's the way he wants to play this, I'll give him something to see.* She moved closer to Justin. "So, how do you gear up for passionate kissing scenes?"

"Is this an invitation—"

"Ease up, cowboy. It's nothing more than professional curiosity."

"You are one interesting woman." He reached for her hand and held it to his lips. His eyes met hers. "First, I imagine I'm alone with an intensely sensual woman whose touch sends electric shockwaves through me. When my imagination and reality meet, like tonight, it results in an explosive, award-worthy scene."

"Oh." Rachel looked away.

"Okay, you two lovebirds," Robert said. "Take your positions."

Rachel placed her laced fingers behind Justin's neck and moved her face inches from his.

"Action."

They spoke their lines.

Their lips met.

Justin kissed her deeply, passionately.

Everything and everyone around her disappeared until a wave of guilt crashed into her chest.

"Cut. That's a wrap."

"I thought I'd won you over." Justin tilted his head toward the sidewalk. "Until I realized you were aiming for the jealous angle. I saw your guy sitting over there. Raw emotions make for great camera shots."

She eyed him warily. "Was that your objective all along?"

He brushed a strand of hair away from her cheek. With a mischievous grin, he turned and strode away.

Her eyes followed him until he passed the crew scurrying to dismantle the set. *He really is a cowboy.* Rachel shook his image from her mind, squared her shoulders, and geared herself for a confrontation with Charlie. She scooted around a cameraman packing his gear, expecting to find him still sitting on the grass. He wasn't. She scanned the exiting crowd. No sign of him.

By the time she covered the distance to the wardrobe trailer, her anger threatened to boil over. She opened the locker, slipped her ring on, and grabbed her phone. No new calls or texts. She changed clothes, dashed to her car, and started the engine.

Her pulse pounded as she drilled her fingers on the steering wheel and waffled between driving to Charlie's to give him a piece of her mind and returning to her sister's home. "If he's going to act like a jilted teenager every time I perform in a love scene ... he can stew in his own immature juices." She put her car in gear and drove straight to Emily's.

Chapter 53

*E*mily stretched her legs across the living room couch, rested her head on the arm, and inserted earbuds. She closed her eyes and laid the back of her hand across her forehead. A long list of obligations wrestled its way to the surface, making it difficult to mentally focus. She willed her mind to dismiss the inventory and concentrate. It worked until a gentle touch on her arm forced her eyes open. "Hey, Sis." She removed the earbuds.

"Are you listening to country-western or pop?"

"A how-to-market-books tutorial." Emily sat up and swung her legs to the floor.

"Isn't ten-thirty a bit late for serious study?"

"Not when it's the only free time on my bloated calendar. How'd the shoot go?"

"Glad it's over." Rachel set her keys and phone on the end table and sat beside her sister. Brownie settled at her feet.

"Did Justin hit on you?"

"Hard to tell." Rachel relayed details.

"Oh yeah, he hit on you big time."

Rachel leaned back. "Charlie showed up."

"I knew reaching out to him was a good idea. Who apologized first?"

Rachel's shoulders slumped. "He disappeared before we had a chance to talk."

"Oh." Emily propped her elbow on the back of the couch. She stared at her sister. Time for a pep talk.

"What?"

"Did I ever tell you about the huge fight Scott and I had two weeks before our wedding?"

"Over what?"

"An offhand remark he made about one of my bridesmaids. A gorgeous blonde who had the hots for him. She moved away six months later. Anyway, my point is watching you in a love scene with a gorgeous hunk like Justin likely shoved Charlie's jealousy button to the edge."

"Or here's another explanation." Rachel scoffed. "He's having second thoughts about marrying me."

"You don't really believe that?"

"Why not?" Rachel fingered her engagement ring. "His mother might have soured him on the whole idea of marriage."

"Charlie loves you way too much to call it quits. You need to call him."

"Why should I?"

"The real question is, why shouldn't you?"

"Because I'm not the one who ran off. Twice."

"Suit yourself." Emily lowered her arm. "All I'm saying is if I were in your shoes—and we do wear the same size—I'd be making that call."

"I'm not you." Rachel broke eye contact. "Besides, maybe I'm the one who's having second thoughts about marriage."

"Not after all those hours Mama Sadie, Pepper, and I have spent planning your wedding—"

"You mean the country-fried spectacle?" Rachel's tone screamed of sarcasm.

"No point talking to you 'til you ditch the mood you're in." Emily pushed off the sofa. "I'm going to crawl in bed beside the man I love." She took a step, then halted. "I suggest you climb into your *empty* bed and remember all the reasons you fell in love with Charlie Bricker."

***

Emily's comment drove a stake in Rachel's heart. She grabbed her phone, headed to the kitchen, and flipped the patio light on. The night air cooled her skin, causing goose bumps to pop up on her arms as she stepped out and dropped into a chair.

Brownie planted a paw on Rachel's lap. Her tail thumped the concrete in a lazy rhythm.

She scratched Brownie's muzzle while watching a drifting cloud dim the moonlight. Deep down, she yearned to hear Charlie's voice. She stared at her phone, her finger poised an inch above his number.

Warning bells erupted in her head. What if she misspoke, said something to upset him? That would definitely push him over the edge. Damage their relationship. Maybe it was best to give him time to deal with his emotions.

The hoot of a distant owl added an eerie vibe to the quiet night. Rachel closed her eyes as images of Charlie danced in her head. His smile and easy-going manner. The way he held her in his arms. Tomorrow she would find him and explain that the love scene with Justin was an act. Nothing more.

Chapter 54

$\mathcal{B}$rownie's whimper pierced the fog in Rachel's head and nudged her awake. She glanced at the clock on the nightstand. "No wonder you're stressed." She slid out of bed, scurried to the kitchen, and opened the sliding door. Brownie bounded out to the back yard.

"I assume there's nothing on your calendar this morning." Emily set a plate of melon and banana slices on Jane and Clair's play table.

"Not 'til tonight's play." Rachel yawned. "I can't believe I slept past ten."

"Based on the dark circles under your eyes, I'm guessing you had a restless night. Exhaustion? Guilty conscience? Or did you and Charlie talk for hours?"

Rachel pulled a mug from the cabinet and poured a cup of coffee. "Thanks for keeping the pot turned on."

Emily's brows went up. "You didn't call him, did you?"

"It was too late."

"Now's a good time."

Rachel stirred honey and vanilla creamer into her mug. "He's entertaining winery visitors."

"My sister, the queen of ridiculous excuses."

Rachel huffed. "You know Saturday is his busiest day."

"You'd best not wait too long."

A muffled bark drew Rachel's attention. "Right now, I have to feed Brownie." She slid the door open, then scooped food into her dog's bowl.

"Since your afternoon seems to be free, will you watch Jane and Clair for a couple of hours? I need uninterrupted time to finish plotting my second novel?"

"On one condition. You stop bugging me about calling Charlie."

"You drive a hard bargain." Emily moved dishes from the sink to the dishwasher.

"Then we have a deal?"

"At least for today," Emily said.

"I'll take my darling nieces to visit their grandma."

"Good idea. Mama Sadie needs serious cheering up."

"That makes two of us." Rachel plucked a banana off the counter and headed to the hall bath. She closed the door behind her and leaned close to the mirror to stare at the dark circles under her eyes. "You're gonna need a ton of concealer." She turned on the shower, shed her pajamas, and stepped into the tub. As hot water rained down her body, she closed her eyes and imagined walking toward Charlie, her wedding gown brushing the white cloth spread along the parking lot aisle. Emily was right. If he didn't call soon, she needed to swallow her pride and make the first move.

***

Rachel held her nieces' hands as they walked into Willow Inn's parlor, where they found Mama Sadie settled on a wingback chair, holding a children's book. Clair and Jane pulled away and made a beeline to their grandma's lap. Rachel sat on the settee and studied her mother's face, scrubbed clean. When she began to read, her voice hinted of cheerfulness, yet her lips failed to curve into a smile.

When Mama Sadie finished the story and closed the book, the twins climbed down and scurried to the toy basket. She followed them with her eyes. "Maggie carried on about you during breakfast."

"Uh oh, what did I do?"

"Oh, nothing much." Maggie's voice sounded behind Rachel. The actress settled on the wingback chair beside Sadie. "Just impressed the dickens out of our director last night. Robert said for someone with no movie experience, you knew how to play to the camera."

"That's a shocker. Especially since love scenes make me more than a little uncomfortable."

"I never liked them much myself," Maggie said. "Anyway, I have a feeling you have a bright future ahead of you."

"Right now, my future is one giant question mark."

Her mother's eyes widened. "You *are* talking about acting, right?"

What are you doing? Mama Sadie doesn't need to add worrying about me to her troubles. "Of course." Desperate to change the subject, she shifted her attention to Maggie. "When do you shoot your next scene?"

"Tomorrow at Brick's house. Like I told your mom, he likely left town to avoid the hassle."

"Bless her heart." A smirk contradicted Mama Sadie's syrupy-sweet tone. "My friend is trying to make sugar out of a mason jar full of vinegar."

"Hey." Maggie knuckled Mama Sadie's arm. "When he returns in a couple of days, you'll find out I'm right."

"And when he doesn't, you'll know I've been dumped like a truck full of old worn-out tires."

Her mother's tone sent a shockwave charging through Rachel. "That's not true—"

"No need to comment, honey." She glanced toward her grandbabies. "Truth is, I was foolish to think I had a future with an upstanding man like Reginald Bricker."

Rachel gripped the settee arm. "He's the fool for letting Cynthia lure him back into her web."

"I know you're angry, but it isn't wise to say unkind things about your future father-in-law." Mama Sadie shrugged. "What I'm trying to say is you can't let our damaged friendship destroy your relationship with Charlie."

Rachel choked back tears. "Maybe Maggie's right about Brick leaving to avoid movie madness."

"I've come to terms that he's gone for good. So please do me a favor and quit fretting about me. After spending thirty years behind bars, I'm an honest-to-goodness survivor."

Clair toddled from the toy basket, carrying a book. "Read me a story, Grandma."

"You picked a good one, sweetheart." She scooped her granddaughter onto her lap and opened the book.

Rachel moved to the bay window overlooking the front porch. Dark clouds drifting in from the west mirrored the gloomy atmosphere in the parlor.

Maggie stepped beside her. "Your mother is an amazing woman."

"She deserves better."

Mittens abandoned her spot on the railing and sprang to the windowsill. Maggie tapped the glass and drew a feline stare. "Seems the inn's watch cat is anticipating rain."

"Thank goodness we filmed the park scene last night."

"Timing is everything." Maggie pursed her lips. "Rumor is you put Justin in his place."

Rachel jerked her head toward Maggie. "What do you mean? And who told you that?"

"The film crew is trained to pay close attention. You'd be surprised how much they catch, especially when they're filming a known womanizer."

"Did my shove clue them in?"

Maggie grinned. "That, plus his over-the-top swagger when he walked away from you. Anyway, kudos for not swelling his already inflated ego."

Rachel shrugged. "Carrie warned me ahead of time."

"I hope you don't let men like him scare you away from the entertainment world. If that's still your dream."

"Funny how dreams live and die with life's changing seasons."

Maggie remained silent for a long moment. "Do you mind if this ready-to-retire lady gives you a piece of advice?"

"Of course not."

"If your dreams are rooted in natural gifts, no one can steal them from you."

Rachel let the comment resonate. "How did you become so wise?"

"Tons of experience and more than a few years under my belt."

Lightning followed by distant thunder conjured images of the night Cynthia barged into her and Charlie's life. Eager to talk to him, she stepped into the foyer and pressed his number. The call went straight to voicemail.

Chapter 55

Rachel parked behind the Willow Falls playhouse two hours before opening curtain and dropped her keys in her purse. She stared at her phone, lying on the passenger seat. Three times after taking the twins home, she had pressed Charlie's number, with no response. *If I don't hear from him tonight* ... She stuffed her phone in her jacket pocket and dashed to the stage door.

After switching on the backstage lights, she stepped onto the stage. Set for act one, it depicted a posh nineteenth-century living room. She ran her fingers along the gold brocade fabric covering the antique sofa as audience raves about the sets and performance came to mind. It still warmed her heart every time someone admitted surprise at finding top-quality theater in a small Georgia town.

A stab of nostalgia rose from her core as Maggie's earlier declaration danced along the edge of her consciousness. Did her dream to act on Broadway sprout from innate talent, or was it nothing more than a fantasy concocted in her childhood imagination?

Tonight's performance was the second time another woman would play Lillian. Perhaps she would regret her decision to abandon the role after the movie crew packed up and left town. Unless her future was destined for films. A figure moving up the aisle interrupted her mental musing. "Hey, Missy."

"Me and Dennis had a big fight." The play's female lead climbed the stage steps. "I don't know if he'll show up tonight."

"He's too conscientious to ditch his responsibility without telling me, and as of ten minutes ago, he hadn't called or texted."

Missy dropped onto the sofa. Her eyes filled with tears. "I'm scared he's gonna break up with me."

"Lovers' spats are normal." Rachel sat beside her protégé and held her hand. "In fact, Charlie and I are dealing with one right now."

The young woman's brows raised. "Really?"

"Uh-huh. A doozy."

"Are you scared?"

Rachel stared at the empty theater and pictured Charlie strolling up the aisle a year earlier, confirming he agreed to play the role of Everett. "Deep love between two people always survives bumpy roads."

"That's kind of what Kat said." Missy sniffed and brushed her fingertips across her cheeks. "She's been like a mother ever since we were in jail together."

"Everyone is delighted you and Kat made Willow Falls your home."

Rachel spotted another figure rushing up the aisle. "I think your young man just arrived."

Dennis dashed up the stairs carrying a bouquet of flowers. He knelt in front of Missy. "I didn't mean what I said. Will you forgive me?"

She slid off the sofa and wrapped her arms around his neck. "A hundred times, yes."

Rachel slipped backstage. Her heart ached to hear Charlie's voice. Yet deep down, a niggling fear gripped her soul. Maybe their love wasn't strong enough to survive a road filled with emotional potholes. Her hands trembled. She clutched a lamppost designated for act three.

The back door swung open. Mirabelle meandered in. She eyed Rachel and halted. "You look pale. Are you sick?"

Rachel released her grip. "I'm fine."

"You're not pregnant ... are you?"

"What? No. Of course not. Why would you even ask such a ridiculous question?"

"I read what goes on with young people these days."

"Every young woman isn't like those you read about, Mirabelle. Besides, you do know I still live with my sister."

"I guess I jumped to the wrong conclusion, except ..."

"Except what?"

"A friend saw your car leaving the winery before the crack of dawn a couple nights ago. But don't you worry, I didn't tell anyone." Mirabelle tucked her purse under her arm and headed to the women's dressing room.

Rachel balled her hands and fought the urge to barge in and give Mirabelle a piece of her mind. *Will I ever adjust to living in a glass bowl?* Determined to keep her cool and avoid a scene, she forced her fingers to uncurl. Within minutes, additional cast and crew members began arriving. She lifted her chin and shifted to director mode.

The increasing flurry of activity did little to ease Rachel's angst. She checked her phone twice, hoping to see a text from Charlie. Each time she shoved it back in her pocket, riddled with disappointment. She peered through a tiny opening between the closed stage curtains and watched guests wander in and fill the rows. Tickets for all except two seats had been sold—the new normal since she and Emily discovered one performance a week generated enough income to cover expenses and pay cast and crew members. In their minds, receiving even small compensation shifted them from amateurs to semi-professionals.

"Everyone's waiting for your pre-performance speech."

Rachel turned toward Mary Dixon, her newly appointed assistant director. "Is it that time already?"

"It is."

"Okay then." She moved backstage and scanned the faces staring at her. *I do love these people.* "Tonight, two hundred and thirty-eight guests are expecting an evening of first-class entertainment. And you ..."

The back door opened, admitting a shaft of light. Charlie stepped inside. He moved behind the crew and leaned his back against the wall.

"I ..." Her voice faltered. She swallowed. "What I mean is ... I'm proud of you and know you will exceed our guests' expectations by a mile. So, go out there and show them what you've got."

Mary slipped her clipboard under her arm. "Okay, everyone, curtain goes up in five."

Rachel waited for the crowd to clear before making her way to Charlie. "Why have you been ignoring me? And why did you disappear after the shoot?"

"We have to talk." He grasped her elbow and led her to a tiny cubby that served as an office. "Look, I admit I acted like a jerk. The mess with Cynthia and Dad. Watching you kiss Justin. The crowds' comments about that love scene."

"You know I was acting."

Charlie ran his fingers through his hair. "That doesn't make it any easier."

Rachel searched for the right words. "You can't come unglued every time I do a love scene."

"The thing is ..." His arms glided around her. He pulled her close. His lips brushed against her ear. "I love you so much it hurts. I don't want anybody or anything to ever come between us."

Every nerve ending in her body came alive. She closed her eyes and melted into his arms. "Is our love strong enough to survive bumps and potholes and whatever else drops in our path? Including a crazy, out-of-control wedding?"

"You bet it is. I arranged a late-night dinner for two after the show."

"A romantic dinner is exactly what we need." Rachel's phone vibrated. She pulled it from her pocket. An unfamiliar number appeared. "Probably a nuisance call." She declined. A moment later it vibrated again. Same number. Then a third time. "Someone is annoyingly persistent."

"Maybe you'd better respond."

"I suppose so." Rachel accepted the call. "Yes, this is Rachel Streetman." She listened. Sweat erupted and ran cold between her shoulder blades. Her hand trembled. "I understand." Her voice shook. "Yes. Okay." She lowered the phone to her side.

Charlie grasped her hand. "What's wrong?"

"My dad." She swallowed the bile burning her throat. "He was ... rushed to the hospital."

"An accident?"

"A massive heart attack." Fear shot through her veins. "We have to leave for Atlanta. Now. In case ... no, he can't die."

"He's tough, sweetheart. Besides, he's too stubborn to give up without a fight."

Mary poked her head around the partition. "Is everything okay?"

"Rachel's father is in the hospital," Charlie answered.

"Oh, my gosh." Mary pressed her hand to her chest. "I'll call Nathan and ask him to notify the prayer team."

"You need to take over Rachel's director duties."

"Of course. Don't either of you worry one second about the play."

Charlie held Rachel's hand as they hurried out the back door and headed to his truck. He drove to the vineyard house so they could pack a change of clothes. Back in the truck, Rachel prepared herself for the painfully long ride to Atlanta.

***

After the call from Rachel, Emily slipped her phone in her pocket and returned to her daughters' bedroom. The pale pink colors, Cinderella castle painted on the wall, and iridescent stars on the ceiling created a momentary refuge from reality.

Scott blew raspberries on Jane's, then Clair's tummy, triggering scrunched noses and heart-warming giggles.

Clair touched her father's cheek. "Do it again, Daddy."

"Time for you and your sister to say your good-night prayers."

The twins climbed into their side-by-side beds and vocalized a few recognizable words in between giggles.

Scott kissed each girl and turned off the overhead light—their signal to lie down—then he slipped away.

Emily tucked them in and moved to the door. She paused to watch Jane rub her eyes and yawn. Clair wrapped her arms around her pink teddy bear. "Good night, precious babies." She pulled the door closed and went to the den where she found Scott sitting on the couch, aiming the remote at the television, scrolling through a list of recordings. "Who called?"

"Rachel."

"During the play? Is there a problem at the theater?"

"Worse." She dropped beside him and relayed the news about Greer.

"That's not good." Scott laid the remote on the end table.

"What's going to happen next?" Emily sighed and laid her head on her husband's shoulder. "A freak tornado ravishing Willow Falls a day before the wedding?"

"That's a little far-fetched."

"So is everything else that's happening around here. Oh, I have to let Robert Nordstrom know what's going on." She sat up, pulled her phone from her pocket, and sent him a text.

"You need to tell Sadie before she hears it from someone else."

"I already called her. Who knows how long Rachel and Charlie will stay in Atlanta? Maybe we should postpone the surprise birthday party?"

"Better to wait a couple days and see what happens."

Her phone pinged an incoming text. "Robert says he's sorry and to keep him in the loop." She tossed her phone aside.

Scott patted Emily's knee. "Know what you need?"

"To watch a funny movie?"

"Pick one out." Scott stood and moved away.

"Where are you going?"

"You'll see."

Emily ambled to a cabinet and scanned the DVD titles from Scott's parents' collection. She selected one and placed it in the player.

Scott returned carrying two bowls and spoons.

"Hot fudge sundaes?"

"With whipped cream. Guaranteed to cheer you up." He sat beside her on the couch and nodded toward the television. "*Arthur.* Mom's all-time favorite comedy."

Emily leaned back and dipped her spoon in the dessert, hoping sugar and laughter would lift her mood as she silently prayed for Rachel's father to recover in time to make it to the wedding.

Chapter 56

*R*achel and Charlie dashed from Piedmont Hospital's parking deck to the Emergency Room. Discovering her father had been moved sent them scrambling to find the Coronary Care Unit. By the time they arrived, Rachel's neck and shoulder muscles screamed with pain. The overpowering scent of disinfectant made her wince.

She clung to Charlie's arm as she eased toward her father's bed and stared at wires from an ECG monitor attached to his chest. An oxygen mask covered his nose and mouth. Fluids dripped from IV bags into the needle inserted in his right arm.

She released Charlie and touched her father's hand.

His eyelids fluttered but failed to open.

"He looks so pale." Rachel's voice escaped in a tortured whisper. "I never imagined seeing him so helpless."

A plump, pleasant-looking nurse approached. "Are you Mr. Streetman's daughter?"

Rachel nodded. "He didn't respond to my touch."

"Pain medication will keep him out for a while. Try not to worry. He's in good hands. Dr. Caruthers is one of the city's top cardiologists."

"I need to talk to him."

"I'll page him for you." She stepped away, then turned back. "Your father's fortunate someone found him in time."

The comment slammed Rachel's chest like a sledgehammer. She clutched the bed railing to keep her knees from buckling.

Charlie gripped her shoulders.

"Did you hear what she said? If someone hadn't found him in time ..." She spun and collapsed into his arms. "What if he doesn't recover?"

"He will, sweetheart. It's not his time to go."

Rachel sniffled. "How do you know?"

"Because someone found him."

She desperately wanted to believe his words. Yet doubt held her mind captive. "Maybe your showing up at the theater tonight wasn't random. I mean ... it's possible ... I don't know what I'm trying to say."

Charlie stroked her back, easing the tension gripping her muscles. "All I know is the urge to hold you in my arms was so strong I had to find you."

"Thank goodness for urges."

He kissed her forehead, then released her and moved two chairs beside the bed.

Rachel sat and reached between the rails to hold her father's hand. "For years I didn't think he had a heart. Now I'm thankful for every beat."

Charlie settled beside her.

"When he came to Willow Falls a couple of weeks ago, he looked thinner than I remembered." She bristled from guilt. "Why didn't I see the signs and insist he schedule a checkup?"

"Does he have heart problems?"

She shook her head. "I've never seen him sick. Except once when he came down with the flu. He stayed home for two days but didn't stop working. He considers illness a weakness."

"Knowing your father, even if you'd known he was headed for trouble and tried to warn him, he wouldn't have listened."

"You're right." Rachel stretched her arm across the railing and rested her chin on her wrist. "Maybe this will scare him into adopting a new perspective."

"Not an easy task for a man driven by success, or who lets his business define him."

"He has to change." She fell silent and focused on the rhythmic beeps punctuated by peaks and straight lines slithering across the ECG monitor. The nurse returned twice to check on her patient before a tall man wearing a white coat—a stethoscope draped around his neck, a chart in his hand—ambled in.

Rachel lifted her chin. "Dr. Caruthers?"

"Yes. Are you Rachel?"

"I am." She stood and introduced Charlie.

The doctor shook their hands, then led them to a small conference room and pointed to a round table. "Please have a seat." He sat across from them. "First, I want you to know your father is a lucky man. Another half-hour, and we'd likely be having a different conversation."

Rachel's breath caught. "Where was he? Who found him?"

Dr. Caruthers flipped a page on his chart. "In his office. Brent Walker called 911."

An image of Greer's favorite rising star—after she resigned—popped into Rachel's head. "The man who needled his way under my skin more times than I can count ... saved my father's life." She eyed the doctor. "What caused his heart attack?"

"We have more tests to run. However, my initial diagnosis is high blood pressure triggered by stress and overwork. Greer and I belong to the same country club, so I'm familiar with his reputation as a hard-driving businessman. Unfortunately, his ambition came close to costing him his life."

Charlie's brows furrowed. "What's the long-term prognosis?"

"His heart sustained a good bit of damage. Which means he'll be forced to change his lifestyle."

Rachel probed Dr. Caruthers' eyes. "What happens if he refuses?"

"Without rest and a change of pace, he's unlikely to see seventy." He leaned forward. "I'll arrange for a counselor to meet with him before he's released. In the meantime, do you have a place to stay?"

She nodded.

"Good. I suggest you both get some rest tonight and return in the morning. I'll talk to you after all the test results come in. A lot of men like him end up driving their family away. Your father's fortunate to have a daughter who cares about him." Dr. Caruthers glanced at his buzzing phone. "If you folks will excuse me." He stood and left the room.

Rachel's shoulders curled forward. "What if abandoning my father's company to follow my own dreams ... what if caring isn't enough?"

Charlie gently pulled her to her feet. "Caring plus a healthy dose of prayer adds power to the miracle of modern medicine."

"Are you preaching?"

"Just stating the facts, gorgeous." Charlie stroked her cheek. "How 'bout we get some sleep and come back in the morning refreshed?"

"Good idea." Rachel held his hand as they walked out of the conference room and headed toward the elevators.

Chapter 57

Rachel climbed into the passenger seat and removed her phone from her purse. Charlie rounded the front of the truck and slid in beside her. "Next stop, your townhouse."

"Hold on." She entered an address and handed him the phone. "Follow these directions."

"To where?"

"The house where I grew up."

"For a drive-by in the middle of the night?"

"Nope. We're going in."

"Your call." Charlie backed out, exited the parking deck, and drove through upscale neighborhoods toward Buckhead. Seven minutes later, he turned onto a long circular driveway fronting a brick mansion. "Wow, I thought my dad had a big house. This looks more like a hotel than a home."

"Only the biggest and best for Greer Streetman."

"No kidding." Charlie dashed to the passenger door and held Rachel's hand as she climbed down. "Do you have a key or are you planning to break in?"

"I'm not crazy." She pulled out a keyring and dangled it in front of his face. "I also know his security code. My mother's birth month and year. I don't think he ever changed it."

"Let's hope not. Otherwise, we'll have some explaining to do when the police show up."

They climbed the steps to double beveled-glass doors. Inside, Rachel punched the number into the keypad and silenced the beeping alarm. "No jail for us tonight." She flipped a switch to illuminate the multi-layered chandelier hanging from the two-story ceiling.

Charlie stood in the center of the marble-floored space, eyes wide.

Rachel moved beside him and followed his gaze to the double staircase anchoring each side of the massive foyer, curving up to meet the second-floor landing. An arched opening beneath the landing led to a hall and beyond the living room. "He's added a few things since I last visited."

Charlie pointed to the paneled room on the right, the walls lined with built-in bookcases and paintings. "His office?"

"The library slash art gallery."

"Impressive." He moved to the dining room entrance on the left and let out a long whistle. "He could seat a small army in here."

Rachel joined him. "Mom hosted what she called very important clients in this room."

"Was everything about business for your father?"

"Pretty much. Except for acquiring expensive possessions. Which is why this looks more like a museum than a warm and cozy home."

"What about your room? Was it also a status symbol?"

"No way. Come on. I'll show you." Rachel clasped his hand and led him upstairs and down a hall to the last door on the left. She brushed her fingers over raised gold letters. "Rachel's Room. I'm surprised he didn't have these removed."

"At least there's a trace of sentimentality in his bones."

She opened the door, revealing a large room with a row of windows opposite the door. A king-size canopied bed, flanked on one side by a round skirted table and on the other by a nightstand, anchored the wall on the right. A desk and a dresser stood on the left. Framed Broadway posters sandwiched a bulletin board.

"You were a serious fan. *Mama Mia. Jersey Boys. Wicked.*" Charlie inched close to the *Peter Pan* poster. "This is personally signed to you by Cathy Rigby."

"My last birthday gift from Mom before she died—and Dad stepped all over my dreams." She lifted a photo off the dresser. "This is me playing Peggy Sawyer in *Forty Second Street* during my senior year at UGA. Before I buckled under Dad's pressure and took a job at Streetman Enterprise." She set the photo down and moseyed to the cream-colored love seat positioned in front of the windows.

Charlie followed and admired the back yard lit by landscape lighting and lights shimmering in the pool. "That's one unique-shaped swimming hole."

Rachel playfully poked him in the ribs. "Is that your country-boy description of a fancy pool?"

"Hey, it is a big hole in the ground, and people do swim in it."

"Mom designed it. She always said curves were more interesting than straight lines. When my friends and I weren't creating plays, we spent a lot of time hanging out in the pool house." Rachel dropped onto the love seat. "After she died, this room became my refuge." She pointed to an array of framed photos on an end table beside the love seat. "Pictures from the happy times, mostly of me and Mom."

Charlie sat beside her and eyed the photos. "Eerie how much you look like her."

"Our resemblance made it easy for Mom and Dad to keep the truth about my birth a secret. If I hadn't found out about Mama Sadie, I'd still be living under the illusion I was born a Streetman." Rachel stared at the corner where her menagerie of stuffed animals once lived—before her father relegated them to the attic. "Dr. Caruthers' comment about men like my father driving their families away makes me wonder if my parents' marriage would have survived long term. Which do you think is worse, losing a wife to cancer or to another man?"

"Cancer would break a man's heart." Charlie remained silent for a long moment. "Losing his wife to another man would drive a stake through it."

"Maybe a wounded ego drove Brick back into Cynthia's arms."

"Good an explanation as any."

Rachel ran her fingers over the smooth fabric covering the love seat. "My father redecorated the master bedroom after Mom died. When she was alive it was light and airy with soft feminine colors. Now, the dark colors and heavy furniture make it look more like a smoking room or an office than a restful retreat. I suppose when he crawled into bed before the redo, the memories were too painful for him to bear." A yawn drew Rachel's hand to her mouth. "I'm exhausted. Is it okay if we stay here tonight?"

"Might as well. I'll bring our bags in. Be back in a jiff."

Rachel sat on the side of the bed and slipped out of her shoes. She pulled the comforter aside and crawled in. The rosette securing the gathered pale-green silk fabric in the center of the canopy caused childhood memories to dance through her mind. Her eyelids grew heavy. She turned on her side and pulled her knees up. Her last memory before plunging into a deep sleep was Charlie setting her overnight bag on the floor.

Chapter 58

*C*onfusion muddled Rachel's brain until her eyes focused and scanned her surroundings. She swung her legs to the floor and noted dust specks floating in the sun's rays streaming through the window. She pushed hair away from her face and dashed to the bathroom before padding into the hall and down to the foyer.

"Charlie, where are you?"

"In the kitchen."

She walked beneath the landing and followed the scent of coffee to the large space worthy of a gourmet chef's approval.

"Good morning, gorgeous." Charlie handed her a cup. "I found honey, but no creamer or milk."

"Dad takes his coffee strong and black." She held the cup in both hands, absorbing the warmth. "Did you manage to sleep?"

"Enough. Last night I counted thirty-three rooms and never made it to the basement. This house is like a baby Biltmore."

"A what?"

"You know. In Asheville. As in North Carolina."

"I've never been there." Rachel sipped her coffee and made a mental note to check it out online. "What time is it? And where's my phone?"

"Half past eight." Charlie pointed to the counter beside the fridge. "Plugged in for a charge."

"We have to go to the hospital."

"You get dressed while I scramble us some eggs."

Rachel set her cup on the island. "I don't have time for breakfast."

Charlie removed a carton of eggs from the refrigerator disguised as cabinetry. "When did you last eat?"

"I don't know. Lunch yesterday?"

"Then we'll make time." He dug in the cabinet under the six-burner stove top and pulled out a frying pan.

Rachel didn't know whether to be thankful or annoyed. "You're not gonna take no for an answer, are you."

"You don't want your stomach to grumble while you're visiting your dad." Charlie cracked eggs into the pan.

"Okay." She sighed. "But we're out of here before ten."

"I promise."

Rachel returned to her room and lugged her overnight bag into the bathroom. She washed her face and stared at her image in the mirror. She owed Emily an update. After showering and dressing, she returned to the kitchen and texted her sister ... then devoured breakfast.

＊

At five minutes to ten, Rachel and Charlie found Greer awake, his upper body raised to a forty-five-degree angle. A nose piece replaced the oxygen mask. Rachel forced a grin. "Hey, Dad. You look a ton better. How are you feeling?"

"Like I don't belong here. Did you drive down this morning?"

"Last night, after Dr. Caruthers called."

He raised the bed to a full sitting position. "You didn't need to make the trip."

"Of course we did." She reached through the railing and held his hand. "This is exactly where we need to be."

"I'm going home today, so you can return to Willow Falls."

Rachel's brows arched. "Is that what the doctor said?"

"It's what I'm saying." He pulled his hand away. "I've never been sick, and I don't intend to let a little incident slow me down."

A shrill beep from the IV pump brought a young nurse wandering in. "It's time for a new dose of goodies, Mr. Streetman." She reset the pump, replaced an empty bag, and injected fluid into a port close to the needle. "On a scale of one to ten, what's your pain level."

"Nothing I can't handle."

"Let me know if it reaches an intolerable level. By the way, your doctor is on the floor. He'll be in shortly to talk to you."

"Good. He can sign my release papers."

"We'll see. In the meantime, let me know what you need." The nurse checked the IV pump once more before leaving.

Rachel watched as the scowl on her father's face intensified.

"What I need is a ticket out of here so I can return to work." The disgruntled patient repositioned his body and winced. "At least your trip gave you a chance to check on your townhouse."

Rachel hesitated, wondering if her father would be upset. "We stayed at your house last night. I wanted to show Charlie where I grew up."

The man turned his head toward Charlie. "What'd you think?"

"Definitely big ... and impressive."

"Like Streetman Enterprise." He launched into an update on his company's latest acquisition until a yawn disrupted his droll monologue. "These drugs make me sleepy."

"You had a heart attack, Dad. You need the rest."

He dismissed her comment with a hand flick. "Nonsense."

"Your daughter is a wise woman," Dr. Caruthers said as he walked in and closed the distance to the bed.

"That's beside the point, Doc. I'm ready to return to work."

"You've never been one to mince words, Greer, so I'm going to give it to you straight. Your heart sustained significant damage, which means, my friend, that you need rest and a lifestyle adjustment."

"Or what?"

"You're headed for another, possibly fatal, heart attack." The doctor continued, revealing diagnosis and proposed treatment.

Rachel saw the color drain from her father's face as his expression morphed from obstinance to confusion to something she had never seen in his eyes. Fear. She gripped the bed rail to steady her trembling limbs as reality set in. The man who measured his worth by the size of his company might be unwilling or unable to change.

"Right now, you need some shut-eye." Dr. Caruthers lowered the bed's head to a semi-reclined position.

Eyelids drooped, then closed. "What'd you do, Doc, slip me a mickey?"

"Something like that." The doctor reached for his stethoscope. "Ticker sounds good for now. I'll check back in a couple of hours." He motioned Rachel and Charlie to follow him.

Rachel held tightly to Charlie's arm as they made their way to the conference room.

After Dr. Caruthers made a note on his chart, he locked eyes with Rachel. "Your father is a proud and stubborn man. I don't know how much influence you have—"

"Very little. If any."

"The point is he needs you or someone he trusts to convince him to view life through a different lens."

"How long will he be here?" Charlie asked.

"At least three more days, maybe longer."

"Our wedding is in a few weeks." Rachel's pulse pounded in her ears. "Will he be well enough to walk me down the aisle?"

"If he takes my instructions seriously and avoids stress, the prospect is good."

Rachel laid her left hand over her right and stared at her engagement ring. She knew her father well enough to realize the chances he would take Dr. Caruthers' demands seriously were fifty-fifty at best.

Chapter 59

*A*n attractive senior woman wearing a volunteer jacket breezed into the hospital room carrying a large bouquet in a cut-glass vase. "Flowers for Mr. Streetman." She set the multi-colored arrangement featuring a red get-well balloon on the tray table and glanced at the sleeping patient. "I hope he feels better soon."

Charlie removed the card from the holder and handed it to Rachel.

Her father's eyes opened. "Who sent the flowers?"

"Your employees." Rachel returned the card to the holder.

"How long did I sleep?"

Rachel glanced at her watch. "Several hours."

He raised the bed to a sitting position. "What time is it?"

"Nearly two," Rachel said.

"No need for you and Charlie to sit here and waste your time watching me." His flat tone matched his detached expression.

"You're my father—"

"I don't need an audience."

Charlie gave Rachel a knowing look and nodded at Greer. "We understand, sir."

Rachel glared at him. *Maybe you do. I don't.*

"I want you to take my daughter back to Willow Falls."

"Why?" Rachel reached under the railing and touched her father's hand. "I mean, who will drive you home and take care of you?"

"Anyone with a car can play chauffeur." He pulled his hand away. "And I don't need anyone to take care of me."

"I know, but—"

"Before you leave town, I want you to do something."

"Anything you need, Dad."

"Go to my home office and find an envelope addressed to you. In my desk. Top right drawer."

"What—"

"Just do it. For me."

"If that's what you want." Rachel leaned over the railing. "There's also something I need *you* to do for me. Listen to your doctor and rest so you'll be well enough to walk me down the aisle."

His eyes narrowed. "I know what I need far better than anyone."

On the verge of tears, Rachel stepped away from the bed.

"We'll follow your instructions, sir," Charlie said as he took Rachel's elbow and steered her out to the hall.

She pulled away from him. "I need to go back in there and talk some sense into him."

"Bad idea." He gripped her shoulders. "Please listen. Your father commands respect for his toughness and ambition."

"What are you trying to say?"

"He doesn't want anyone, especially you, to see him weak and needy."

Tears erupted and spilled down her cheeks. "Men are sometimes too stubborn for words."

"That stubborn streak is what will keep him alive. Now, let's go find out what's in his desk."

***

By the time they parked in front of her father's mansion, a dull ache assaulted Rachel's chest. "What if he sent me to find his will or instructions about his funeral?"

"Whatever it is, he considers it important." Charlie rounded the front of the truck, opened the passenger door, and held his hand out. "We'll find out what it is together."

She grabbed her phone and stepped down. Her fingers entwined with her fiancé's as they entered the house, turned off the alarm, and moved through the foyer. Memories from her childhood flooded her mind the moment they stepped into his office. "For a couple of years after my mother died, I spent most Saturdays and Sundays in this room, waiting for my dad to stop working. I'd often curl up on that couch to read a book or dream about being a famous actress."

Rachel approached the desk and sat in her father's executive chair. She set her phone down, gripped the drawer handle, and pulled it open. Inside she found a greeting-card-sized envelope, the flap side turned up. She flipped it over and gasped.

Charlie moved to her side. "What is it?"

She traced her name. "My mother's handwriting." Her fingers trembled as she removed a folded sheet of pale pink paper. "Her signature stationery." Rachel's vision blurred with tears. She handed the letter to Charlie. "Read it to me."

He unfolded the paper. "It says, *My Dearest Rachel. I'm penning this letter to let you know I love you with all my heart, with every fiber of my being. The years I spent watching you grow from an infant to a little girl to a young lady were the happiest in my life. The most difficult part of losing my battle with cancer is knowing I will never see you become the woman you were meant to be. To watch you, my beautiful, talented daughter, pursue and achieve your dreams.*

Charlie paused and took a deep breath. "*During my final days, I spent precious moments with a close friend who taught me about the gift of eternity. She prepared me to leave this world with a sense of peace and an obligation to tell you the truth when you were old enough to understand. Which is why your father promised to give you this letter on your sixteenth birthday.*"

My sixteenth birthday? Rachel reached for a tissue and nodded for Charlie to continue.

"*From the day Greer and I married, I yearned for a child. For years I tried in vain to get pregnant. Eventually, we came to understand it wasn't possible. So, we set out to find a baby everyone would think was our own. From the moment I first held you in my arms, you were a part of me. I knew your father wanted to groom you to follow in his footsteps, but I encouraged him to let you find your own path. If he doesn't, please be kind to him, but promise you won't let him lead you where you don't want to go.*'"

Charlie swallowed, then continued. "*There is something else you need to know. You have a sister, an identical twin. Another couple adopted her. They didn't know about you until I sent them a letter through the adoption agency. I asked if when you turned sixteen and wanted to meet her, would they allow it? They wrote back stating, yes. If they heard from you. I know this comes as a shock, but it is meant to bring fullness to your life and to let you know how much you were and are loved. Until we meet again in paradise, your mother."*

Rachel sat in stunned silence until anger bubbled and threatened to explode. She swiped her tears away. "How dare he break his promise to her. Emily and I would have found each other years ago. I would have followed my mother's wishes and ignored my father's plan for my life. I would have applied to Julliard." She leapt from the chair and dashed to the window overlooking the driveway leading to the four-car garage. "My father is a cruel, selfish man. That letter would have changed my life."

Charlie slid his arm around her and pulled her close. "He had no right to keep it from you. But he did, and I'm glad."

She pushed his hand away. "How can you say that?"

"Think about it. If you hadn't gone to work for Streetman Enterprise, we'd never have met."

"Of course, we would have. In Willow Falls, after you started working on the winery."

Charlie shook his head. "Who convinced my superstitious dad to close the deal on the property after Emily's parents' accident spooked him?"

"Brent and me."

His brows raised. "Who?"

"Okay, me. Brent would have blown it."

"The night you met my dad at Cut's Steakhouse, he had planned to chuck the deal and bid on a property seventy miles from Willow Falls. The fact is, Miss Ex Streetman Enterprise VP, *you* are the reason Willow Oak Winery exists. And your dad's decision made it possible for us to meet and fall in love."

Silence enfolded the moment as she faced Charlie. "Are you suggesting I forgive him?"

He stroked her cheek. "Forgiveness is good for the soul, yours and his."

His comment rang true. Yet anger clung tightly. "Part of me still wants to give him a piece of my mind. Except I'm afraid the stress will kill him." She broke eye contact. "I'll let him off the hook after he tells me why he kept the letter a secret."

"That's fair."

She returned to the desk. "As soon as we pack our bags, we need to return to the hospital and confront him."

"Not a good idea. The hospital part is too in his face."

"What do you suggest I do? Write him a letter and tell him to stash it in a drawer for fifteen years?"

"He knows you've read it, Rachel. Call him. His cell is on the table beside the bed."

She drew in a deep breath and slumped back in the chair. "If you think that's the best approach."

"It's the only one that makes sense."

She stared at her phone for a moment, pressed his number, and engaged the speaker.

He answered after the second ring. "You read it, didn't you?"

"Yes." She struggled to tamp down her anger. "Why didn't you honor my mother's wishes and give it to me years ago?"

"By the time you turned sixteen, I had begun grooming you to take my place. The truth is I didn't want to lose you to your childhood fantasies."

Her brain ached to chastise him, but her heart prevented the words from rolling off her tongue.

"I had no right to keep it from you."

"No, you didn't. Even though in the end, everything turned out okay."

"Now you know your mother was by far the better parent. Maybe one day you'll be able to forgive me."

Rachel closed her eyes, and for the second time since discovering she had a twin, spoke words that poured from her heart. "I love you, Dad, and I forgive you."

"I love you too, Strawberry Girl."

"You take care of yourself."

"My doc just walked in. I'll talk to you later." Her father ended the call.

Charlie pulled Rachel into his arms and held her. "Your relationship with your dad just moved to a whole new level, sweetheart."

Tears spilled down her cheeks. She pressed her face against Charlie's neck and wept as years of pent up anger and resentment toward the man who adopted her melted and washed away in a river of forgiveness.

Chapter 60

*E*mily stopped beside Redding Arms' front desk and read the sign displayed on an easel. *Antoine's Amazing Beauty Bash.* A red arrow pointed right. She turned the corner and passed the elevator. As she neared the ballroom, female chatter drifted into the hall. Inside, she stood along the back wall beside Kat. "Turnout looks great."

"Except for Robert Nordstrom's audition, this is the hotel's biggest shindig. I couldn't squeeze one more table in here without violating safety regulations."

Emily scanned the room filled with women sitting in semi-circles at round, cloth-covered tables. A lighted mirror and makeup assortment were set in front of each chair. "Obviously, Pearl's idea is a huge hit."

"It's definitely bringing in a good chunk of change." Kat pointed to the camera slung on Emily's shoulder. "I take it you're here as a reporter."

"This will make a great feature story for this week's edition." Emily slid the camera off her shoulder and aimed it toward two of Robert's camera operators adjusting their equipment. She strolled through the room, snapping photos and recording comments until Antoine, dressed in shiny black slacks and a purple silk shirt, motioned her to the back of the room. "Your camera tells me you are Madame Emily and not Mademoiselle Rachel."

"Correct. I'm amazed at how much you and Pearl accomplished in such a short time."

Antoine fingered the lavalier attached to his lapel. "My list of contacts and connections is quite long."

"I noticed two director chairs on the stage. Are you and Pearl both demonstrating?"

"My dear, all these ladies paid to learn from a master. So, I will perform magic on two women whose transformations will showcase my skills."

Emily suppressed a giggle. "Have you selected your models?"

"Not yet." He pressed a finger to his earbud. "My microphone's going live in one minute."

"Good luck."

The lights flickered. "Ladies." Kat's voice boomed over the loudspeakers. "Please welcome our host and makeup artist extraordinaire, the great Antoine."

The roar of applause and cheers accompanied the man as he pranced between the tables and stepped onto the makeshift stage between a pair of free-standing screens. "*Merci*, my lovelies. This evening I will show you how to change your lives forever. My dear friend, Pearl, and my assistants will circulate among you to offer help while I reveal beauty secrets I have shared with countless stars. Before I begin, I will select two perfect models."

Hands shot up amidst a cacophony of pick-me requests.

Antoine rapid-tapped his palms. "*S'il vous plaît*, Madams and Mademoiselles. You must let me proceed."

The crowd quieted as their hero stepped down and meandered among the tables eyeing candidates. He stopped beside a plain young woman who worked as a hotel housekeeper. "Come, let me make you beautiful."

She pressed her hands to her cheeks. "Me?"

"Yes, my precious." He led her to the stage, then returned to the audience and resumed strolling. "Ah yes," he said as he stopped behind Mirabelle. "My second model must be the woman who inspired this *magnifique* affair." He led her to the second chair and turned to face his audience. "As instructed, you have each come with your face washed as clean as a fresh canvas awaiting the brush of beauty."

Kat scooted beside Emily and whispered, "The man's a trip."

"He's definitely one of a kind." She zoomed her camera lens and snapped shots of Antoine working his magic while explaining his technique until movement on her right drew her attention.

"I need you to come with me," Rachel whispered.

"I didn't expect you back this soon."

"Change of plans." Rachel led her to a bench in the hall.

"What's wrong?" A chill crept up her spine. "Please don't tell me your dad's gone."

"He's in bad shape but still alive. He's also the reason we need to talk." Rachel removed an envelope from her purse. "For the past two hours I've waffled back and forth between showing this to you and keeping it a secret."

Emily eyed the envelope. "What is it?"

"A letter from my mother. I didn't know it existed until today. You need to know what she wrote." She released it into her sister's hand.

Emily unfolded the letter and focused on the words written by a woman who had died twenty years ago. As she read the last paragraph, she gasped. Her hand flew to her throat. "They knew. All those years I begged for a sister, and my parents refused to tell me. How could they?"

"I asked myself the same question. Then I realized they wanted to protect you."

"By keeping me in the dark?"

"When your parents didn't hear from me, they had to think I had no interest in meeting you. Think about it. If you knew I existed, then believed I didn't want to find you—"

"My heart would have shattered into a million pieces."

"Which is why your mom and dad didn't tell you."

Emily wiped a stray tear and handed the letter back. "Why did your father give it to you after all these years?"

"I suppose to assuage his guilt in the face of mortality. Other than telling Scott, this should remain between us. I don't want Mama Sadie or anyone else thinking less of my dad."

"I agree." Emily slumped against the wall. "You and I have a complicated history."

"The stuff of soap operas."

"I should write a book about it. Or at least a short story. Without revealing the real characters or divulging secrets."

Rachel slipped the letter back in the envelope and dropped it in her purse. "Do you think anyone would read it?"

"Are you kidding? Everyone in Willow Falls."

Chapter 61

The front door thudding closed sent Brownie scrambling to the foyer. Emily stopped typing.

Rachel breezed into the den. "One more shoot in the can, so to speak."

"How did it go with Justin?"

"It wasn't a romantic scene, so no drama." Rachel dropped onto the couch. "Tomorrow we film our breakup, my last shoot for *this* movie."

"Have your dreams shifted from stage to film?" Emily set her computer on the end table beside her recliner.

"Don't read anything into my comment."

"Do you think you'll miss it?"

Rachel shrugged. "Hard to tell, with everything else going on. Have you talked to Mama Sadie?"

"Kat and Pepper treated her to the works at Pearl's. Called it her birthday present. She still thinks we're taking her to your new house for a family celebration."

"What time are you and Scott picking her up?"

"Seven, to give guests time to arrive. Everyone's parking in the upper lot."

"I'm sorry I couldn't help you decorate."

"Not a problem. Charlie and Jack filled in for you. Speaking of Charlie, has he heard from his dad?"

"Not a peep." Rachel's chin tilted down. "I hope Brick is suffering from a big-time guilty conscience."

"A lot of good that will do." Emily laced her fingers behind her neck and stretched her shoulders. "All I can say is, thank goodness only a handful of us know the original reason for tonight's party."

273

"We need to make Mama Sadie feel like royalty."

"The setting will definitely create the right mood."

Rachel's brows lifted. "Did you guys do more decorating than you and I planned?"

Emily grinned at her sister. "You'll see."

"In that case, I need to change clothes and scoot on over before my curiosity goes bananas." Rachel stood. "Text me when you have our guest of honor close to the winery."

"Will do."

***

With each step up to her mother's apartment, Emily's anger at Brick deepened. She stopped at the landing and filled her lungs. She stood there a long moment pursing her lips before releasing the air. Mama Sadie opened the door before she knocked.

Emily stared at her mother's new hairstyle and eyes, beautifully accentuated by subtle eyeshadow and liner. "You're absolutely gorgeous. And the dress ... teal is the perfect color for you."

"Birthday gifts from Pepper and Kat. Guess they figured I needed one more makeover before giving in to old age."

"Are you kidding me? Don't you know fifty is the new thirty?"

"Glory be, honey, if that were the case, I'd still be in prison."

"You're a scream, Mama Sadie." Emily escorted her mother down the stairs.

Scott opened the back door. "Wow, you look like a million dollars."

"Thanks to Pearl." She slid into the car. "I don't care what anyone says. She's every bit as good as Antoine."

During the drive to the winery, the three laughed and exchanged stories about Jane and Clair's antics. When they turned off County Road and parked in the lower lot, Sadie turned serious. "Why are you stopping here? It's a long walk up to the house."

Emily peered over the front seat. "Before we head up, Charlie wants your expert opinion on a new look for the dining room."

"If you ask me, it was pretty as a picture before. Why did he go changing it?"

"Good question," Emily said. "We're about to find out."

Charlie's vineyard protectors Buster and Merlot accompanied them as they covered the distance to the tasting room door. Inside, one overhead light cast a dim glow. At the foot of the dark stairwell, Mama Sadie clutched the railing. "I guess Charlie forgot to turn on the lights."

"That's a guy for you," Scott said as he held his arm out to his mother-in-law.

When they reached the top and stepped into the dining room, the lights switched on. Twenty-two of Mama Sadie's closest friends and family members shouted, "Surprise!"

The birthday girl pressed her palms together and touched her fingers to her lips as friends rushed to embrace her.

"Talk about a room fit for a queen," Scott said. "You outdid yourselves."

"A labor of love." Emily eyed the banner reading *Happy Birthday to our Beloved Sadie* suspended over the buffet set along the wall of windows and the table in the corner displaying an array of wrapped gifts.

"Your hard work deserves a glass of Georgia wine. Back in a sec." He headed to the self-serve bar set up on the floor-to-ceiling cabinet.

Emily stepped into the room and drank in the view. The chairs had been slip-covered in shiny gold fabric, with white satin ribbons tied around the backs. Floral centerpieces and flickering candles graced each table. Blue and gold streamers crisscrossed the room.

Rachel approached. "She looks fabulous. And did you see the look on her face? All the people she loves the most are here ... Missy, Dennis, JT, Jack ..."

Emily listened to her sister reel off the names while also listening to Kat and Pepper smother Mama Sadie with compliments.

Maggie wandered over. "Your mother is fortunate to have a loving family and so many close friends."

"Thank you for coming," Emily said.

"I wouldn't have missed this for all the bling in Hollywood. Have you seen Patsy's cake? It's a work of art."

"This little town is filled with talented people." Rachel nodded toward the gift table. "Word is our resident artist created a special painting."

"A Naomi Jasper original," Maggie said. "Perfect gift for a woman as special as your mother. Excuse me while I join her adoring fans."

Mama Sadie's smile as she responded to love from her friends tempered Emily's anger toward Brick. "After tonight, I think she'll be okay."

Scott returned carrying two glasses of Champagne. He gave one glass to Emily, the other to Rachel. "Congratulations for pulling off the surprise. Even Mirabelle's on her best behavior."

"I'm amazed she kept tonight a secret."

"My threat to remove her name from her Willow Inn suite worked wonders," Emily said. "Again."

Charlie stepped beside Rachel. "First Willow Oak party since the grand opening. Next event is our wedding."

"At least we don't have to keep that event a secret," Emily said with a grin.

"No kidding." Rachel snickered. "By now, I suspect the entire county has heard about it. Patsy will have to bake a much bigger cake."

"You mean *cakes*." Emily slipped her hand around Scott's bicep. "Let's mingle with Mama Sadie's extended family."

A half-hour later, Emily approached Pepper and Kat. "It's time for the official welcome, and I can't find my mother. Have either of you seen her?"

Kat nodded. "She headed down the hall a few minutes ago, after her phone rang. Unfortunately, innkeepers and hotel managers are never off duty."

"Of all the nights for a problem to pop up," Pepper said. "Hopefully, something minor."

"Guess we'll have to wait a bit longer." Emily passed by Scott, Charlie, Mitch, and JT involved in a heated debate about the Atlanta Falcons' season potential. She joined Rachel in a discussion with Missy and Dennis about movie versus play-acting. The dining room buzzed with activity and laughter ... until all heads turned toward the dining room entrance.

Chatter evolved to stunned silence.

Emily's knees threatened to buckle as she gasped, then pressed her hand to her lips.

Chapter 62

Rachel's heart leapt to her throat at the sight of Charlie's dad and her mother standing at the dining room entrance. She gripped the back of a chair to steady her quivering limbs.

Gasps and whispers rippled through the room.

Brick escorted Mama Sadie to a table beside the buffet. He pulled a chair out. She sat, then laced her fingers and laid her hands on her lap.

Emily touched Rachel's shoulder. "Do you have any idea what's going on?"

"Not a clue."

Charlie approached his dad. They exchanged words. Charlie stepped away.

Brick faced the guests. "I can tell from your expressions that I'm the least popular man in town. And for good reason. I'm surprised Mitch hasn't handcuffed me and hauled me off to jail."

Silence permeated the room.

He shoved his hands in his pockets. "The first time I laid eyes on this property, I knew it had potential. When I purchased it, I had planned to let Charlie manage the vineyard and winery so I wouldn't have to move here and give up my big-city lifestyle. Then something happened. I discovered I liked this crazy little town, especially after Willow Falls became more than a spot on the map no one outside a five-mile radius knew existed. So, I bought that house over on Main Street and moved in. Mind you, I didn't sell my home back in Atlanta. A lot of memories live there. My sons growing up. The happy days when we were a family of four."

Brick shrugged. "When Cynthia and I married, I believed we would spend the rest of our lives together until she abandoned our family and ran off with another man. When she showed up here ... I considered it a sign we were meant to be together. Truth is ... well, Cynthia did a number on my ego. You all saw her. She's beautiful and sexy. Although, the rumor about her boosting the wealth of at least one plastic surgeon is true. Anyway, she and I left Willow Falls and headed to Atlanta ... to the home we once shared."

Emily clutched Rachel's arm and leaned close. "He's going to break Mama Sadie's heart all over again. Charlie has to stop him."

"I don't think this is what it seems. We have to let it play out."

Brick pulled his hands from his pockets. "A few minutes ago, I apologized to Sadie for leaving town without telling her. Now, I want everyone here to know that Cynthia slept in the guest room the entire time we were in Atlanta. Nothing happened between us. However, something did happen to me. I discovered that every ounce of romantic love I ever had for my ex-wife was gone ... vanished forever."

Silence continued to enfold the moment.

"But there is another woman who captured my heart." Brick's face lit with a smile. "She's funny and charming and beautiful inside and out. And she's braver than anyone I have ever known. Right here, right now, in front of our family and friends, I want to apologize again for the lousy way I've treated Sadie. I won't blame her if she kicks me in the butt and tells me to scram. But if she can find it in her heart to grant me one more chance, I promise I'll never leave her again."

Rachel pressed her hand to her chest.

Brick knelt on one knee. "Sadie, I want you and everyone here to know that I don't need a rainbow, or a four-leaf clover, or a lucky penny to know I have fallen madly in love with you."

Rachel's heart pounded against her ribs.

Brick slipped his hand into his pocket and removed a turquoise box. He lifted the lid and held it out. "Sadie Liles, you will make me the happiest man alive if you become my wife and let me spend the rest of my days making you happy."

The guests held their collective breath.

Sadie unlaced her fingers and touched his cheek. "My dinner invitation still stands."

"Is that a yes?"

"Glory be, Reginald Bricker. Of course, it's a yes."

Tears spilled down Rachel's cheeks as she watched her future father-in-law slip the ring on her mother's finger then kiss her.

Guests erupted in cheers and applause.

Emily sniffled. "This couldn't be more perfect."

Rachel dabbed her fingers under her eyes. "Maybe they're real after all."

"What?"

"Fairy tales and happily-ever-afters."

Chapter 63

*R*achel stood at the kitchen island and drizzled dressing into a bowl filled with baby lettuces. "I hope everyone likes this." She transferred the greens to six plates and topped the salads with grated gorgonzola and dried cranberries.

Emily stood by with a grin. "I can't believe my sister actually made the dressing."

"All I can say is thank goodness for online recipes. Help me carry them to the table."

Emily followed Rachel to the dining area. She set the plates down, then caressed the table's satiny-smooth surface. "This is one amazing wedding gift."

"Brick had it custom made in France's Bordeaux region. Imagine the stories it could tell." Rachel's eyes drifted to the living room. "Charlie's dad and our mother look adorable together."

"I don't know who my girls love more, Grandma Sadie or Grandpa Brick."

Rachel uncorked a bottle of Cabernet Sauvignon. "At least they'll have one grandmother and grandfather to spoil them."

"Don't give up on your dad just yet. He is home from the hospital, right?"

"A lot of good it'll do." Rachel poured wine into six glasses. "According to Nancy—"

"Your former assistant?"

Rachel nodded. "And bridesmaid. Anyway, she sent me a text saying he showed up at work yesterday. Less than a week after a near-fatal heart attack, and he's back at the grindstone. His stubborn pride is going to kill him."

"We need to pray he comes to his senses." Emily followed her sister back to the kitchen.

"I'm not convinced anyone or anything can break his stubborn streak." Rachel removed a pan of rolls from the oven. "These are store-bought, but the package claims they're just like grandmother used to make." She transferred them to a basket and handed it to Emily.

The glass door leading to the deck swung open. Charlie stepped in, accompanied by the sizzle of hot meat and the scent of rosemary and garlic. "Steaks are ready."

Scott followed, carrying a platter of sweet potatoes. "This guy knows his way around a grill. I hear men make the best chefs."

"Pepper would beg to differ." Emily thumped his arm. "Or should I say Executive Chef Pepper."

"I admit there are exceptions," Charlie said. "We need to serve dinner while these babies are still hot."

After everyone gathered around the table and Charlie blessed the food, he raised his glass. "A toast to the first official dinner with Willow Falls' newest engaged couple and to the incredible woman who is about to become my mother-in-law and step-mom."

Glasses clinked.

Mama Sadie spread a napkin on her lap. "I do declare, Charlie. I don't know if I should introduce you as my son-in-law or step-son."

Brick laughed. "Since you look young enough to be his sister and are a mere thirteen years older than he is, I'd stick with son-in-law."

Charlie chuckled. "Hey, Dad, are you bragging about robbing the cradle?"

"An old codger winning the heart of the prettiest lady in Georgia ought to have bragging rights."

Baby Jane looked at Brick. "Grandpa, what's a codger?"

Laughter erupted as Brick's attempt to answer the question resulted in a Jane and Clair giggle fest.

Dinner continued amid light-hearted conversation about the surprise birthday party, the upcoming wedding, and Willow Falls' reaction to the movie invasion. As Rachel savored her last bite of steak, she imagined her father sitting at the table, enjoying these moments with the family.

Somehow, she had to find a way to make him understand life offered far more than working twenty-four-seven.

Brick patted his stomach. "Charlie, I have to admit, that's the best steak I've ever tasted."

"I can't take all the credit. Rachel found the recipe in *The Wine Lover's Cookbook*. The secret is fresh rosemary and aged balsamic."

"Good reference for a vintner."

Rachel laid her fork across her plate. "Speaking of recipes, I suggest we have coffee and dessert in the living room."

"If you don't mind waiting a few minutes, Sadie and I have something to tell y'all."

Rachel glanced at Charlie, then back at his dad. "Sure."

Brick reached for Mama Sadie's hand. "My beautiful fiancée and I decided we've been single far too long. Which means a lengthy engagement is out of the question."

"Brick and I have talked it over. Monday, we're going to Atlanta to get married in a civil ceremony."

Emily's eyes widened. "Don't you want a storybook wedding to match your fairytale romance?"

"Honey, I don't need a fancy event to feel like Cinderella. Besides, planning another wedding close to Rachel and Charlie's is too much." Mama Sadie stood and lifted Clair from her booster seat and nodded toward Brick. "Come on, Prince Charming, let's take our sweet grandbabies to the living room and read them a story."

The abrupt change of subject gave Rachel pause. "Emily, you and Scott go on in the living room. Charlie and I will clear the table." She gathered a stack of dishes, carried them to the kitchen, and set them in the sink. "It's not right."

She moved to the door and watched the pink glow cast by the setting sun. "I understand why they don't want to wait. Still ... Mama Sadie's already given up so much."

"They made the decision." Charlie stepped behind her and wrapped his arms around her waist. "Besides, they're right about this town not needing another out-of-control wedding anytime soon."

"Even though she claimed it didn't matter, I'm positive I saw a hint of disappointment in her eyes." An idea crept in and took root. "But what if ..." She spun around, locked eyes with Charlie, and let it roll off her tongue. She waited for his reaction. "What do you think?"

Charlie's face inched close to hers. "You're a true romantic, Rachel Streetman, and an amazing daughter."

"Are you saying it's okay with you?"

"If they're willing, so am I."

She kissed him. Then again. "We have to go tell them."

They held hands and joined their guests in the living room where Scott sat on the couch with his arm around Emily's shoulders. Mama Sadie and Brick sat on the floor, each with a granddaughter in their lap. Rachel settled in front of them.

Charlie joined her. "My fiancée has come up with a great idea she wants to run by you two."

Rachel eyed Brick, then her mother. "Charlie and I have talked it over, and ... we want you to get married with us."

Emily gasped and covered her heart with both hands.

Mama Sadie's eyes widened. "A double wedding?"

"A glorious, foot-stomping, country wedding with two brides and two grooms."

Her mother laid the book on the floor and shook her head. "Your suggestion is thoughtful, honey, and means the world to me. But I don't think it's right."

"How could anything be more right?" Rachel grasped her mother's hand. "Mother and daughter marry father and son. That's the stuff movies are made of."

"That's a mighty generous offer," Brick said.

"I don't know." Sadie stared at her new fiancé. "Their wedding is just around the corner, and I don't have a dress—"

"Not a problem," Rachel said. "We'll go to Atlanta and buy one off the rack. Who would you want in your wedding party?"

"I suppose Pepper and Kat. Maybe my new friend, Maggie."

"Perfect." Rachel said. "We'll take them with us to hunt for the perfect wedding gown."

"There's more than a dress to think about," Sadie said hesitantly. "There's invitations—"

Emily scooted to the edge of the couch. "This is the best idea ever. And who needs invitations? We have Mirabelle."

Brick laughed, and everyone joined him.

Mama Sadie's brows rose as she shifted her eyes from Brick to Emily. "You both think it's a good idea too?"

"I think it's a great idea, Mama Sadie."

Sadie stroked Clair's silky red curls and eyed Rachel. "I wouldn't want to spoil your special day."

"Nothing would make me happier than to make it *our* special day, one we'll both treasure for the rest of our lives."

Mama Sadie reached for Brick's hand. "What do you think?"

"I'd be mighty proud to watch you walk down the aisle dressed in a beautiful white gown."

Mama Sadie splayed her left hand. "Years ago, I dreamed of falling in love and having a big fancy wedding."

Rachel caught her mother's eye. "Are you saying yes?"

"Honey, I'd be proud as a peacock to share a wedding with you."

Clair touched her grandmother's cheek. "What's a peacock?"

"A big, beautiful bird—"

"You're not a bird." Clair giggled. "You're a grandma."

Laughter filled the room.

Rachel tweaked Clair's cheek. "You're right, sweet girl, she's the best grandma and mama in the whole wide world."

Brick clasped his son's hand and pulled him into a hug. "This is one fine family you and I are marrying into."

"You bet it is."

Chapter 64

*E*mily closed the Caravan's power liftgate and started the engine, excited about their little adventure. "Buckle up, ladies, we're heading to Atlanta."

"We need to buy Pastor Nathan a gift for letting us use the church minivan." Rachel closed the front passenger door and buckled her belt. "There's no way six of us would fit in Charlie's truck."

"I'm surprised but delighted you asked me to be in the wedding, Sadie," Maggie said.

"Glory be, honey, along with Pepper and Kat, you've become one of my best friends. Besides, now that you're buying one of Greer's condos and making Willow Falls home, you're like regular folks."

Maggie smiled. "I like the sound of that."

Emily drove to the end of Main Street and turned onto County Road. "The wedding has again become the town's number one topic of conversation." The thought warmed her heart.

"It's way more than a wedding," Pepper said. "It's the biggest social event since Alicia Adams and her Atlanta news crew showed up last year. Now *everyone* in town is planning to attend."

"Including the entire movie crew," added Rachel. "Brick had to rent a second tent and another truckload of chairs."

Kat laughed. "I've been in my share of weddings, but never one like yours. I'm telling you, this one will be worthy of another *Around Georgia* segment."

"No way." Rachel glanced at Kat. "Alicia's attending as my bridesmaid, not a television reporter."

"I'm just saying, mama and daughter marrying daddy and son is way more than a little country shindig."

"Speaking of dads," Pepper said. "Your father is kind to let us stay at his house tonight."

"I didn't exactly give him a choice." Rachel shrugged. "Besides, he has eight bedrooms—"

"Eight!" Kat guffawed. "For a man who lives alone? What a waste."

"His house is more of a status symbol than a home. Anyway, when I told him Maggie Warren was joining us, he agreed. I hope hosting half the wedding party will convince him to take care of himself long enough to show up and walk me down the aisle."

"Why wouldn't he?" Maggie's tone hinted surprise. "He's your dad."

"I'm not saying he doesn't want to." Rachel sighed. "It's just ... he's a serious workaholic."

"Let me guess," Maggie said. "He's too proud to admit he's sick."

Rachel nodded. "And stubborn. He considers illness a weakness and work the reason for living."

"I've met a lot of men like him during my career. Directors. Actors. Producers. Do you mind if I talk to him? Maybe help him understand there's life beyond work?"

"Be my guest. But don't be surprised if he doesn't respond."

Maggie smiled. "I'll put all my acting skills to good use and give it my best shot."

***

Two hours after leaving Willow Falls, and happy to be at their destination, Emily parked in front of a bridal shop. Inside, the owner escorted them to a private salon furnished with an off-white, antique sofa and four easy chairs. Two dressing rooms, the entrances covered with gold silk curtains, flanked a raised platform. Soft background music created a welcoming atmosphere.

"Thank you for trusting us with your special day." She pointed to a coffee urn and six cups and saucers, sitting on a table beside a plate of scones. "Please help yourself to coffee while my assistant, Amanda, takes good care of the bride." The owner stepped away.

Pat Nichols

An attractive woman with short, dark hair pressed her palms together and eyed Mama Sadie. "Based on the description your daughter provided, I'm assuming you're the bride."

The soon-to-be bride grinned. "That would be me."

"I've taken the liberty to gather an assortment of off-the-rack options for you." Amanda escorted her customer across the room to a wheeled garment rack holding an array of gowns.

Rachel plated a scone and sat on a chair beside Emily. "This is as exciting as the day you and Mama Sadie helped me choose my gown."

"You tried on at least a dozen dresses before you decided. How many do you suppose it will take before our mother decides?"

"Maybe five?"

"Sadie's a no-nonsense kind of gal," Kat said as she poured a cup of coffee. "I'm guessing she'll take her time looking at the dresses and go with the first one she tries on."

"I agree with Kat." Pepper eyed the refreshments. "At the most, she'll try on two."

"We're about to find out how well you two know her." Rachel bit into a scone.

Amanda pulled the first dress from the rack and displayed it on a headless mannequin. Emily watched her mother view the gown from every direction before asking to see the second. Halfway through the selection, she stood back. "That's the one."

Mama Sadie followed Amanda to the dressing room. Ten minutes later, she emerged and stepped onto the platform in front of a three-way mirror. Dressed in the white gown, form-fitted to the knees, then flaring to the ankles, with a lace bodice and three-quarter sleeves, she was the perfect image of a twenty-first-century Cinderella.

Rachel moved to the platform. "You look stunning."

"All those years in prison ... I never expected to look or feel pretty again." She stepped off the platform and embraced Rachel. "Bless you, child, for sharing your wedding with me."

Rachel returned the embrace. "I love you, Mama Sadie."

Kat sniffed. "Like I told you, she picked the first dress she tried on."

Sadie released Rachel and reached for Emily. She smiled at her friends and brushed away a tear. "Why waste time messing around. Amanda, do you have those bridesmaid outfits ready?"

"Yes, ma'am. They match the dresses your daughter ordered, each in a different color. As soon as I help you out of your gown, I'll bring them out for you ladies to try on."

***

An hour after the bridal attendants were fitted with their gowns, Emily climbed into the driver's seat and swiveled toward the back. "It took way less time to shop than any of us expected. Which means we have time for lunch."

"We don't mess around." Kat buckled her seatbelt. "I'm starving. Do you have someplace in mind?"

"The Cheesecake Factory at Perimeter Mall is a few blocks away. The same restaurant where my other mother and I ate during our last shopping trip before ... the accident." Emily's breath caught in her throat.

"All those memories." Rachel reached across the console and touched Emily's arm. "Are you sure that's the best option?"

Emily swallowed her sadness and took Rachel's hand. "It's the perfect place to begin a new chapter with the sister I didn't know existed, my first mother, and three special friends."

"Well, okay then," Rachel said. "Cheesecake Factory needs to welcome six ladies in the mood to celebrate. After we eat, we'll have time to wander around the mall."

"My first shopping trip with my two beautiful daughters and my three best friends," Mama Sadie said. "Life keeps getting better and better."

Chapter 65

Moments after Emily parked in Greer's driveway, she gawked at the brick mansion spread across the massive space. "That's the biggest house I've ever seen." She climbed out and stood in front of the van.

Rachel joined her. "Wait 'til you see the inside."

Maggie rolled her overnight bag from the rear. "From the outside, it rivals every Beverly Hills mansion I ever visited."

Pepper stepped up beside Rachel. "Is this where you grew up?"

"Sure is."

"I'm surprised you're not spoiled rotten."

"After my mom died ... truth is, it became more like a prison than a home."

Kat guffawed. "It for darn sure doesn't look like the jail where Sadie and I spent time."

Mama Sadie bumped her friend's arm. "You should know better than anybody the impact of psychological prisons."

"Don't give me a hard time, girlfriend. I'm just saying, from the looks of it, we'll need maps to find our way around."

Pepper released her suitcase handle. "Instead of standing here staring like a bunch of sightseers, we should go ring the doorbell. Unless Rachel has a key."

"Today, I'm as much a guest as all of you. So, doorbell it is."

A uniformed housekeeper responded. "You must be Miss Rachel and guests."

"I am. And you are?"

"Nellie. I've been working for your father for the past year."

"Pleasure to meet you, Nellie."

"Likewise, Miss Rachel. Please come in, ladies." She stood to the side.

Kat stepped in and emitted a long whistle. "It feels like we need to check in or at least sign some kind of guest book."

"There's nothing to sign." Nellie's eyes widened. "You're Mr. Streetman's first guests since I took this job."

"Where is my father?" Rachel asked.

"In his office. The one downtown."

"Why am I not surprised?"

"He said he'd be home by six," Nellie said. "When y'all are ready, I'll set some food out for you. First, let me show you to your rooms."

The women followed Nellie to the second floor and their assigned quarters.

Emily hoisted her suitcase onto the king-size sleigh bed in an elegant guest room, then dashed next door to Rachel's room. "Wow. This is triple the size of my childhood bedroom. I can't imagine living in such luxury." She peeked into the bathroom. "I had to walk down the hall to brush my teeth and go ... well, you know, heed the call of nature. Although, the distance between your bathroom and bed is about the same as mine was from bed to bath."

"You're hilarious." Rachel opened her suitcase.

Emily crossed the room and dropped onto the love seat in front of the window. "How did we grow up in dramatically different environments and turn out so much alike?"

"The miracle of genetics, I suppose. This house overflowed with laughter and joy before my mother died." Rachel plucked a framed photo off the dresser. "That great big foyer downstairs was where my friends and I performed little plays for our audience of one. Mom would sit on the stairs and cheer us on. I'm still amazed at how much we favor her."

"Your parents selected you well."

Rachel held the photo to her chest and sat beside her sister. "I'm sorry I didn't have the chance to meet your mom and dad."

"You'd have loved them. Growing up in a small town was like living with one big extended family." Emily hiked a knee on the couch and turned toward the window. "Do you suppose your father returned to work because he's lonely in this gigantic house?"

"If that were the reason, he'd have been here to greet us."

Mama Sadie breezed in, followed by Pepper and Kat. "We're unpacked and ready for the grand tour."

"Is Maggie coming along?"

Mama Sadie shook her head. "She claims she's seen more than her share of fancy houses. She'll join us in the kitchen after a bit."

Rachel returned her mother's photo to the dresser. "This is a good place to start."

For the next hour, Emily took in every word as Rachel escorted everyone except Maggie through three floors and entertained them with stories from the years before she turned twelve. When they arrived in the kitchen, they found Maggie sitting at the island, chatting with Nellie. "How'd you enjoy the tour, ladies?"

"Kat hit the nail on the head about needing a map." Mama Sadie climbed onto a stool beside Maggie and kicked her shoes off. "I'm keeping my cell phone handy in case I get lost."

"I imagine you ladies worked up an appetite." Nellie scurried to the refrigerator and transferred platters of sandwiches, fruit, and vegetables to the island. "We have soft drinks and coffee or wine and Champagne."

"My father tends to like Champagne to celebrate special occasions," Rachel said.

"He does?" Nellie's cheeks flushed. "I mean, he hasn't celebrated anything since I've been working for him. At least not here in the house."

"Well, by golly." Rachel snapped her fingers. "We'll make tonight a first."

"A first for what?" Greer strutted in and tossed his keys on the counter.

"Hey, Dad. We're celebrating a successful shopping trip. You know everyone here except our new friend."

Maggie slid off her stool and approached him, her hand extended. "I'm Maggie Warren. Thank you for inviting us to stay in your lovely home."

He sandwiched her hand between both of his. "The pleasure's all mine. I watched a couple of your movies. The last one ... I don't remember the name. The one ... the one about the blind girl ..."

Emily did a double-take as she listened to him babble on. She cut her eyes over to Rachel. From the look on her face, she was probably thinking the same thing—*Is it possible the man of steel is attracted to a famous Hollywood star?*

Nellie set seven flutes on the counter and presented the Champagne to Rachel. "Do you want to remove the cork?"

"I think our host should do the honors." Rachel carried the bottle to her father. "How about a toast to two brides, one matron of honor, and three bridesmaids. Pepper, Kat, and Maggie are Mama Sadie's attendants. And Maggie's buying one of your condos."

His brows arched. "A vacation getaway?"

Maggie shook her head. "I'm retiring and returning to my small-town roots. Willow Falls is my new home."

"One sold, four to go." Greer pulled the cork and filled the flutes. "Nellie, we're a glass short."

"There are seven, sir."

"Counting you there are eight of us. Grab another glass."

Nellie clamped her arms to her side and stared wide-eyed at her boss.

The man does have a heart. Emily smiled at Rachel as she scooted to the cabinet and removed a glass.

Greer filled it and handed it to Nellie. "Cheers, ladies."

Maggie clinked her glass to Greer's. "I noticed some spectacular paintings in your library. How long have you been collecting?"

"For years. One of my favorite pieces is a Naomi Jasper original."

Maggie placed her hand on Greer's arm. "Which means more than real estate connects you to Willow Falls."

"Would you like to see it?"

"I'd love to."

Emily suppressed a laugh as Rachel gawked at her father. He pressed his hand to Maggie's back and guided her from the kitchen.

"That woman knows how to work it," Kat said.

Emily scooted close to her sister. "What's with your father?"

"I think that man's an imposter. The real Greer Streetman thinks movie watching is a colossal waste of time."

"Maybe he's a closet fan," Emily teased. "Who could miss the giant flat-screen television in the master suite?"

"Whatever's going on, I hope the real Greer doesn't show up." Rachel sipped her Champagne. "If I'd had the slightest inkling he'd respond to Maggie, I would've sent her to visit him in the hospital. If we're lucky, she'll help him adopt a whole new outlook on life."

Chapter 66

Rachel motioned Charlie to a corner table in the Redding Arms dining room. He leaned down and kissed her cheek, then sat to her left. "When is he coming down."

"Any minute now. He checked in late last night. I had breakfast with Alicia and Nancy this morning."

"Your reporter friend obviously knows the town." Charlie reached for his water. "How'd your former assistant react to all the craziness going on?"

"Like a proper fan. She wants her picture taken with the stars. I told her she could pose with Maggie at tonight's rehearsal dinner. The rest she'll have to finagle on her own. She signed up for JT's noon tour. Alicia joined her, said she wanted to see what's changed in the past year." Rachel caught sight of her father at the dining room entrance. "He's here."

Charlie stood. "We're glad you made it."

"Why would I miss it?" He held his hand out to Rachel.

She rose and embraced him. "Thanks for coming, Dad."

He sat beside her. "Sharing a wedding with your mother and your fiancé's old man is unique. Are you double honeymooning as well?"

"Hardly. Charlie and I are flying to France the day after tomorrow. We're starting in Paris, then touring a couple of wine regions."

"Good choice for a vintner." He eyed Charlie. "Where's your dad taking his bride?"

"Hawaii. Sadie couldn't get a passport in time to leave the country."

"Not only has she never flown," Rachel said, "she's never ventured beyond Georgia's borders. He's opening up a whole new world for her."

The waitress rushed to their table. "Everyone's super excited about tomorrow. Chef Pepper plans to close the dining room after breakfast.

The staff's making a heap of sandwiches for hotel guests who show up for lunch. Today, everything on the menu is available."

After ordering and handing their menu to the waitress, dad turned to daughter. "Is the entire town shutting down for your wedding?"

"I know it seems crazy, but yeah."

Her father frowned. "The perfect setup for unscrupulous tourists to rob everyone blind."

"Same concern Sheriff Mitch had," Charlie said. "Which is why he hired neighboring deputies to patrol the streets."

"The price of progress."

"Small-town enthusiasm still rules the day around here." Charlie propped his arms on the table. "How long are you staying in town?"

"That depends. I returned to work the day after I left the hospital."

"We know," Rachel said.

"The office grapevine reaches far and wide."

Rachel raised her brows.

"Don't look so shocked, Strawberry Girl. I know Nancy used to keep you tuned in, and I have my own resources."

"Let me guess. Your faithful assistant."

He nodded. "She's worth her weight in gold. Anyway, after I left the hospital, I couldn't accept the fact that I was not a hundred percent. Ambition and pride are tough to deal with."

How will he recover if he can't even say the word sick?

The waitress returned with their orders. "Chef Pepper says welcome back to Willow Falls, Mr. Streetman. She hopes you enjoy lunch."

"Tell her thanks."

Rachel toyed with her salad and stole glances at her father as he bit into his chicken salad sandwich, aching to hear more but afraid to ask.

He swallowed, then reached for his water. "I'm taking time off from the office."

"Did I hear you right?" Rachel did a double-take. "You're taking a vacation?"

"That's not what I said. I'll work remotely."

Rachel locked eyes with him. "I can't imagine you staying holed up at home with the office a couple of miles away."

"Which is why I'm taking one of my condos off the market. I can work from Willow Falls as easily as Buckhead."

Charlie eyed him. "Which condo?"

"Across from the *Willow Post*."

Rachel stared at him. "The unit next to Maggie's?"

"That's the one." He glanced at his Rolex. "I have a one o'clock appointment with Nathan to look at furniture."

"Supporting our local economy?" asked Charlie.

"The man who functions as pastor, mayor, and the town's only furniture store owner deserves my business. Plus, a thriving town will give me a good return on my investments."

"You know the rehearsal begins at three," Rachel said.

"Which is why I need to leave now. Lunch is on me. Charge it to my room."

Rachel watched her father stroll out of the dining room. "Well, I'll be. Her ploy must have worked."

"Whose ploy to do what?"

"Maggie's. To break down my father's tough, all-work-no-play philosophy."

"Trust me, sweetheart. It'll take more than a pretty woman's sweet talk to transform Greer Streetman."

"You didn't see how he looked at her the day they met."

Charlie tipped his water glass toward Rachel. "If Maggie succeeds, I'll treat you to a trip to Italy for our first anniversary."

"Hmm." Rachel grinned. "Maybe you should start practicing."

"To do what?"

"Speak Italian."

Chapter 67

*E*mily slipped away from the attendants fussing over Rachel and Sadie and moved to the window in Charlie's office. Her heart filled with joy as she took in the scene below. The pair of white tents covering the lower parking lot. The sea of wooden folding chairs filled with guests. Scores of residents standing and sitting in the grass. A long row of buffet tables laden with food filled the space between the vineyard and winery. Movie crew golf carts transported guests from their parking spots along County Road.

Pepper slid in beside her. "Willow Falls' version of a royal wedding. Not as fancy but every bit as fascinating and a lot more colorful. Rachel's choice of bridesmaid dresses is unique. Same style, each a different color."

"Like a beautiful rainbow," Mama Sadie said as she joined them. "A good sign, according to Brick."

Emily adjusted her mother's veil. "Everything about today points to a beautiful, bright future."

"I had to pinch myself this morning to make sure I wasn't dreaming." She lifted her left hand. "Then I looked at this beautiful ring and knew it was real." She directed her attention to Pepper. "Will you take the ladies to the dining room for a few minutes? I want some time alone with my daughters."

"Of course, I will." Kat moved to the door. "Come on, ladies, let's check out the scene from the dining room."

When the three were alone, Mama Sadie stepped in front of a freestanding, full-length mirror. "Fifty-year-old, first-time bride marries daughter's groom's daddy. Makes for a good story, don't you think?"

Emily moved to her right. "And great material for a writer."

"Or a Hallmark movie." Rachel stepped to Sadie's left. "We are an amazing trio."

A smile lit Mama Sadie's face as she held her daughters' hands. "This day, this moment is a blessing beyond anything I ever imagined. The first time I met Brick, I thought, glory be, what a charming man. I was surprised when he invited me to escort him to the town's big July Fourth celebration."

Emily squeezed her mother's hand. "You obviously swept him off his feet."

"It took a year before he kissed me proper. Despite the difference in our ages and backgrounds, we're good together."

"Yes, you are." Rachel kissed her mother's cheek.

Pepper flung the door open. "I'm sorry, Sadie. Kat and I tried to stop her but—"

Cynthia breezed into the room. "I told them I'd make a scene during the ceremony if they didn't let me through."

Emily gasped.

Rachel's mouth fell open.

Mama Sadie's expression remained neutral. "It's okay, Pepper. You can leave us." She waited for her friend to close the door before releasing her daughters' hands. "I reckon we shouldn't be surprised you showed up."

Cynthia glanced around the room. "Fancy office. Charlie's or Brick's?"

"Charlie's." Rachel's eyes narrowed. "Why are you here?"

"Despite the fact that I'm not welcome in Willow Falls, I needed to show up and make peace with my son. Make that *sons*. I spent the last half hour with Charlie and his brother Ronnie. Or should I say Brick's best man." Cynthia eyed the boxes of bouquets covering the desk. "Colorful flowers. Sadie, I imagine there are doubts in your head about Brick and me. After all, we did leave town together."

Emily's hands fisted. "Stop right there—"

"I'll handle this, honey." Mama Sadie kept her eyes focused on Cynthia. "I spent thirty years in prison. I can deal with whatever she has to say."

"Your mother is a smart woman." Cynthia leaned back against the desk. "Everyone knows I showed up in this burg to sweep my ex off his feet. And why not? I'm single again, and as far as I knew, so was he. In case you're wondering, the insane letter-writing campaign made me that much more determined to achieve my objective. When Brick agreed to return to Atlanta with me and invited me to stay the night at our old house, I expected to win him over."

Emily's eyes narrowed. *What is she trying to prove?*

"Brick insisted I sleep in the guest room farthest from the master suite. In my mind, he was toying with me—playing hard to get. So, I spent a week trying every feminine ploy in my arsenal to wheedle my way into his bedroom and back into his heart. Nothing worked." She turned and plucked a photo of Rachel off the desk. "Nice picture. At first, I thought I'd lost my appeal as a woman, and after all the work I had done." She sighed. "Until the night Brick told me about you, Sadie. I saw something in his eyes I'd never seen before. In that moment, I recognized the truth. I didn't fail."

Mama Sadie remained silent.

Cynthia stepped away from the desk. "You had already captured his heart." She locked eyes with Sadie and reached for her hand. "I want you to know he adores you with every fiber of his being. You are his true soulmate."

"Thank you for telling me."

"Brick's a good man, Sadie. Crazy superstitious, but good. All I ask is for you to love him with all your heart."

"I promise." She embraced the woman she had replaced in Brick's life.

Cynthia pulled away and moved to the door. "Maybe one day you and I can become friends. Oh, and in case you're wondering, I'm not foolish enough to show my face down there and subject myself to more ridicule. I'll watch the wedding from up here and disappear after all your guests leave." She opened the door and pushed past the bridal party gathered in the hall.

Kat dashed in. "Do you want us to hogtie that woman and keep her away from your man?"

Mama Sadie shook her head. "Cynthia didn't come here to cause trouble, and she's planning to stay out of sight."

"Call me skeptical," Kat said. "Are you sure we can trust her?"

"She bared her soul. So yeah, we can trust her."

"Good to know, because it's time for this wedding to begin." Pepper distributed bouquets, then led the entourage through the restaurant, down the stairs to the tasting room.

Mary greeted the women. "Wow, Rachel and Sadie, you're both beautiful." She plucked the newspaper's camera from the tasting bar. "Although today I'm the pastor's wife and your wedding coordinator, I'm still a reporter. Emily, stand in front of the stairs with your mother and sister."

The three moved into position. Mary snapped a photo. "Next week's front-page story. And now on to the tents."

Outside, Emily hesitated. She looked up and spotted a lone figure standing at the window in Charlie's office. As a mother, she understood the sacrifice Cynthia had made. For a split second, she was tempted to motion her down.

Kat nudged Emily's arm. "Don't feel sorry for her. She's doing the right thing. Besides, women like her are survivors."

"How did you know what I was thinking?"

"Like I've said lots of times, one good thing I learned in prison was how to read people. Now, let's go get your mama and sister married."

Chapter 68

Rachel's heart skipped a beat at the sight of her father, standing at the edge of the first tent, smiling. "Hello, Strawberry Girl."

She straightened his bowtie. "You look handsome all dressed up in a tuxedo."

"And you are stunning. As beautiful as the mother who adopted you, the day she walked down the aisle." He held his arm out, bent at the elbow.

Rachel placed her hand on his forearm.

He covered her hand with his. "Charlie's a lucky man. I'm glad you ignored my warning to stay away from him."

"To tell you the truth, my desire to defy you drove me into his arms. Then something wonderful happened. I fell in love with him."

Greer chuckled. "Despite the fact we're not blood-related, your stubborn streak proves we're father and daughter."

"Today wouldn't be the same without you, Dad. Thank you for being here for me."

He squeezed her hand. "Nothing could keep me away."

Rachel's pulse quickened when Agnes Peterson began playing the processional on a baby grand piano. Maggie moved down the aisle first, followed by Kat, Nancy, Alicia, and matrons-of-honor Pepper and Emily. She held her breath the moment Agnes transitioned to the bridal chorus, signaling Mama Sadie to begin her stroll. Faces beamed. Heads turned as eyes followed the first bride. When she stood beside her groom, the crowd turned toward the back.

Rachel and her father stepped into the aisle. She smiled, knowing she was moments away from becoming one with the man she loved with all her heart. She glimpsed the best men—Scott and Charlie's brother Ronnie and groomsmen, Mitch, Dennis, Jack, and JT—all looking handsome in charcoal tuxedos.

As Rachel moved down the aisle, her eyes met her groom's and didn't stray. When her father placed her hand in Charlie's, her heart was so full of love she thought it might burst.

"Hello, gorgeous," he whispered.

She gazed deep into his eyes. "Hello, handsome."

***

The party following the ceremony was a spirited blend of elegance, pot-luck supper, and country-style hoedown, with pop and romantic songs replacing square dance tunes. Rachel clung to Charlie's arm as they circulated and chatted with guests clamoring for their turn to congratulate the newly married couple and offer homespun advice on marriage.

Mirabelle pushed her way to them and leaned close. "I've been paying attention to your father and Maggie Warren. There's something brewing with those two."

Charlie laughed. "You have some imagination."

Mirabelle propped her hands on her hips. "What I have is eyes."

Patsy Peacock stepped beside her. "Are you giving our newlyweds a hard time?"

"You can vouch for me." Mirabelle lowered her arms. "You saw Rachel's dad and Maggie hanging out together—"

"For goodness sake," Patsy said. "They're both in the wedding party, so naturally they're spending time with each other."

"I know what I saw, and I'm telling you there's a lot more going on. Him moving in next door to Maggie. I'm going to do my own investigation." Mirabelle spun away.

Patsy shook her head. "The town crier is at it again. By this time tomorrow, she'll have everyone believing Greer and Maggie are days from eloping. Anyway, congratulations you two, the ceremony was beautiful. And you, Rachel, are stunning."

"Thank you, Patsy. The cakes you created are works of art. I almost feel guilty cutting them."

"I don't mean to brag, but they'll taste every bit as good as they look."

Gertie moseyed over. "It was a hoot seeing all those signs in downtown windows: *Closed. Gone to the Wedding.*"

Rachel chuckled. "Only in a small town."

Emily and Scott approached. "What do you think about your southern-fried wedding now, Sis?"

"Two years ago, my family consisted of me and one overbearing father. Now it feels like everyone in Willow Falls is at least a distant cousin."

"Are you bragging or complaining?" Emily teased.

"Given a choice between the two, I'll take the crowd."

Charlie beamed. "My bride has finally transitioned from city slicker to country girl."

"Not entirely." Rachel thumped his arm. "There's no way I'm raising goats and chickens in our back yard."

From the corner of her eye, Rachel spotted Robert Nordstrom approaching. He stopped beside Emily. "I've attended a lot of weddings, but never one as laid back and fun as this one."

"Thank you for loaning us your golf carts and drivers," Rachel said.

"You should see County Road. Cars are lined up for a mile."

Emily, Scott, and Gertie stepped away.

Robert fingered his beard. "Everybody's talking about your no-gift request. I've also heard snippets of conversation about doing something special to commemorate today. Interesting concept. Before I forget. I have something for you." He removed an envelope from his coat pocket and handed it to her.

Rachel stared at the envelope. "Should we open it now?"

Mary approached. "Sorry to interrupt, but it's time to cut the cakes."

"Looks like we'll have to wait." She gave the envelope to Charlie. He slipped it into his tux pocket. They held hands as they strolled past the gazebo and joined the other newlyweds at a table displaying two six-tier wedding cakes and four sheet cakes.

The moment Rachel and Charlie slid a knife into their cake, guests applauded.

"Do you suppose they're happy for us or eager to taste Patsy's masterpiece?" Rachel pushed a small piece into Charlie's mouth.

He swallowed, then returned the gesture.

She licked her lips. "Lemon with buttercream frosting. Perfect." Rachel watched her mother wipe a dot of icing from the corner of her husband's mouth. Then Brick kissed her. She kissed him back. The crowd applauded again.

"Oh my. I do believe my mother and your father are starting their honeymoon early."

The music stopped. "Ladies and gentlemen," announced the DJ. "It's time for the official dance."

Charlie stroked Rachel's cheek. "*Our* honeymoon will have to wait until I dance with my beautiful bride."

The two newly married couples joined the wedding party gathered on the gazebo. The DJ announced the father-daughter dance. "Through the Years" began to play. The crowd parted. Greer gathered Rachel into his arms and whispered, "Have I told you how proud I am of the woman you've become?"

She choked back tears. "Thank you. I love you, Dad."

Moments later, the DJ invited Charlie and his new stepmother to the floor. The song morphed into "The Way You Look Tonight."

Brick cut in on Charlie. Charlie tapped Greer on the shoulder. He placed his daughter's hand in her new husband's hand. "Take good care of my Strawberry Girl."

"Yes, sir. I promise."

When the next song began playing, the gazebo filled with couples. Emily and Scott moved close to Rachel and Charlie. Their sitter stepped up with Jane and Clair. They scooped their daughters into their arms. Before they spun away, Emily leaned close to her sister. "Cynthia kept her promise."

"Is she still sitting at the window?"

Emily nodded.

Rachel stepped back and grabbed Charlie's hand. "Come with me, sweetheart. Someone needs a piece of our wedding cake."

They rushed from the gazebo. Charlie placed a slice on a plate and grabbed a fork before they wove through the crowd and climbed the private stairs to his office.

Cynthia turned toward them, her cheeks tearstained.

Rachel knelt in front of her and held her hands. "I want you to know I love your son with all my heart."

"Thank you for this moment. It means more than you'll ever know."

"You told Mama Sadie you hoped to one day become friends. I'd be honored if you'd extend that invitation to me."

"We'll see what the future brings. Right now, you two need to scoot back to your reception before someone comes looking for you."

Charlie helped his bride to her feet. "Thank you for keeping your promise, Mom."

"Call it my wedding gift to you, your father, and two beautiful brides." She sniffled and turned back toward the window.

Rachel clung to her husband as they stepped out of the office. At the bottom of the stairs, Charlie gathered her in his arms. "I didn't think I could love you more, but what you just did for my mother ..." He kissed her deeply, passionately.

When their lips parted, she pressed her fingers to his lips. "And I thought Brick laid a big one on Mama Sadie."

"What can I say, gorgeous, you're the gift that brings out the best in me."

"Speaking of gifts, do you mind if we open Robert's envelope?"

"Might as well." He pulled it from his pocket, ran his finger under the flap, and handed it to Rachel.

After unfolding stapled sheets of paper, her hand flew to her chest. "Oh my."

"What is it?"

"A contract for a role in his next film." The decision was no longer hers alone to make. She looked deep into her husband's eyes. "What should I do?"

He smiled and stroked her cheek. "Sign it, Mrs. Bricker, and follow your dreams."